ALSO BY MEG M. ROBINSON

<u>Chloe Chadwick Series</u>

Finding Salus

Waking Salus

Remembering Salus

Saving Salus

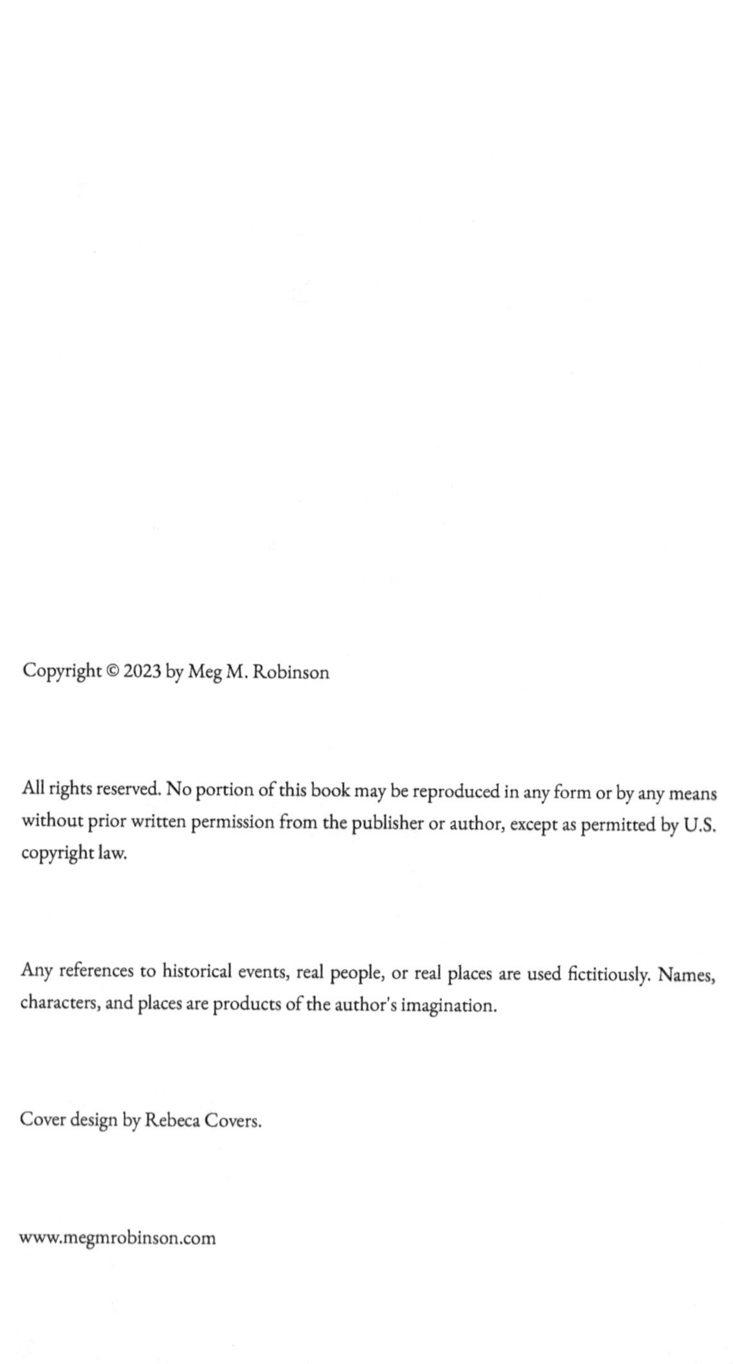

SEEKING ETERNITY

IMMORTAL LOVE BOOK I

MEG M. ROBINSON

ARCANE CROW PUBLISHING

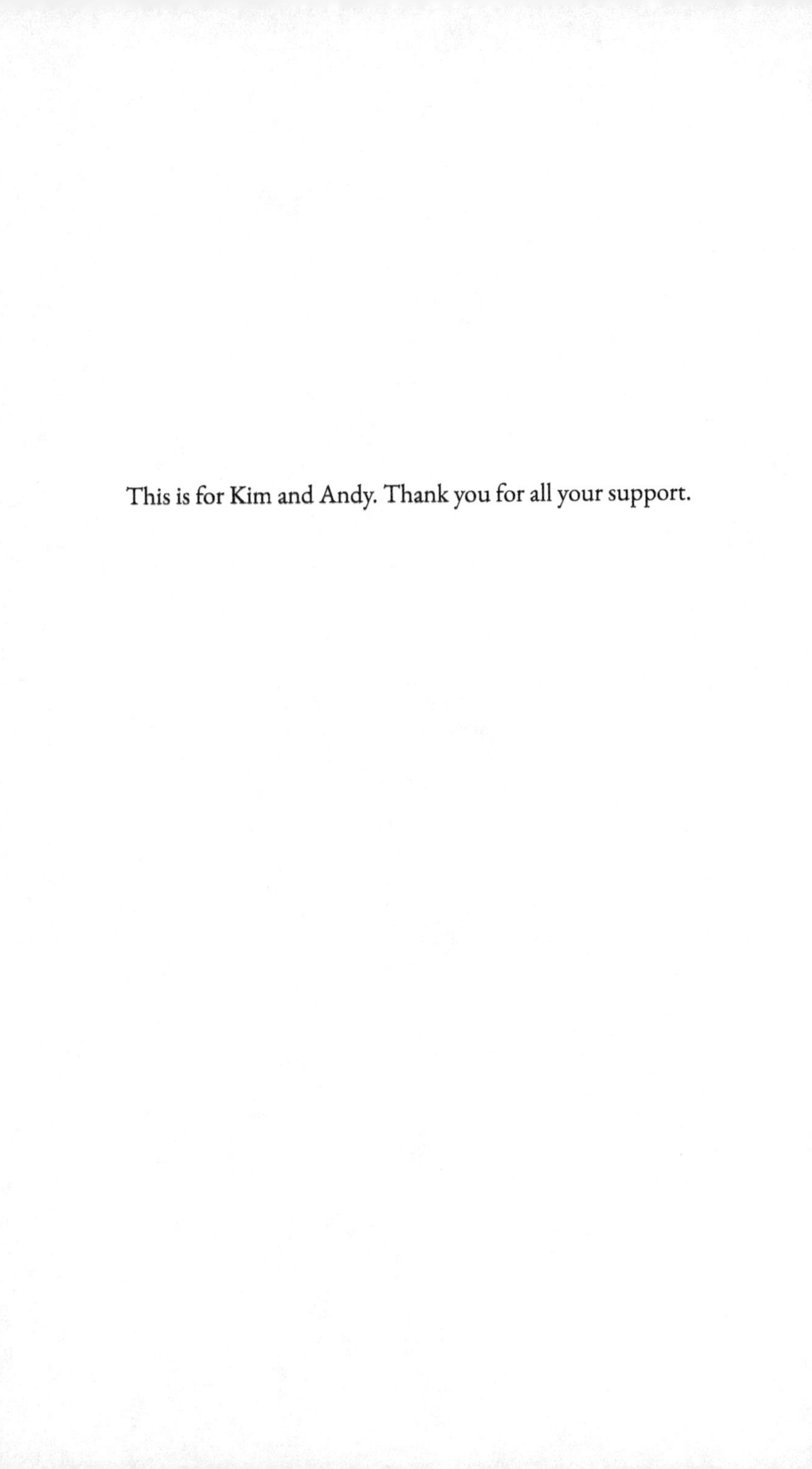

This is for Kim and Andy. Thank you for all your support.

CHAPTER I

Paige always hated when eight-thirty rolled around on Friday night. Sure, most people her age thought the evening was just starting at that hour, but it signaled the end of her favorite time of the week. Because Friday nights were when she visited the British Museum.

She knew she was considered dull and a nerd by her peers. At twenty-four she should be going on dates or partying, they said, but that wasn't what she wanted. Paige loved history—the older the better—and there was no place she enjoyed more than the British Museum, regardless of what exhibits were on display.

As always, she was a little sad as she walked out of the building and into the warm night. She was dressed casually in jeans, a tee-shirt that proclaimed that archaeology rocked, and a pair of dingy sneakers. Fashion wasn't something she ever concerned herself with, as she preferred to be comfortable. She was pretty enough, she knew, with her vivid red hair, fair skin, and green eyes, but her appearance had never been a high priority for her. Which was why the slender woman had pulled her mass of hair—which fell to her waist in a riot of curls—into a quick braid, so at least she wouldn't have to worry about it getting in her way, which it often did.

Despite the hour, Paige wasn't concerned to be walking home by herself. She enjoyed the exercise, and she'd never had anyone bother her along her route. Not seriously, in any case. An inebriated boy, barely old enough to drink, had hit on her one night, but it was half-hearted at best, and easily ignored.

She paused at the bottom of the museum stairs to pull out her phone and earbuds, inserting the latter before she selected a song and hit play. As the first notes of "Welcome to the Jungle" by Guns N' Roses sounded in her ears, she smiled. Music, like history, never failed to lift her spirits. Humming along with the song, she started the familiar walk home, half-zoned out. Because of that, she never heard the sound of footsteps in the alley ahead of her.

She did, however, sense that she was no longer alone, but by then, it was too late.

A man reached out as she stepped past a building. A hand clamped roughly over her mouth, while his other arm snaked around her waist, holding her as tightly as any constrictor.

He jerked her away from the streetlights and further into the shadows, overpowering her without a problem despite her panicked struggles. With her arms pinned to her sides, Paige wasn't able to even grab her keys to use as a weapon. All she could do was whimper and yell, though the hand over her mouth muffled any noise she made.

Only once they were far enough away from the street and hidden behind a dumpster did his grip loosen. Even then, it was only to release one of her arms.

His face pressed close to hers, close enough that she could smell the sour scent of the alcohol he'd been drinking, overpowering the pungent odor of sweat. He hissed in her ear and made her shudder. "Your money and phone, now!"

She must have moved more slowly than he wanted, because he suddenly twisted and shoved her hard against the building. The brick was unyielding against her back and her head struck the wall, causing her to bite her tongue as sharp pain radiated through her skull and her belly clenched against the sudden nausea it produced.

To further drive his command home, she had a fist slam into her stomach before he demanded, again in that hissing voice, "Now! Or I'll do worse than punch you!"

Physically unable to comply with her limbs leaden and trembling, Paige's thoughts screamed in her head. *Help me! Someone! Please!* But, knowing no one could hear her, she struggled to bring a hand up. Even she couldn't have said if it was to give in to the mugger's demands or to push him away, but she didn't get the chance to do either one.

Paige couldn't see anyone behind the mugger, yet he was ripped sharply away from her, slamming into the building across the alley. Astonished, she could only watch as the man was pinned four feet off the ground by an unseen force.

She knew she'd hit her head pretty good—it was throbbing in time with her heartbeat, overshadowing the aches in her back and tongue—but she didn't think it was serious enough for her to be hallucinating. Her legs gave out then, and she slid down the wall until her butt hit the pavement, her eyes fixed on the thief.

A man strolled toward them—for no other word suited his almost lazy stride—glancing dismissively at the would-be mugger before he turned to Paige. "Are you all right?" His voice was clipped, his accent as English as hers, though a bit more upper crust.

Recovering, or trying to, she only stared up at her rescuer. With the shadows that permeated the alley, she couldn't make out more than his height and build. He was tall, several inches above six feet, and it didn't look like he had an ounce of fat anywhere on his body. It was the way he stood that truly caught her eye, though. His stance was one of a man who was in control and knew it.

When she didn't answer right away, he crouched down in front of her, ignoring the panicked curses of the mugger. He studied her face before asking again in a more gentle tone, "Are you all right?"

Fingers trembled as she lifted her hand, gingerly touching the back of her head. He seemed to understand because he nodded. He reached out, paying no attention to her flinch, and gently touched her forehead. Instantly, the pain lessened and the rolling of her stomach calmed.

"Better?"

Tentatively, she inclined her head. When it didn't cause further agony to explode within her skull, she managed a tiny smile. "Much," she said, her voice hoarse from her futile screams.

"Good. You should get out of here before I let him go. He'll most likely just run away." He glanced back to the mugger, then made a disgusted sound. "Especially since he's already pissed himself, but there's no sense in taking that chance."

He rose and offered a hand to her. She saw light glint off a ring on his middle finger as she took the offered assistance. The moment that she put her hand in his, she felt light-headed. When she swayed halfway up, he tightened his grip.

"Careful now," he warned.

Paige nodded slowly before she asked, "H-how did you do that?" She refused to look at her assailant, and instead just nodded her head slightly in that direction.

Her rescuer said blandly, "Magic." Rather than sarcastic, something in Paige told her that he spoke no more than the truth. She certainly didn't have any other explanation for how a grown man was being held to a wall without anyone touching him. "You really should go now, though." To help encourage that very course of action, with his hand still on hers, he led her to the mouth of the alley. A streetlight shined directly on him now, and she felt her heart give two rapid beats.

He was gorgeous. Probably in his mid-thirties, every feature on his face was perfect, from the regally arched brows, right down to the hint of stubble covering his cheeks and chin. His hair was dark brown, just long enough on the top to be mussed, but stylishly. His skin was lightly tanned, which only made his eyes seem darker. She was certain that they were brown, too, but in this light, they looked almost black. Though he was dressed in what could only be termed as casual, the jeans and button-down shirt looked amazing on him.

Even as she felt herself staring again, he released her hand and gave her a gentle push. "Go on. Get home and tend to your injuries."

She realized then that though the pain wasn't nearly as intense as it had been, she did still hurt. Home would be very welcome. Home and a shower, as the encounter with the criminal had left her feeling dirty down to her skin. She nodded and smiled. "Thank you for rescuing me."

"Don't mention it." His tone suggested he meant it literally. Without waiting to see if she left, he turned to walk back down the alley, disappearing into the darkness. When she heard a whimper from the mugger, she decided to take his advice, moving as quickly as she could for home.

When Paige arrived home fifteen minutes later, she saw her dad's car parked out front. Tension she hadn't realized she was still holding onto started to dissipate. She was *home*, and home meant safety.

Since her mother had died when Paige was a baby, it had just been her and her dad and they'd always been close. Sure, he was often overprotective, but Jacob Williams had already lost one of his ladies, he would tell her, and he wasn't going to lose his other. Besides, after the incident in the alley, she could use some of his coddling. Never before had she been so happy with her decision to continue living with her father for a few years.

"Dad?" she called once she was inside, quickly shucking her bag and dropping it by the front door.

"In the kitchen."

Paige hurried back and zeroed in on her father. When he turned at her footsteps, she walked right up to him and wrapped her arms tightly around his waist.

Now she was truly safe.

He saw just enough of her face before it was pressed against his chest for his welcoming smile to switch to a concerned frown. "Hey there. What's wrong, pumpkin? Did something happen at the museum?"

Now that she was home, tears began to fall and she nodded. Jacob's arms came up to enfold her in a hug, but he squeezed too tight at first, the pressure irritating her sore back. She yelped, and he transferred his hands to her shoulders and eased her away so he could see her face. The sight of her damp cheeks made him frantic. "What happened?"

She sniffled and wiped impatiently at the tears as she looked up at him. The sight of his loving face, with his crazy carrot-red hair and pale blue eyes, was comforting. "I was mugged."

"What?" he roared, body tensing with the desire to hunt down the person who'd dared to hurt his baby girl. The fact that she was, technically, an adult didn't factor into it. She was his little girl and all he had left. "Where? What's he look like? I'll tear him apart!"

Not at all frightened by his anger as she knew it was on her behalf, she nodded and said, "Not far from the museum. He wanted my money and phone. He...he slammed me against a wall, but I'll be okay, Dad." Trying to dispel a bit of his worry, she worked up a trembling smile. "A man rescued me. He got the guy away from me, then he made sure I was all right and helped me up." And because it was her father, and she was closer to him than anyone else, she gave a tiny laugh and let herself add, "And I think he did it with magic!"

She wasn't serious, had even begun to doubt what she had seen and was chalking it up to the head injury, but her father's mood, his entire demeanor, switched in an instant. The concern was gone—or smothered. In its place was rage and...disgust? It made no sense to Paige.

"Dad?" she asked uncertainly, baffled by the sudden shift.

"We do *not* discuss magic in this house!"

The vehemence in his voice caused her to take a startled step back. "What? Why?" True, she'd never heard him mention magic once, and he watched nothing that could even remotely be considered fantasy, but he'd never expressed the level of hatred for magic that he was displaying now.

Rather than answer her, he demanded, "How did he find you?"

Paige frowned in confusion at the shift in subjects. "What? Who? The mugger?"

"No. The witch," Jacob hissed, making the last word sound like the world's worst slur.

Bewildered, she shifted tender shoulders in a shrug. "I don't know. We were hidden from the street and the mugger had my mouth covered so I couldn't scream, except in my head."

His eyes narrowed. "You screamed for help in your head?" The question sounded accusing, further confusing her.

She took another step back, aware that she was trembling and the throbbing in her skull was returning. "I think anyone would have in that situation. Everyone would hope for help. Why are you so angry?"

"You used magic!"

For a second, she stared at him in shock. "What? N-no, I didn't. I couldn't!" she protested. "Magic isn't real, Dad!"

"It is! You did! You scream in your head and a witch just *happens* to stroll by and see you hidden away?" He shook his head and sneered. "No, you used magic. I won't have it. Get your things and get out of here. I want nothing, absolutely *nothing*, to do with witches or magic. You don't know what magic does to you. I won't—" He broke off and shook his head again. "No, I won't have magic in this house," he snarled.

"Dad!" she cried in shock. "Don't do this!" she begged. "I didn't do magic! I *can't* do magic! It's not real! You can't do this, Dad. Please, don't—"

He cut her off with a slice of his hand through the air. "I don't want to hear it. You have until I get back to get your things."

Tears streamed down her face as she was suddenly staring at his back as he stormed out of the house. The sharp slamming of the door made her flinch.

None of this made sense! Her normally loving and calm father was acting totally irrational and not like himself. She'd never seen him like this before, not even the one time he let himself get completely drunk as he mourned his dead wife. All her life it had been just the two of them, and they'd always been close. So for him to kick her out just minutes after she'd been attacked? It was inconceivable. So much so that she couldn't work up any anger—not yet—for his demand. That would come, she was sure, but right now confusion and hurt overshadowed everything else.

Paige wished she could convince herself that he was just upset and would calm down, but she knew him too well. Once his mind was made up, he didn't change it. Ever. She'd never met anyone as stubborn as her dad. Maybe, just maybe, he'd cool off in time, but she was positive that it wouldn't happen tonight. Worse, she knew if she tried to argue, to reason with him, he'd only dig his heels in deeper and it would be much more difficult to get him to come around in the future.

Minutes passed as Paige stood there, shoulders hunched with defeat, too stunned to move. She didn't have anywhere else to go. She had a few friends, yes, but they didn't have the space for a houseguest, even a temporary one. While she had a job she enjoyed at the library, she was only part-time at the moment and couldn't afford a place on her salary, not alone.

Slowly, her thoughts turned to her unnamed rescuer. Her tears dried up and her back straightened. She knew where to go. She had no idea *how* she knew, especially since she didn't even know his name, but that was hardly the weirdest thing that had happened to her tonight. What mattered was that she somehow knew *exactly* where to find her mysterious savior.

Impulsively, she decided to go to him. She'd demand some answers, and maybe, if she was lucky, she'd find a place to stay until her dad came to his senses.

Was it a foolish choice? Possibly, but she didn't have a lot of options.

Paige picked up her bag and marched to her bedroom. She grabbed both her suitcases out of the closet and loaded them and her backpack up with the things she wanted to keep. She didn't think her dad would toss her possessions, and hopefully she wouldn't be gone long, but she was too practical to take the chance. Her clothes, toiletries, laptop, and the photo album that held pictures of her and her parents were the first to be packed. The small wooden jewelry box that once belonged to her mom and still contained her jewelry was a must as well. As an afterthought, she grabbed a few of her favorite books—history and what her dad called 'girl fiction'—but everything else she could either live without or replace. Besides, her bags were full by that point.

It was awkward to roll both suitcases behind her with her bag on her back, but she managed to get out the front door. There were always cabs around this stretch of road so she shouldn't have to walk far before she could finally sit down. Fortunately, she found a ride in less than a minute. After loading herself and her things into the cab, she rattled off an address she'd never before seen or heard. The cab driver gave her a look.

"You sure you want to go there? It'll be more than an hour, and not cheap," he said with no small hint of doubt.

It would take a chunk of what little money she had, she knew, but she didn't have any alternatives. "Positive," she told him in a curt voice.

He only shrugged and started driving, leaving her to dwell on the drastic change her life had taken, all in the space of an hour.

CHAPTER 2

Paige spent the entire ride turning the entire situation over in her mind. Somehow, she was absolutely positive that the address she'd told the cab driver was where she'd find the man who had rescued her. But other than a vague answer of 'magic,' she had no explanation for how she'd obtained that knowledge. Nor could she come up with any logical reason why her dad would have reacted like he had. Given how close they'd always been, Paige had expected him to be angry on her behalf, but loving and reassuring toward her. It had begun that way, true enough, but what could have possibly happened to make him kick his only daughter out, minutes after she'd been attacked?

What had made him so cruel?

His reaction had also made her begin to rethink her doubts about magic existing. No one had that intense of a response to something imaginary. But if he'd known about magic, how had Paige grown up clueless? *Why* had she not been told that it was real? Then she wondered, had her mom had magic? Had *she* been a witch? If so, it might explain a few things. It might explain why her dad thought she had done magic.

But it didn't explain why he hated magic so deeply.

It was just over an hour later when the taxi stopped. The cabbie looked out the windshield skeptically, then back to Paige. "This is the address. You sure you want me to let you out here?"

She leaned forward and peered out the window. A tall stone wall gave way to an immense iron gate with a call box beside it. Beyond, she could see a large expanse of overgrown lawn in front of a big three-story home that looked like it hadn't been lived in for generations. Her confidence almost failed her before she steeled herself, lifting her chin and straightening her back. She'd get through this. Even if her unknown rescuer turned her out, she'd manage. She wasn't the sort to just lie down and accept defeat, and she wasn't going to begin now.

She just wouldn't think about how this estate was the only thing she'd seen for miles.

"Positive," she said before she paid and got out.

The cabbie showed a hint of concern and helped her get her things, even though she told him she could manage. He was reluctant to leave, but she insisted. After waiting for him to drive off, she took a deep breath, moved to the intercom, then, ignoring the pounding in her head, pushed the call button.

There were several minutes in which nothing happened, other than Paige's mind filling with all manner of disturbing scenarios. If no one was here, she could spend days wandering the countryside, alone and without any food. The mystery man could open the gates only to set dogs on her. And those were two of the kindest outcomes she thought of. Finally, there was a reply from the intercom. "What is it?"

Though the voice was impatient and, without a doubt, unfriendly, it was familiar and Paige felt something loosen inside her. It was her rescuer. She was still clueless as to how she'd managed to find him, but she wanted to weep with relief. Something tonight had actually gone right.

All too quickly, that relief cooled. How to get him to let her in? She was a complete stranger, and showing up here like this, he'd probably think she was some weird stalker or something.

Before she could think too much and give up, she hit the button to reply. "Um...hello. It's Paige. I'm the one you rescued earlier tonight. I was wanting—hoping," she corrected, "that I could come in."

As she spoke, lightning flashed, and less than a second later, it was followed by the loud crack of thunder. She glanced up to the dark skies, brow furrowed in concern. If he said no, she was going to be cold and wet on top of everything else. She didn't know if she could handle anything else tonight. It had already been the most eventful night of her life.

While she waited for his response, she could sense his surprise, even without a face to watch or a voice to listen to. Probably just a fanciful notion, based on her dad's rantings about magic, she decided. Seconds, then minutes, passed in silence. Just as the first drop of rain hit her nose, the gate began to open.

There was no other response, not so much as a single word, but Paige didn't hesitate. The rain started coming down hard and fast. She wanted to get inside before she got soaked to her skin, though she doubted she'd make it. For the moment, that immediate concern overrode—mostly—her fear of what she'd say or do to convince the man to let her stay. Or if she *should* stay. Especially with the estate looking so abandoned and inhospitable. She only knew one thing about this man, but since it was that he'd helped a woman who had been in desperate need of it, she felt like she had to take this risk.

With her luggage, Paige couldn't really run, but she moved as quickly as she could manage, taking in the sight of the structure and grounds surrounding it. Grass sprung up in random places along the drive, and the yard looked as though it had never been tended. The house itself was in serious need of a good cleaning, the bricks gone black from years of neglect. Some parts of the wall were completely covered by ivy, which had tried its best to take over. The front door, at least, was in its proper place and looked sturdy enough. She saw one broken window, and the others were so caked with grime they didn't even reflect the next bolt of lightning. However, the sudden flash did reveal the silhouette of a bird, perched on the edge of the roof. A crow or raven, maybe? A shiver ran through her, and she had to wonder if it was a bad omen.

To distract herself from her worries, she focused on the house. Oddly, if the structure had been taken care of, it would be the sort of place Paige would normally love. It had to be more than two centuries old, and she'd put money on it being closer to three. Who knew what sort of treasures could lie inside? Probably filthy treasures at this point, she thought, but that would be easy enough to remedy.

Her steps slowed when she neared the door, apprehension taking over once more. For a second, she wanted nothing more than to turn around and run back down the drive. To simply go home and have her dad tell her he hadn't meant any of it, that she could absolutely stay in the home she'd grown up in. On the heels of those thoughts came another. She was no coward, and this man had answers. More, she had found him for a reason, so she wasn't going to tuck tail and run. She was better than that. Yes, she'd received a punch in the gut tonight—literally—but she was going to do herself proud. Right now, pride was essentially all she had.

Head held high, she stepped up to the door. Before she could ring the doorbell, it opened. There stood the man from the alley, her rescuer. He was in the same pair of jeans and button-down shirt, was still the sexiest man she'd ever seen, but now he looked absolutely pissed. Not that she could really blame him. It was late, and she was an intruder.

"What the hell are you doing at my house? For that matter, how did you find me?" he demanded, his body filling the doorway, arms folded over his chest. At the moment, he looked less like her savior and more like a scoundrel, but it did nothing to detract from his appeal.

Since he clearly didn't want her inside, she stood on the partially shielded stoop, water dripping from her hair, with one stray drop falling from the tip of her nose. Despite her best efforts to beat the rain, she was soaked through, and she wanted to scream at him. To ask why he'd save her from a mugger just to let her get pneumonia. But anger wouldn't get her out of the weather.

"I don't know," Paige admitted, in the calmest, most serene voice she could manage. She'd had enough of temper tonight, especially male temper, to do anything to encourage it. "Somehow I just knew this address, and that it was yours."

There was no attempt to hide his skepticism. He arched a brow and gave her a hard look. "Explain."

She really wished he'd let her come inside, as she was getting wetter by the second, but she knew better than to press. Yet. She could sense that he was wary of her and wanted to be left alone. There was an undercurrent of interest, though. Not the interest of a man who sees a woman he desires, but like she'd done something curious. She had no idea how she knew those things, but she decided to trust her instincts.

"I really can't explain much more than that," she continued reluctantly. "I...I needed someplace to stay, and suddenly it came to me where I could find you. I've never been to this part of the country. I haven't even traveled much outside of London, but I just somehow knew your address and was able to give it to the cabbie. I knew it would lead to you."

He was silent for several moments. "And just why did you come here?" he asked, not yet relaxing, but he wasn't scowling at her any longer. "Even if I accept that you knew I was here, why me? What do you want?"

Paige normally wasn't one for over-sharing. She was friendly, yes, but tended to keep her personal business to herself. Something had her telling him the whole truth, regardless of how personal and embarrassing it was. "When I got home, when I mentioned to my dad that I was attacked, he was worried...at first. Then I told him how I thought my rescuer—how you—had saved me with magic." The memory of her dad's anger made her swallow and blink to fight back tears. "I was just joking, I didn't really believe it, but he went kind of mad. Said he wouldn't have magic or...or witches in his house. He told me to go, and he didn't just mean for a little while, either. He wanted me to leave for good. To move out."

Paige saw as much as felt that he wasn't sure if he could believe her. When he started to speak, she hurried on. "He called me a witch, because I thought how much I wanted help with that mugger, and then you found me. I can't say if I am a witch, but if that's the case, if you did use magic to save me, you're the only person I've ever met who knew about magic besides my dad. I had to come here. Please. Please don't send me away." She forgot her calm facade enough that a plea slipped into her voice. She hated herself for it, but couldn't take it back.

He looked unmoved but asked, "What's your name? And your father's?"

"I'm Paige, Paige Williams, and my dad's name is Jacob Williams," she answered, relieved that he had yet to shut the door in her face. Relief turned to confusion when he was surprised at hearing the names. It was almost as though they were familiar to him. She kept her questions to herself, instead holding her breath to see what he'd say.

"Are you hoping that I will teach you magic?"

She blinked. It wasn't something she had thought about consciously, but now that she *was* thinking about it, she very much wanted to learn if she had magic of her own. And if she did, she certainly wanted to learn to wield it. "I...yes, I suppose I am."

The thought that she could have magic sent a thrill running through her and dried her tears before they could fall. Not that she'd truly notice a tear with the rain dripping down her face.

Even as he began to respond, she swayed on her feet. Paige remembered that she'd suffered a head injury, and hadn't had time to tend to it, or even rest. She had been too worried in the cab to focus on what was, at the time, a minor concern. Adrenaline and stubbornness were likely the only reasons she was still upright.

Before she could fall, he muttered a curse and scooped her neatly off her feet. She gave a soft squeak of surprise as he turned and carried her into a parlor, with her too stunned to do anything but let him. Though the sofa he set her on looked reasonably clean, the rest of the room and entryway were as dingy as the exterior of the house. She saw several cobwebs, and most of the surfaces in her line of sight were covered in a thick layer of dust. Even the wallpaper was grimy, and she absently wondered how long it had been since anyone had bothered to clean the house. More, she wondered how dust could accumulate like it had in an occupied home. But her antique-loving eye could see the beauty that lay beneath the dirt. If she squinted a bit.

A careless flick of the man's fingers toward the fireplace had flames leaping up, and the sudden display of magic made her jump.

"You haven't tended to your injuries, have you?" he snapped.

Sheepishly, she shook her head. "I didn't get the chance. I got kicked out only a few minutes after arriving home."

He gave an annoyed growl, one that intensified when she tried to get up. He stopped her with a mostly gentle shove to her shoulder. "Where do you think you're going? You've probably got a concussion."

"But I have to get my things out of the rain!"

His jaw clenched, but he turned on his heel. A moment later, she heard the door slam before he brought the suitcases and bag into the parlor. She was happy to see he didn't drop them, but set them down easily despite his irritation.

In the short time it had taken him to bring her things inside, she'd sat up but remained sitting on the couch. She didn't want to push him, and she did feel rather wretched. Aside from the pounding headache, her back was sore and her cheeks hurt from where the mugger's hand had clamped down on her mouth. It wasn't as intense as it had been before her good Samaritan had done whatever it was he'd done when he touched her, but it still wasn't pleasant.

He sat down beside her and gently placed his hands on her head. The headache began to ease immediately. She closed her eyes, sighing softly with relief. The other injuries were minor and more easily ignored. She might be stiff tomorrow, and would certainly be bruised, but that was preferable to dealing with a concussion. By the time he spoke, she could barely tell she'd been hurt. Part of her wondered why he hadn't done that when he'd eased the pain before, but she was too grateful to question him.

"Headache gone?"

"Yes, thank you," Paige said, her eyes open now as she smiled gratefully at him, which had dimples flashing in both her cheeks.

He gave a noncommittal sound and leaned back, studying her. "I could be persuaded to take you on as an apprentice, Paige, but it does come with some conditions."

Her mind hadn't made the connection between learning magic and becoming an apprentice, though now that it had occurred to her, she almost giggled. She'd be the sorcerer's apprentice. On that thought, she sobered. She would also be agreeing to working with a man who was, in a real sense, a total stranger. Yes, he'd saved her then taken care of her injuries, but she really didn't know anything about him. On the other hand, she had nothing to go back to. No home, no family. Not anymore. And while she'd liked her job, she hadn't loved it. She'd rather work at a museum, dealing with history. So if she did agree to this, and he turned out to be a horrible person, she wasn't really any worse off. And, hopefully, she would know more about herself. She'd discover things she couldn't learn in the library or any museum.

Magic. Just thinking the word made excitement race through her, and she knew she couldn't turn down this opportunity.

She drew in a slow breath and fought to remain calm. "What conditions would those be, sir?"

He scowled. "First, you don't call me sir. My name is Julian. Julian Mooreton. I don't care if you call me Julian or Mooreton, as long you don't call me sir."

Paige grinned and nodded. "That's easy enough, now that I know your name."

"Second...there are a few rooms here which are private. I never want to discover that you've been snooping. You're a stranger, Paige, and some of what I do is sensitive."

There was an instant nod of agreement. "Of course. I would never snoop through your things," she promised. Though she found herself exceptionally curious as to what, exactly, he did.

Her easy acquiescence had him giving her a sharp, suspicious look, but he continued. "Third, you'll be asked to assist me when needed, with magic and research. I'm not a slave driver, so you won't be worked to death, but it is something that's required of you as my apprentice."

She'd expected that anyway and gave him another dimple-filled smile. "That sounds lovely! It's just a chance to learn something," she replied eagerly.

As though he wanted her to take a moment before agreeing to something, he added, "You'll also be required to clean up after yourself. I don't need someone underfoot who will be leaving messes all over my house."

Paige blinked, then hid a smile. The house was nothing but a mess, at least from what she'd seen so far so she wasn't sure how he'd miss one more mess. Given her love of history, and the fact that this house was centuries old, she planned to do what she could to clean and restore it.

There was no doubt in her mind that it would be beautiful if it only had a bit of care. She nearly laughed as she wondered what his reaction would be to seeing his neglected home clean and shining again. She nodded. "Agreed."

He sighed and got to his feet. "Then come with me. I'll show you to your room." He picked up her suitcases, leaving her just the bag to carry. With each step that took her to her bedroom, she felt lighter and happier than she'd been in a very long time.

CHAPTER 3

The room given to Paige was tidy, though it held some of the dust she'd seen in the rest of the house. The sheets on the bed were clean, at least. They did smell a bit musty, but it was nothing she couldn't live with for a single night. And while she worried she wouldn't be able to sleep due to everything that had happened to her, after changing into pajamas and lying down, she was out within minutes.

The next morning, she woke not long after dawn and made her way downstairs in search of caffeine and Julian. Despite the house being in such dire need of cleaning, it was old and full of antiques, so she all but tip-toed around until she located the kitchen. To her surprise, it was not only clean, but occupied.

Julian sat at the small table in a little breakfast nook. He cradled a mug of coffee in his hands, but across from him was another, still hot and steaming.

"Good morning," Julian said before he sipped from his cup, eyes fixed on her.

Paige hovered in the doorway for a moment before she nodded and moved to take the other seat. "Morning," she replied softly. She wasn't quite certain how to act around him today. Last night she'd been caught off guard by her father and the mugging, and hadn't thought her plan through, not fully. Despite him agreeing to teach her magic, it was entirely possible she'd just made the worst mistake of her life. But what other choice had she had? A hotel? She would have only been able to afford a few nights. Apprenticing to Julian might not pay at all, but it sounded as if room and board would be included, so it couldn't be all bad. If nothing else, it would give her time to figure something else out if needed.

"Did you sleep well?" he asked as she stirred sugar and cream into her coffee.

"I did, yes. Very well. Thank you." They were both being so polite it almost hurt. She hadn't expected it from him. In the aftermath of the attack he'd been nice enough, but she wouldn't have called him polite. Stiff, certainly, but that wasn't the same thing.

"Good. I imagine you have quite a few questions?"

She sipped her coffee, though it wasn't truly necessary for her to wake up. The offer of answers alone was sufficient to jolt her to full coherence. "I do, yes. Before yesterday, I'd never heard of witches or magic in anything but a fictional setting. It was a little shocking, actually, to hear that they exist." She smiled weakly. "I thought the mugger floating against the wall was all just some hallucination brought about by a concussion until my dad started in on witches."

"It isn't only witches," Julian said as he got up and moved to the oven. He opened the door and drew two cloth-covered plates from within before nudging it closed. "Do you need to wake up a bit more, or do you want to begin now?" he asked as he set a plate in front of her before he retook his seat.

She pulled the napkin off her plate and saw that he'd made sausage, eggs, and toast. They were still warm, so she assumed he'd been expecting her. At first she wondered how he could have timed it so precisely, but fell back on her new catch-all explanation—magic. "No, I'm awake enough. Please, I want to know everything."

One corner of his mouth twitched upward. "You will not learn everything in a single morning, but I can tell you the basics of what else exists."

"That will do for now, thank you," Paige said with a smile before she started eating. It was decent, though hardly the best she'd ever eaten. Still, it was hot and filling, and she wasn't about to complain about his hospitality. Especially when her current situation still felt so uncertain. Like one wrong move would result in her with nothing and no one.

"First, I would suggest you forget what you've read or seen in a TV show or movie. While some of it is at least vaguely factual, most isn't. If you try to take those stories as truth, you'll end up confused or simply wrong."

She nodded. "That makes sense." Besides, there was very little consistency in those works of fiction. Each author or screenwriter had their own take on the world of the supernatural.

"There are three types of people who live on Earth. Humans, the Arcane—which includes witches as well as the other types of supernatural people—and the gods. I'm not going to go into any great detail about the Arcane as a whole right now, but we all have some sort of power, whether it's an innate ability like the shapeshifters or true magic like with witches. We also live a great deal longer than humans." He canted his head slightly. "If you are a witch—and I suspect you are—you have almost another ten centuries to live."

Paige stared at him, forgetting to chew for a moment. She swallowed quickly, barely managing not to choke on her sausage. "Ten centuries? As in a thousand years?" she asked, her voice a little higher pitched than it had been a moment before. Later, she would wonder how that fact took precedence over the bombshell that gods existed, but for now, it did.

He chuckled and nodded. "A thousand years," he confirmed. "There are a few types of supernaturals that live longer and a few that are essentially immortal, but a thousand years is fairly average." He paused a moment, then asked, "Do you need a minute, or would you like me to go on?"

Slowly, she shook her head. Truthfully, she did want a minute to process, but if she was this shocked so soon into his explanation, there was bound to be more. It would be better to hear it all at once. Or so she hoped. The other option was that she would suffer from information overload and break her mind. "No, please, continue."

He studied her for a long moment before he nodded. "For now, I'll focus on witches. We are people who have power of our own and can harness it to do magic, such as starting the fire last night, levitating people, or, in your case, telepathy. Exactly what can be done depends on the person, but we can all do magic. Other members of the Arcane can't, not like us. They might be able to shift forms, have heightened physical attributes, or perform a type of magic that is extremely limited, such as affecting a single element."

She took a slow breath and nodded. "And you mentioned gods, plural?" she asked, fighting to keep her voice steady. "They're real, too?"

He felt a surge of respect for this young woman. She'd been mugged, kicked out of her home, abandoned by her only family, and thrust into an unfamiliar world, but she wasn't crumbling. She was doing her best to pick herself up and move past it, to thrive. While he largely just wanted to be left alone, had never wanted an apprentice, he couldn't find it in himself to make her leave. No, he would do as promised and educate her.

"Are you familiar with Greek mythology? Or perhaps Egyptian? Any of the polytheistic religions, really."

Paige had to laugh despite feeling like she was drowning. "I spend every Friday at the British Museum. I've seen all sorts of exhibits that have art and artifacts that mention or portray the gods." She sobered when she realized what he was getting at. "Those are the gods you meant?"

"Indeed. They all exist, though a few of them have been killed or faded through the millennia. I wouldn't suggest calling out to any of them, though. Having them take notice of you isn't always a good thing," he warned. "Like people, not all gods are good."

She swallowed as she remembered some of the stories where various gods toyed with humans or tortured them for one silly reason or another. "And all of these...people...they live together on Earth, hiding from humans? How? Shouldn't people—the humans—notice some of this?"

"No, they shouldn't notice. There is only one law that all members of the Arcane must follow, and that is to make sure we don't reveal ourselves to humans. We have the power, yes, even the experience, but we're grossly outnumbered."

Her brow furrowed. "But what about that man in the alley? Wasn't that breaking the law?"

Julian shook his head. "First, he was drunk. Second, I ensured he wouldn't remember being pinned with magic. Lastly, our law is more concerned with large groups of people, or the world as a whole. A single individual isn't as much a concern, especially if they're not powerful or influential." A faint smile curved his lips. "If he did remember and started telling people what had happened, what do you think would happen?"

"Oh. Yes, people would think he was insane or had simply drank too much, wouldn't they?"

"Precisely. As to the other part of your question, not all of us live on Earth. Some—like demons—live in other dimensions, or places that aren't quite dimensions, but other planes of existence. I'm sure you've heard of Olympus, for example." She nodded and he went on. "The Arcane largely reside on Earth, however, and yes, they live together. For the most part, we live as humans do. We have jobs and families, just like anyone else. We pay taxes, we vote, we do everything humans do."

"I'm trying to picture shapeshifters or witches who are hundreds of years old working as accountants or cops, and it's not easy," she admitted.

"That's exactly what some of us do, though," Julian said with a shrug. "Some of us do have jobs that are out of the ordinary, if you're only used to human professions. Some are, technically, illegal. We have specialists who forge identities for us, for example. If you're two hundred years old, you can't exactly show a birth certificate with your actual date of birth, after all."

Paige leaned forward, her food forgotten, her arms folded on the table. "What sort of out of the ordinary jobs?"

"Healers, potion makers, demon hunters, or demonologists, just to name a few."

"And what job do you have?"

"Demonologist. So you'll be learning quite a lot about demons, dimensions, and ancient languages." He cocked a brow. "Are you okay with that?"

It took everything Paige had not to let out a cry of happiness as she nodded eagerly. "I love ancient history, so learning the languages would be...fantastic." It was too tame a word, but she couldn't think of one to properly convey how she felt. "As far as demons or dimensions? I want to learn everything about my new world I can."

"I think you mean that," he murmured. "Very well. Meet me in the parlor in an hour. That's the room with the fireplace from last night. I'll show you around the house, then we'll get started. And no, we will not dive right into demonology."

Disappointed, Paige said, "We're won't?"

He reluctantly smiled. "No. Instead, we're going to find out where your magical talents lie."

All disappointment faded in a flash. "Oh, well, that's fine then."

"Good. Then eat up. I'll see you in an hour," he told her before he rose and left the kitchen.

Paige looked at her plate. It didn't really appeal to her any longer, but she knew she needed to eat. Her mind was filled with hope and questions, and she needed fuel if she was going to be up for learning everything Julian had to teach her. And she intended to learn it all.

Julian wasn't sure what to make of the woman in his kitchen. When he'd first heard her telepathic cry for help the night before, he'd just been wandering around London. He had actually wanted to be alone, but figured he could save her, then move on with his life. He certainly hadn't expected to see her show up at his front door mere hours later, soaked to the bone and pleading for assistance.

He also hadn't expected to be intrigued by her or to feel the first stirrings of desire he'd experienced since his wife died. Not just the physical need for release, but true desire. He'd shoved it firmly aside and focused on the woman's story and the possibilities that had brought her to his door.

While he'd told her he was going to test her to see what abilities she had, he was certain he knew at least some of them. For her to have known where to find him, and with such apparent ease, there was at least one power she had to be skilled in. Still, he would check. And yes, he'd teach her, just like he'd promised, but it wouldn't be anything more than that. If he could help it, the only thing between them would be the bond between teacher and student. He *liked* being alone, and having a young witch who knew nothing in his space was going to try every bit of patience he possessed.

He hoped it was only her ignorance that would cause him trouble, but something deep inside him told him that would only be the start of it.

CHAPTER 4

Paige took the hour Julian had given her to finish eating then take a shower. After she was clean and in fresh clothes, she went downstairs to the parlor. She made a wrong turn—twice—but found it, only to realize she had beaten him there. She sat on the same sofa he'd laid her on the night before, but didn't have time to do anything else before he walked in.

"Ah, good. You're here. Come on, there are a few rooms you need to be aware of," he said, motioning for her to follow him.

She rose and hurried out after him. "Such as?"

"The library, for one, and the rooms that I told you are private, but most importantly, my workshop." He glanced at her, his voice going serious. "The workshop is just that, a place for work. You'll become familiar with it, since that's where we'll be doing most anything that deals with magic or demons, but I'd rather you not go in there when we're not working. There are quite a few extremely old books and scrolls, as well as some artifacts, and I'm quite particular about how they're handled."

Paige nodded. "I understand. I'll be careful when I'm in there," she promised, hoping her eagerness didn't show. Old scrolls and books? Her fingers itched to get a hold of them.

"Good." He led her down the hall and opened one of the doors, gesturing for her to go inside. "You're welcome in this library whenever you like. While there are a few first editions, nothing in here is truly irreplaceable. You'll find copies of most of these works at regular bookstores, and I encourage reading and learning in all its forms. So long as you're careful with the books and get something from them—even if that's simple enjoyment—then you can take whatever you like."

Paige peeked inside and was both thrilled and horrified. It was a large room, full of floor-to-ceiling shelves that were crowded with books. A spiral staircase led to a second level, and after taking a few steps inside, she could see the second floor was just as full. But even a quick glance showed that it was woefully disorganized, and it looked like no one had been in here in years, judging by the amount of dust that covered every available surface.

"I do enjoy reading," was all she told him, not willing to criticize his housekeeping. He nodded and drew her out of the library to continue on.

They went upstairs and he stopped by two doors placed close together. He touched the knob on the first door. "This is my bedroom. I like my privacy, though it's not entirely off-limits. You might need to come find me at some point or another. Though I do, of course, ask that you knock rather than barging in." He shrugged and moved to the second door, but didn't even touch the knob, just stared at the wood. "This room is strictly off-limits. If I find you in here, you're gone." His head slightly turned toward her, just enough to let his gaze shift to meet hers. "No arguments, no questions. You'll simply be evicted from the house and I won't teach you another thing. I'll make sure no one else will, either," he told her, his voice flat, clipped, and dangerously serious.

The warning made Paige very curious, but she could tell he wasn't exaggerating what his reaction would be. "I understand. I won't go in there."

"Good." He said nothing else as he went back downstairs, but they didn't stop on the first floor, instead going down one more level.

The stairs ended at a door, which made Paige wonder just how large this workshop of Julian's was. When he opened the door and they stepped inside, she was a little disappointed to see it was only about as big as the parlor. It was, however, pristine. This was clearly where Julian spent most of his time, and one of the few places important enough for him to bother cleaning.

The workshop was rectangular and, aside from the door and wall it stood on, covered in heavy shelving. Most of those shelves were packed with books and scrolls, most of them clearly old, perhaps centuries old. A few shelves held jars full of what she could only guess were bits for potions or spells, along with various odds and ends that Paige couldn't hope to name. She'd certainly never seen any of them in any store, even holistic healing shops. There were a few things that looked so alien that she wondered if they'd come from one of the dimensions Julian had mentioned.

In the center of the room was a large, heavy wooden table. It was scarred from use and covered with papers and books. It only had two chairs; one was an ordinary chair, though a mismatched cushion had been added, while the other was heavier and looked much more comfortable. The padding on it had been in place for so long that it had faded and taken the impression of the body that occupied it so often.

"Have a seat," Julian said as he relaxed into the well-used chair. To Paige's relief, his voice had thawed, so he no longer sounded quite as untouchable as he had in the upstairs hall.

"This is your workshop?" Paige asked as she looked around at everything she could see as she settled into the other seat.

"It is. And it's warded, which is why it's the perfect place to test your magic."

Her gaze whipped back to him. "What do you mean?"

"No magic you can use in here will harm anything or escape this room. I, along with people who owed me favors, worked hard to ensure that this is as safe a place as possible when it comes to using magic. Fire won't hurt the books, for example, which was honestly my biggest concern."

"I'm going to use fire?" Paige asked excitedly, fixating on that single word.

"Perhaps," Julian said with a slow shrug. "We don't know yet where your talents lie, after all. You could always have an affinity for, say, water instead of fire. Or no elemental ability at all. The powers a witch can have are many and varied. That's why we're here."

"Oh. That makes sense." She supposed it did, anyway. She was hardly an expert on witchcraft. "How do we begin?"

"You're going to attempt to use various types of magic, but I have a feeling that I know the direction at least some of your powers lean, since you called to me telepathically without knowing what you were," he explained.

"Telepathically?" She grinned. "That is so cool."

"It can be." He stretched his hand out, palm up. "What I want you to do is take my hand and try to read my thoughts. Likely you'll only get what I'm thinking about at the moment, but that's enough for our purposes."

"But *how* do I read your thoughts?" she asked with a frown as she slowly stretched her hand out and laid her palm over his. It was warm and rougher than she'd expected, but not unpleasantly so. It also sent a thrill of desire through her, followed immediately by a thought. *"I'd better be careful and shield a bit. I don't want her hearing..."* The voice in her head trailed off and Paige realized it hadn't been her thought. After a moment, the voice turned wry and almost amused. *"You figured it out already, didn't you?"*

Paige jerked her hand back, eyes wide. "Was that...were those...your thoughts?"

He nodded. "They were. You did that effortlessly, too. I think it's safe to say you're going to be a skilled telepath. Before we move onto the...flashier magics...let's try the other mental magics."

"I...um...wow. I never dreamed that I'd be able to read people's minds," she stammered, surprised by the feeling of rightness the prospect of being a mental witch brought. And how having his thoughts in her head hadn't felt intrusive like she might have expected.

"You will hear plenty, I'm sure, though not everyone will be as easy to read or will be shielded. I'll teach you how to do that later so you can prevent your thoughts from being heard." He actually smiled then, though it wasn't as open and bright as hers tended to be. "Right now, I want you to take my hand again, but instead of trying to read my mind, focus on my emotions." His smile grew tight then, but he left his hand out. "If you can read emotions as well, then you'll be what's termed an empath."

He seemed less happy than he had about her reading his mind, but his hand was steady as she placed hers into it. "Okay," she murmured. She tried doing it with her eyes open, but she was too caught up in studying his face to focus on the task set to her. When she closed her eyes, she was still distracted by the feel of his hand against hers, but it was more manageable. Now it was one distraction rather than two. She breathed slowly and focused her thoughts on his emotions, into feeling what he felt. She didn't have to try long before she became annoyed, tense, and there was an odd fluctuation between resigned and hopeful.

Her teeth clenched as the annoyance became her own, her body tensing. "This is ridiculous," she muttered, but when she tried to pull her hand back, Julian's fingers closed over hers.

"It's not. Relax, Paige. It's not your emotions you're feeling. It's easy to get overwhelmed the first few times you feel the emotions of others," he said, and the annoyance disappeared, replaced by a hint of surprise.

"What? Oh! Oh, I'm so sorry, Julian, I didn't mean—"

His hand opened and he shook his head. "It's quite all right. It's nothing to apologize for. Like I said, it's easy to get overwhelmed. I have yet to hear of an empath who didn't feel someone else's emotions as their own at least once." He drew his hand back. "That was actually quite good. There's one more mental magic I'd like to test you on, though." He rose and moved to one of the shelves, taking a small, leather-bound book down. Once he'd retaken his seat, he set the book on the table. "Have you ever heard of psychometry?" When she only shook her head, he explained. "It's the ability to touch an object—sometimes a person—and get impressions off that object. Some can get impressions from a location just by being in it. Emotional imprints from people who touched it or stood in it, perhaps, or places an object had been. It varies from object to object and place to place." He pushed the book a little closer to her. "I'd like you to touch this book, to hold it, and see if you can get anything from it."

This time Paige hesitated, not because she was reluctant, but because pieces were starting to put themselves together in her mind. "I don't think I need to."

He frowned. "What do you mean?" he asked, but there was a light in his eyes that she interpreted to mean the question was more test than true query.

She looked up from the book and met his gaze. "I knew where you lived. I knew your address. You didn't tell me, and it's doubtful you were thinking of your address when you helped me up in that alley. Even if you were, I didn't hear your address like I heard your thoughts a minute ago."

Something close to a smile flickered on his face for a fraction of a second, and he nodded. "I see. Yes, that would most likely count as psychometry. But let's just be certain. We don't know precisely what happened before. Adrenaline can cause a person to do astonishing things, both for humans and the Arcane. Just like someone could lift a car off a child, sometimes witches can perform magic they otherwise wouldn't be able to."

She nodded. "All right." She reached for the book with both hands. Half of her expected to get something the moment she touched the leather, but she didn't. It wasn't more than a minute before she had a sense of knowing, however. "It's a journal," she murmured, her head tilting as she focused harder on the book. The rush of facts didn't end, but was joined by images. A man sitting at a desk, writing with a quill by candlelight. The same man carrying the journal as he walked through the streets of some city, centuries ago, she guessed. The man sitting at the bedside of an old, ill-looking woman, writing as she spoke.

The images vanished when Julian pulled the journal from her fingers. "I said your name a couple of times," he explained when she gave him a confused look. "I suppose it's safe to say that you got something more from it than just that it was a journal?"

Paige flexed her fingers and nodded. "I saw a man writing in it, carrying it, transcribing an old woman's words..."

Julian looked pleased. "It belonged to the man who taught my mentor. He traveled the world gathering information about demons. So you did very well."

She felt her cheeks flush with pleasure. "Thank you. What's next?"

"Now we move onto other magics. Physical magics. Elemental, healing, things like that."

A smile curved her lips. "I can't wait."

Unfortunately, those trials didn't go as well. When they tested her ability to move things with her mind, she struggled with even lifting a piece of paper. They tried elemental magics next. To her disappointment, she couldn't make so much as a spark or drop of water. The other elements he coached her through went no better. When he decided to give teleporting a shot, she couldn't move an inch without doing it the old-fashioned way, but gave herself a mild headache trying.

The last bit of magic they tested was healing. Paige was shocked when Julian took a dagger off a shelf and pulled the sharp tip of it across his palm.

"Julian! Oh my god, why did you do that?" she asked, standing quickly and rushing around the table to take his hand in hers, putting pressure on the cut.

He gave her a look that was a cross between amused and baffled. "I told you we were going to see how you were at healing. You can't do that without something to heal."

She blushed and nodded. "Oh, yes. I forgot for a moment," she mumbled, embarrassed.

"No, it's fine. But why don't you go ahead and try to heal the cut?" he suggested. "Since it's there."

"Yes, that's true. What do I do?"

"Healing something visible like this is relatively simple. Focus on it, direct your magic to seal the wound shut, to regrow the skin."

She had to take a few deep breaths to steady herself before she could focus on what she was supposed to be doing. She wanted, desperately, to heal the wound and ease his pain, but she felt none of the power she'd felt when she was using the mental magics. "I'm sorry, but I don't think it's working."

"It's fine, Paige. Not everyone has a talent for healing," Julian told her, patting her hand before using his own power to heal the small cut. "Like I told you before, we all have different talents. A lack of ability in one type of magic doesn't mean you're inept. For example, I'm friends with a woman called Suni. She's an amazing healer, probably the best in the world. I wouldn't be surprised if she could heal anything short of death. But she can't do half of what you can do without any sort of training. We all have our talents. If we were all equally as good at everything, how boring would the world be?"

She smiled faintly and took a step back. "That's a fair point." She sighed. "What's next?"

"Next? We get to work. Strengthening your magic, teaching you about demons, and instructing you on how to be my apprentice." Julian smiled. "You better sit down, because you've got a lot of work ahead of you."

Just twenty-four hours ago, this would have seemed crazy to her, but the part of her that craved knowledge absolutely couldn't wait.

CHAPTER 5

Three years later

Music poured out of the speaker on the table. Paige absently hummed along, but she didn't really hear it. She was too absorbed with her task and thoughts to pay it much attention, but she enjoyed having the background noise whenever she worked, especially when she was cataloging thousands of books.

The 'public' library was still a chaotic mess. It had been just as bad as she'd originally thought when she'd first been shown the room. There hadn't been order to anything, and the dust was as thick as she'd estimated. While it was now clean, it was still disorganized. Other rooms had been a higher priority, and her magic lessons had taken up quite a bit of her time.

Paige had found a very thorough, very exacting teacher in Julian, but she couldn't have been happier about that.

Under his tutelage, she had strengthened her own powers, though she was disappointed that she was still hopeless with any of the physical magics. Not too disappointed, however. The powers she did have were impressive—to her, in any case—and could be a lot of fun. They could absolutely be convenient. It was hard for her to lose anything, for instance, which had come in very handy when she was still learning her way around the big house. All she had to do was focus on the object and she would get an impression of where it was. Things she handled a lot were easier to locate, but as long as she'd touched something, she was generally able to find it.

And, just as he'd promised, magic wasn't all she learned from him either. He was not just a demonologist, but, judging by the number of people who called or came to him for help or advice on the subject, one of the best on the planet. Because of his specialty, a good number of his books and other texts weren't in English, which meant she'd been picking up bits of several languages, just like he'd warned. Old languages, mostly. And just as she'd promised, she loved every word she learned. True, they weren't easy to learn, but she studied hard and truly enjoyed the process.

More, she learned about Julian, going off observation and her own empathic skills. He was careful to keep a shield on his mind to hide his thoughts from her, but she still figured out much about him. While he was a demanding teacher, he was never harsh. Though he was very particular in his work—and how she assisted in that work—she liked the fact that he never treated her as though she were lesser than him. He even, on occasion, seemed to truly appreciate her help.

Paige smiled as she thought of his reaction when he'd seen her first efforts to restore the house. Since she'd had to quit her job, being so far away, she'd needed something to occupy her time between lessons and the things she studied on her own. The parlor had been scrubbed to within an inch of its life until it looked completely out of place in the otherwise rundown home. She'd also attacked the garden she found behind the house with glee. She loved flowers, so it had pained her to see so many overgrown bushes and strangled flowers. It had taken her weeks to make it look halfway presentable again. A full year until she was happy with it.

Julian had been gruff and snapped at her at first when he'd seen those two areas, but she'd felt his surprise and reluctant admiration, even as he complained. There was shame, too, that he'd allowed it to reach such a state, but he'd adjusted. In time, he'd started visiting the garden more, which pleased her.

The biggest surprise about him, however, had come by accident. After she'd gotten several other rooms cleaned, and his surprise had changed to pleasure, she'd tentatively asked if she could give his bedroom the same treatment. It made the most sense for her to go after the rooms they used before dealing with guest rooms. After a long pause, he'd agreed, but warned her not to go into the adjoining room, or open anything that was locked. That was easy enough for her to concede to—she wouldn't have done so anyway—and she got right to work.

When cleaning up, she'd found a woman's wedding ring hidden behind the bed, tucked in a gap between the floor and the wall. Upon touching it, she had gotten one of the strongest impressions she'd ever received from any object. Except this one gave off conflicting emotions. Pure joy came first, followed immediately by great sorrow. It had left her breathless and astounded once she'd sorted through the flashes of images.

Julian had been married. To a human, it seemed. One who had died of old age long before Paige had even been born.

Forcing herself back into the here and now, Paige shook her head. She couldn't blame Julian for being so closed off, given what he'd suffered. And he had opened up some in the last three years. Nor was he surprised any longer when he would walk into a room and see her there. All in all, things were good. She had even stopped mourning the loss of her relationship with her father. It had taken a full year for her to accept he wasn't going to change his mind, but she wouldn't allow herself to think about it too often.

Only one thing marred her new life. Despite his grumpy nature, she'd fallen in love with Julian, but he barely seemed to notice she was even female. Her attempts at flirting had gone equally unnoticed, whether it was a subtle innuendo, teasing comment, or time spent making herself look appealing. Because of that, she'd learned to block her own thoughts so he didn't catch a stray longing. Shielding was now an ingrained habit.

She paused midway through the shelf she was working on and frowned. No, that wasn't the only blip in an otherwise happy life. The past year, Julian had become extra secretive. He'd been working on something new, something that felt important. He didn't ask for her assistance like he normally would, and hadn't even given her a clue as to what he was working on.

Not to mention that a few months ago, he'd gotten a phone call in the middle of dinner. Whatever had been said, he'd disappeared. He'd returned unharmed, but wouldn't say anything about it other than he was helping a friend in America. That was the most surprising, since he had told her he hadn't left the country in years.

She shrugged to herself and continued sorting. There wasn't really anything she could do about it. She was here for Julian, regardless of whether he saw her as an apprentice, friend, woman, or anything else. And worrying wasn't going to solve the problem either.

"Paige?"

She'd gotten used to telepathic communication in the three years she'd been here. It no longer phased her at all. In fact, it was more convenient than cell phones. But it came just infrequently enough to make her curious. *"Yes? Is there something you need?"*

There was a brief hesitation. *"Can you come down to my workshop?"*

"Of course. I'll be there in a minute."

Leaving everything where it was, she got up and made her way to the workshop. It had once been a wine cellar, she'd learned, but Julian had converted it into a workshop before covering it in wards and other magical protection. It was a fascinating room, and she come to love spending time in it, despite how disorganized it appeared. One of these days, she was going to convince Julian to let her organize it properly, but he insisted he knew where everything was. Wryly, she had to admit that he usually did.

Paige stepped into the room to find Julian sitting at the table. He was frowning and visibly antsy, and though he was more likely to frown than smile, fidgeting or showing any sign of nerves was completely unlike him. And that wasn't the only thing unusual about the sight presented to her. For the first time that she'd seen, the table wasn't cluttered. A single book sat in front of him, and he absently drummed his fingers on the thick leather cover. She couldn't see the title of the book, though she could tell it was old. Since most of the books he kept in this room were more than half a millennium old, that didn't narrow things down at all.

She caught the waves of uncertainty and frustration pouring off of him. "Is everything okay?" she asked, stopping just inside the door.

He waved a hand at her chair. "It's fine," he replied, but the word was more clipped than usual.

This was new, and she got nervous. Her mind came up with all sorts of reasons for him to call her down here. Was he kicking her out? Had he decided he couldn't teach her anything else since the physical magic just wouldn't come?

She sat, but couldn't relax. Briefly, she thought about taking a peek in his mind—she thought she *might* be able to penetrate his shields if she tried—but dismissed it as rude. Surely he wouldn't keep her in suspense long.

As seconds, then minutes ticked by, the idea of finding out for herself what was going on surfaced again. Before she could talk herself into it, he straightened.

"I need your help."

Paige blinked at him. "Of course." She'd been helping him for three years, so she didn't understand the buildup. "What do you need me to do?"

He ran a hand through his hair, then over the stubble on his cheeks. "Before we get into that, I want to give you the option to back out of helping me now."

She frowned. "Why would I back out? I'm your apprentice, Julian. I've happily helped you every time you've asked since day one." Though she knew he didn't like what he called 'cheeky apprentices', she pressed on. "What's so awful about this help? You're acting like you don't actually want me to help."

"Because I don't," he snapped. He pushed back his chair and started to pace.

No, he didn't want her help. He didn't want to involve anyone, even his now-invaluable apprentice. It was too dangerous, and he'd become...fond...of Paige. Not only was she extremely competent, she was sweet, a hard worker, and...no, he wouldn't go there. Still, want or not, he needed her if he wanted to get past the wall he'd hit in his research. And he *had* to succeed. While giving up normally wasn't in him, with this particular task, he simply couldn't fail.

"You do a lot of reading, studying, when you're not with me, yes?" he asked when he stopped pacing.

"Yes. Though usually it's books in the library, since you won't let me take any of these books out of the workshop."

It was a stringent rule of his, for the safety of the volumes and one of the first things she'd learned. He needed to reconsider his rule about her being in here without him. She'd learn more if she had more time to study these books. "Have you come across anything about magical objects or relics?"

Paige cocked her head. It was a hint, but not nearly enough of one. She had no idea where he was going with this train of thought. "Of course. Not as much as I would have liked, but I've seen some references here and there. Why?"

When he spoke, there was a hesitation, and she knew that it wasn't what he had originally intended to say. "The help I'm going to ask you is going to be dangerous, Paige. Potentially fatal, though I doubt it will come to anything that extreme, but it is possible. You didn't sign on with me to be put in danger, so I want you to decide if that's something you're willing to risk. If you're not, that's fine. We'll continue as we have been."

But Paige didn't want things to continue as they were. She wanted to find out what he was working on so diligently by himself. She wanted to make sure he took care of himself. It was painfully obvious he wasn't sleeping well, and he'd only picked at meals the past few days.

And she wanted him to notice what was right in front of his face. She wanted him to notice her.

She gave a small sigh before she worked up one of her serene smiles. It was getting harder to do, but she managed. "I'm not going any-where, Julian. And I do *not* want to continue as we have been."

The vehemence of her voice surprised him, and his brows lifted. "Well then. Before I ask for the help, you'll need a bit of a history lesson." She brightened instantly and he couldn't help but chuckle. "You wouldn't find history so interesting if you'd lived through it," he told her, as he often had, before retaking his seat.

She gave him an impish grin. "Sure I would. I'm living through history now. Everyone does, they just don't realize it."

He conceded the point with a nod. "Fair point. All right, then. Thousands of years ago, magical objects—relics—were everywhere. I can't say they were as widespread as, say, cell phones are today, but they weren't uncommon by any means. Not just the small charms you've seen, either, where the magic is for convenience only. Not even what is considered a powerful relic by today's standards, such as things which can give control over an element, but truly powerful relics. Godlike, you could say. Some were actually made by the gods, in fact. Most were created by a single sect of witches in Greece, however. At the time, they alone seemed to have the knowledge of how to imbue objects with magic to rival that of their deities. This is where legends of objects with immense power came from, because they did exist, in some form or another. Magical swords and armor, cups and cauldrons that could feed or heal or extend life indefinitely."

Intrigued, she sat forward, arms crossed on the table. "So things like Excalibur and the Fountain of Youth were real?"

"Indeed. Perhaps not exactly as they are portrayed in legends, but yes," he confirmed.

"Where is this sect now? Do you have any books written by them?" she asked excitedly.

His brow furrowed with displeasure and he shook his head. "Unfortunately not, but that's the next part of the story. I know you're familiar with the Greek gods."

"Of course."

"Then you should be familiar with a recurring theme in multiple myths. Specifically, where some deity or another is jealous or wary of another's power. Such as Cronus when he swallowed his children to attempt to prevent them from taking his power."

She nodded. While that was one of the more famous examples, she was aware there were several others.

Julian smiled, but there was no trace of humor in it. "Mortal-made relics were no exception. As long as the relics made were something easily managed by one of the Arcane, everything was fine. But when these artisans began making objects that could grant immortality or truly resurrect the dead, things only the gods should be capable of, things changed. Zeus claimed it was an act of hubris for us to not only be able to create such things, but to actually do it. Most believe they were viewed as a threat to his rule." He shrugged, though given all he knew of the king of the gods, that was the reason he believed to be true. "Regardless of why, he had every member of that sect of witches killed, destroyed every word they'd written on how to create powerful relics, and destroyed the relics he deemed too powerful for mortals."

The expression of shock and sorrow on her face was one he understood too well. He, too, mourned the lack of such amazing objects, more than she ever could. The lack had cost him the only woman he'd ever loved. At the memory of his wife's death, pain tightened his chest, so sharply that he knew Paige had felt it. The sympathetic expression she wore only confirmed it.

Quickly, he went on. "The creation of relics themselves weren't banned, just those that rivaled the gods. Unfortunately, the loss of every single person who knew how to create them meant that for more than a thousand years, only low-level relics were made. We had to start from scratch. Think of it like someone destroying all cars and information on them, so to create one you first had to learn—again—how to make a wheel, the combustion engine, and so on."

"That's horrible," she whispered. "Was anyone using the relics against the gods?"

He shook his head. "Not that I'm aware of, though it was, of course, quite a bit before my time. I have no doubt that for every king or leader, there is someone who feels they could do a better job, but to the best of my knowledge, only another god would challenge a god." The grief on her face made him continue. "Obviously, not all relics were destroyed. The more common ones were left alone—you've seen some of those—but at least a few of the legendary ones survived, though not intact."

Pure curiosity wore at the sympathy until Paige resolved to listen and not dwell on things that happened years before she was born. "How do you know some survived?"

"I have a piece of one."

Paige frowned. "A piece?"

He nodded. "The ones they couldn't destroy, they split into pieces and hid so they could never be found and reassembled."

Understanding dawned. She had worked closely enough with him for long enough to understand how his mind worked. "So you want to find the other piece or pieces of the relic you have and make it whole again, and the danger you mentioned is the gods trying to stop us?"

"That's part of it, yes," he confirmed with a nod. "But I'm also not foolish enough to believe that there won't be dangers in simply finding these pieces, either. No doubt they were put in hard to reach or dangerous places, perhaps even with guards, to ensure that they were never found."

"That makes sense." Suddenly, she laughed, and he gave her an astonished look. "Sorry, sorry," she said, waving a hand and trying to get her laughter under control. "I just pictured us as Indiana Jones. Too bad that your hair is too dark for you to be Indy," she explained with a grin.

Reluctantly, he felt his lips curve. "And you don't look a thing like Short Round." His smile disappeared. "But you aren't too far off. Traps are certainly possible. That's why I wanted to give you the opportunity to back out."

"I'm not backing out," she told him firmly. "But why would you think I would have backed out before I knew what we were going up against?"

"I was trying to give you plausible deniability, my dear."

The endearment, however casually it was given, or impersonally, still made her heart skip a beat.

"Well, I don't need it. You're stuck with me, Julian, but I'm not sure how I can help. I don't know anything about relics, and while I do know about history, I don't know that I'm knowledgeable enough to be of any use in this."

"I'm stuck with you, hmm?" he murmured. He saw her cheeks flush with color and tilted his head as he considered her.

Paige hadn't physically aged, not even a day, since she'd moved into Mooreton. She was still the vividly beautiful and vivacious girl he'd rescued. No, he corrected, not a girl. She was a woman. Even with the jeans, tee-shirts, and hoodies she preferred, her womanhood was never in question. And her hair was amazing. Brilliantly red, it formed a curly halo around her face. Rarely was it ever fully contained and brought to mind images of that hair spread out across his pillow or caught in his hand. Briefly, he longed to see if it was as soft as it looked, but no sooner than the thought had occurred, he stamped it down. It felt disloyal to his wife, to his Mary, despite the fact that she'd been dead more than two hundred years.

While he hadn't been celibate in those two centuries, sex was an impersonal act now, and a rare one, at that. It fulfilled a bodily need and nothing more. When he gave into those needs, he never allowed anything that could be considered intimate. He never kissed a woman, and he never slept with the same woman twice. Doing anything else felt wrong.

It took a moment to realize Paige was saying his name, and he snapped back to the present. "Sorry," he said, voice gruff. "You don't need to know the history of relics, or about the relics themselves. You only need to have your ability to touch an object and get impressions from it." One corner of his mouth turned up in a tiny smile. "You found me, after all."

Unconvinced, Paige frowned. "Yes, but it's one thing to touch something belonging to a person and find their home, and another thing entirely to touch something and locate missing pieces of it. Especially since it's probably been warded or enchanted or something. If they didn't want these things being reassembled, I can't imagine they would leave any of the pieces unprotected."

"Yes, likely the warding is impressive and nigh impenetrable," he agreed, "but I don't think it's impossible." He hesitated before admitting, "I've reached a dead end, Paige. Unless your magic can give us some sort of direction, I don't know that I'll ever find any of the rest of the pieces."

Conflicting emotions wound through her. On one hand, this obviously meant a lot to him, but she didn't want the weight of his hopes piled on her shoulders, especially since she didn't know how much help she could be. What if she failed? On the other hand, she loved him, and he had taught her everything she knew about witchcraft, so how could she refuse?

To give herself a little more time, she asked, "Do you know what the relic does? Or rather, what it will do once it's reassembled?"

He hesitated. "I think I do..." She arched a brow questioningly, and he sighed softly. "If I'm right, this is part of an amulet of immortality. One very creatively named the Amulet of Life."

She gaped at him. Witches lived long, and she knew other beings could live even longer than that, but true immortality? She thought that was reserved for gods and very few other members of the Arcane. "Are you sure?"

"As sure as I can be with only a fragment of it."

She drew in a slow breath. "I'll do what I can. Give me the piece and we'll see what I see." The relief on his face made her momentarily uncomfortable. What if she couldn't do what he asked her to do? No, that wasn't what was bothering her, not really. This was one of her strengths. It was his motivation that had her hesitating. True, if he'd had this amulet centuries ago, his wife wouldn't have died, but that didn't explain why he wanted it now. Traveling through time wasn't possible, as far as she knew, so why the fierce desire for something to grant immortality?

She pushed her misgivings away. If he needed this, she'd do what she could to help him get it. "Where did you get this piece, anyway?"

He rose and moved to the one wall without shelves. She felt the tingle of magic as he opened a hole in it—she *knew* he had a safe in here!—and retrieved a box. "Would you believe I inherited it?" he asked and returned to the table. "It was hidden away with a bit of jewelry in my mother's things. I only discovered it a year ago," he admitted.

Well, that certainly explained the change in his personality this past year.

Paige watched every movement closely as he unlocked the box with a small gold key, then took out a bundle wrapped in several layers of black silk. Carefully, he unfolded the cloth before he placed it on the table and gently pushed it across to her.

Her first glimpse left her disappointed. It looked so ordinary. It was made of tarnished silver, and looked to be a quarter circle with a little piece cut out of the point. She could see that there were many symbols carved into it, but even with all her studies, only a few looked even close to familiar.

"How did you realize that this was magical?" she asked, unable to hide how let down she was by its appearance.

Luckily, that amused him. "It doesn't look very impressive at all, does it?"

She made a noncommittal sound and gently tugged the silk toward her so she could get a better look.

He slid his hands into his pockets and watched her. "I would have just set it with the other things I was left that I don't need and never use, but then I touched it." He grinned when she gave him a startled look. "I may not have your abilities, Paige, but I didn't need them for that. There's still magic in it. It's faint, almost nonexistent as far as I can tell, but when I touched it, I felt what little remains. I only know that it's a relic—an amulet, to be precise—because of a journal that my mother's great-grandmother wrote."

"You have a journal that old?" she asked, more excited about that than the lackluster amulet. Yes, old history books fascinated her, but a journal was on a whole other level. It was written by a person about their life, their experiences. It was so much more personal than a book that coldly chronicled events, though she loved both.

"I do, but it's written in ancient Greek, and not all of the writing has survived. But later, if you want to look at it and practice translating it, you're welcome to." He shrugged. "Maybe you'll find something I missed."

"I knew I should have focused on my Greek," she muttered. He only smiled, so she drew in a slow breath. "Well, no time like the present, right?" she asked, giving him a cheeky grin. After he gave her a nod of approval, she reached out and picked up the amulet piece.

Once again, Paige's world changed in an instant.

CHAPTER 6

The moment Paige's fingers wrapped around the relic, her head flew back and she screamed with pain. Her body bowed upward, so sharply it reached a pose impossible for most. The agony caused her to tremble, hard enough for it to be visible. Her eyes—wide open but unseeing—began to glow, emitting a bright emerald light.

Later, he couldn't have said whether the contortions of her body or the shining of her eyes unnerved him the most. In the end, it didn't matter. Neither were natural. Julian rushed around the table to her side. He reached her just as her awkward pose knocked her chair backward, but he managed to catch her an instant before she hit the floor. The tension thrumming through her body made it difficult to hold her, so he carefully lowered her to the floor.

"Paige! Let go of the amulet!" Julian told her, not realizing he yelled the command.

She didn't seem to hear him. Instead, she half-screamed, but instead of English, she was speaking Ancient Greek. That by itself wouldn't be too surprising, as she had learned some of the language, but the words were spoken fluently. More unusual was that she didn't speak with an accent, which was something even he had yet to accomplish.

Fortunately, the words were clear enough that he could make them out, even if they were being yelled.

"It hurts! Gods, it burns! Why are we being ripped apart? Why? It hurts!" she shrieked as she writhed helplessly against him.

Shifting her in his arms, Julian reached for the hand holding the amulet. Her fingers were clamped so tightly around it that her fair skin looked positively bloodless. Hoping this would end once she was no longer touching the relic, he started to try to pry her fingers open. Though normally he was physically stronger than her, he found it nearly impossible to open her hand. The relic either somehow gave her strength, or it was simply refusing to give up the contact. If it was the latter, she was in serious trouble.

Her screaming about the sensations rushing through her was endless. Each cry tore into him, filling him with guilt and protectiveness for the woman in his arms. He should never have asked her to do this, but because he had, she was suffering. And given that he knew how strong a woman she was, for her to be reacting like this meant it had to be more intense than any person should ever have to bear.

"Dammit, Paige! Drop the amulet! Drop it!" The agonized rantings continued as though he hadn't spoken. He switched to Ancient Greek and repeated his command. Nothing.

"They're missing! All missing! We should be together! Not separated in pain and fear!" she screamed. She repeated herself over and over as Julian managed to get one finger partially off the relic. Then the words ended abruptly and his eyes lifted to her face. Her mouth was open, her eyes still glowing green, when she started to seize.

He was afraid if he didn't get the amulet away from her, and soon, that it would kill her. He whispered an apology to her before he used all his strength, physical and magical, to force her fingers away from the relic. Slowly, her dainty fingers began to open. He could hear a muted crack and felt at least one delicate bone break, which made him wince. Still, the relic dropped free of her hand and fell to the floor. The moment it was no longer in contact with her skin, she slumped in his arms, barely conscious and breathing rapidly.

The object of his obsession was left where it had landed, ignored, as he picked her up and laid her as gently as he could on the table. Quickly, he healed her broken finger before he stroked her now damp hair back from her face. "Paige? Can you hear me?" he asked quietly.

Dull eyes turned to him, but he wasn't sure if she really saw him. She made a sound he couldn't decipher.

His concern spiked. "Paige?"

"'m here," she slurred weakly, her voice rough from the force of her screams. The words were in English again, and he sighed with relief.

He nodded. "Good. Just lay still. I'm going to get you some scotch. It'll help." There was no response other than the slow closing of her eyes. Not wanting to leave her in her condition, he teleported the bottle and glass to the table and, with hands that weren't quite steady, poured. He helped her lift her head and offered the glass to her lips. "Sip slowly. You don't want to choke." She managed to get two swallows down before she turned her head and refused more. "Just lay there and rest for a few minutes," he murmured.

She nodded and he stepped back. He picked up the silk and used it to wrap the relic piece up once more before it was put back into the box, then into the safe, away from her. His task done, he returned to his seat while she half-dozed on the table. He didn't say anything, not wanting to disturb her if she was actually resting. This was a new experience for him, which meant he wasn't exactly sure what the relic had done to her. Worse, he wasn't sure how to help her other than to give her time to recover.

It was half an hour before she moved or spoke. Slowly, she rolled to face him, though it took most of the little energy she had left. "Saw it," she said, speaking quietly and slowly. Anything else would aggravate her already raw throat.

Julian frowned and leaned toward her. "Saw what?"

"The amulet. As it used to be. And its destruction."

For a moment, he couldn't react. Obsession warred with guilt until finally the obsession won out. He told himself that if she didn't tell him, then all her pain had been for nothing, but he wasn't sure if he believed it. "Tell me," he said quietly.

"It was round, with dozens of symbols, front and back...Had a stone in the center, big as my thumbnail...Something shimmery and iridescent. Pretty. Hung on a chain. 'Bout this big." She managed to lift a hand inches off the table and held her thumb and forefinger an inch and a half apart.

She fell silent and Julian forced himself to wait, to let her breathe. He knew that talking had to be exhausting for her. His patience was rewarded a few minutes later. "It's in five pieces now. It feels...alive. It knows it's not whole." She swallowed and closed her eyes. "Took two gods to break it. They were afraid of it, or angry at it," she mumbled, her words getting more slurred. "One piece is in the dark. Another's cold. So cold..." She trailed off and went silent for so long that Julian said her name. "Hmm?"

"You were telling me about the pieces of the amulet?"

It took a moment for her to remember. "Oh. Right. One felt wet, another felt hot."

He fell back in his chair, mildly stunned. Yes, her description of where the pieces could be found was incredibly vague, but in the hour since she'd first seen the piece, she'd given him more than he'd found in a year of research. He had something to go on now. Excitement stirred inside him.

"Do you think you can you get me locations? More exact ones?" he asked.

One eye cracked open, and he was struck by how glassy it looked. And how she suddenly looked scared. Before he could retract the question, she nodded. "Can try. Later."

"Yes, later," he agreed quietly. "You should sleep."

He rose to help her, but she shook her head. "'m fine," she told him, trying to sound firm, but she couldn't manage it. Still, she did get herself vertical and swatted weakly at his hand when he reached out to help.

He paused before he nodded and stepped back. It bothered him a great deal not to help her, but he'd already caused her unnecessary pain today. He couldn't bruise her pride as well. Better his take a beating since this was his fault.

It took her a minute to slide off the table, and though he was sure she was going to collapse, she stayed upright.

He was struck again by guilt as he watched her shuffle away. "Call me if you need anything," he told her. "I'll be listening." Even in her weakened state he should be able to hear a mental call from anywhere on the estate, as long as he was listening for it. He would definitely be listening.

"'kay."

When he could no longer hear the sounds of her feet brushing along the floor, he sank back into his chair and poured the scotch. The first drink slid down his throat, but it did nothing to warm the cold knot in his belly.

He'd been selfish, and incredibly so. That he had no way of knowing that she'd react to the relic like she had was no excuse, not really. He knew her strengths were in the mental magics, and this particular ability was innate and came so easily to her. He should have guessed that a strong witch would have a strong reaction to a powerful relic.

And you knew that the relic was extremely powerful if even you received a little zap, his subconscious whispered to him, and he flinched. But he couldn't deny the truth, nor lie to himself.

He took another sip and stared at the spot where she had seized in his arms. Maybe he could find another way. Maybe there was someone who could use what she'd already discovered and build on it. Surely Paige wasn't absolutely necessary to finding the other pieces.

What Julian wouldn't admit, even to himself, was how much it had hurt him to see her suffering like that. It was a pain he'd have gladly taken on himself in his quest, but to see her writhing, screaming, had torn at a piece of him. The place where his esteemed apprentice resided. He knew that when he went to sleep that night, he was going to see it over and over in his dreams. But maybe it was a fitting punishment for a selfish man. He certainly deserved no less.

When he slept, Julian had the nightmares he was expecting, had, in fact, taken no precautions to prevent them. Besides, he didn't believe any magic could prevent a dream he knew he had earned.

Once again, he saw Paige, her body rigid with the torment thrust upon her by the relic. Only this time, he wasn't able to get her fingers open. This time, she screamed until the pain was so intense that she could only twitched helplessly. This time, he watched as that small piece of carved silver drained her magic, then her life. He watched as that eerie green glow faded until her eyes stared unseeing at the ceiling and her body lay still in death. And, holding her lifeless figure, he screamed in rage to the heavens.

It was still hours before dawn when he jerked awake, the sound of his dream grief echoing in his head. He remembered all too well the feeling of loss he'd experienced when he'd lost Mary. In his nightmare, it had felt twice as acute, which only added to his guilt. Even awake, his heart pounded and it took quite some time for him to calm down.

But he didn't sleep again.

The moment Paige closed the door to the workshop, she leaned heavily against the wall. She should have accepted help. Her limbs felt so weak, so shaky, she wasn't sure how she was going to get up the two flights of stairs to bed. Yet pride prevented her from going back for help.

Slowly she made her way upstairs, though the trip that should have taken just a few minutes took her more than twenty. She had to stop and rest multiple times, and once sat down on a stair halfway up the steps until she had the strength to continue. Finally she made it to her bedroom and absently closed the door behind her.

Never had her bed looked as it good as it did now. She shuffled over and fell into it face down, not bothering to change clothes or even take her shoes off. It would all be wasted energy, and she didn't have any to spare.

Paige sighed and drew her pillow to her, half laying on it, half cuddling it. Her whole body ached. Never in her life had she felt like this, not even after the mugging that had led her to Julian. But the physical discomfort was the least of it. She felt a bone-deep loneliness, a sadness that far surpassed anything she'd experienced before. She wanted a hug, to hold and be held in return, but there was no way she was going to get that from Julian. Not with the distance he continued to keep between them.

To distract herself, she let her mind wander back to what she'd seen, the impressions she'd gotten when she touched the piece of the relic. A lot of it was hazy or jumbled. There had been so much information pouring through her that it was difficult for her to separate one image from another. The one thing that had been clear was the pain. It wasn't caused by the strength of the magic in the relic, but was more...a memory of the relic. Memory of a pain she didn't know objects could feel. She didn't know how they could have memories either, but nothing else made sense.

Thinking too hard of the pain made her aches intensify and she tried to focus on the places. Dark, cold, hot, and wet weren't much help. They weren't any help, actually. But the visions slipped away when she thought too hard on them.

In the morning, she'd try to sketch the amulet as she'd seen it. She wasn't a great artist, but it might give Julian something more to go on.

She sighed and gave the pillow a weak squeeze. She was too tired to try to figure any of this out. All she wanted was to slip into sleep. Preferably a dreamless sleep, but there was no way she had the energy to shield her mind.

Exhausted, she closed her eyes, and let the darkness slide over her and take her under.

CHAPTER 7

Normally, Paige was awake early every morning. Frequently, she woke when it was still dark, so she could take her first cup of coffee as she watched the sun rise. It was her favorite time of day, when everything was still and quiet and beautiful. It felt like she was the only person in the world, as if that exquisite fading of colors from black to pale blue was entirely for her.

This morning, however, her internal clock failed her and she slept in. When she woke, she saw that she had slept more than twelve hours. She had never in her life slept that long at once, even when she'd been ill. Worse, she still had almost no energy. It took her almost half an hour to rouse herself enough to leave the bed, and with each minute that passed, she grew more despondent. How had simply touching the amulet piece caused her to feel this wretched?

Her movements were slow because each step took so much out of her. She refused to lie uselessly in bed, though, no matter what she'd been through the day before. She had a journal to read, and she still wanted to do that sketch. Hopefully Julian would have made coffee, too, which was certainly worth getting up for. As she struggled down the stairs, she tried to reach out with her mind to contact him. It was then she noticed lethargy wasn't her only problem. Panicked, she realized her magic wasn't working either. She nearly slipped on the next step and, one hand holding the rail in a death grip, had to sit down abruptly to prevent herself from tumbling down the stairs.

Not having the senses she'd become so accustomed to was devastating, and she was unsurprised to feel wetness on her cheeks. To her, empathy and telepathy, those magical senses, were every bit as important as sight or hearing were to others. She fought to tamp down the hysteria that threatened to overwhelm her. Wrapping her arms around herself, she started to rock and stare at the floor without really seeing it. The only thing she could focus on was what was missing, and why. Had touching the amulet done something to her? Had it taken her magic? More importantly, was it temporary, or was she now the human she'd grown up believing she was? She didn't want to go back to being human. She loved being a witch. She loved learning magic from Julian. There was no way she could handle losing what had become such a part of her identity.

That was how Julian found her twenty minutes later. Worry poured through him as he rushed up the stairs, crouching on the step beneath her so he was at eye level. "Paige? What is it? What's wrong?"

Paige was so caught up in her loss that it took a full minute for her eyes to actually focus on his face, and a moment longer for her to seem to recognize him. "It's gone, Julian," she whispered, and he heard the anguish in her voice.

"What's gone?" he asked as gently as he could, wiping tears off her cheek with his thumb.

"My magic," she told him, voice cracking. "It's gone. I can't feel you. I couldn't call out to you."

He was nowhere near her level when it came to empathy, but he still felt how much the lack bothered her. A quick check was all that was needed for him to know she was absolutely depleted. It was honestly a shock she'd managed to get out of bed, as drained as she was. But sharing his power was possible. Witches often lent each other power when casting magic. All it really required was physical contact—and even that wasn't strictly necessary if the one giving the power didn't mind having it forcibly and painfully yanked from them. But it was a slow process in a situation like this.

A kiss would be quicker.

An image of his dead wife slipped into his mind. It wasn't quite as sharp as it used to be, which only heaped guilt onto guilt.

"No, it's not gone," he assured her. "You're just drained, like a dead battery. It'll come back on its own, though it may take a few days." He hesitated. "Or I can give you some of my power." The hope in her eyes seared him, so he added quickly, "It requires...contact...to work."

"I don't care what it takes, Julian. I feel blind. I can't stand this. Please, help me," she pleaded with him as she gripped his sleeve.

Before he could talk himself out of it, he gave in. He had to make this right. This was his fault, after all. If something in the back of his mind was eager for this, he ignored it.

His hand cupped the nape of her neck and he pulled her in to meet him. The instant that their lips touched, he felt as though he'd been struck by lightning. He almost forgot to transfer the power he'd promised. When he did remember, it was little more than an afterthought. How could he focus on that when her lips were on his? When he could feel the pulse in her throat quicken and smell the gentle floral scent of her? When he could taste her?

Julian was drawn further into the kiss, his lips softening against hers, though he didn't try to deepen it. He savored the feel of her mouth, letting the kiss go on much longer than he'd intended, or was necessary. But it felt so good, so right. It was only when she made a small sound of pleasure that he came back to himself.

He jerked back so abruptly that Paige almost fell against him. As soon as he was sure she was steady, he straightened and retreated a few steps.

She touched her lips lightly with her fingertips as she watched him, just as affected by the kiss as he was. And she knew, unquestioningly, that he was affected. All of her senses had returned to her, and she felt the conflicting emotions inside him. The longing, the guilt, the bewilderment...and the loneliness.

It was the guilt that caused his voice to be so curt, so unfriendly, when he asked, "Better?"

Paige's hand dropped to her lap and she nodded. "Yes, thank you. I can feel again."

Where he sounded upset, she sounded dazed. Looked dazed, too, Julian noted. Still, he'd achieved his goal. The fact that he wanted to kiss her again pissed him off, though. He gave her a short nod then turned and stomped away, knowing that she watched him go.

He retreated to his workshop, certain she wouldn't follow him there. Right now, he just needed to calm down. Specifically, he needed his unruly body to calm down. The kiss, innocent as it may have been, had left him aroused, which was part of the source of his anger. He didn't want to be turned on by Paige. Despite being a widower for half his life, and knowing that he was never going to get his wife back, it still felt disloyal to be so attracted to anyone else. He knew it didn't make sense, and his friends had told him many times that he needed to move on, but something always held him back.

Trying to push thoughts of Paige—and his wife—aside, he threw himself into work. He grabbed the journal he'd been using solely for research on the relic and started adding the incident from the previous night. It wasn't likely he'd forget a single instant of what had happened, but he tended to err on the side of caution when it came to anything magical.

Unfortunately, the little Paige had given him wasn't much to go on. One of the pieces was wet? That could mean anything, and searching every ocean, lake, river, stream, and swamp in the world was an impossible task. Likewise, dark could be in any of a million places. No, he'd need to narrow it down quite a bit before he could even think about going after any of them.

He'd tried using the piece he had to track the others, but the spell had completely failed. While not unexpected, it was disappointing. The gods didn't leave much to chance, and he was sure the pieces were warded from magic of all kinds, but especially magic meant to locate them. That would make things too easy and they intended these relics to never be found.

It would have been helpful if his ancestor had left some indication of where she'd found the piece currently in his safe, but for some reason, she hadn't deemed it necessary. He wasn't sure it would've helped in any case, but all information, however trivial, was welcome.

After retrieving his one book that went into any depth on relics, he settled in to read, to see if he'd missed something, anything, that might help.

Half an hour later, his phone rang. He'd been so absorbed in the book that he jumped a little. Happy no one was around to see, he answered.

"Hello?"

"Hey Julian, you got a sec?"

He almost smiled at the voice on the other end. Marco was one of his oldest friends, and though they didn't see each other much, they did talk quite frequently. But then, as a demonologist, his knowledge was especially useful to Marco, who was the commander of the Venatoribus Noctu, an Arcane group whose sole purpose was to protect the Earth from demons. Yet the calls were generally social enough that just hearing Marco's voice helped dispel some of the last of his bad mood.

"For you? Of course. What are you hunting today?"

"Fire demon. I *hate* fire demons. Especially this one." He sounded disgusted, but Julian wasn't sure if it was with the demon or himself.

"What's so bad about this one?" Julian wondered. It was hardly the first one the Hunters had fought.

"Damn thing doesn't seem to realize that it doesn't have to be on fire twenty-four seven. I mean, how many demons *never* conserve their power by letting their flames turn to embers? And he's hot enough that nothing gets through to his skin."

Generally, the Arcane didn't use guns, but demons were the one exception. "He's melting bullets before they reach him?" Julian asked with some surprise. Most fire demons couldn't burn quite that hot.

Marco growled. "It's hard to believe, I know, but I emptied a couple of magazines into him, and all I got for my trouble was a fireball to the arm and my hair getting set on fire. Do you know just how *bad* burning hair smells?" Marco demanded.

Julian mostly stifled a laugh. "And magic isn't doing any good on him?"

"None that I've got to try on him, and I brought in an ice elemental. You got any ideas, Mr. Wizard? Because this jackass has seriously pissed me off. I want him dead. Last week."

"Hmm. Have you met Jeff Anderson yet?"

"Who? Oh. The dude who offed Gurnov last year?"

"That's the one. He's a fire elementalist. I haven't seen it, but apparently he can do the full turning into flame thing. He could probably help you out since the fire won't be able to harm him."

Marco considered. "Never thought I'd literally fight fire with fire, but that just might be the ticket. Got his number handy?"

"I do." He rattled it off. "You might have to talk his wife into letting him help, though. She's a little protective since he almost died fighting Gurnov."

"That's fine. I know how to charm the ladies when I need to. Hate to cut this short, but I wanna get this demon taken care of. Talk to you later, man."

"Not a problem. Good hunting."

When Julian hung up the phone, he felt lighter, better. He could actually think clearly now. Paige shouldn't be involved in anything else concerning the amulet. It was, obviously, too dangerous for her. His nightmare had only reinforced that opinion, and seeing her so helpless as she sat on the stairs...

No, he shouldn't think of that.

A quick mental search, a light one, found her in the garden and he gave a half-smile. She'd wasted no time in repairing the garden once she'd moved in, and truth be told, he did enjoy it more now. Before, he simply hadn't had the time—or desire—to deal with what he had considered a frivolous problem. Especially since the garden had, prior to that, been Mary's domain.

But Paige had improved the entire house and made it look presentable again. Except for one room, the room that had been Mary's sanctuary. He would allow no one to disturb that room, not even Paige.

Especially not Paige.

Rather than ask her to join him or teleporting to her, he gave himself a few minutes by walking out to the garden. He found Paige sitting on one of the stone benches, a freshly cut white rose in her hand. Since she had a look of intense concentration on her face, he didn't announce himself right away, but waited and watched.

The rosebud was still tightly furled, and Paige was staring at it intently. Physical magics were her weakness and her powers weren't fully recharged quite yet, but she was determined to make the flower bloom. It was, she thought, a much wiser thing to be focusing on than Julian's mind-scrambling kiss. Especially since he had run away immediately afterward.

The petals twitched but refused to obey her magic, so she sighed and dropped her hand with the flower into her lap. It was just as well. Her focus really wasn't what it should be for such things. Her mind kept wandering back to the feel of his lips on hers. She smiled wryly and shook her head. She'd dreamed of him kissing her many times, but she never imagined that their first kiss would be of necessity. It was, she thought bitterly, no different than if he'd given her mouth-to-mouth resuscitation.

Movement against her fingers made her look down at the flower. She saw that the petals were fully open now, resulting in what was, in her opinion, the most beautiful rose she'd ever seen. She let out a soft cry of happiness and lifted the flower, brushing a finger delicately over the petals.

"Given what you did for me yesterday, it seemed a shame for you not to have your blossomed flower," came the clipped voice from behind her.

Some of her happiness dimmed. So she hadn't caused the flower to open. Even worse, Julian still didn't sound happy. He was using that uptight voice she hated. Although...

Paige twisted to look at him then cocked her head. He didn't *feel* angry anymore, though there were still threads of guilt woven through his mind.

"Thank you. I knew better than to try, at least not today, but..." She shrugged.

"I understand perfectly." Julian walked over and sat down on the opposite side of the bench, glancing at the rose, then to her. "I've been thinking..." He saw her lips twitch before she could prevent the response. "Yes, I know I tend to do that a lot," he said dryly. "But my point is, given how strongly—and violently—you reacted to touching the relic, I have no right to ask you to try again, even if we did wait for you to recover fully."

Paige opened her mouth to protest, but he lifted a hand to forestall her objections. "You've already given me more information than I had, and it's a starting point. I'll find another way to track the pieces down."

She arched a brow and for a moment he glimpsed the steel core that had allowed a scared woman who was alone to come to a stranger's house and ask to stay.

"That's stupid. And you're stupid if you really decide not to let me help," she told him, shaking her head.

Her words baffled him. She was calling him *stupid?* He honestly didn't know how to respond since it was so completely unexpected. He couldn't even be angry. Paige was sweet. She didn't go around insulting anyone, but especially not him.

"Pardon me?"

The sheer indignation in his voice made her smile a little. "You heard me, and I know you're fluent in English, so there's no point in pretending that you didn't understand me." She lifted the flower, brushing the silky petals against her cheek while she talked. "You said it yourself, I gave you more information than you had, and you had a *year* to work on the problem before you finally asked me for help. Beyond that, it's not like you browbeat me into helping you. You simply asked and I agreed. Willingly."

She faltered for a moment and bit her lip uncertainly. When she continued, her voice was quieter, and more solemn. "I've touched it already. It felt almost alive, so it *hurt* when it was ripped apart, and I felt that too. I felt that it wants to be whole again, not scattered around the world in pieces. Even if you hadn't asked me to help, I would. There's no other option for me," she admitted.

"Be that as it may..." Now he broke off, unsure how to counter her last argument. In her case, he'd probably say the same and consider it to be a damn good argument.

In the silence, Paige gave him a sad smile. "Face it, Julian. I'm going to help you whether you like it or not. This amulet is something you need, so you don't lose anyone else you love."

Instantly she knew that she'd misspoken, and the frigid mask that covered his face confirmed her misstep. Julian was a very private person and had never told her about his wife.

"Julian, I'm sor—"

He cut her off and got to his feet. He stared at her coldly for a few seconds before disappearing.

Paige ran her hands through her hair. "Damn. You're an idiot, Paige," she murmured to herself. How many times, she wondered, could a woman screw up with a man in one day?

She looked back at the house and longed for him as the rose slipped out of her fingers, forgotten.

CHAPTER 8

She'd had enough. Three days had passed since the incident in the garden, and while Paige was fully recovered from her brush with the amulet, things with Julian were still at an all-time low. He hadn't spoken to her since leaving the garden and had, in fact, been making an effort to avoid her. Normally, she saw him multiple times each day, but she'd only seen him twice since the day in the garden.

She'd attempted to speak with him, but he always seemed to be leaving the room when she'd entered. Finally she'd gotten tired of the rejections and focused on doing the sketch of the amulet. It took her more than an hour and, while it did give the correct dimensions, it was a rudimentary sketch at best. She knew she didn't have the symbols perfect, but she'd also gotten little more than impressions of alien scribbles in her vision.

After that, she'd worked in the library and stewed. But as the days passed, her remorse at hurting him shifted to annoyance. Paige knew she'd screwed up and had inadvertently hurt him, but enough was enough. He was three hundred years old, not three. He should be better than this. They had work to do, and she was going to get it done.

She reached out with her mind and located him in his workshop, which didn't surprise her. She was pretty sure he'd even been sleeping there the past few days, which heightened her annoyance. Julian was an adult, but instead of talking about the elephant in the room, he was resorting to childish hiding. Rather than let him see her irritation, she schooled her expression into a calm one, and ensured that her mind was shielded. Only then did she go downstairs and, for the first time, step into his workshop uninvited.

The only sign he gave that he knew she was there was a slight stiffening of his shoulders, but she could feel he was shielding as hard as she was. She walked over to her chair and sat down, but he still made no effort to acknowledge her presence. When a minute passed, then two, a small sound of annoyance slipped past her lips.

"Julian, this is ridiculous. You can't keep ignoring me. I live here and I'm your apprentice and I'm sorry that I said what I did."

Coolly, he looked up, one brow arched, a bored look on his face. "And just how did you find out about her?" he asked, leaning back.

She hesitated, but she couldn't lie to him or ignore the question. "When I first cleaned your bedroom, I...I found a ring, a woman's ring, hidden behind the bed. When I touched it..." She shrugged. "I knew."

There was the slightest wince from him. "So you've known for quite some time, then."

She nodded slowly.

"And the ring? Where is it?"

"I put it back where I found it. It's tucked in a crack between the floor and the wall. I didn't want to hurt you. That's the only reason I didn't say anything then, I promise."

He gave a terse nod and made a note to retrieve Mary's wedding ring as soon as he could. It had about killed him when he lost it, but all his attempts to find it had come up empty. He couldn't believe it had been behind his bed the whole time.

Silence stretched out and made Paige more uncomfortable. "I wasn't snooping, Julian, just cleaning, and I really am sorry that I found out, but I couldn't prevent it. More, I am so sorry that your wife died, and wish I could do more than give you words."

As Julian watched her and saw the sincerity on her face, something in his chest loosened. He nodded. "It wasn't your fault," he conceded. Anger still simmered in his chest, but it was a mere fraction of what it had been. Nor was it truly directed toward Paige. "But in the future, if you ever discover something about me from your powers, inadvertent or not, let me know immediately. I don't like surprises like that."

Relieved, Paige nodded eagerly. "Absolutely." She wavered a moment, then asked, "Are we all right, then?"

His answer didn't come immediately, but finally, he nodded slowly. "We're all right."

She relaxed and gave him a brilliant smile that had him shifting uncomfortably in his chair at his physical reaction to it. Luckily, no one but him had to know that her smile was, literally, arousing.

"Good. Then can we please get back to work? I made a sketch of the amulet," she told him. She shifted to pull it out of her pocket, unfolded it, and set it on the table between them. He drew it toward him, but she wasn't done. "I also need to see the genuine article again," she said, holding out a hand.

All at once, the sketch and her smile were forgotten. "Now wait a damn minute—"

"I'm completely back to my normal self, I promise. My magic is how it was prior to touching it," she was quick to assure him, but he scowled.

"That may be, but I still think this is a bad idea, Paige. It nearly killed you last time. I'm not going to risk it finishing you off this time. I know a shapeshifter who's a very good tracker. He might be able to use what you discovered to track the pieces down."

Hand still extended, she smirked. "Really? He can use the fact that we know a piece is somewhere hot to track it down?" she asked, brows lifting, but they both knew the answer: he couldn't. "There are millions of possibilities for each piece, Julian. We need more than a single aspect of the environment each is in. Especially when that aspect is so vague. I'll take precautions this time, since I know just how strong my reaction will be. And I won't just absorb everything that it has to give me like I did last time. I've been...practicing," she admitted. At his questioning look, she shrugged. "I found things the past few days that I could get an impression off of, and worked to focus on just one piece of the information. It took me a bit to sort things out, but I can do it now."

"Explain," he demanded, trying to ignore his rising hope.

"Instead of just taking everything from the amulet, including the pain it felt, I'll just pick one of the locations I sensed and focus on that." He arched a brow and she continued. "I'll try to zero in on the piece that's in the dark and block out everything else. Like watching a single movie instead of dozens at once. I'm hoping that by doing it this way, I'll bypass the pain and keep from having my head bombarded by everything. No pain, no overwhelming information, just what we need, one piece at a time."

He was reluctantly impressed and thought about her plan. If—and it was a big if—she could actually narrow down her focus like that, it just might work.

"Okay." She started to smile but he shook his head. "I'll give you one more chance with the amulet, but just one. *If* you can do this, then we'll revisit the idea of doing it again. But if it turns out like last time, then that's it. You never handle the relic again and I call in the shifter. Do we have a deal?"

Confident that she could do this, she nodded. "Deal."

Silently, he got up and retrieved the relic piece from the safe. When it was once again set in front of her on its bed of silk, she started to shield her mind, ignoring the fact that this time Julian was standing beside her. Not taking any chances, she supposed. She'd rather believe he was just being cautious than believe he didn't have any faith in her abilities, but had a feeling it was more the latter.

Once she was sure her mind was as protected as it could be, she picked up the relic.

Julian watched her closely, prepared to do whatever he had to in the event that she failed to properly protect herself. Even with all her shielding, he saw that the relic was powerful enough to make her body go rigid, but was relieved to see that it wasn't the unnatural contortions he had witnessed before. Her eyes began to glow again, that same unearthly green from before. Dimly he realized that without the writhing that had come with it last time, the effect was actually rather pretty. It made her look almost alien, but it also made her look strong, powerful.

With him standing watch, Paige fought not to let herself be helpless against the amulet's memories. She bit her lip, hard enough to taste blood, and focused on just one of the pieces, the one hidden in the dark. Slowly, so slowly, those impressions became clearer.

Her voice was strained when she spoke, but it was in English, rather than Greek, so Julian made no move to retrieve the amulet. There was a moment of concern when she didn't speak in sentences, but short phrases with long pauses, but it was most likely—he hoped—a result of her focus in protecting herself.

"Jungle. Green and humid and hot. Full of life. Far from an immense river. Big cats. Leopard? Jaguar? Cheetah? Not sure." She shook her head slightly and moved on. "Stone structure. Temple maybe? Small. Protection underground. Dangerous. Goes deep." She swayed in her chair then shuddered. "So deep. Trapped. Guardians outside."

Her breath caught and her eyes widened as the glow brightened until she shone like a beacon. To his horror, she reverted back to Ancient Greek. "Find me! Save me! Please! I'm alone in the dark! Find me!"

"Stop it, Paige! That's enough! Let go!" Julian demanded as he reached for her hand. Before he could even start to pry the amulet free of her hand, her fingers opened and the amulet fell. He caught it just before it hit the floor, then set it on the silk and ignored it.

Paige slumped back in her seat, breathing heavily, her eyes back to their normal, unlit green. She smiled, weary but pleased. This time she wasn't half-unconscious and didn't seem to have suffered for her attempt, other than being a little out of breath.

"How do you feel?"

"Actually? I feel pretty good. My magic is intact, but some of the emotion is lingering," she admitted, placing a hand over her chest to ease the ache she felt there.

He frowned. "What do you mean?"

"The loneliness." She rubbed her arms as though cold. "I felt how lonely it had been, trapped and separated for thousands of years. So *I* feel like I've been through all that. Like I'm alone and trapped."

"You're not alone, Paige. And you were...kind of brilliant," he grudgingly allowed.

She cocked her head, surprised by the compliment. "I was?"

Uncomfortable, he walked around the table and sat down, putting some distance between them. "You suffered greatly after touching that relic, enough that you could have died. But you found a way to safely try again. And not only did you go through with the attempt, despite the risks, you also got useful information. Possibly even information that no one else could have gotten."

She gave him another one of those smiles that quickened his pulse, so he hurried on. "I have an idea of the general area you might have been talking about. But I'm not sure how much I can narrow it down." He pulled out his phone and played with it for a moment. "Describe the cat you saw."

"One of the bigger cats, but definitely not a lion or tiger. Wrong size and coloring. It—they—were yellow, with spots, but it was more like spots within larger spots."

He turned the phone around to show her a picture of a feline. "Is this it?" He swiped. "Or this?"

"The first one," she said after studying the black spots on the cats.

"Jaguar. So right away we're in South America."

Paige brightened. "And the jungle I saw, could it be the Amazon Rainforest?"

"It would stand to reason, yes. It's certainly hot, green, and humid, as well as populated by jaguars. The stone structure probably is a temple, too. There are certainly enough of them in South America. Then there's the river, of course. No one can deny the Amazon is an immense river."

His voice was getting distracted, but she only smiled. This was the voice he got when he was deep in work mode. For the next hour she retrieved books for him, both from the shelves in the workshop and the library upstairs, while he tried to find something, anything, to narrow it further. He showed her pictures of different temples in the area, but she rejected them all. Some were close in appearance to the one she'd seen, but none was quite right.

"Maybe if I went to the Amazon, I could sort of zero in on it? Like a compass?" she suggested finally. "It wants me to find the other pieces, so maybe it'll give me more when I'm closer or give me an idea of direction."

He frowned. "Maybe...but I've got another idea. The shapeshifter I mentioned. Unfortunately Wade's a wolf, not a jaguar, but he's a very skilled tracker."

She looked skeptical. "You think he can sniff out the location? Do you realize how big the Amazon is? I don't think any wolf has a nose that good."

He smiled. "Possibly, but Wade's brand of tracking isn't just done with his nose and eyes. Besides, even if you can act as a compass for this, it might still be good to have him along. He's a good man to have in a fight or emergency."

Part of Paige wanted it to just be Julian and herself, but she knew it was wiser to have someone else go with them. Especially since she would be utterly useless if they were attacked. She half-wished that she'd taken some sort of self-defense class, but she'd been too focused on learning magic instead. "You trust him?"

"He's one of my best and oldest friends."

Paige sighed. "All right." Then she smiled slyly. "But now he gets to be Short Round and I get to be Willie."

Julian let out a burst of surprised laughter. "Go on, Willie. I'm going to put the relic away, then pay Wade a visit. Something like this shouldn't be done over the phone."

"Agreed." As she walked out of the workshop, she mused aloud, "I hope I'm not allergic to wolves..."

Julian chuckled and shook his head as he dialed Wade's number. He wished he hadn't kissed Paige. He really did like her and considered her a friend, not just a student. This attraction he felt for her could only spoil things. When it ended badly, as it only could, he'd lose a friend and the best assistant he'd ever had. The thought bothered him a great deal more than he liked.

"Hey, Julian."

"Hello, Wade. You're not busy at the moment, are you?"

Wade sighed. "Unfortunately not. Had a job, but it ended a week ago," he complained.

"I might have another one for you."

"Oh? What kind of job?"

Instead of answering, Julian disconnected and teleported himself to Wade's rustic cabin home in Washington state.

"The dangerous kind," he told the wolf with a smile.

CHAPTER 9

While not shabby by any means, Wade's cabin wasn't one that most people living in modern times would prefer to live in. Which was fitting, since it had stood, more or less the same, for almost three hundred years. Julian could have managed to teleport if Wade had moved, but not nearly with so much ease. Besides, the place suited the wolf.

The cabin wasn't large, only three rooms, which consisted of a bedroom, bathroom, and large open area that was made up of a living area and kitchen. Recently it had been upgraded to solar power, so Wade had electricity for the first time since it was built. According to Wade, the only reason he'd added that 'luxury' was to have hot showers and run his computer, but Julian wasn't sure he believed the wolf. Two chairs sat in front of a stone fireplace, with an end table between them. In the kitchen, he had a table with another two chairs, further reinforcing the fact that Wade didn't get a lot of company. Despite that—or because he sprawled out when he slept—Julian could see through the open bedroom door that Wade's bed was king-sized.

Wade was just standing up, barefoot and dressed only in a pair of jeans. He was nearly as tall as Julian, with hair as light as Julian's was dark. His features were more rugged, but women seemed to enjoy them, nonetheless. Though Wade tended to act like he wasn't educated around people he didn't know, his gray-green eyes belied that to those who bothered to look. His torso was tattooed, front and back, with all manner of images. Once Julian had asked what they all meant. Wade had cryptically answered that they were his prey. His tone had prevented Julian from pressing further.

"Haven't I told you to warn me first?" Wade demanded. "I *am* a shifter, you know, and we tend to like to be free, if you know what I mean." The lewd roll of his hips helped confirm exactly what he meant, though Julian was well aware of the fact that shifters were more comfortable with nudity than most people.

After a brief moment, both men laughed, then gave each other a one-armed man hug.

"How you been, Julian?" Wade asked as he dropped back into one of the chairs.

"Depends on the day you ask," he admitted as he sat down. "I told you I took on an apprentice, right?"

"Sure. Some chick, right? Pam or Phoebe or something starting with a P?"

Julian made a noncommittal noise. "Paige, yes. She's an excellent student, and very helpful, very useful."

Wade arched a brow. "She's been there what, two years now?"

"Three."

"And the best you can say is she's helpful? Is she a bitch or stupid or something?"

Julian bristled. "She's neither of those things. She has this sort of...serene way about her, so she's the furthest thing from a bitch she could be. And she's extremely friendly and likes to help people." Wade made a 'go on' gesture and Julian sighed, knowing what the wolf was pushing for. "She's got red hair. Lots of it. Falls to her hips, or damn near. Green eyes, fair skin."

The shifter let out a low whistle. "Niiiice. I'm partial to red heads. You know what they say, right? Red on the head means fire in the bed," he said with a grin and brow waggle that would have looked absurd on anyone else. Julian wasn't quite sure how Wade managed to pull it off. "You'll have to introduce me to her—then make yourself scarce."

Though Wade was joking—mostly—the same way he'd done hundreds of times, Julian didn't take it as well as he'd taken other jokes. His arm flew out and Wade was suddenly pinned to the ceiling, looking thoroughly surprised.

"You will not touch her!" Julian growled.

Wade had *never* seen Julian act like this. Julian simply didn't lose his temper. When he got pissed, he got icy. And for him to act this way over a woman? It was unheard of. Though for all Wade knew, this is how Julian had acted about Mary if another man had flirted with her. But Wade wasn't upset. Quite the opposite, in fact, though he hid his amusement.

He put his hands up in surrender. "Got it. Paige is off limits. I won't lay a paw on her," he assured Julian, keeping his voice calm.

The sudden rage that had gripped Julian faded, and he realized what he had done. Shamed at his lack of control, he lowered Wade back to his chair and looked intently at the cold fireplace. "I apologize, Wade. I don't know what came over me."

Wade absently rubbed his shoulder, which ached a little from the contact with the ceiling. "Apology accepted, but I think we both know what came over you. What's been going on with you and this Paige?"

"Nothing."

"Bullshit," Wade said, unconvinced.

Julian looked back to him and sighed. Wade was worse than a dog with a bone when he got fixated on something. He wouldn't just give up. "If we're going to talk about that, I'm going to need a whiskey." He'd prefer scotch, but knew Wade was a whiskey man. When in Rome.

"Isn't it handy that I happen to have a couple of bottles on hand, then?" he asked with a toothy smile.

After they each had a glass, and Julian's had been emptied and refilled, Wade asked, "So? What's going on? I've *never* seen you react to a woman like that before. You haven't even gotten that worked up on the few occasions that you've talked about Mary." Which made it all the more intriguing to a curious wolf like Wade. True, he'd never joked about making a move on Mary when she'd been alive, but it was still interesting.

Julian scowled before he finally shrugged. "I'm not sure, to be honest. You remember how I told you I met her, right?"

Wade grinned. "Yeah. You played white knight, then she showed up on your doorstep. Not likely to forget that."

Rolling his eyes, Julian continued. "She was...she had a bad magical reaction the other day."

Wade's brows furrowed in concern. It reminded Julian why they were friends. He wasn't just a rough wolf with a deeply lecherous side. He gave a damn, too. "She okay?"

"Mmm. She is now, but it left her physically weak and almost completely drained of magic. And since she's a powerful empath and telepath, it left her sort of head-blind. Imagine losing your sense of smell, Wade, and I think it's a pretty accurate comparison."

The thought made Wade shudder, and he shook his head. "No fucking thank you. But I feel bad for her now."

"So did I," Julian admitted. "Which is why I offered to help. To give her a little of my magic so she wouldn't be so empty until she recharged naturally." Wade nodded, but didn't interrupt. "Problem is...the only way I knew how to do it, quickly and without it causing her pain, was...well...with a kiss," he said, mumbling the last three words.

"'Scuse me? Don't think I heard that last bit," Wade said, and he knew if he were in wolf form, his ears would be perked all the way forward.

"I said a kiss, dammit!"

"That's what I thought you said," Wade said smugly. "So I'm guessing it was a good kiss?"

Julian wanted to growl, but held it in. He'd already lost control once, he wasn't going to do it again, no matter how much he didn't want to talk about this. "Don't get the wrong idea, Wade. We weren't pawing at each other on the staircase. It was innocent."

"Innocent doesn't mean it wasn't good," was the retort.

"Fine, it was a good kiss, okay? But it shouldn't have happened."

"Maybe, maybe not, but it did happen. Was that the only kiss?"

"Yes," he snapped. "The only other times I've touched her were completely chaste. Helping her when she was weak or injured."

Wade cocked his head. "Maybe you should start at the beginning."

"Since it's all part of the whole and the reason I need your help, then it's probably a good idea." But Julian hesitated. He trusted Wade, but this was still dangerous information to have. However, he didn't give

Wade the same offer he'd given Paige, didn't give Wade the chance to back out. If he tried, Wade would be insulted, he knew. They'd been friends for too long, and Wade thrived on danger. So he took a breath and dove in. "I found a piece of a relic."

Some might not have grasped the significance of that statement, but Wade knew Julian wouldn't be bringing up some insignificant object, and he was well aware of how rare the powerful relics were. He whistled low and shook his head. "Dangerous thing to find, but you said piece. I'm guessing you want to find the other pieces, right?"

Julian smiled tightly. "I do. This one apparently conveys immortality. So I asked Paige to help, since she's extremely skilled with psychometry. If she could touch a stranger once and find him an hour from London with nothing else to go on, without any training whatsoever, I thought she could get something from a piece of a powerful magical object."

"Did she?" Wade wasn't a witch, but the thought of actually seeing a legendary relic was damn tempting. Everyone knew they had once existed, but the only objects that existed now could easily be mimicked by an Arcane's natural powers. There were few members of the supernatural community who wouldn't want to see one, regardless of the danger that came with it.

"In a way. The moment she touched it, the relic...invaded her. Apparently it has life, of a sort, so she felt it being broken into pieces. She went rigid and her eyes bloody glowed, Wade. She could've been in a pitch black room and lit the whole place up with her eyes alone."

Wade grimaced and shook his head. "That sounds disturbing."

"It was, though when she wasn't in agony, it's actually..." Julian thought she'd been absolutely gorgeous with glowing emerald eyes, but that was something he was going to keep to himself.

"Actually what?"

"It was brilliant. I'd never seen anything like it." Which was part of the truth, and all he wanted to share.

"I'd kind of like to see that. But go on."

"Well, she didn't get much. Mostly it was just pain, but she did get a little information before she started having some sort of seizure. I honestly think that if I hadn't gotten the amulet out of her hand, it might have killed her," he admitted. "As it was, I had to break one of her fingers to do it."

Wade's eyes went sympathetic. "Damn. I take it this was what left her so drained?"

Julian nodded. "So you can see why I felt compelled to share some of my magic with her?"

"Hell yeah. But still, this seems like a major reaction for a single kiss."

"It wasn't just that. I told her that she was done. I wasn't going to let her handle the amulet again, but she refused to be put off. Said she'd started it and she was going to finish it. She..." He sighed. "She said that she didn't want me to lose another person I loved."

Wade winced. "I didn't realize you'd told her about Mary."

"I hadn't. Her powers did."

"Ouch. Let me guess. You froze her out after that?"

Julian's shoulders hunched defensively. Wade knew him entirely too well. "Until she forced me to pay attention, yeah. We're okay now.

Other than the fact that I'm lusting after my bloody apprentice," he muttered.

Julian expected sympathy from Wade since the shifter knew the whole story with Mary, and how he'd shunned romantic relationships, staying loyal to her memory. He should have remembered that Wade was one of those pushing him to move on and live his life.

"About time, I say. Are you wanting my advice?" Wade asked, taking a drink and looking entirely too pleased for Julian's taste.

"I suppose I must be," Julian answered wearily.

"Well, I say go for it. You've gone two hundred years with only your hand for any real sort of companionship." Julian didn't even flinch at that crude statement. "I've heard you talk about Paige, and it's clear that you like her as a person. I might even go so far as to say you're friends, not just teacher and apprentice." His voice gentled. "I know you loved Mary, Julian, but would she really want you to live the rest of your life alone? Or would she want you to be happy and maybe find someone else?"

He wanted to yell at Wade, to throw something and argue, but he knew Wade only spoke the truth. "You make it sound like she's a sure thing," he said hotly, wanting *something* he could use to argue with.

Wade shrugged. "Nothing's a sure thing, Julian. But if you don't try, you can't succeed." He was a perceptive wolf, and he saw that his friend needed time to think it over, so he changed the subject. "What is it you need from me on the relic front, though? You said Paige didn't get much?"

"Not the first time. The second time, she managed to shield herself and narrowed things down. One of the pieces is in the Amazon Rainforest, away from the river itself and inside a temple that no one has found—at least not publicly." He drank, trying to relax again, but finding it difficult. "She's hoping that once she's in the Amazon, she'll be able to act as a sort of compass, but I'd rather have a tracker with us."

"And another fighter, I'm assuming?"

"It couldn't hurt," Julian admitted. "She's not the best with physical magics and has never trained to fight. Could you come with us?"

That toothy grin reappeared. "Depends. You know I'm a mercenary, not a charity."

Julian chuckled. "I was planning to pay you. Especially since you've been to the Amazon and I haven't."

"Excellent. My rates start at ten thousand a day. That's with the friend discount."

"You know I'm good for it." Longevity and a unique skill set came in handy when it came to finances. And he also knew that Wade was full of it. He might charge that much for hunting down a dangerous bounty, but he'd never charged Julian even a fraction of that.

"Awesome. How you planning to get down there?"

"Plane. I could teleport us, but taking two people and whatever supplies we'll need will tax my powers, and since we don't know what we'll be up against, I'd rather not take that chance."

"You'll need to get a private plane, then, since you can't get weapons on a commercial flight, and trust me, we'll need them," Wade told him.

Julian smirked. "Easy enough. I have never flown commercial in my life and I don't plan to start now."

"Works for me," Wade said cheerfully. "Let me get you a list of things you'll need. I don't wanna hear you whining because you forgot something and want mine."

"You're such a giver," Julian said dryly as Wade started writing. As the list grew longer and longer, he arched a brow. Luckily, he was a wealthy man, otherwise the sheer length of the list would have him paling. "We'll leave in a week from today and meet you in Manaus," he said after Wade had given him the list. "And yes, I'll have a plane waiting for you nearby. Just text me which airport works best for you."

"Can't wait," the shifter said sincerely. "Sounds like fun. And I'll get to meet the woman who's driving the super serious Julian up a wall."

"Don't push it," Julian warned. "See you in a week."

He teleported back to Mooreton, appearing in the hallway. He startled Paige, who squeaked when she nearly ran into him. "Good god! Don't scare me like that!" she told him as she leaned against the wall, waiting for her heartbeat to settle down.

"Sorry," he said contritely.

She waved a hand dismissively. "Did your friend agree to help?"

"He did. We'll leave for Brazil in a week."

To his shock—and secretly to his delight—she did some sort of happy dance, shaking her hips and butt while punching her hands in the air. "Yes! I'm going to Brazil!" she sang happily.

He allowed her a minute of celebration before he cleared his throat. "Do remember that it won't be a walk in the park."

"Oh, I know. But it'll be worth it." She stopped and frowned. "I don't know what I need to pack for this," she worried aloud. "I've never been anywhere but England."

"Wade does." He held up the list. "He wrote it all down." He grinned. "Didn't want to hear me complaining when I was suffering and wanted his supplies. Because of some of them, we'll be going on a private plane."

She gaped at him. "Not only am I leaving the country for the first time, flying for the first time, but I'm going on a private plane? Julian, I want to thank you, sincerely, for putting that amulet in my hand."

He shook his head and gave the list to her. Her eyes widened as she looked it over. "We don't have most of this, and it isn't going to be cheap, Julian," she warned him.

Unconcerned, he shrugged. "So?"

"I can't afford my share of this!" She did have a little money, left over from when she'd worked three years before, but not much. Since she rarely left Mooreton, there hadn't been anything to spend it on, not since Julian insisted that room and board was payment for assisting him. All the groceries she'd bought the last three years went on a credit card he'd given her for that purpose. But that had been food for Julian as well as herself, so she hadn't felt too guilty about it.

He scowled. "I say again...so? Use the card. I assure you I can afford it. And you going with me is helping me, so I need you properly outfitted." He saw she still wanted to protest, so he added, "This isn't your responsibility. Again, you're helping me, so just buy the damn supplies with my card."

Paige's expression turned mulish for an instant before she smiled sweetly. "You'll need to come with me, you know."

"What? Why?" Regardless of Wade's advice, he could use some distance from her.

"Well, I can hardly know what hiking boots are comfortable for you or try your clothes on for you." Seeing that he wasn't convinced, she added, in a saccharin tone, "Of course, I could try, but I can't guarantee that you won't end up with Hawaiian shirts or pink boots." She knew that he'd never be caught dead in either of those, so as an argument, it was pretty effective.

He sighed in defeat. "Fine. We'll go first thing tomorrow. Just no more cruel threats, okay?"

She gave him another amazing smile and nodded. "Promise!" Then she turned to continue down the hall, singing under her breath and half-dancing.

As he watched the twitching of her jean-clad ass, he thought that Wade might be right. Maybe he should give himself a break... and give a relationship with Paige a chance.

CHAPTER 10

As usual, Paige was awake when Julian managed to drag himself out of bed. He hadn't slept well, too busy thinking about two things; Paige, and what could go wrong on their trip. So when he came downstairs and found her offering him a cup of coffee, doctored to perfection, he was grateful.

After the first cup, he was able to communicate in actual words instead of grunts, and by the third he felt that he was ready—probably—to go shopping with Paige. He just hoped she wasn't one of those people who took an hour to decide between two choices. He wasn't a fan of shopping, so he wanted this done with as quickly as possible.

Though Paige had driven his car plenty—she was the one who ran to the nearest village to get groceries—he insisted on driving today. Knowing Paige, it was likely to be the most control he had all day. She had decided they would get the boring stuff out of the way first, so they could enjoy the rest of the day. Apparently, that meant first aid supplies, sunscreen, canteens, and other hiking gear. He could admit that wasn't really exciting, but none of it was, in his opinion. This trip was going to be work, and most likely dangerous work.

After that, and before he could get distracted, he dragged her to a camera store and insisted that she buy herself a nice camera. His excuse was that it was a big trip for her, in several ways, and she'd probably want pictures to remember it with. In reality, he still felt guilty about the danger he'd put her in and hoped that the gift would help ease it. She argued that it was too much and wasn't needed, but when he saw how much she wanted it—though she tried to hide it—he wore her down. The smile she gave him was repayment enough.

They walked out of the store with Paige cradling the shopping bag to her chest, grinning like a loon. The smile disappeared when she almost ran into her dad.

Jacob had aged in the three years since she'd seen him, which shouldn't have really been possible. There was more gray in his hair, more lines on his face. But the angry expression he wore hadn't changed since the night he'd kicked her out.

"Dad..." she began, though she had no idea what to say to him. But he wasn't looking at her. He was glaring at Julian.

Julian's expression was inscrutable as he inclined his head to the older man. "Jacob," he said in a neutral tone.

That surprised Paige, who looked between the two men. "You know each other? Julian, why did you never say anything?"

He didn't so much as glance at her, just shifted one shoulder in a shrug and kept his eyes on Jacob. "It served no purpose for you to know."

"So. You've made your choice and stayed with his sort, I see," Jacob said bitterly.

"You didn't give me much of a choice, dad," Paige said quietly. "I had nowhere to go, and he was nice enough to take me in and help me."

Fearing where the conversation was going to go, Julian quickly surrounded them with a bubble that would prevent any humans from overhearing what they said.

"You could've come back. All you had to do was promise that you would never use magic! That you'd never associate with the likes of *him* again," he snapped at her.

The pure hatred for magic that was clear in his voice made Paige take a step back. She might have taken another, but Julian's hand lightly touched her back and she drew comfort from it.

She drew in a deep breath and lifted her chin. "You told me not to come back. I'd just been attacked, and all you cared about was magic. How could you hate it more than you loved me?" she asked, despising the slight tremble in her voice, the burn of moisture in her eyes.

"You don't know what it's done to me! What it did to your mother!" Jacob yelled, his face turning red.

Paige fought back the tears, but one slid down her cheek despite her efforts. Her chest felt hot and tight and she knew that this might be the last time she ever saw her father. All over a prejudice she had been ignorant of and still didn't understand. "How could I? You never told me anything about it! You can't hide these things from me then expect me to understand."

Julian broke in. "Jacob, you can hardly blame her for what I did, and Elizabeth wouldn't want you to act like this. More, this is hardly the time or place for such a discussion. You are, however, welcome to come by Mooreton anytime you'd like to visit Paige."

Jacob whirled on Julian, and Paige feared that he'd take a swing. "You don't mention her! Don't you dare say her name. You may have known her, but she wasn't your wife." He clenched and unclenched his fists before he turned on his heel and stomped off.

Paige's eyes closed, dislodging another tear to slide down her cheek. When Julian comfortingly rubbed his hand over her back, she sagged against him. Unsure, he supported her, but didn't move to embrace her, though he sensed she'd more than welcome a hug at this point. Forcing a lighter note into his voice, he said, "He'll calm down, Paige. And we have some shopping left to do. The fun stuff, right? Though I still absolutely refuse to let you put me in a Hawaiian shirt."

She laughed—just a little—as he'd hoped, and dashed away her tears. "I'm still going to try," she assured him.

Over the next few hours, they bought the rest of what they'd need and her mood had improved somewhat. True to her word, she had tried to get him to try on a Hawaiian shirt in blue and white, but he'd staunchly refused. Instead, she bought herself a bathing suit that had a pink and black hibiscus print. It wasn't the same, but it amused him and cheered her a little. As did being able to buy several outfits in what she called rainforest chic. They looked like cargo pants, tank tops, and long-sleeved tan shirts to him, but if it made her happy, he didn't care what she called it.

Once they were back home, her mood had plummeted again, the drive giving her a chance to dwell on her father and his words. They unloaded the car in silence and brought everything up to her room.

After everything was laid out beside her bed, she expected Julian to leave. When he didn't, she asked, "Was there something you needed?"

He hesitated, then nodded. "You to smile again."

That took her by surprise, so for a moment she only blinked at him. Finally, she tried to force a smile, but he shook his head.

"A real one." He motioned for her to have a seat on her bed while he took the chair by the window. "Your father is a good man, Paige."

She sank to the bed and nodded. "I know. Or I did. I can't see how a good man would do to me what he did, though."

"You should know, better than anyone, that emotions don't always make sense. He has his reasons for hating magic, and that hatred makes him illogical about it."

"But why? Before that night, I'd never heard that magic existed, much less that my father knew it." She frowned. "You know him. Do you know what happened?" she asked, grabbing her mother's jewelry box off her nightstand.

"Some," Julian admitted. "Both he and your mother are—were—witches. From what I remember, your mother had powers similar to yours, while your father tended toward elemental powers. I know they were trying to do something, some bit of magic that was more his purview than hers, and she died because the magic backfired or something along those lines. But I don't know the details."

Her thumbs brushed against the box's lid before she opened it. Just touching things that had belonged to her mother, that she'd worn, helped to center her. "Did you know her well?"

"No, not well. We were just acquaintances, really," Julian admitted and shook his head.

"Can you tell me anything about her?" Paige asked, blindly picking up a ring to run her fingers along the cool metal. She wasn't sure whether to smile or cry when she saw she held her mother's favorite ring. "Dad never talked about her much."

There were tears in her eyes again, so he chose his words carefully. "She was like you in some ways. Every time I saw her, she always seemed so at peace. Nothing ruffled her. And she was always smiling, laughing. I never heard anyone say anything negative about her, before or after her death."

Paige sniffled and lifted the ring, pressing it lightly against her lips. She had no memories of her mother. Having to rely on stories told by others and photographs was a poor substitution. Which was why she occasionally liked to simply touch these things her mother had owned. It was a way for her to feel connected to the woman she'd never known.

Julian suddenly straightened in his chair and his eyes widened. Waves of excitement rolled off of him.

She looked behind her, then back to him, bewildered. "What? What is it?"

"That ring, can I see it?" he asked and rose to walk over to her.

"The ring?" Paige blinked at it, then at him, before she slowly placed it in his outstretched hand. She was reluctant to give it away, even temporarily or to a person she trusted completely, but knew he wouldn't do anything to damage it.

He held it between two fingers and lifted it so he could examine it. A smile curved his lips and Paige frowned, not understanding the fuss about a simple ring. The emerald it held was small and the band was made of white gold. It wasn't an expensive ring. Simple and pretty, yes, but no more than that.

"Do you realize what you have here?" he asked, not taking his eyes off it.

"Um...A ring that my mum owned and passed to me?"

His bark of laughter made her jump. "Not just a ring, my dear." Suddenly, he frowned. "You didn't get any impressions off of it?"

She shrugged, too surprised by the path the conversation had taken to notice he'd slipped 'my dear' in there. "Sometimes, but nothing much. I know my mum wore it, and loved it, but that's about it."

"Curious," he murmured. "Paige, I think this may be a relic. The moment I saw it, I knew it was magic. Strong magic. There's certainly magic around it."

"That's ridiculous. I've never reacted to it like I did to the piece downstairs," Paige argued with a firm shake of her head. "There's never been anything remotely close to what happened with your piece. And if it *was* magic, do you really think my dad would have allowed it in his house?"

"Only if he knew it was there. How often did he ever look in your mother's jewelry? Or did he put it away, so it wasn't a painful reminder?" he asked gently.

That much was true, but it was still hard for Paige to believe it could be a relic.

"Will you allow me to take it, just for a little while, to study it?" he asked. "Understanding one relic might help me understand another."

Automatically Paige started to refuse, but the hope in his eyes had her considering his request. Finally, she gave in and nodded. "I will, just...please, Julian, don't lose it. I don't know what I'd do if I didn't have it."

Julian grinned at her. He was so caught up in the promise of what was to come that he impulsively took the last step between them and kissed her. It was brief, over almost before he realized what he was doing, but his heart had quickened some by the time he took a quick step back. A primal part of him was pleased to see Paige was equally as affected, her eyes dilated, lips parted.

He cleared his throat and took another step away from her. "I promise I won't lose it. Thank you, Paige." He almost said more, but thought better of it. A nod was given to her before he left the room. Before he could do something else without truly thinking it through.

She watched him go then lifted her fingers to her vibrating lips.

One of these days, she hoped to get a real kiss from him. Not one caused by necessity, or so brief that not even one heartbeat passed between the beginning and the end.

Maybe one day...

CHAPTER 11

Paige didn't see much of Julian in the days leading up to their departure, but the tone of this absence was much different from the last time. He spoke to her when he saw her, was friendly, even, he was just too caught up in researching for the trip. And examining her ring whenever he had a spare moment. It was typical Julian, really, and so normal she felt relieved. Mostly.

She didn't mind his preoccupation. She was too excited about their trip to mind much of anything. The night before they left, she barely slept an hour, too full of anticipation. To her, it was better than the night before Christmas. Not only was she leaving the country for the first time, but she was going on an adventure to find a magical artifact. She'd be going to a place that likely hadn't seen people in hundreds of years. Maybe thousands. It was like a dream come true, and she couldn't wait to dive right in.

Soon enough, their bags were put into the car and they were off to the small airport where a jet was waiting for them. Julian was amused at her enthusiasm and impatience when she hurried them onto the plane, but it was her reaction once on board that made him chuckle.

Mooreton, now that it had been cleaned up, was far from a hovel, and it did hold several impressive pieces of furniture and art. Yet even after living in such an impressive place for three years, Paige still looked overwhelmed by the comfort and luxury of the jet. The seats were large and plush, but there was also a sofa big enough to sleep on, a full bathroom and bedroom, and even a kitchen area. She saw two TVs with accompanying electronics, too. All in all, they had everything they'd need for the sixteen hour flight. For that matter, she thought they had enough to live on this plane.

Like a kid, she wanted to sit in every seat, touch everything she could, push every button. Somehow, she refrained. Instead, she dutifully stowed their gear before sitting down, almost bouncing with excitement.

The one dim spot was that Julian had insisted she bring her mother's ring. Thinking that it could be a relic made her wary, so it was on a chain around her neck rather than around her finger. She'd worn it in the past without any ill effects, but she couldn't bring herself to wear it now. Not after what had happened with Julian's relic piece.

Paige wasn't at all nervous about flying as she buckled up. Any nerves she felt were all about what would happen once they were back on the ground. As the plane started down the runway, she all but pressed her nose against the window to watch as the world started to recede beneath her.

"Is it everything you hoped it would be so far?" Julian asked a few minutes later, smiling at the joy she found in something as simple as a plane taking off. He was used to luxury and magic, had become jaded to them both. Seeing her like this helped remind him of the joy life could hold.

"Better," she assured him with a grin, turning back to face him.

It was only then that Julian saw that she wasn't wearing her mother's ring, and he frowned. "Why aren't you wearing the ring? You brought it, didn't you?"

Lifting a hand to touch the ring that lay beneath her shirt, Paige shrugged, guilt crossing her features. "I don't know. I've always loved this ring, but since you told me it might be a relic...part of me doesn't want to touch it," she admitted.

He shook his head. "I would say that you have absolutely nothing to worry about, Paige. You said yourself that you've touched it numerous times, and it's never bothered you, right?" When she reluctantly nodded, he went on. "Why would it start now? Likely, the other one only affected you so strongly because it was broken into pieces. That, and I would guarantee that the amulet is a much stronger relic than the ring. And if the ring *was* going to affect you negatively, I don't think that wearing it on a chain instead of your finger would prevent it. It would only need to touch your skin. So please...put it on your finger." He thought of an argument then that might sway her and added, "It would certainly be safer on your finger, too. We're going to be hiking through the Amazon. A chain could easily get snagged and break."

Mentally cursing that he was right, Paige undid the necklace and, after a brief pause, slipped the ring onto her finger. She held her breath for a moment, but nothing happened. She didn't feel any different. "I guess you were right."

He smiled.

"What did you find out about it, anyway?"

It was his turn to hesitate. "It is definitely magical, and has enough power that I'm fairly certain it is a relic. Unfortunately, as you know, records regarding relics, especially specific relics, are scarce at best.

Only a few are mentioned in any of the materials I have, and none of the descriptions matched the ring," he said, nodding at it.

Deflated, she slumped back in her seat. "I was hoping for more."

"So was I. There's a chance that we'll find out what it does the old fashioned way." At her confused look, he added, "By trial and error, when the ring does whatever it is that it was meant to do."

That wasn't reassuring. What if it was meant to turn the one wearing it to ash? Yes, that was extremely unlikely given that it had been her mother's, but they had no way of knowing for certain. "I guess..."

They both went silent, and Paige turned her attention outside the plane again, fascinated by the sight of the clouds and the world below.

While she watched the earth passing beneath them, he watched her. Memories of their two kisses started to sneak into his consciousness, and he had to subtly shift his sudden erection into a more comfortable position. Not that it helped much.

He could deny it all he liked, he could try to remind himself that he still loved Mary, but facts were facts. He wanted Paige more than he remembered ever wanting another woman, including his wife. Sighing softly, he closed his eyes. He tried to convince himself that it had just been too long since Mary had been alive and he was misremembering, but he knew that wasn't true. More, he had half convinced himself to shuck the cloak of grief he'd worn for too long, but actually doing it wasn't as easy, not when regret and sorrow tried to pull it back over him.

Paige cocked her head as she felt the turmoil within him and she looked back, concerned. "Julian?"

"Hmm?"

"Is everything okay? You feel...conflicted."

His eyes opened and the heat within them made her breath catch. Before she could speak again, he reached over, undid her seatbelt, and plucked her out of her chair, pulling her into his lap. She felt the hardness beneath her butt and squirmed before she could think better of it. Her heart pounded with anticipation, hoping—praying—that this was going to lead where she thought it was.

He groaned and slid his fingers into her thick hair before he kissed her as she'd been longing for. There was nothing innocent this time in the firm press of his lips against hers. It was hot, demanding, and it made Paige's head swim with a mixture of joy and lust.

She wrapped her arms around him, as much to anchor herself as to hold him, and sunk into the kiss. She'd only had one brief serious relationship before she came to live at Mooreton, so she knew she wasn't exactly experienced, especially next to a man who was centuries old. Desperate to not disappoint him, to make sure he wanted to do it again, she poured everything she had into that kiss.

Rocked by the intensity of her reaction, Julian forgot himself, forgot all of his arguments against this very thing. He urged her lips to part, groaning when she gave in without hesitation. Diving deeper, he plundered, reveling in the taste of her and the feel of her soft body pressed against his. Never pulling his mouth from hers, his hand lifted to her breast, cupping it through her shirt. She moaned and pressed against his palm, all too happy to take things further.

"Please..."

The husky whisper jarred him out of his lust-fueled haze, and he pulled back, his hand dropping to the arm of his seat.

The sight of her was almost more than his self-control could handle. Her lips were slightly parted and swollen from their kissing, her hair mussed from his hands. But it was her eyes that nearly undid him. Half-lidded, filled with heat—and something else he didn't want to explore at the moment. She clearly didn't want to stop.

But then, neither did he.

Gently, he unwound her arms from his neck and set her back in her seat, ignoring the confused hurt that replaced the desire in her eyes.

"I'm sorry—" he began, voice rough.

"I'm not," she shot back.

"I shouldn't have manhandled you like that," he continued as though she hadn't spoken. She scowled as he turned his seat and reclined it back. "I'm going to sleep."

Paige started to snap at him, but caught herself just in time. "Fine," she said, careful to keep her voice perfectly neutral, though her nails bit harshly into the palms of her hands.

Though he closed his eyes, it took him a long time to actually fall asleep. His body wouldn't cooperate. Neither would his mind. He had wanted the kiss. He still wanted it, and more. Something about that single word—*please*—had reminded him of his past, though. He wasn't sure why. But Wade's words played over in his head. It truly was time for him to live again. If he could only figure out how to do it.

Those thoughts bounced around in his brain for hours, but eventually he did sleep. And dream.

Julian knew it for a dream as soon as it began, so it didn't worry him. His dreams never had. Even recently, when he'd begun dreaming about Paige, he'd only felt the slightest stirring of guilt.

Dreams weren't real, after all.

So when he found himself in his garden with a familiar redhead, he simply allowed himself to go along for the ride.

He walked toward Paige, who sat on a stone bench with her back to him. Her marvelous hair was unbound and fell to her hips, so from behind it acted as a cloak, hiding most of her from view. When he got closer, he could see she wore a dress made of some thin, clingy fabric in a green that matched her eyes exactly. The paleness of her skin only made it seem more vibrant. Her head slightly turned and he could see a smile teasing her lips.

Giving into temptation in a way he wouldn't allow himself when awake, he leaned down, needing to touch her. He swept her hair to one side and kissed the nape of her neck, lips curving against her skin when she shivered.

"I've been waiting for you..." she murmured even as she tilted her head, encouraging more of the gentle affection.

The thought made him harden in a rush that nearly left him dizzy. He nuzzled her throat, then nipped it lightly before he stepped around her. "Have you? Did you dress for me, too?" he asked, as he greedily drank in the sight of her. The dress was cut low enough to reveal the swell of her breasts—the fabric clinging to them in a way that he thoroughly approved of—and short enough to show off long, slender legs and bare feet.

She smiled up at him, her eyes moving over him with as much hunger as he felt. "Of course."

Slowly, he lowered himself to his knees in front of her before gently tugging her to the edge of the bench. "Good," he murmured, before he rubbed his cheek against one of her breasts. Her nipple puckered, visible even through the dress, so he turned his head to capture it through the cloth and suck teasingly. When she moaned and cupped his head, he drew harder, faster, until she was making small, eager noises for him.

Drawing back, he circled his thumb around the other nipple. "Have I told you how absolutely beautiful you are?" he murmured as he took in the flush on her cheeks, the way her lips were parted with her building need.

She gave him a sultry smile. "Not yet."

He bent his head to kiss the exposed tops of both breasts. "Consider it said, then, because you are exquisite."

She tried to draw him up for a kiss, but he shook his head and leaned back. Hands that weren't quite steady drew her dress upward until it was bunched up around her hips. Beneath, she wore nothing but the subtle floral fragrance that was hers, and hers alone. His cock throbbed and it took every bit of control not to shove his pants down and yank her onto him.

He groaned and repeated, "Exquisite," as his thumb brushed over her inner thigh.

She was breathing more heavily now, and he saw that she was already aroused, already damp with need. He lowered his head and pressed a tender kiss between her thighs, making her breath catch.

"Please," she whispered, her fingers tightening in his hair.

He smiled at the lust-filled plea and couldn't resist giving her what she asked for. Slowly, thoroughly, he began to love her with his mouth. The first pass of his tongue over her, that first taste, made him ache, and while he had intended to go slow, be tender, he was desperate for more. He'd denied himself for too long. Now that he'd given in, he couldn't stop. More, he didn't want to stop.

Julian's mouth worked her until she was squirming and her hands had moved to his shoulders. She held on so tightly he could feel the press of her nails through his shirt, and that display of how much she wanted this, wanted him, only spurred him on. His fingers replaced his tongue, and he gently slid one, then two of them inside her. It was almost too much for him. She was so soft and hot that he needed to be inside her now. Somehow, he held off and began to work her desire higher. He stroked expertly, curling his fingers to find that sensitive spot within, and was rewarded when she cried out and threw her head back.

But it wasn't enough for him. He wanted to see her lose it. He wanted to hear her scream as she came for him. And gods, he wanted to feel her wrapped around him when she did.

His lips found the swollen bundle of nerves and he began to suck in time with the press of his fingers—and the throbbing in his groin—until he sensed more than saw her body bow with the force of her first release. She cried his name as she trembled above him, and he just craved more.

After the first climax subsided, she tried to weakly pull him away, to escape the sensations that were almost overwhelming, but he refused until she'd come a second time.

He had to catch her before she could just slide bonelessly off the bench, and drew her down so they knelt in the grass together.

"I need you, Paige," he murmured as he lazily brushed his lips over the rapid pulse in her neck, his hands locked on her hips.

"I know," she responded in a low, sexy voice that made his cock jerk. He stopped breathing for a moment when he felt her fingers undoing his jeans. She tugged them down until he was bared to her. She bit her lip as she wrapped her hand around him, slowly stroking until his eyes met hers.

"Paige," he groaned as she bent down and dabbed her tongue over the tip of his cock, tasting the moisture already gathered there. To his delighted shock, she took him into her mouth and began to slide her lips and tongue over him.

Part of him wanted nothing more, but he managed, with more willpower than he thought he possessed, to gently push her back after just a few moments of that delicious torment. Her mouth felt amazing, but he wanted all of her. When she gave him a confused look, he nudged her until she was laying back in the grass. "If I hadn't stopped you, I wouldn't be able to do this," he told her, settling between her thighs, his hard length brushing against her core.

Her eyes fluttered closed as she gave a breathy, "Oh. Okay. Yes." Her voice was as dazed as her eyes and he felt satisfaction swell in his chest that he'd done that to her. So when she lifted her arms to hold him, he claimed her lips in a fierce kiss.

He started to thrust forward, to finally bury himself so deep inside her that he'd feel like he was part of her...

The plane touched down on the runway in Brazil, the small jolt startling him just enough to fracture the dream and wake him.

It took a moment for him to fully come back to reality, but his body was still back in the dream, aching for what he'd almost had. He wanted to rage at the timing and scrubbed his hands over his face. Not wanting Paige to pick up on what had happened, he shielded his mind and emotions as strongly as he could manage as he slipped into the small bathroom to compose himself.

He shielded so strongly he didn't realize Paige had woke at the same time he had, or that she was panting with need just as he was.

CHAPTER 12

Neither Paige nor Julian mentioned the intense dream they'd had. They had no idea they'd shared the dream, but it was too intense, their relationship too uncertain, for either to give even a hint of their desires to the other. No one even spoke as they freshened up, gathered their things, and got off the plane.

Wade was waiting for them, dressed in black cargo pants, a tee-shirt, and hiking boots. He leaned against a rugged-looking off-road SUV with his arms crossed, sunglasses on to shield against the bright morning sun. "About time you slackers got here. I've been waiting two hours," he called jokingly. When Julian just grunted and Paige only gave him a faint smile in response, Wade cocked his head, confused and curious. "Bad flight?"

"No, it was fine. We slept for most of it," Julian answered, his clipped voice back in full force, while Paige just flushed pink.

Wade glanced between them, and when they got closer, he could smell the arousal on them. More, he could feel the tension sparking around them, so he let the subject drop. He was many things, but he wasn't cruel and he wasn't about to embarrass a woman he'd only just met. But he'd damn well pin Julian down later and try to find out what had happened to make them both so glum. "Right, well, I'm going to assume you're Paige. I'm Wade, tracker extraordinaire. You guys eat yet?"

Julian shook his head while Paige answered, "No."

"Okay, well, there's a restaurant nearby. The food's not that bad. We can get you guys fed, then figure out what our plans are. Sound good?"

"That's fine," Paige agreed when Julian only shrugged. Her stomach was tied in knots after that dream. What she was hungry for wasn't food, but knew they'd need to eat before venturing out into the Amazon. She wasn't a lazy woman by any means, but something like this was bound to stretch the limits of her endurance. Plenty of fuel beforehand would be an excellent idea.

The shifter studied them both for another minute before he helped them load their bags into the back of the SUV. Silence filled the vehicle as they drove the short distance to the restaurant, then took a seat outside so they were close to the vehicle. No one should have any clue what they were up to, but years of tracking down dangerous people had made Wade cautious, even paranoid. Since it had kept him alive this long, he didn't see any reason to change.

The atmosphere was subdued as they ordered. Paige wasn't familiar with Portuguese, so Wade translated for her then gave her order to the waiter. Afterward, he tried to make conversation with them both, only to get single syllable answers. It wasn't until the pair had gotten coffee and food that he made any progress.

"So what's the plan? You have a starting point?"

"Unfortunately, not much of one," Julian admitted. "We do need to get away from the river, though, and we can avoid all the ruins that have been documented. They'd just be a waste of time."

"You sure? There could be a hidden room or something. God knows they're always discovering new things about old places. Things even we have forgotten."

Paige shook her head. "I saw the outside of the temple, too. And Julian showed me pictures of all the known ones he could find, and they weren't right. Some were similar in design or decoration to the one I saw, but none were exact."

"Oh." Wade frowned as he ate. "Well, even discounting anything close to the river, it's still a big fucking area to search. We could spend several of *our* lifetimes trying."

Julian glanced at Paige, just for a second, before he asked, "You sense anything?"

She went still, head tilted as she reached out with her magic. Both men watched her, silent now so they didn't break her concentration. After a few minutes, she made an annoyed sound and shook her head. "I don't feel it. I know it's here, but that's it. I don't know that I can feel anything unless I'm touching the piece we have. To be honest, I'd have been shocked if I could feel it without that one in my hand." She glanced at Julian but was no more eager for eye contact than he was. "I couldn't sense your piece unless I was holding it," she pointed out.

He grunted. "It's at home in the safe. I didn't want to be traipsing around the Amazon with that in our pockets. It could get lost too easily, and we don't know how well others could sense or track it, and through it, us."

She frowned and shook her head. "But I'm not going to be of any use if I don't have it so I can link to the other pieces," she argued.

Wade added, "And without some direction, we may as well be sitting back twiddling our thumbs, Julian. Again, the Amazon Rainforest is fucking huge. More than two *million* square miles. Lifetimes, remember?"

Julian scowled and continued to eat.

Hesitantly, Paige tried again. "Julian—"

"If we don't make any progress within twenty-four hours, I'll retrieve it. But I can't believe that there's only one way of finding the damn thing," he snapped.

Paige and Wade exchanged a glance before the latter nodded slowly. "Sure thing. In the meantime, do we want to get a hotel? It'll give you guys a place to shower or rest before we get going." They shouldn't need either, considering the plane they'd just stepped off of had both shower and beds, but maybe an hour or two would settle them down a little.

Julian started to speak when Paige held up a hand. Both men looked at her and found her with an unhappy look on her face, her eyes unfocused with deep concentration, brow furrowed with concern.

There was a tickle in the back of her mind. At first, she'd dismissed it as paranoia since she was in an unfamiliar place, surrounded by a language she didn't speak, but that wasn't it. She felt like someone was prodding at her head, poking it like a curious child. Paige shielded, immediately and strongly, and waited for the cold rush of fear, but it didn't come. She was concerned, definitely, but the probing didn't feel malicious. That, strangely, only made her worry more.

"Someone's trying to get in my head," she told them absently, even as the sensation subsided. "I think I shielded before they got anything."

"Are you sure?" Wade asked, closing his eyes as he sniffed at the air. There were so many people around, and, being in a restaurant, his sense of smell was hindered, but he tried anyway.

Julian didn't question her. He knew just how strong her telepathy was.

"Positive," Paige answered. "I felt them sort of nudging at me. But when I shielded, it went away. I don't think they wanted to get caught."

"There's danger," Wade growled softly, the hair on the back of his neck standing up. Wolves—especially this wolf—were attuned to danger, an instinct they had honed over millennia. It wasn't a scent, and it might not even be anything in their immediate vicinity, but it was coming.

"Damn," Julian said, digging out some cash and dropping it on the table. "No hotel. Get to the car." No one argued, they just hurried for the vehicle, piling in. By unspoken agreement, Wade jumped into the driver's seat.

Paige expected him to race away from the city, but was surprised when he kept to a more reasonable speed. Julian surreptitiously watched behind them for signs of anyone following them, while Paige kept her senses open for another intruder.

Once out of the city, Wade picked up a little bit of speed. They weren't being followed, as far as they could tell, but he didn't seem to want to take any chances. But just a few minutes outside of the city, he pulled over and glanced back to Paige. "Look to your right."

Confused, she did as he asked and gasped softly as she got her first glimpse of the Amazon river. Two sections of the river merged together here, but rather than the water mixing, they flowed alongside one another, resulting in the river looking dark on one side, light on the other.

"How is that possible?" she asked, fumbling for the camera Julian had given her and taking several shots.

"It's *Encontro das Águas*. Meeting of the Waters." He grinned. "It's a pretty popular tourist attraction, and I figured that you'd never seen anything like it before."

"I haven't. It's brilliant! Thank you, Wade," she told him, giving him a bright smile. She ignored the short, quickly hidden burst of annoyance she felt from Julian. He wasn't going to ruin her first experience as a tourist with his grumpiness.

"Anytime, Red," Wade told her before putting the SUV into motion again. Tourist time was done, and the brief stop had been a risk. Now it was time to get to safety and start hunting for the relic.

No one relaxed, not until they were a good hour away and well off the main road. Wade pulled in front of some brush to help hide the vehicle from anyone who might follow them, then turned to face his companions. "I think we need to revisit this twenty-four-hour plan. If someone started poking around less than an hour after you hit the ground, then we don't have time to wait. And just randomly searching isn't exactly a speedy process."

"You're not wrong, but if we have that piece on us, it could make us easier for them to locate. It could become a damn beacon, for all we know," Julian disagreed.

"Maybe, maybe not. But the longer we're out here, the better a chance they have of finding us. Which puts us—*all* of us—in danger," he said, inclining his head purposefully toward Paige.

She wanted to be offended, but she knew she was the weak link if it came to violence or a magical confrontation. The moment they were done with this and she had some free time, she was going to learn how to defend herself. Just because she couldn't throw a fireball didn't mean she couldn't learn how to throw a punch.

"He's right," she said quietly. "I don't think that anyone can sense it, though, not unless they're really powerful or somehow linked to it. You had that piece in the house for a year and I only had no idea it was there until you told me," she pointed out.

"Just make sure you shield it really, really well before you bring it back here, just to be on the safe side. But hell, if Paige can't sense these things when she's deliberately looking for them, then how can whoever's following us sense it with it shielded and without knowing what they're looking for?"

Julian sighed, then nodded. "Fine. Don't go anywhere."

"Wouldn't dream of it."

The moment Julian disappeared, Wade turned off the SUV and climbed out, stretching his legs. "You okay, Red?"

Paige frowned at the spot where Julian had sat, but slowly nodded. "I am. I'm just wondering who would want to get inside my head," she answered, slipping out of the vehicle. "I don't think they were in your head, or Julian's, at least. I have a feeling I'd have noticed if they'd tried." It wasn't something she was positive of, as not many people came to Mooreton, but given that telepathy was her strength, it only made sense that she would figure it out.

"Maybe it was just a guy who thought you were hot and he was checking to see if you were single," Wade teased with a bump of his shoulder against hers. When she laughed, he felt like a hero for having brought her out of her funk. She had looked so frustrated with her own skills, so he was happy to cheer her up. "But don't worry about it too much, okay? You're in Brazil, in the middle of the Amazon. Try to enjoy it." He was going to try to take his own advice. This trip had a bad feeling to it, and he was keeping alert for signs they were being followed, but he liked Paige. Liked her and had a feeling she was a lot stronger than she gave herself credit for. He was looking forward to seeing her find that strength.

She smiled. "You're right. I've been looking forward to this since we realized the piece was here. And speaking of..." She reached back into the vehicle and grabbed the camera. After taking several steps back from Wade, she lifted it and grinned. "Have to get a shot of our fearless guide." When he struck a goofy pose, she couldn't help but giggle, even as she took a shot. "Okay, funny man, now a real one, please?" she asked, but her voice was lighter now, amused, so his smile for her next shot was genuine.

After she got her picture, Wade dug in his pack and pulled out a sheathed knife. "Here," he said, handing it to her. She took it, but with a confused look on her face, which made him grin. "For protection. It straps to your thigh. Julian and I aren't going to let anything happen to you, Red, but I want you to have a way to protect yourself. Just in case."

Paige hesitated, but ultimately nodded. It took a minute for her to figure out the straps to get it in place on her thigh. It felt awkward, but Wade relaxed once it was in place, so she said nothing. "Better?"

He nodded. "Much. Now, let's get to work, so we're ready to go when he gets back."

They worked with light-hearted banter, and neither noticed the presence that crept in, watching them.

CHAPTER 13

Julian teleported himself directly to his workshop and got the relic piece out of the safe. He scowled at it for a moment, certain he was bringing a target back with him. No one should know he had this, but he didn't know of any reason why someone would be probing Paige's mind, either. She hadn't had the chance to make any enemies, and while she was powerful in her own right, she didn't radiate pure magic like some people did. Her talents were much more subtle than that. Even he might have missed it when they'd first met if she hadn't been screaming for help.

What really worried him was the fact that her ability to block the intrusion wasn't likely to put them off, either. If anything, it was bound to make whoever it was more intrigued by her. Not everyone knew how to shield their mind, even if they had the potential to do it.

He unwrapped the silk around the relic and meticulously crafted a shield around the tarnished silver to prevent anyone else from sensing it. Normally he could just use his will, his intent for such a thing, but since he wanted to ensure it was a strong shield, he cupped his hand over the metal and chanted in a low voice. Afterward, not wanting Paige to touch the relic itself by accident, he rewrapped it and slipped it into a velvet bag.

He'd been gone longer than he intended, but he wasn't going to take any chances. Not with the relic, and not with Paige's life. She'd come so close to dying once already, and he still hadn't shaken the guilt of that. He doubted he'd ever fully shake it.

Finally, he was as satisfied as he was going to get, and returned to the Amazon. Paige and Wade hadn't wasted the time he'd spent shielding the relic. They were both out of the SUV and they'd gotten their bags—and his—ready to go. They turned when they sensed that he was back, and Paige walked over to him, her expression cautious.

His fingers tightened on the bag holding the relic. "Before I give you this, I want you to make damn sure that you're prepared," he warned, desperate to avoid harming her with the object. With his obsession.

She arched a brow and extended her hand. "I am. I'm at least as well protected as I was the last time I held it. I promise. Now please give it to me so we can get away from here and put more distance between us and whoever was being nosy."

"Speaking of, do you know who might have been doing that?" Wade asked as he hitched his pack into place.

"Not sure. No one should know I have this except for the two of you. Maybe it was just a curious local," Julian answered, but his voice was skeptical.

"Maybe," Wade said, equally unconvinced.

After studying Paige's face for a moment, Julian reluctantly opened the pouch and silk and placed the wedge of silver in Paige's palm.

There was no surprise this time when her eyes glowed, though Wade's brows shot up and he gave a low whistle. "Impressive," he murmured. "And a little creepy."

Julian tuned him out to watch Paige. Her fingers closed around the object, and though a light tremor went through her, she didn't seem to be suffering. In fact, she was more relaxed than she'd been the last time. Grudgingly, he allowed that maybe Paige was getting better at this. That or she was just getting used to how the relic affected her. It could even be the shielding he'd placed on it, though that should only prevent detection. Whatever the reason, he was relieved that holding it was so much easier on her now. But an uneasy feeling remained. Magic was unpredictable, he knew, and relics like this were more powerful, and thus more unpredictable, than most. Despite his desperate desire to find all the pieces of this relic, part of him wished Paige had been less insistent about helping him.

The green glow was cut off when she closed her eyes, and the men watched as she slowly turned, pausing now and again, as though she were getting her bearings.

"It knows," she murmured.

"Knows what?" Wade asked.

"That another piece is nearby."

She moved as if in a trance, each step painfully slow, each turn careful. It took more than fifteen minutes for her to be even remotely certain of what she was sensing. The relic had feelings, yes, but it wasn't quite like anything people felt. More, though she felt a pull toward the piece here in the Amazon, it wasn't the only pull she felt, just the strongest one. All four of the lost pieces were in her mind, each trying to draw her attention to them. Finally, her eyes opened and she nodded to the trees ahead of her. "It's in that direction, but it's not close. I feel it like a tug that comes from here," she told them, placing her other hand over her solar plexus.

Wade pulled out his GPS unit, making note of the direction and plotting a path. "Got it."

"Let's put the relic away," Julian said, reaching for the hand that held it.

A mutinous look on her face, Paige snatched it back, cradling it against her chest. "No. I need to hold it." She needed to feel what it felt, needed to be connected to the other pieces. She couldn't let them be alone any longer.

His brows arched. "You need to?"

She hesitated, then told him, "So I can act as a compass."

He was pretty damn sure it wasn't the truth. He knew her too well, and she was a horrible liar. "Paige, we can get it back out if we need to, but for right now, you need to put it away," he told her gently. "Maybe it can't be tracked normally, but perhaps someone can track the influence it has on you."

She made a sound of distress, and her whole manner had him worried. Had they traded physical danger for mental? Was the relic trying to control her? Or was the feeling it gave Paige addicting somehow?

"C'mon Paige, we can't go until it's put away. Can't have you wandering around the jungle with glowing eyes, now can we?" Wade asked with forced cheerfulness.

Between the two of them, they managed to get her to let go of the relic, and Julian quickly took it from her and tucked it away. His pocket, so if she did try to go for it, there would be no way for him to miss the attempt.

She swayed with its absence, and Wade reached out to steady her. "Whoa...careful there, Red. Hold on to me if you need to." Her face was paler than normal, and he could feel a fine trembling in her limbs as he held her upright. It made him question the wisdom of this whole venture, especially the part where Paige had to lead them through the Amazon.

When she gripped Wade's arm to keep herself upright, a surge of jealousy tore through Julian and he clenched his teeth. "Let's go," he snapped, picking up his backpack.

Wade gave him an amused look, but released Paige and offered her pack to her, too. She was slower, even with Wade's assistance, but soon enough, they were ready to go.

"I'll take point," Wade said as he started away from the road and into the jungle. A machete hung from his side, but for now was unnecessary. The trees and other plant life weren't thick enough yet to prevent them from passing. This part of the Amazon was still close enough to civilization that people did, occasionally, venture here, which made travel somewhat easier. But he knew the deeper they went, the more overgrown and wild the plants would get.

Paige gave Julian a quick glance then fell in behind Wade, while it took a minute for Julian to follow.

Over the next few hours they wound through areas so wild Paige found it hard to believe anyone had ever walked there, though she knew they had.

At one point Wade had warned her to keep back, and though confused, she'd complied. She was startled by his quickness as he grabbed a snake that had been hanging from a low-lying branch, completely camouflaged. As it had thrashed in his grip, he had efficiently decapitated it with his machete, explaining that it had been extremely poisonous, as well as aggressive. That sight made her shudder and look away, though she couldn't protest his actions. She'd never been around blood or death, and her only experience with violence had been her mugging. But the incident did serve to remind her of just how dangerous the Amazon could be.

The rest of their hike that day wasn't unpleasant, though it was physically demanding. Paige kept in shape by doing yoga three times a week, but she wasn't used to any sort of grueling activity. That point was driven home when they came across a fallen tree that was as big around as she was tall. Walking around it wasn't really an option, so they had to climb over it. She was struggling to pull herself up when she slipped. Before she could even cry out, Julian was there to save her with a well-placed hand on her butt. It did stop her downward motion, but made her face flare red. Not with embarrassment, either, though that was present as well with Wade looking at them. No, this was the most intimate touch Julian had given her since the plane, even if it was given with the best of intentions. It tempted her to struggle with obstacles more often.

"Careful," he told her, voice gruff, as he gave her a little boost up. He perhaps gave her too strong of a boost, needing to get his hands off her before he touched her a great deal more.

"Whoops. Yeah, don't wanna slip," Wade said, reaching for her hand and pulling her over the tree. He noted the blush and hid a grin.

Determined to help Julian—and Paige, it seemed—Wade didn't venture as far ahead once they were past the obstacle. Instead, he walked beside Paige and struck up a conversation with her. Well, less conversation and more outrageous flirting. She'd been in a mood since they made her give up the relic, then off-center after the incident with the fallen tree, but gradually he accomplished two things—he cheered her up and made Julian jealous. Every time he would glance back at

Julian, his friend would glare at him, silently promising retribution. Eventually Julian couldn't stand any more and pushed between them, long strides carrying him ahead.

Paige looked distressed, but Wade just grinned and grabbed her arm to keep her from catching up with him. "Don't," he told her in a low voice.

Surprised, she stopped and looked up at him. "Why not? He's upset."

"No," he calmly corrected, "he's jealous."

She scoffed. "No, he's not. He wants nothing to do with me except as his apprentice. He's made that very clear." Though she studied Julian's retreating back and wondered if that was entirely true. His words didn't always match with his actions, and those were all she had to go on since he hid his emotions behind a wall of magic when around her. And he had kissed her, even if he'd apologized immediately afterward.

"Trust me, Red, he's jealous. Which isn't a bad thing."

They started walking again as she gave him a curious look. "It's not?"

"Oh no, it's a good thing, I promise. A very good thing."

She mulled over that for a few minutes, not quite understanding how jealousy could ever be a good thing. She also didn't want Julian to make a move just because he didn't want another man flirting with her. It would be better if other emotions, if true affection, drove him. Finally, she shook her head and asked in a quiet voice, "What was he like? Before his wife died?"

Wade debated for a moment before deciding to answer her question. "He was a lot like me, actually. Which meant he was amazing, if I do say so myself," he said, puffing out his chest. She laughed softly and he grinned in return. "But no, he wasn't as uptight as he is now, though he's always been a brilliant nerd. Now, keep in mind that I hadn't known him long before Mary died, but he was a lot more easy going. Always good for a laugh and ready to have fun. He spent a lot more time with people, too. Oh, I know he sees people now, aside from you, but how often do those visits not involve his work?"

"Very rarely," she had to admit.

"And how often have you heard him laugh or do something just for the hell of it?"

"He's laughed a couple of times, but...I think he has a purpose for everything he does."

"Exactly. He just doesn't see the fun in life anymore. It's all work for him now," he said, and she was struck at how sad he sounded for his friend.

It was getting late and she knew that they'd stop soon, but before they did, she asked, "Can you tell me something he did before? Something he did just for the hell of it?"

He thought for a moment, then laughed. Julian heard and paused long enough to scowl back at them. "Once, when Mary was gone—visiting her family, I think—he shanghaied me. Literally, I might add," he said, grinning. "He just had an urge to visit China and didn't want to go alone. So he just teleported in, snagged me—right out of a bath, no less—and popped us over to Shanghai. Which meant, of course, that I was buck naked, but he didn't care. He was nice enough to find me something to cover my ass with, though. The fact that it was a sheer scarf covered in flowers did nothing to help my ego, let me tell you. The local ladies loved it, though." And he missed those times. He liked Julian now, he really did. The man was his closest friend, and he'd do anything to help the man, but he wanted the Julian back who actually lived, not just existed.

She laughed and shook her head before sobering. "I can't imagine him doing anything like that, now," she said with a sorrow-filled sigh.

"Give it time," he recommended, giving her shoulder a comforting squeeze.

She was smiling up at him when Julian turned back to them, so his words were sharp when he told them, "We'll make camp here for the night."

Paige frowned a little at the tone of Julian's voice, but Wade fought not to smile. The little redhead was getting under Julian's skin in a major way, and Wade couldn't be happier for his friend. He wondered just how much it would take to push Julian back over the edge between living and surviving.

Julian set about placing protective magic around their campsite while Paige and Wade set up the tent and found enough dry wood for a fire, but it wasn't until after they'd eaten that Julian seemed to cool off. Unfortunately, it didn't last long.

There was only one tent, and though it was big enough for all three of them—Paige had made sure to get one that was—Julian wasn't happy about the sleeping arrangements. It had seemed safe enough when they'd bought it, but after the impromptu make-out session on the plane, and the dream that had followed, he just didn't like it. No matter how they arranged themselves in the tent, he'd suffer. But he couldn't ask anyone, even himself, to sleep outside. It was too risky. There were too many dangerous insects and wildlife to sleep unprotected. He was genuinely surprised they hadn't run into more than a single snake so far. And while he could, technically, teleport out and retrieve another tent, it was an unnecessary waste of magic. Especially since they'd already had someone magically interested in them. If they were attacked in the night, he didn't want to be drained because he couldn't sleep in the same tent as an attractive woman.

It got worse when they went to climb into the tent. Julian knew it wouldn't be smart for him to sleep next to Paige, but neither could he stand the thought of her sleeping next to the charming wolf, especially after they'd been laughing together all day. In the end, he decided to be in the middle and resigned himself to a sleepless night.

"Good night Julian, Wade," Paige said as she got settled, a tiny smile on her lips.

"Night Red."

"Good night."

Within minutes Wade was asleep, and despite her excitement, Paige followed not long after. Julian, however, was still awake hours later.

CHAPTER 14

I t was the sound of birds that woke Paige. She smiled without opening her eyes, just listening to the natural song playing all around her. Smelling the warm, green scent of the rainforest. For several minutes she just laid there, utterly content, before she realized she had needs to attend to. Needs that were forgotten when she realized just why she was so comfortable, despite being in a tent.

She was laying half-atop Julian.

His thigh was between her legs, her groin pressed firmly against it. Her breasts were crushed against his chest and side, while his shoulder acted as a pillow. More, his arm was around her, holding her securely against him. It wasn't a bad position to wake up in, but it was certainly awkward, given their history and his reaction to their kisses. He wasn't likely to be pleased if he woke up and found them like this.

She sighed and debated what to do when she heard a smothered chuckle. For one horrified instant, she thought it was Julian, and felt her cheeks heat up. Then she saw Wade watching her and grinning.

He mouthed, "Need some help?"

She nodded, wanting nothing more than to get up before Julian woke. She certainly didn't want to wake him in the process.

Wade silently stood and reached down to simply lift Paige off of Julian with no apparent effort. Once she was on her feet, she smiled gratefully.

It was only once they were out of the tent that either spoke. "Thank you. I wasn't sure how I was going to get up without waking him," she told him as she poked at the cold ashes from last night's fire.

"Personally, I don't know why you didn't kick me out so you could give him a special wake up call," Wade said, shrugging.

Paige's shoulders hunched in both frustration and embarrassment as she glanced at the tent. She'd only known Wade for a day, but she had few friends she could talk about this sort of thing with. More, Wade did seem to care about Julian and want to help her. "He doesn't want me," she told him miserably.

Wade snorted. "No, he doesn't *want* to want you."

Paige blinked, then gave a short laugh. "Somehow, I think I understood what you meant."

"Good. But yeah, lack of wanting isn't the problem, Red, I can promise you that," he told her as he got the fire going so they could have coffee and a hot breakfast.

"Then what is? Because every time we've...um..."

He chuckled. "I know he's kissed you."

She blushed harder. "Not just kissing, but not much more, if you catch my meaning?"

Intrigued, he murmured, "Well, I'll be. I didn't figure he'd do anything else without being hit on the head with a blunt object. Or taking a century to work his way up to it."

"What do you mean?"

Aware that he was again betraying a confidence, but wanting to see Julian move on and be happy, he lowered his voice. "It's not you. He somehow got it in his head that wanting you is being disloyal to Mary."

Astonished, Paige pointed out in a hushed tone, "But it's been centuries! Humans move on after a few years. Some don't even take that long."

"I know. Believe me, I know. I've tried to get him to move on for all of those years," he promised her. "He's a very loyal man, though, and stubborn as a mule."

"So it's hopeless," she whispered, feeling defeated.

"Hardly," he said dryly. "If there's been more than just the one kiss, and more than just kissing, then there's definitely a chance. You just might have to be the one to make a move. Surprise him, so he doesn't have time to talk himself out of getting what he actually wants," he suggested.

She thought about that for a moment. "Do you really think that would work?"

The sound of the zipper on the tent door interrupted them and they looked over to see Julian, a grumpy look on his face.

"Is there coffee?"

"Soon," Paige promised as she hastily started making it.

With the three of them working, coffee was soon ready, along with a breakfast of biscuits and eggs. After eating their fill and getting packed up, Julian dug out the relic and handed it to Paige without a word.

This time Wade was more prepared for the glowing eyes, and they just waited patiently as she communed with it, as Wade had started to think of the process.

Paige was starting to understand the relic better. The feelings and images she got from it were clearer than they'd been when she'd held it in England. They were also stronger, perhaps because of the proximity to another piece. She didn't know how an object could long for anything, much less be lonely, but she couldn't deny that, somehow, it did.

"It's closer, but I think we're still a few days away at this rate," she admitted. "That way," she pointed before willingly giving the piece back to Julian. They were still on course, at least, but Julian looked annoyed at the thought of spending three or four days like this. And while she had pointed northwest, it was unlikely they'd be able to go too far in that direction before the terrain made them veer off course.

Wade again took point, and this time Julian made no move to stop him. That was largely because Paige stayed between them this time, not speaking to either of them much. Julian was relieved, because it gave him a chance to think.

He'd woken briefly a few hours before dawn to find Paige cuddled up against him. It hadn't made him uncomfortable or guilty—though he'd wondered about the latter—but instead it had felt...nice. He hadn't slept with a woman pressed against him since Mary. There had been sex, yes, but he'd never stayed overnight with any of them, and he'd forgotten how pleasurable it could be, even without sex. He'd struggled with how right it felt, but in the end made no move to separate her from him.

Hell, he could even admit to himself that part of the reason why he woke up so grumpy was that he woke up alone. That did cause some guilt, but upon thinking about it, he realized that he was feeling less guilty than he had even just a week ago.

Were Wade's words actually making sense to him?

Ahead, Paige's thoughts weren't so dissimilar to his. She, too, had enjoyed cuddling against him—or would have if she hadn't been worried about his reaction if he'd woken up. But more, she was mulling over what Wade had told her. She glanced back at Julian, unsurprised to see him lost in thought. *Could* she make the first move? It really wasn't her forte. She wasn't sure what she should do if she decided to listen to Wade's advice. Had he meant she should just kiss Julian and hope for the best? Or should she actually try to seduce him? Both thoughts brought color to her cheeks and set warmth blooming low in her belly. She couldn't say she was against the idea of seducing him, it would just be a first for her.

Wade was the most cheerful of the three. In fact, when he wasn't looking at either of his companions, he was grinning, sometimes even whistling, as he led the way through the jungle, hacking away at vines and branches so they could pass. He knew, even without Paige's telepathy, that they were both thinking about the other, and felt pleased at that fact. With a silent laugh, he wondered if he should ditch bounty hunting and take up match-making. Nah, he decided. Just because they were thinking about it didn't mean that anything would come of it. But he could hope.

The biggest downside to this trip wasn't his companion's moods, but the natural dangers of the Amazon. In his position in the lead he'd already steered them around, or taken care of, several threats, including a giant centipede that would have freaked Paige out, and a poison dart frog that she probably would have fallen in love with because of its bright blue coloring. He considered showing it to her so she could take a picture, but didn't want her to get anywhere close to something so deadly.

There was more light up ahead and he frowned when the trees parted and he could see the chasm in front of them. It had to be a hundred feet across, maybe more, so jumping was most definitely out. "Hey, we got a problem," he called back to the others.

When they joined him, Paige made an unhappy noise. "There's no way we can cross that!"

Julian shook his head. "Not necessarily. I could teleport us across it."

"Yeah, but how drained would that leave you? Didn't you say you wanted to conserve power whenever you could?" Wade asked.

"Yes, but—"

"Let me do some scouting. Could be there's an easy way across which would save you the trouble."

"Then we should all go."

Wade shook his head. "Nope. I can move faster by myself—and on four legs."

Knowing that Wade was right, Julian nodded. "Okay, but if we don't hear from you in half an hour, we're coming after you."

"Fair enough." He shucked his pack and leaned it against a tree. "If you're shy, you might wanna look away," he told Paige with a wink as he started stripping. Clearly, he had no modesty, because he didn't wait for her to react before pulling off his pants.

Not that he particularly had any reason for modesty, Paige thought, given the strength and definition in those muscles, and that golden skin. He was definitely a catch. Oddly, the sight of him didn't cause her blood to heat with desire like the simple thought of Julian did. She did find his tattoos curious, though. They weren't done in any single style and covered a fair bit of his body. She could see more ink than bare flesh, actually.

Julian scowled and Paige let out a squeak of embarrassment when she realized she was staring and clamped her eyes shut. Still, the lure of actually watching a shapeshifter turn from human to animal was more than she could handle. She cracked an eye open—only so Julian wouldn't notice—and watched Wade's body grow fur as it contorted and shrank, until the man was replaced by a beautiful gray and black wolf. Larger than his natural counterparts, he was leanly muscled. While he was primarily gray, he had black streaks down his side, and a mask that covered his eyes and half his muzzle. He shook himself before he let out a little yip and Paige opened her eyes fully, smiling with delight. "Wade, that's brilliant!"

Wade woofed in reply and wagged his tail to show he agreed with her, before he took off at a dead run along the chasm.

Once the sound of his paws striking the earth had faded, both Paige and Julian realized that they were alone. Julian did his best to ignore her and sat down on a rock to wait.

Paige watched him surreptitiously as she thought about what to do. If she was going to take Wade's advice, now was the perfect time. She walked over to him and waited until he looked up at her. What she had intended to say wasn't what came out of her mouth. She meant to be charming and flirtatious, though she wasn't experienced with being either, but instead, she heard herself ask bluntly, "Do you want me?" The moment the words were out of her mouth she blushed, but also lifted her chin, not retracting the question.

Too shocked by the question, and the boldness with which Paige had asked it, Julian could only widen his eyes and stammer for a moment. "Do I *what?*"

She drew in a deep breath, then repeated more slowly, "Do you want me?"

"What kind of question is that?" he demanded.

"The kind I'd like an answer to. Do you want me?" she asked, the words carefully spaced. "I should hope it's not a difficult question, all things considered. And I think I deserve to know the answer. You haven't exactly been clear about it the last few weeks."

He lunged to his feet and answered angrily. "Yes! Okay? Are you happy now? I want you!" Happiness shone on her face, which perversely made him add, "But I'm not going to do anything about it, so get those thoughts out of your head right now." He wasn't sure why he said it, not when he'd been pondering the possibility of beginning something with her, but he also couldn't take it back.

She stepped closer, until they were toe-to-toe. "What if I want to do something about it?" she challenged, hands on her hips.

That left him speechless, as his mind was suddenly filled with images of her seducing him. Her sitting on his lap and kissing him senseless. Or walking toward him in nothing but lace and shadows, her steps confident, hips swaying. The best one was of him stepping into his bedroom to find her beneath the sheets, wearing nothing but a smile. Consequently, all the blood rushed out of his brain and to a part of his anatomy that was much lower.

He was saved by Wade's return and was too worked up to even notice when his friend shifted back to human. A comfortably naked human.

Wade pursed his lips as he watched the two witches. "So…I found a bridge," he told them as he started dressing.

"That's nice," Paige said, refusing to back down, even with Wade present. In fact, it was Julian who took a step back then moved to grab his pack. She let out a breath she didn't realize she'd been holding, and turned to the half-dressed Wade. "It wasn't far, then?"

"Nope. Not even half a mile. Just hope you guys don't mind old rope bridges."

She paled slightly, which was a feat with her normally fair skin. "I've seen too many movies *not* to mind them."

He grinned. "Not to worry. I tested it. Rope seems sturdy, so do the boards. Doesn't look like it's been up that long, actually. Probably replaced sometime in the last year. It'll be fine."

His reassurances fell flat when Paige actually saw the bridge. It looked just as unstable as she'd feared. Boards, slightly warped by heat and moisture, were laid unevenly across thick ropes, so there were gaps between most of them. There were, at least, ropes strung higher to give something to hold on to. Scared, but not wanting to slow them down, she cautiously followed Wade out onto it.

About three quarters of the way across, the pressure of her foot on a weak spot had a board cracking and giving way beneath her. She felt herself start to fall and let out a little scream. Before either of the men could reach her, she caught herself on the rope and clung to it with all her strength.

"Paige! You all right?" Wade yelled, turning to start back for her.

Julian was quicker and gently used his magic to lift her to the next board, which was more solid.

"I'm...I'm fine," she told them breathlessly while she waited for her heart rate to return to normal. It took another minute before she could loosen her hold on the rope and take another step. By the time she reached the other side, she was calmer, but still pale from the experience and trying to ignore the slight shaking in her limbs.

"Next time, I'd very much like to teleport across, thanks," she told them as she sat down and dug out her canteen.

Julian smiled a little and Wade chuckled before ruffling her hair. "I don't see why," he said, giving her shoulder a squeeze. "You went across like a champ. Some people would've flat out refused to step foot on that thing. Or refused to take another step after a board broke on them. You did great, Red."

Reassured, Paige gave him a weak smile. "Thanks."

Julian frowned. "We should get going. Get more distance behind us before we camp for the night."

"You're right." Paige sighed and pushed to her feet. "Let's get going. I'm okay now."

CHAPTER 15

For two days they traveled through the rainforest. Each morning, Paige would check their heading, then they'd walk in near silence, only speaking when necessary. This was largely because the tension between Julian and Paige was at an all-time high. Even Wade had toned down his teasing in light of how uncomfortable the other two were. Still, when the silence was broken, it was always Wade trying to brighten their moods or warn them of danger.

Luckily, there was little reason for conversation beyond Paige correcting their direction. There was one instance where she nearly stepped on a caiman, thinking it was a log, but Julian noticed what it was just in time to snatch her up by the waist and pull her back. She had squeaked in surprise and stiffened, but when he'd said, "Caiman," she'd remembered her reading on the dangers of the Amazon and stopped all thoughts of struggle. Instead, she'd clung to him and stared at the ground, half-expecting to see it crowded by the reptiles. He hadn't put her down until he'd teleported the reptile somewhere far from Paige with a flick of his fingers.

Afterward, their day had continued as normal, other than Paige having to fight not to look back at Julian. It was a fight she lost as often as she won. She liked watching him normally, but there was something about seeing him out of his element that made him even more appealing than usual. Perhaps it was the scruff he'd accumulated being away from civilization, or the fact that he didn't appear as polished as he did at home in England. It could also have been the ease in which he'd picked her up. Strength was definitely sexy. It could even be as simple as their conversation weighing on her mind. Whatever it was, she wanted to be near him, to watch him.

The next morning, they woke up to find they weren't alone.

The sun had been up for half an hour when they began to stir. Paige was the first one out of the tent, but her cry of surprise was enough to have both men rushing out behind her, Wade armed with his machete, Julian ready to tackle the threat magically. What they saw stopped them both in their tracks.

Monkeys had invaded their camp. To save on space in the tent, they'd left most of their things just outside by the fire, and two of the packs had been opened, some of the contents strewn about. A monkey, Paige thought it was a capuchin, was perched atop one of the packs, still yanking things out of it. Another had unearthed a bag of trail mix that Paige had in her bag, opened it, and was happily pulling out dried bananas to eat. Two others were playing tug-of-war with the satellite phone. In the trees, another half dozen monkeys watched, more cautious than their companions.

Paige couldn't do anything more than stare at the mess the monkeys had made, but after a long moment, her lips began to twitch.

Wade wasn't so subtle. Once it sunk in that they weren't being attacked, he bust out laughing and lowered his machete. "Well, damn. Of all the things I thought might happen to us out here, this wasn't anywhere on my radar," he said when he stopped laughing long enough to breathe.

Even Julian couldn't hold on to his initial annoyance and smiled.

"Is this common?" Paige asked, bewildered by the lack of fear the monkeys were showing. "They aren't running away. The one in my trail mix is staring right at us as he eats, but he's not the least bit afraid of us."

Wade shrugged. "It's not uncommon. They might steal food from a house, and I've heard of some stealing things from tourists and actually ransoming them back for food."

"That is...adorable. Kind of," she decided, before remembering she'd put the camera in the tent with them the night before. She moved slowly, not wanting to startle the monkeys, and ducked back inside to retrieve it. Then she proceeded to take multiple pictures of every monkey she could find before grinning. "I'm going to have some awesome pictures by the time we get back home. But I do have one question."

"What's that, Red?"

"How do we get our stuff back?"

"Shoo them away. Possibly bribe them with food," Julian said with a shrug. "Depends on how determined they are, I think."

"They might go away when we get closer, but somehow I doubt it's going to be that easy," Wade added. He started for the monkeys, making loud noises and waving his arms to try to startle them away. Paige bit back a laugh when one of the monkeys simply looked at him, unimpressed. She started snapping more pictures as Wade yelled and stomped and acted like a crazy man in an attempt to rescue their things.

Julian had a different method. He levitated their things, the ones that weren't serving as monkey perches, toward the tent, then starting lifting the monkeys up and into the trees. Most dropped the things they were holding, surprised when objects moved on their own, but the monkey with the bag of food clung tightly to it. No way was he going to lose the food he'd stolen fair and square. Eventually, Julian decided to just let him have it. The phone was a different story. For a brief moment, it was caught between the two monkeys and his magic, before their fingers slipped and he managed to retrieve it.

By that time, Paige was sitting on the ground, laughing so hard that she had to hold her aching sides. Never in her life had she expected to watch two grown men trying to outwit a gang of monkey thieves, but she knew it would go down as one of her favorite memories. She just wished she'd thought to get a video instead of just pictures.

When the monkeys had all retreated to the trees, some of them screaming down at the trio, Wade offered Paige a hand up. "Laughing at us, are you, Red?"

"You should have seen yourselves! Especially you! Those monkeys weren't at all scared of the big bad wolf," she told him with a big grin. "I think that's why Julian didn't even try that approach with them."

"My way was more effective," Julian agreed with a smug smile. "But we should get repacked and eat. We've got a long day ahead of us."

The others pitched in to help sort out what things went in which bag before settling in for breakfast. They ate quickly and packed up camp before loading up their bags. With only a brief hesitation, Julian returned the relic piece to Paige. Her gasp had both men stepping toward her, but she shook her head, absolute delight showing in her luminous eyes. "No. No, I'm fine. It's just stronger. Much, much stronger." She shivered and took a step forward. "So much stronger. We're close," she murmured before moving at a quick pace into the rainforest, not even waiting for the guys.

"Hey!" Wade exclaimed, taking a few running steps to catch up with her, with Julian right on his heels. "You need to wait for us," he chided, and though she gave him a sheepish look, she didn't slow.

"Sorry. We're just really close. I feel...urgent."

Julian shook his head, but there was concern in his eyes. "That's not you, Paige. It's the amulet."

"Maybe, but I still feel it. I'm not sure I could separate it from my feelings if I tried."

He wanted to take the relic from her then, to save her from its influence, but when he started to say something, Wade stopped him. "We're not going straight, Julian. Not by any stretch of the imagination. And if we're that close? We need her to guide us or we're going to end up way off course." He dropped his voice and added, "We'll keep an eye on her, and we're going to be right here with her the entire time."

Julian paid more attention to where they were going and realized that Wade was right. Without her acting as a guide, they might never find where they were going, or would simply backtrack endlessly.

It was a good thing that the men were following Paige so closely because a few minutes later she stumbled right into a bullet ant nest. Wade was the first to notice the inch-long black insects. He darted forward, wrapped an arm around her waist, and dragged her back. He wasn't quick enough to prevent several ants from climbing on her. One started to move up her pants, while another few ventured further up her body. A couple fell off and landed on Wade as he jostled Paige.

Her scream of pain when the first ant bit her shook Julian to the core. He rushed over, slapping at the other ants, but one got her on the arm before he got them all off. Unfortunately, the pain from the bites was so intense she was unable to focus enough to help him and just trembled in Wade's arms.

Wade didn't let go of her until they were a safe distance from the colony, only then gently setting her down on a log. He'd been stung, too, once on his side and once on his arm, but only clenched his jaw at the intense pain and leaned against a tree to keep watch while Julian tended to Paige. It was all he could do not to scream at the feel of the venom working through his veins, turning them to fire. For the next few minutes, minimum, he knew he'd be absolutely useless. And that was only if Julian would be able to neutralize the venom from the ants. Otherwise, he'd be in for a day full of suffering. Even his shifter healing wouldn't completely deal it with it, not right away.

"I know it hurts. I know. It'll be better in a minute, I swear," Julian murmured to Paige as he located the ants and got them off her. His magic wasn't great for venoms, but he did what he could anyway, easing the worst of the pain. She wouldn't suffer like most victims of the ants, at least. After, he gathered her into his arms, letting her cling to him as she struggled to calm down and let the rest of the pain abate. "There, it's getting better, isn't it?" She was relaxing, bit by bit, but he found himself shaking lightly with concern for her. Bullet ants wouldn't have killed her unless she'd been allergic, but it was a sort of agony he had never wanted her to suffer.

"Some. Yes. Thank you," Paige whispered, her face pressed against his shoulder. But without the burn of the ant completely clouding her mind, she picked up on Wade's pain and twisted in Julian's arms to look at him. "You got bit!" She tried to climb out of Julian's arms, which tightened around her for a few seconds before letting go.

"Yeah, but it's not a big deal, Red. I'll survive," he said, his voice tight, his body thrumming with tension.

"Don't be a twit," Paige argued. She saw the tiny mark on his arm from one of the ants and laid her fingers gently over it. Slowly her magic soothed, though he didn't, couldn't relax just yet. Not for the first time, she wished she could actually heal, rather than just tricking the mind into ignoring pain. "Was there another one?"

Wordlessly, Wade pulled his shirt up enough to show where an ant was still attached to his side. She let out a soft cry and slapped it away, then stomped on it when it landed on the ground. She couldn't do anything more for him than she had, so she looked over to Julian with a helpless look on her face. He crouched beside her and laid his hand on Wade's arm, giving him the same treatment he'd given Paige.

With each breath Wade took, the pain eased until it was bearable, but he still felt a dull ache when Julian drew his hand back. "It's better. Much better. Thank you," he panted softly as he drew Paige into a one-armed hug and kissed her hair. "You okay? I'm sorry I didn't see them in time."

Julian's jaw clenched at the affectionate gesture, but he said nothing. Right now he wouldn't begrudge her anything that made her feel better, even if it was a kiss from another man. Though he could admit to himself that if Wade had aimed for her mouth, he wouldn't have been quite so agreeable. But a kiss to her hair he could handle.

She nodded and looked back to Julian, giving him a warm smile that was only lightly tinged with the lingering pain. "I am. Thank you, both of you." The smile dimmed. "I should have paid more attention to where I was going. What *were* those things?"

"Bullet ants. Generally agreed to have the most painful sting of any insect," Wade said, pulling out the flask he'd filled with whiskey. He took a drink then offered it to Paige.

Slowly, Paige took it. "I'm not going to argue with that." She took a tiny sip and made a face as it burned down her throat, but it settled nicely in her belly and dulled the memory of the pain. She gave the flask back to him. "But I mean it sincerely. Thank you both."

"You are more than welcome, Paige. I'm just glad it wasn't worse than it was," Julian told her with a gentle smile. "You want to take a few minutes and rest before we get started again?" he asked them both.

Wade shook his head, and after a moment, Paige did the same. "No, I'd like to keep going. We're too close to stop now." For that matter, if they stopped now, she wasn't sure she'd be able to continue, not for a while. She rubbed a thumb over the relic, surprised she hadn't dropped it when they'd been stung. "Very, very close."

"All right, but let me know if you need a break."

She smiled. "I will."

Close ended up being almost an hour away. They approached an area that looked impassable due to dense foliage, but rather than swerving around it like she'd done multiple times in the last few days, Paige walked right up to it. Julian saw her frown, but couldn't quite make out the soft words she said. Her hand touched the knife strapped to her leg, then frowned harder.

Wade and Julian exchanged a look before Wade spoke. "Everything okay, Red?

She whirled so quickly toward the wolf that her braid nearly smacked Julian in the face. "Give me your machete."

Wade's hand went protectively to the handle of his blade. "Uh...as much as I hate telling a lady no, I'm gonna have to ask why first."

She rolled her eyes then motioned to the vines and branches in front of her with a sharp, deliberate motion. "Those? We can't exactly walk through them." She paused. "Well, I can't, at any rate."

"Why don't you let me? Don't want you to get hurt." Before giving her a chance to argue—which he was sure she'd do—Wade glanced at Julian, who drew her back.

It was just as well that he took over, she thought after a minute. He was making quick work of the plant life and only stopped when the blade clearly hit stone. It surprised him, but Paige just pulled away from Julian to impatiently shove at vegetation until they could see the wall beyond. There was no writing of any sort, nor did Paige see anything that could be used to open it.

"This is the door, I'm sure of it. It's what I saw when I first found the piece," she told them, running her fingers across the stone. "The vines weren't here, and it didn't look quite so worn, but this is it."

Wade suddenly tensed and tilted his head back to sniff at the air. "We've—"

He was cut off as a jaguar leapt at him from the side. Quick reflexes kept the large feline from latching onto his throat, but those sharp teeth sank deep into his forearm as he was shoved back against the stone.

There was just enough warning to let Julian step between Paige and the jaguars, shielding her with his body. His blood froze when he saw there were several of the beasts, and that was just the ones he could see.

Normally they were solitary creatures, so seeing more than one was dangerous enough, and there was no telling how many were nearby, waiting. Fortunately, they had stone at their back, so they couldn't be surrounded. He hoped.

Wade flung the jaguar from him with a roar that was more wolf than man. "Get the door open," he snarled as he moved in front of the others, his body language feral and aggressive.

The jaguars paced slowly, not in any rush now that it was obvious their prey was trapped within the semi-circle of predators.

Paige turned back to the door, her fingers holding tightly to the piece in her hand as she struggled to make sense of what was essentially nothing. But as she looked, she noticed that there were a few indentations. Most looked like natural wear on the stone or where someone had hammered at it, trying to open it. One of them even looked a little like a slot. She bit her lip then lifted her hand and, once the piece got close to the slot, her hand moved as though pulled.

The moment the piece was set into the narrow groove, there was a grinding sound and the door began to open inward. She put her shoulder to it but was only able to hasten the movement fractionally. "Inside! Hurry!" she yelled once she was able to slip through the opening.

Julian lifted his hands and a faint shimmering appeared in the air in front of him. "Get in, Wade. I'll follow!"

Wade was set to protest when one of the jaguars tried to charge them and hit an invisible wall. The impact made Julian grunt softly and the muscles in his arms corded from the strain the magic put on his body. Understanding what Julian had done, Wade ran to join Paige. "I'm in!"

Julian backed up slowly until he was almost even with the door, which now stood wide open. He heard the grinding again and risked a glance back. Paige had the relic piece in her hand again and a horrified expression on her face. Apparently, when she'd grabbed the relic, the door had begun closing again.

Hoping it would be a blessing rather than a curse, Julian held the barrier until the last possible moment, then let it drop and dove through the opening. He cut it close enough that he felt stone scrape both sides of his body before he hit the ground hard.

The instant that Julian had cleared the door, Wade shoved at it with all his strength, trying to get it closed before one of the jaguars decided to follow them in. Before it could shut completely, four razor-sharp claws curled around the edge of the door.

Seeing the problem, both Julian and Paige lent their strength, pushing as hard as they could. When they did manage to get it closed, they heard a pained, muted roar on the other side, one quickly followed by several others.

Wade slid down the door until his ass hit the ground, then blinked.

Paige's eyes weren't glowing any longer, which left them in complete darkness.

CHAPTER 16

"Shit!" came the uncharacteristic curse from Paige as she dropped to her knees. They stung as they hit bare stone, but she ignored them and started to search blindly for the relic she'd dropped at some point while trying to close the door. Her hand brushed it and she breathed a sigh of relief.

Julian quickly healed the scrapes from the door, then dug in his pack and pulled out his flashlight. Paige followed his example after tucking the relic into her pocket. Wade went for his headlamp instead, leaving his hands free.

Wade's movements were slow and a little awkward, and when Paige shined her light over him from her position on the floor, she let out a cry of dismay. "You're hurt!"

A crooked smile curved his lips. "Eh, 'tis but a scratch," he told her with a bad English accent, despite the fact that his arm was ripped open and bleeding. But compared to the bullet ant, it did feel more like a scratch than it might have otherwise.

Without even looking back, Julian snorted. "You could be headless and you'd say that."

"True," Wade allowed without hesitation.

Paige frowned at them both and knelt beside Wade. "It's silly to suffer when you've got two witches here. Especially when he's capable of healing you and I'm capable of easing your pain," she scolded as she set her light aside and laid her hands on him. She watched his face, his eyes closing, as she nudged his mind and made the pain of the claw marks lessen.

Julian laid his hand on Wade's shoulder and pushed magic into him, knitting the ragged flesh back together. The blood would still need to be washed off, but now Wade could use his arm properly and he wouldn't be in danger of having the cuts get infected.

Paige gave Julian a grateful look, infinitely pleased that at least *one* of them could heal properly. "How's that feel?" she asked with a smile, before frowning. "And be honest. If he missed something, we want to know so we can take care of it."

Wade got to his feet and gave her braid a light, playful tug with his formerly injured arm. "It's fine, Red. Promise. Besides, we should get moving."

"I suppose..." He offered her a hand and she took it before rising.

Julian hadn't been idle while Paige was noticing Wade's injuries, but had examined the temple room they found themselves in. It wasn't large, maybe only eight feet by twenty, with walls that were entirely carved with writing and pictures. Aside from the door, it only held a set of rough stone steps that led underground. There were no altars or windows, there wasn't even any dust. Until they'd opened the door, it had apparently been sealed tight. But it wasn't the steps he had his light trained on, but a section of wall just above it, and the writing carved into the stone.

The other two stepped up beside him and Paige frowned. "I don't recognize that writing. It definitely doesn't look like it belongs in this area, but...it's familiar, but not at the same time. Do you know it?" she asked with a glance toward her mentor.

"I do. It's a much older form of Greek than I've started to teach you," Julian answered.

"Well, what's it say, then?" Wade asked.

There was a sigh from Julian. "Basically? If we go down there, we die. It's pretty descriptive about it, too," he admitted. "The gods will smite us, we'll get tortured, etcetera."

"So, death to all who enter here, huh?" Wade said with a shake of his head. "The gods don't like changing things up, do they?"

"No, for such long-lived beings, they don't change often, and not without being dragged into it."

"Tell me about it," Wade muttered.

"The way I see it," Paige began, "if we go back outside, the jaguars will kill us. If we leave and just teleport home, then there's no chance of finding the piece of the relic. We'll just be giving up." She motioned to the writing. "Chances are, part of that warning is to scare people away, and it wasn't written with the idea that someone who had a piece of the relic in hand would be reading it. So I think we should continue on." She bit her lip and looked at them. "If you two want to, I mean." She knew it was dangerous, and while Julian desperately wanted the completed relic, Wade was just helping them. Putting him in danger without his consent seemed wrong.

Wade grinned and even Julian looked amused. It was Julian who said, "I'm the one who started this whole thing. If you're both willing, then I'm more than happy to continue on. Especially since I think that you have the right of it, Paige."

"Hell, I'm always down for adventure. Let's go," Wade said, grinning and starting down the steps.

"Wait! Be careful!" Paige cried. She just got another grin, which made her roll her eyes.

"He'll be fine, Paige," Julian murmured. "He's a survivor, that one, and this is hardly his first adventure, as you keep calling it."

Worried and uncertain, Paige nodded, then followed him downward. Trekking through the rainforest was one thing, but being inside an unexplored temple? It was nerve-wracking, even with Julian and Wade there. Each step she took had her wondering if she was going to set off some sort of trap. When she didn't, she wasn't sure if she should be relieved or worried. There was no way it was going to be easy.

But it was also thrilling. To be in a temple that probably hadn't had anyone in it for thousands of years was something she could have only dreamed of before. Now she was living it. Sure, they were here specifically for the piece of the amulet, but there was no telling what other ancient treasures they might find or secrets they may learn.

The steps seemed to go on forever, and every noise, even the lightest scuff of a boot against stone, sounded thunderous to her ears. Not to mention there were spiderwebs on almost every surface. Adding to Paige's trepidation was the fact that not all of those webs were empty, and not all the spiders inhabiting them were small. She saw one with a body as big as her fist. What confused her, though, was that there were webs at all. There wasn't any dust, which meant the temple had been airtight, but there were spiders? Had they been placed here intentionally? Then again, given the pack of jaguars outside, she couldn't discount it. Spiders could be simply another way of protecting the contents of the temple. And if that were the case, these spiders should be considered dangerous.

The deeper they descended, the colder it got. It made sense, Paige knew, but she had to wonder exactly how far down the steps went.

Wade stopped at the bottom of the steps, scowling. There were three hallways leading off from the steps, and from their vantage point, they all looked identical, right down to the carvings above the doorways. He stepped to the entrance of each one and sniffed before he gave a low growl of annoyance. "There's no difference in how they smell. They just smell like stone and spiders."

"How are we supposed to know where to go?" Paige asked as she took one step toward the rightmost tunnel and peered down it.

"I don't think we're supposed to." Julian shook his head and considered. "No doubt this is another security measure. Let people get lost in a maze of identical hallways until they starve to death. I wouldn't be surprised if there was magic in place to make it impossible to navigate properly."

"Like the Greek labyrinth?" Paige asked.

"Exactly, and we don't have a magical ball of string," Julian agreed.

"I just hope we're the only things alive down here," Wade said dryly.

"You mean besides the hundreds of spiders I've already seen?" Paige retorted.

He flashed her a grin. "Yeah." He shrugged. "Let's just pick a direction and see where it goes."

"Why don't I see if the relic can help first? It's led us this far, after all."

After a moment, Julian nodded. "It can't hurt. Then, if we don't get anywhere, we can try Wade's idea."

Paige nodded and pulled the relic out of her pocket. Her eyes turned luminescent once more, but she frowned. "I know it's close, closer than it's been, but I don't feel like it's pulling me in any particular direction. It feels like the other piece is just sort of...all around. Everywhere, or nowhere."

Not truly surprised, Julian nodded. "Then we pick a direction and see where it leads," he said before he went down the left passage.

The others followed, keeping close in case of an attack, but with enough space between them that if one encountered a trap, there would be a chance for the others to avoid it. They came to a four-way intersection, and after a moment, Julian turned to the left. "If we keep following the left wall, we should be able to backtrack easily enough," he explained.

As they walked, Paige kept hoping to see something to give them some sort of clue, but the carvings were gone and the walls were smooth beneath the webs.

They reached a T and Julian turned left once more. He'd only taken a few steps before the floor fell out from under him, revealing a hole as wide as the hall and a good fifteen feet across. Paige screamed and tried to grab him, but it was Wade who made contact, latching onto Julian's wrist.

"Damn boy. You need to lose a pound or two," Wade grunted once he was sure Julian wasn't going to fall, but the witch wasn't looking at him.

Only two inches beneath Julian's dangling feet was a pit of razor sharp spikes, each one coated with some gleaming substance. A type of poison, he was sure, and not a mild one, given his luck. "I'll consider that if you get me out *before* I end up impaled," he said, glancing back up to the wolf.

Wade lifted Julian out of the pit, and the moment his feet were on solid stone again, all three retreated a few steps. To their astonishment, the floor lifted back into place, leaving no sign of what was hiding beneath.

"Perhaps...we should leave markings? Just in case?" Paige suggested, rather than give into the urge to throw her arms around Julian.

"Smart idea, Red." Wade said before he frowned. "I'd rather not dull my knives. Either of you got something we can use?"

"One moment," Julian said. There was a brief swell of magic around him before he turned his hand over to show a large piece of charcoal. "This should work, I believe," he said, before kneeling. He drew a large X and the floor and wrote 'Spikes' beneath it. To be safe, both walls were marked with an X as well.

With that route impassable, they turned around to take another tunnel. As they walked, they marked the walls and floor, using arrows to point back the way they'd come. They also marked dead ends they came across, and there were quite a few of those. All three were surprised when they didn't come across any other traps. Not until, after half an hour, they found themselves back at the pit trap.

"How the hell did we manage this?" Wade growled. "I've got a pretty good sense of direction, and we shouldn't be here."

"No, we shouldn't," Julian agreed. "I've been paying close attention and we shouldn't be anywhere near here." He sighed. "Like I said before, it's likely there's some magic down here that distorts things."

Paige nodded. "It must just be part of the defenses down here, along with that spike pit. We'll just have to find some other way of navigating. Besides, the markings are still there, so nothing is messing with that. We can still avoid traps."

"We can avoid repeat traps," Julian corrected.

"It's still better than just wandering around aimlessly. Unless you think you can counter the magic that's turning us around?"

He hesitated, then shook his head. "I could certainly try, but I think it might be wasted energy. The piece was shielded to be untraceable, and nothing I did could get around it. I see no reason to assume that this magic would be any less powerful."

As much as she wanted him to be wrong, it was a logical point, and he'd already had to use magic several times today. He was also the only one in the group who could heal. The last thing they needed was for one of them to be injured and Julian too depleted to heal them. "True. All right, let's try this again."

Each turn chosen was done so carefully, with all three of them trying to spot their markings before they'd gone too far down the wrong corridor. One turn led them into a small room with no other exit. Unlike everything else they'd seen in the temple, this room wasn't empty. Pedestals and tables held all manner of things, from delicate looking jewelry to life-sized stone statues, exquisitely carved. The room all but shimmered with the gold, silver, and gems packed into it. They all looked pristine, though they were covered with what looked like red dust.

"Oh, it's so beautiful," Paige breathed, in awe of the history and beauty of the things in front of her. She started to step forward, but Wade grabbed her pack and yanked her back before she could take more than a single step. She twisted to look at him and saw his free arm was lifted to cover his nose and mouth.

"Julian! Get back," he snapped, voice muffled from his arm.

Curious, but not about to argue, Julian moved back until he was even with the other two. "What is it?"

"Poison." He slowly lowered his arm and sniffed before his nose wrinkled and he sneezed. "Sorry, Red, but if you'd gone into that room, if you'd touched *anything*, you'd be dead," he told her with no trace of his usual humor. "That powder, the one covering every damn thing, was a trap. You pick up something shiny, you absorb the poison through your skin, you die. And it's not an easy death, either."

Paige paled and nodded slowly. "You saved me, then."

Julian frowned. "What sort of poison?"

Wade's face was uncommonly serious when he turned to Julian. "Something I'd hoped was long gone. Mixture of powdered gorgon blood and nightshade, with something else tossed in for extra pain. I've seen it, once, which is the only reason I recognized the smell. It paralyzes you—and I mean every part of you, including your heart and lungs—and turns your skin to something close to stone, which makes it damn hard for anyone to treat you, if they even have time to try. It works quick and magic doesn't help."

Paige shuddered and took another step back from the room. "Let's go. I don't want to be so close to this any longer."

"I don't blame you, Red." Without another word, Wade turned to venture back into the maze.

They ran into a few more minor traps, of the cliche variety, according to Wade—arrows shooting out of the wall, a second pit trap, and flames coming out of the floor. Wade's reflexes saved him from getting impaled by the arrows, while Julian caught Paige when she almost fell into the pit. The flames almost turned Julian and Wade into barbecue, but Julian was able to shield them enough that they just got singed. They also got turned around by the magic of the temple more than once, which had all three frustrated, their tempers at the snapping point.

Then there were the spiders.

They had found themselves by the poison treasure room again when Wade froze. Paige was the first to notice and stopped. "What is it?" she asked tiredly.

"Something's coming," Wade growled, drawing his knife.

"Do you know what?" Julian asked, searching the end of the passageway for signs of movement.

Wade didn't answer immediately. "Spiders, I think."

The sounds grew loud enough for Julian and Paige to hear a skittering across stone, and it was getting close.

"That doesn't sound like the little spiders," Paige said quietly. Though she'd never used a knife as a weapon, she slowly drew the one Wade had given her. Most likely she'd hurt herself more than any of the spiders, but if they were as big as they sounded, she wanted options.

"No, it doesn't," Julian agreed grimly.

The spiders came into view, and Paige whimpered when she saw half a dozen spiders, the smallest of which had a body the size of a soccer ball. And they were all headed toward her and her companions. They crawled along the ceiling and upper walls, but as they got closer, a few scrambled lower along the walls, with one veering onto the floor.

Wade threw his knife and there was an unearthly shriek from the spider on the floor as it was fatally impaled. This seemed to enrage the rest of the spiders. They moved faster, closing in on the trio.

Julian threw a blast of magic at one of the arachnids, knocking it off the wall. It landed on the floor and flailed for a moment before it righted itself, though two of its legs were useless. Julian hit it again and it flew back, then lay limp, its legs curling up in death.

The rest of the spiders reached the group, and the two still on the ceiling dropped down onto them. One landed on Julian's shoulder and tried to sink its fangs into his neck. He managed to get his hand up, so the almost inch long fangs dug into the side of his hand instead of his jugular. He flung his arm sharply, sending the spider flying until it hit the wall with a meaty thud. But these weren't fragile spiders, and it got up entirely too quickly, racing back toward Julian until he hit it with a fireball, then another, and another, until it stopped moving.

The other spider landed on top of Paige's head and she screamed, stumbling back a few rapid steps until her back hit the wall. She slapped at the arachnid—barely remembering not to use the hand holding the knife—until a lucky shot from the flashlight knocked it off her so it landed a few paces from her feet. Instinct had her lifting the knife then bringing it down as she dropped to a crouch, sinking it into the gray and black body. Fear had her stabbing over and over until it finally clicked in her head that the thing was quite dead. Relief allowed her to ignore the gore that had splattered on her hand and face. For now.

The last two spiders were taken care of by a well-placed machete of Wade's and several more blasts of magic thrown by Julian. Once the last of the creatures was dead, Julian turned to Paige, his eyes widening slightly when he saw the dead spider. "Are you okay?" he asked, moving to her side.

Paige nodded, the motion jerky. "I am. I really don't like spiders," she said quietly, trembling lightly as she moved away from the corpse. "Can we go? I want to put more distance between us and...them," she said, nodding toward the remains of the spiders.

"Of course. Wade, you ready?"

The shifter had retrieved his knife and pulled out a cloth to wipe it off, but he stepped closer to Paige first, cleaning her face then offering the cloth to her. "For your hand," he murmured.

Paige glanced down numbly and wiped the blood from her fingers then the knife.

Both men watched her for a moment before Wade nodded to Julian. "I'm ready. And I'm with her on wanting to get the hell out of here. I don't mind normal spiders, but these are just freaky."

"Indeed," Julian agreed. "Let's go."

"Wait," Paige said, grabbing his arm. "Didn't one of them get you?" she asked, shining her light on his hand, which was dripping blood on the stone floor.

He grimaced and looked at his hand. It was a neat wound, especially compared to what the jaguar had done to Wade's arm, but now that he wasn't worried about Paige, it had begun to throb. Since he had no idea what kind of spiders they were, he didn't want to take chances.

"It did," he agreed before he focused on himself. He didn't sense any poison spreading from the wound, so healed it, resolving to check again when they either stopped for the night or were home. "I think I'm okay," he assured her.

Paige insisted on checking for herself, but finding nothing alarming, she nodded and they continued on.

Another hour and they found what seemed to be a safe section of hallway and sat down to rest.

"How long have we been in here?" Paige asked as she sipped water from her canteen.

Wade checked his watch and groaned. "Three hours. It's getting close to dusk, which is why it feels like we've been in here forever."

"Are you serious?" she asked, astonished. "Are we going to camp here tonight?"

"It would be the smart thing to do. None of us are at our best while we're tired or hungry, and you're both still recovering from the bullet ants," Julian said. "I don't think we need the tent, since we're sheltered and it's a comfortable temperature here, but we should take turns standing watch."

Wade snorted. "Damn straight we're standing watch. Aside from Paige's spiders, there could be gods knows what else down here. Just because we haven't seen it doesn't mean that it's not waiting."

"I'm trying not to think too hard about that," Paige muttered as she pulled her sleeping bag from her pack. The hallway was big enough for them to sleep side by side, so she stretched her bag out along one wall, but only after poking and prodding to make sure she wouldn't accidentally trigger something in her sleep. "Anyone have any ideas on how to find the end of this maze?" she asked, pulling out a bag of jerky.

She wasn't hungry so much as exhausted, but knew if she didn't eat, the boys would complain, so she nibbled on the jerky as they talked.

The others situated their bags as well, with Wade taking his share of the jerky. "Not sure," he admitted. "Most everything down here smells and looks the same. If we keep marking walls, we're bound to find new hallways, but there's no telling how big this place is."

"We can try the relic again tomorrow, see if we've gone far enough for it to try to guide you," Julian suggested, but no one seemed enthusiastic about their chances there.

"Maybe we'll just get lucky and stumble on it," Wade said with a quick grin. "I've always been a lucky kind of guy."

"You'd have to be, not to have more people punching you in the face," Julian said dryly, though Paige could see the humor in his eyes.

"Nah, who wants to punch something this pretty?" Wade asked with a dramatic gesture toward his face.

Paige giggled and shook her head, stretching out on her bag. "I'm going to try to sleep. Wake me up if anything exciting happens." Though she sincerely hoped they would have a quiet night.

CHAPTER 17

Paige woke to someone shaking her shoulder gently. "Paige? It's time to get up. We're going to pack up and try to figure out this labyrinth."

The voice was low and soothing, just deep enough, smooth enough to make her want to curl into the person it came from. "Julian?" she murmured without opening her eyes.

"Yes, it's me."

She stretched slowly, catlike, and felt the slight breeze caused by rapid movement as Julian rapidly backed away. When she opened her eyes, he was several feet away, his back to her. She blinked in confusion as Wade chuckled.

It wasn't difficult for him to see why Julian had retreated, not when the way she'd moved had pulled her shirt taut across her chest. "Morning Red. Sleep well?"

"Wait, morning? No one woke me for my watch?"

Wade grinned. "Nah. Wasn't any point, and you needed your sleep. But up and at 'em."

Paige scrubbed her hands over her face and yawned before she sat up and reached for her canteen. "Give me five and I'll be good to go."

True to her word, she was up and packed in five minutes. She gratefully accepted the thermos of lukewarm coffee that Julian handed to her and greedily drank. After, she brought out the relic and held it in both hands, focusing.

"You sense anything?" Wade asked after a minute.

"Yes, but it's not very clear," she murmured. "I think we need to go that way," she said, opening her eyes and nodding back the way they'd come the night before. To her surprise, neither of the men looked skeptical, but given how they'd gotten so easily turned around, she supposed that going back made as much sense as anything else.

After the relic was tucked away, they set off, walking carefully to avoid stepping right into a trap. In the next half hour, they hadn't come across any of the marks they'd left the day before. Another thirty minutes after that, she spoke up. "Does it seem like we're in a new part of the temple? Not like it was built after the rest, but...new to us?"

"It does. I don't smell us here." At Paige's baffled look, Wade laughed. "Even when we just walk by, our scent is still left behind. I'm not catching any trace of it, so yes, I think this is a new part of the temple."

"That's good, right?"

"It certainly could be, but we won't know unless we find the relic here," Julian answered.

"I suppose you're...right..." Paige trailed off, her steps slowing until she just stopped. She looked down the passage they were about to pass and frowned.

"What is it, Red?"

"I'm not sure," she murmured. "But I think we need to go that way."

Julian studied the passage, which looked identical to the rest. "How sure are you?"

"I'm getting more positive by the second." She turned and started down the hallway, though to Julian's relief, she didn't race across it. She drew the amulet piece out and held it tightly in her hand as she walked.

A few steps behind her, Wade whispered to Julian, "Is it just me, or does her whole eye glow thing seem brighter than it did an hour ago?"

"No, it's not just you. I hope it's just because we're getting close."

"We are," Paige said as she stopped in front of a doorway. The feeling of urgency she'd been getting from the relic stopped and was replaced by a strong vibration that felt almost hopeful to her. It was extremely distracting, so she put the piece back in her pocket.

The instant her fingers left the silver, she froze.

There was someone watching them.

She could feel the brush of their mind against hers. Unwilling to alert their watcher that she was onto them by saying or thinking something to the men, she cautiously reached out toward it with her magic, trying to figure out who kept trying to peek into her thoughts. There was surprise from that mind, before it seemed to vanish.

"Paige...Paige, what's wrong?"

Julian's voice seemed to fade in, and she blinked at him. "What?"

He frowned. "Are you all right?"

She rubbed the back of her neck. "There was someone watching us. Again."

Instantly, Wade lifted his head, trying to scent anyone nearby. "I only smell us down here," he informed her.

"I'm telling you, they were here. I felt their mind. When I tried to peek and see who it was, they felt surprised, then disappeared," Paige insisted. "And I think it's the same person as before, from the cafe."

"I believe you, Paige," Julian told her. "Minds can travel further than scents can. You said they disappeared, though?" She nodded. "Then perhaps we should try to hurry?"

Paige started to nod, then smiled. She motioned to the room before shining her light inside. The room was large, probably thirty feet square, if not bigger, but empty aside from a pedestal at the far end—and the slice of silver that rested atop it. "It's there."

Not expecting to actually have reached their destinations, their bodies went tense with readiness as they peeked into the room. Julian scowled and reached out an arm to stop Wade as he started inside. "Wait. There's some sort of magic here in the doorway," he warned.

Yielding to Julian in matters such as this, Wade backed up, drawing Paige with him.

"Do you know what kind?" Paige asked.

"Not yet. Give me a few," he said absently.

Not willing to let a moment of rest pass him by, Wade leaned against the wall and pulled out an energy bar. He munched on it while Julian ran his hands just beyond the magic and muttered to himself.

It was a few minutes later that his hands suddenly dropped and he let out a loud curse that wasn't English.

Wade leaned toward Paige and stage-whispered, "I have no idea what the hell he just said, but he sounds angry."

"He does," Paige murmured, "but I'm not sure what he said either. I think that was Sumerian, but I'd be lying if I said I was certain."

"Yes, it was Sumerian," Julian confirmed as he turned back, and that anger was visible. "We can't get through this doorway," he told them.

"What? Why not? We've come so far!" she protested.

"I'm not a hundred percent certain, but from what I can tell, that doorway will kill any person who passes through it," he told them as he started to pace.

Beyond the anger, Paige felt the frustration, the defeat coming off of him. Her heart ached and she stepped toward him. "Julian..."

"I'm okay," he told her a moment later. "Just because we can't pass through the doorway doesn't mean that we can't still get the relic. We *are* witches, after all," he said with a faint smile.

"Oh. Yes, I suppose that makes sense. It'll have to be you, though." Never before had she truly resented the fact that she couldn't physically manipulate the world around her, but it stung to let someone else, even Julian, retrieve the amulet she was so connected to.

"I'd step back. Just because I won't be physically going in there doesn't mean there won't be some sort of backlash," he warned, and Wade and Paige both took a few steps back. Anxiety slid through Paige and part of her wanted to tell him to stop, but she knew he wouldn't. Not when he could literally see his target.

Once assured they were safe, Julian focused on the piece of silver only feet from him. Though he didn't expect it to be easy, he was still annoyed when the relic didn't simply lift off the pedestal at the touch of his magic. He extended a hand to focus and strengthened his pull. He worked harder and harder until his arm trembled and sweat beaded on his brow, but the relic didn't so much as twitch from his magic. When that did nothing, he tried to teleport the piece from the pedestal to his hand, but that, too, wasn't as simple as he would have liked.

Only after several minutes of trying did Julian drop his hand, admitting defeat. Paige offered him a canteen and he drank greedily. "They must have the relic warded against any magic that would move it. That or the pedestal, or hell, the doorway could hold the ward, too. Either way, there's no way I can get it with magic."

"We'll find another way. There has to be some way to get it," Paige said hopefully.

Julian wasn't so sure. These pieces had been hidden by the gods, so why would they make things easy? Their intention had no doubt been to make things as impossible as they could, and he said as much. "I'd try teleporting in, but I have a feeling it would have the same effect as stepping through the doorway. The gods aren't fools to ignore such a simple loophole. And they made the room large enough that I don't think anything we have with us could reach it while still being able to retrieve it," he explained.

"Maybe we're overthinking this," Wade said thoughtfully.

"What do you mean?" Julian asked.

"You said no person could get through, right?"

"That's right."

"Well, you're both people, but I do have an animal form. Perhaps it's just meant to keep literal people out, not any living thing."

"I don't know..." Paige said uncertainly. "I felt your mind as a wolf. You still felt like a human. It seems like an unnecessary risk."

Julian added his protest to hers. "She's right. You're not purely animal. We can't chance it."

Wade wasn't the sort to wait around, and he liked taking risks. They were exciting. If he could take a risk while helping two friends? That just made it all the more appealing. "So...what? You just want to abandon it until you can train Lassie to retrieve it?" Wade asked sarcastically. "Well, fuck that." There was no stripping to warn them that he was going to shift this time. Between one moment and the next, he was simply a wolf with tattered clothes hanging off him. He gave himself a quick shake to ensure that he wouldn't trip on any scraps of cloth, then, before either witch could stop him, he leapt through the doorway. They knew the moment he touched the magic, because the whole chamber flared a bright yellow for a few seconds, intense enough to sting their eyes. Worse, Wade yelped and spasmed in mid-air before falling hard on his side and going utterly still.

"Wade!" Paige screamed, and it took everything she had not to rush through the doorway to try to help him.

Julian must have sensed her need, because he wrapped his arms around her to keep her in place. "Look, he's breathing," he murmured against her hair, and she stilled until she saw that furred side move. What truly astonished her was the fact that Wade wasn't just alive, he was struggling to his feet, his movements slow and full of pain.

Unshielded, Paige could feel the hurt radiating from him, and knew that this was at least as bad as the ants had been. Worse, really, since it encompassed his entire body.

"Forget the relic, Wade, we need to get you out of there," Julian snapped, but the wolf ignored him.

"Wade, please! The relic isn't worth more than you. Get out of there so we can help you," Paige pleaded.

Wade did nothing to acknowledge that he'd even heard them. He limped over to the pedestal and sniffed it before he very carefully took the piece between his teeth. The moment he touched it, his body stiffened and he whimpered, the sound tearing through Paige like a knife.

To Paige's eye, it looked like every step, every movement hurt worse than the last, but somehow he managed to keep upright. She clung to Julian, not caring that she had tears sliding down her cheeks. It was bad enough when he'd been stung saving her from the bullet ants, but this? This was so much worse. If he didn't make it...No, he'd make it. He had to.

Wade remained stiff as he painstakingly made his way back to the doorway, but stopped in front of it.

"Come on, Wade. We're not worried about the relic, we just want you safe," Paige whispered to him, but she understood his hesitation. Would the doorway hurt him leaving the room as well, or was it one way only?

Pain-filled eyes fixed on Paige before Wade jerked his head and released the relic mid-motion, sending it flying through the doorway. There was no magical reaction to it, just the clinking of metal hitting stone. Neither Paige nor Julian so much as looked toward it, their eyes fixed on Wade as he swayed on his paws. Slowly, he began moving again until he passed through the doorway. There was a low whimper, but no yelp this time, and he didn't stop moving until he was past the magical barrier. Once through, he collapsed on his side before he flashed back to human.

Neither witch paid any attention to Wade's nudity as they knelt beside him, pulling him further from the doorway. Julian laid his hands on Wade's back, since he was turned away. He glanced at Paige, letting her know silently what he needed. She mirrored Julian's position, lending her power to him, in case his own wasn't enough to heal Wade.

Even with the two of them it took several minutes before Wade was breathing more easily and the tension caused by pain started to ease. The doorway had damaged quite a bit inside him, both physically and magically, so repairing it was a slow process.

"Thanks," Wade whispered weakly.

"Just don't scare us like that again!" Paige said, her voice trembling with concern. She looked up at Julian. "We need to get him to a bed where he can rest for a few days."

"I can teleport us home. It'd be best for him," Julian said as he grabbed Wade's bag so it wouldn't be left behind. He did have the good sense to grab the piece that Wade had retrieved and shoved it in a pocket—wanting it separate from the one Paige carried, for now.

Except when he tried to send them back to Mooreton, nothing happened, and he uttered a low curse.

"What's wrong?" Paige asked.

"I can't teleport. It could just be this specific location, to prevent people from teleporting to the relic, but I can't move us a single centimeter," Julian explained.

Wade forced himself onto all fours, but his limbs trembled with the effort even that much activity caused.

Paige noticed and let out a soft cry of distress, reaching to help support him. "Wade! What are you doing?" She was still too concerned to care much that he was naked, though her cheeks did pinken.

"We need...to move. Only way Julian...can teleport us," he said, exhausted by even those few words.

"He's right," Julian said reluctantly as he bent to help Wade up. "The sooner we leave this area, the sooner we can get him into a bed."

"I suppose," Paige murmured.

"Pants first?" Wade asked, forcing a smile to his lips. "Don't want to shock Red too much."

Paige's cheeks darkened, but Julian only chuckled and nodded. "Of course." He passed the pack over to Paige. "Can you grab them?" he asked, still supporting Wade.

She nodded and dug through the bag until she found Wade's spare pants. She thrust them at Julian who took them and helped Wade get them on. A few minutes later they were ready to go and, with Wade holding onto both Paige and Julian, they started back, paying close attention to the markings they'd left behind.

Their progress was sluggish. Not only did they have to be sure they didn't trigger any of the traps, but Wade's condition slowed them considerably. Five minutes later, Julian pulled them to a stop. "Let me see if we're far enough away to teleport."

Paige looked at Wade's pale face and nodded. "The sooner the better," she agreed.

Julian closed his eyes to help focus his power, and though he felt the magic start to take hold, it didn't quite work. "Not yet," he told them grimly before they resumed their forward progress.

They passed the treasure room, the pit trap, and finally the first corridor they'd seen, yet were still unable to teleport.

"Really hope…we don't have…to go outside," Wade mumbled.

"Maybe the jaguars will be gone?" Paige suggested hopefully.

"Maybe," Julian said, though without any real conviction. "Let's try just going upstairs to the entrance before we worry about that."

It had felt like it took forever for them to descend the stairs the day before, but going up them now took much, much longer. By the time they reached the top, even Paige and Julian were exhausted, their muscles protesting the activity.

"Try again," Paige urged.

Julian nodded and pulled on the magic, relieved when he felt it respond. "Hold on," he said, tightening his hold on Wade and reaching across to touch Paige's hand. A moment later, they were back in Mooreton.

CHAPTER 18

There wasn't much of the day left when they returned to Mooreton, but what remained was spent tending to Wade. Though he insisted that he could walk, he was half carried, half levitated up the stairs and into one of the guest rooms. Julian helped him to the en suite bathroom for a shower, but stayed just outside, giving him some privacy while Wade scrubbed away the Amazon. Afterward, once Wade had donned a pair of loose cotton pants, Julian helped him to bed, where Paige got him settled and fussed over him.

"I'm okay, Paige. Seriously. You don't need to go all mother hen over me. Just need a beer, half my weight in burgers, and a full night's sleep, then I'll be good to go," Wade assured her, multiple times, until she finally believed him and went to get him something to eat.

Both he and Julian watched her go. The moment the door closed behind her, Wade turned to Julian. "You're crazy if you don't—"

Julian lifted a hand and shook his head. "Don't start. I'd hate to beat an already wounded man."

Wade grinned and shrugged. "Can't blame a wolf for trying." He sobered. "It's good you took me with you, though. I don't think you and Paige would've managed to get the relic without me."

"No, probably not," Julian agreed. "But you also wouldn't be laying in that bed with barely enough strength to even take a shower by yourself."

"Maybe, but I signed up for it. And I went through that doorway despite your bitching. Not only that, but you know I take risks every day when I'm on the job. So stop blaming yourself. I'll be fine. Tomorrow you'll be wishing I was back in bed being all helpless."

"You're probably right about that," Julian said dryly. "Eat, then get some rest. I want the normal you back as soon as possible, no matter how annoying the normal you is."

Wade saluted him. "Will do, boss."

Julian shook his head and slipped out of the room.

A few minutes later, Paige came in with a bowl of chicken soup and some buttered toast. Wade complained about what he called invalid food, teasing her about it until she smiled. She refused to leave until he'd eaten, then she'd tugged the blankets up almost to his chin. Even then, he had to badger her into leaving. He appreciated the mothering, and knew part of it was just her nurturing side coming out, but another part was guilt because he'd gotten hurt helping her and Julian.

Paige remembered little of the night after that. She knew she'd showered—bathing off several days' worth of grime—before falling face first into bed without dressing, but it was all a bit hazy.

Ten hours later, she woke and felt better than she had in weeks. Full of energy, she decided to make breakfast, hoping the activity would occupy her mind so she wouldn't dwell on the relic or Wade's injury. She sang aloud as she cooked, though neither of the men were awake yet. Julian wasn't one to sleep in, though, and walked in grunting for a cup of coffee before the eggs had finished cooking.

At her insistence—though he grumbled—he went to wake Wade and help him downstairs. She wasn't going to have them talking about the relic on empty stomachs after the time they'd spent in the Amazon.

They all sat at the table in the breakfast nook, with the men scooping piles of food onto their plates, which made Paige smile.

"You feeling better this morning, Wade?" she asked as she spread jam on a piece of toast.

"Yep. Back to my normal self. Maybe not quite ready to run a marathon, but anything short of that and I'm good to go," he said, flashing her a playful grin.

"Good. But don't ever do something like that again. You scared me."

"And me," Julian added with a dark look for his friend.

"I know, I know. But we couldn't just turn back when we were right there," Wade protested. "It would've pissed me off to go through all that, to get right outside the door, and go home empty handed. It would've pissed both of you off, too."

"Maybe, but you're still more important than any relic," Paige told him with a shake of her head.

"As much as I hate to admit it, she's right," Julian added with a hint of a smile. Most wouldn't have noticed it, but both Paige and Wade knew him well enough to recognize the minute change in expression.

"Yeah, yeah. But hey, now that we've gotten it, when are we going to see if Paige can do that voodoo that she do?" Wade asked, shoveling in more eggs.

Julian shrugged. "I suppose as soon as we're done eating. Assuming you're up for it, Paige?"

"Of course. I'm just as eager to find out what comes next as you two," she answered with a smile. She was nervous about the other pieces, but hid it. There was no reason to have Julian trying to leave her behind again, which he would if he knew she had misgivings, but she couldn't help but wonder. What if the piece in the Amazon had been the easiest to get to? There was a piece that was somewhere wet. For all she knew, it could be at the bottom of the Mariana Trench, and that truly would be impossible for them to retrieve. At least with any magic or technology she was familiar with. But it also served no purpose to worry until she had to, so she focused on her breakfast and the men in front of her.

"Then what are you waiting for? Eat faster," Wade said with a wolfy smile.

Twenty minutes later in the workshop, Julian pulled out the new fragment and set it on the table for them to examine.

Paige didn't sit as she normally would, instead badgering Wade until he'd taken her seat. She had argued that he was still recovering his strength until he'd given in. Only then had she stood back, hands clasped as Julian picked up the piece.

"It looks very similar to the first piece," he murmured. "Same shape, same metal, same look to the symbols, same little notch cut out."

Wade grinned. "I haven't really looked at the piece you already had, so I'll have to take your word on it. Paige?"

Julian studied Paige's face for a long moment before he stood and offered the piece to her.

She took a deep breath, shielded her mind, then reached out and took it. The reaction was wholly different from the first time she'd touched the other piece, or any time since. There was no jolt of power strong enough to arch her body or make her scream. There was no pain of any sort. The only thing that was the same was the emerald gleam of her eyes, the longing and loneliness from the metal.

Her head tilted, and she reached into her pocket to pull out the first piece. As soon as she had both the pieces out, her hands were drawn together like the pieces were magnets. When the edges touched, they fused together, leaving no seam or any sign to show that they had ever been separated. It was a half-circle now, with a smaller half-circle piece missing from the middle of the flat edge.

There was only a second for her to be pleased before the amulet reacted. She cried out and her body jerked before every muscle in her body went taut, causing her body to contort and start to tumble downward.

Even recovering from his ordeal, Wade had wolf-like reflexes which made him quicker than Julian. He jumped to his feet, knocking his chair backward as he grabbed her. Not knowing what to do, he just kept his arms around her and looked at Julian with a shocked and confused expression on his face.

Julian was beside them in an instant, a hand lifted to her cheek. "Focus, Paige. Don't let it rule you. Let it flow over you and past you. Just focus," he told her, voice quiet but firm. "Remember how you protected yourself when it was just one piece. Control the information, don't let it control you."

Something he said penetrated her mind and there was the tiniest of nods as she forced herself to comply. Bit by bit she began to relax until Wade could sit her on the edge of the table. His chair was still upended, and he didn't want to risk letting her go long enough to right it.

She was hyperventilating, but it was still an improvement, so Julian just reached for her clasped hands, holding them as he stared into her eyes and tried to lend her what strength he could.

"I'm good. I'm fine," she panted. "Cold. Freezing. Icy bottom of the world. Cold, cold, cold, cold," she chanted before her teeth started chattering. That worried Julian enough, but then her breath started to come out as a wispy fog. It was just little puffs, but the fact that it was visible in a warm room concerned him more.

"What's wrong with her?" Wade asked quietly, touching her cheek lightly. "She doesn't feel cold."

"No, but another piece of the relic is," Julian murmured. "We knew one of them was somewhere cold." She started to shiver hard and he rubbed her hands briskly. "If she doesn't let go of it soon..."

Wade nodded in understanding. The relic could freeze her to death.

"Paige, sweetheart, it's warm enough here, and you need to stay here. You need to focus and protect yourself," Julian told her, not noticing the endearment he used.

Later, Wade would wonder if it was the instructions or being called sweetheart by Julian that steadied Paige enough to focus.

The chattering slowly stopped and she nodded, the motion short and jerky. "Cave. In a cave, in a frozen land. It's so cold there," she panted.

"That's enough, Paige. You can let go of the amulet now. We've got enough. Just let go," Julian told her, gently pulling at her fingers, which opened and released the amulet piece to him.

She slumped against him, her breathing gradually returning to normal. "Was...it really enough?" she asked, recovering more quickly now—though she could admit to herself that she forced herself to sit upright and not lean against Julian. She didn't want his pity.

"I think it's pretty clear that the icy bottom of the world is Antarctica," Wade said with a grin. "Just gotta find a cave near the south pole and we'll be golden, huh?" Then he sobered. "You okay though, Red?"

"I am. Still a little cold, but I'm warming up. And that sounds accurate to me," she told him, giving him a weary smile. "I don't know if it's exactly the south pole, though."

"We'll figure it out. Either way, we'll need to get some cold weather gear. I know it gets cold in England, but I don't have anything even remotely suited for Antarctica, so we'll need to go shopping again," Julian said once he stepped back, hoping the thought of shopping would cheer Paige up. He put the amulet in the safe before focusing on Wade. "You don't have to come with us, Wade. You did more than we could have—"

Wade cut him off with a snort. "Boy, you keep that up and you're gonna piss me off. I'm coming. To find this next piece and any others that need finding. You think I'm not gonna see how this plays out? That's like walking out of a movie thirty minutes in. Besides, my mama didn't raise no quitters."

Paige giggled, and the sound improved the mood of both men, who couldn't help but smile at her.

"Very well. But we will take a few days first. For the shopping and for both you and Paige to fully recover. And that is *not* negotiable," Julian said.

"No argument here. I'll go grab the gear," Wade offered.

"Can I come with you?" Paige asked. "I like shopping."

Again struck by a surge of jealousy, Julian frowned but said nothing. He wasn't sure why he was upset, anyway. He hadn't decided if he was going to touch her, and Wade *was* a good man, once you got him to be serious about anything. Paige could do worse...

He couldn't finish the thought. The idea of Paige with anyone else made him livid.

Paige frowned and glanced at Julian, but he shielded his emotions before she could get more than a quick hint of what he was feeling.

Wade fought not to grin, but failed. "Imagine that. But yeah, you can. Probably best anyway. Any coat I'd get for you would either swallow you or be too tight. Meet you outside. And Julian? We're taking your car." He snuck a wink to Paige, then walked out, whistling.

"You need anything besides the obvious?" she asked Julian. "Wade looks about your size, so clothes should be easy enough."

"No, have fun," he told her, before retreating to his books.

She hesitated a moment at his clear dismissal then sighed and followed Wade.

As they walked to the car neither spoke—Paige because she was thinking, and Wade to give her space. It was the former who broke the silence first. "I asked Julian if he wanted me," she blurted out.

Wade let out a surprised laugh and held up a fist toward her. She grinned a bit self-consciously as she gave him a fist-bump. "Nice going, Red. When did you do that? And what'd he say?"

"When we reached that canyon and you were off looking for that absolutely dreadful bridge." She sighed softly. "At first he dodged the question, but then he said he did, but that he wasn't going to do anything about it."

Wade muttered something uncomplimentary about his friend and climbed into the car. Then his mood improved slightly. He'd always loved Julian's car. Though he was partial to tough vehicles with four-wheel drive, there was something about the 1960 Aston Martin that made him almost gleeful.

Paige's lips twitched as she joined him. "I asked him what he'd do if I decided to do something about it."

He whistled. "Good one."

"Well, it might have been." She smiled sly. "But we were interrupted before he could say anything, by a wolf returning and becoming a naked man."

He had the grace to look sheepish. "Oops. Sorry, Red. Didn't mean to get in the way."

"I know. And I'm not upset. Quite the opposite. I...want to try to make the most of our few days back home." At first she'd hesitated, thinking that they needed to focus on the relic, but there wasn't much else for them to do but recover, and her logic was that getting things settled between her and Julian would make them less distracted in Antarctica. Besides, she didn't want to waste any more time.

"Oh?" He arched a brow. "How so?"

Paige's cheeks went bright red. "I...um...I've decided to seduce him. Not sure on the how yet, but..." She shrugged and stared out the window, embarrassed.

He grinned. "You want some advice from a guy? Especially a guy who's known Julian for a couple of centuries?"

Embarrassment was quickly surpassed by the need to help Julian forget about his wife—and her love for him—and she nodded. "Please."

"While we're out shopping, get some lingerie. Something wicked, and as red as your hair..."

<h1 style="text-align:center">CHAPTER 19</h1>

They returned in just enough time for dinner, though Wade insisted that he cook, since she'd made breakfast. Paige was a little skeptical, but Wade promised that he knew how to cook steak and potatoes like a champ. Julian tried to bow out, but Wade browbeat him into joining them.

While Wade dealt with that, Paige retreated to her room. She didn't need to rest, she needed a distraction. If she didn't get her mind off what could potentially happen later, she might explode. So she spent the time until dinner by looking at the photos she'd taken in Brazil. It was painfully obvious that she was far from a professional photographer, but overall, she was happy with the pictures. She'd gotten several good ones—including a few of their primate intruders—and a fantastic shot of Julian. In it, he stood confidently, staring into the wilds of the rainforest, with the lush green spread behind him. It was perfectly him, and she made sure to save that one.

Only after she'd gone through all the pictures—and deleted the ones that were out of focus or dominated by random fingers—did she join the men downstairs.

It was a quiet affair, for the most part. Julian was lost in thought—which switched between their next trip and Paige—while

Paige was simply nervous about what she had planned for that night. She was no virgin, but neither had she ever set out to intentionally seduce someone. It had always happened organically, or she'd been the one being seduced.

Wade, of course, had no problem carrying on conversation and did most of the talking, usually with a grin on his face. Julian was in for a big surprise later.

After what felt like an eternity had passed, everyone went up to bed. Before entering his room, Wade gave her a grin and mouthed 'good luck' to her.

Having Wade *know* that she was, hopefully, going to have sex soon was a little mortifying. With her inexperience, and since she'd never been a party girl, talking about sex wasn't something she was entirely comfortable with. Still, if his suggestion worked, the embarrassment would be worth it.

In her bedroom, she changed into the lingerie she'd bought—after making sure Wade was nowhere close to the store. It was nothing like anything she'd ever worn before, or even thought about wearing, really, though she had to admit it did make her feel sexy. Self-conscious, yes, but sexy.

The red teddy was sheer and embellished with black lace, as were the stockings and excuse for panties that went with it. It had looked fantastic on the mannequin, and the deep red color looked wonderful against her fair skin.

She hoped it was enough to push past Julian's hold on the past.

Paige brushed her hair out so it hung around her in loose waves that fell to her hips, and dabbed just a hint of perfume at her throat and between her breasts. After examining herself in the mirror, searching for faults, she slipped into a robe, which she closed and belted.

When she passed Wade's door, she refused to even glance at it, and continued on to Julian's room. She took several calming breaths, then knocked. It took him only a moment to open it, though he was frowning. Frowning and wearing nothing but a pair of gray cotton pants.

"Is everything okay?" he asked.

At first, she didn't hear him. She was too struck by the sight of him shirtless. Somehow in the three years she'd been there, she'd never seen him with his shirt off, and boy, was it a revelation. Though he was certainly a scholar, he didn't look like the stereotypical book nerd. He was fit, with a flat belly, and well-muscled arms and chest. He wasn't muscular enough to be bulky, but the overall package made her feel a little warm, with the heat centered between her thighs.

She'd known he was handsome, but she'd had no idea that under his clothes he would be so unbelievably hot. She wanted to get her hands on him more than ever, to touch all that skin, to follow the narrow trail of hair that led down his belly and disappeared into his pants.

"Can I come in?" she asked, proud that her voice was steady. Mostly.

He hesitated before he stepped back and motioned for her to come in.

She gave him a faint smile and brushed past him. His room hadn't changed, other than there being a few more books spread around. The covers on his bed were drawn down, the sheets rumpled, so she knew he had been in bed when she knocked.

Halfway to his bed, she stopped and half-turned to look back at him. He clearly wasn't sure what to do, but closed the door as he stared after her.

"Is something wrong? Are you worried about the trip to Antarctica?"

Slowly, Paige shook her head. "No, nothing's wrong..." Her unsteady fingers went to the sash of her robe while her heart pounded wildly in her chest.

"What are you doing?" he demanded, but it didn't stop her. She could hear how his voice had thickened, could feel a sudden surge in his emotions, even though he prevented her from feeling what those emotions were. But she was a smart girl and could only be one of two things.

It definitely wasn't anger.

She shrugged the robe off her shoulders and let it slide to the floor. Nerves started to fade at his reaction and the slip in his shielding that gave her a glimpse into the man.

Eyes widened as he took in her body wrapped in sinful red. It should have looked stark against her pale skin, but instead it made her look luminous. With her hair down like it was—something she rarely did—she looked both softer and like sex made flesh. Never before had he seen a woman look as stunning or tempting as she did. The lingerie accented more than it hid and his mouth went dry with need. His pants did nothing to hide his sudden arousal, and for the first time he truly felt like all the blood had rushed out of his head and into his pants. After a couple of tries, he did actually manage a coherent statement. "You should go. Now."

She started for him—and where the hell had she learned to walk like *that*, he wondered, with her hips swaying erotically—as she shook her head. "I'm not going anywhere, Julian. Not unless you can tell me, honestly, that you want me to go. Not unless you can say that you don't want me. Not unless you can prove that you think this is a bad idea." Stopping in front of him, she gave him a siren's smile. "I don't think you'll be able to, though."

"Why?" he rasped, staring at the breasts that were only barely hidden by lace. His hands were fisted at his sides, because if he didn't keep his arousal in check, he'd grab her and throw her onto his bed.

"Because I can *feel* how much you want me right now." She swallowed and took another step, so they were toe to toe. "And it's almost as much as I want you."

He didn't—couldn't—stop her as her arms slid around his neck and she went up on her toes. Her body pressed lightly against his as she arched up and laid her lips against his.

It began sweet, almost innocent, but it caused his tightly held control to disintegrate. She felt so hot and soft against him and made him crave more. He groaned and wrapped his arms around her, pressing her more firmly against him as he plundered her mouth. The intensity of his response delighted Paige and sent a bolt of desire through her. When one of his hands slid down to cup her backside and pull her tight against his erection, she whimpered with need.

Again and again his tongue thrust into her mouth to play with hers until they were both breathless, all while he held her tightly. They broke the kiss, but neither would release the other as they panted and stared into each other's eyes.

"If you're going to change your mind, Paige, do it now. Because after this, I'm not letting you out of my bed until dawn," he warned her in a rough voice.

She shook her head slowly. "I'm right where I want to be," she whispered. "Or close enough," she added with a pointed look behind her and at the bed.

His eyes darkened with lust and he all but tore the lingerie off of her, which thrilled her further. There was no more room for embarrassment, no room for anything but passion. And she'd never had a man so desperate for her that he ripped the clothes off her. She loved it.

When he had her nude but for the stockings, he gripped her rear and lifted her up, so it was more natural to wrap her legs around him than not. The intimate press of him between her legs, with only his thin cotton pants separating them, made her moan and squirm against the hard ridge nestled against her.

He sucked in a breath and tightened his hold. Already he was so hard it was painful, but he couldn't bear to stop, not now. "Don't do that or I'm going to drop you," he warned, even as he hurried to the bed so he could lay her on it. He quickly pushed his pants down and kicked them off, leaving him as nude as she was. Paige's soft sound of pure feminine approval had him groaning even as he studied her.

The lingerie had hinted at how beautiful she was, but seeing her like this? She was perfect, from her wild red hair down to her unpainted toes. He couldn't quite decide exactly where he wanted to begin. Part of him wanted to go slow, to make it as good for her as he could, but he wasn't sure he was strong enough to draw this out.

A knee rested on the bed beside her as he trailed a finger across her cheek. "I've dreamed of having you like this," he admitted, bending his head to circle a nipple with his tongue. Her breathing quickened and he scraped his teeth gently over the tight peak, which had her back arching toward him.

"So have I," she breathed, unable to believe that she was finally in bed with him, that her hands were roaming over his warm skin, exploring him, learning his body.

He paused for a moment then nuzzled her breast, murmuring, "I should have guessed." With her powers, it would be more surprising if they hadn't shared dreams. Somehow, knowing he hadn't been alone in that dream on the plane didn't bother him, but instead made him ache even more for her. Made him want to discover if reality could be even better than dreams.

His fingers slid between her legs and found her then, and she didn't think to question what he meant. All her thoughts fragmented when he rubbed against the small bundle of nerves, drawing a helpless gasp from her. Shifting upward, his mouth found hers once more at the same moment his fingers slid lower. Hips lifted encouragingly while her hands pressed against his back, her short nails biting lightly into his skin. He doubted she even realized she was doing it, and her uninhibited passion had him nearly desperate to bury himself within her.

"I'm sorry," he groaned against her lips, fingers stroking more quickly over her slick flesh.

"For...for what?" she asked, her mind delightfully muddled.

"It's going to be quick. This time."

The idea that there would be other times made up for any disappointment Paige might have had, but in truth, she wanted him just as much. More, really, since she was feeling not just her need, but his as well. The combination threatened to swamp her, and she held on to sanity by her fingertips.

"Yes," she told him urgently as she hooked her legs around his hips to draw him closer. "Gods, yes."

He groaned at the easy acceptance and shifted so that he pressed against her, making her tremble with anticipation. Forcing himself to at least start slowly, uncertain just how experienced she was, he began to ease into her. His good intentions vanished before he had made it halfway into her. She was so slick and hot around him that he thrust deep with a low hiss of pleasure. To his satisfaction, she moaned and arched up to meet him.

Reality was absolutely better than his dreams had been.

When he started to move within her, he knew it would be over too quickly, but he was determined that she was going to have her pleasure before he found his. They found a rhythm together, so quickly it felt natural, right to be here with her like this, and he gave into the urge to kiss her again. He drank down her moans and cries, giving her back his groans. One of his hands found her breast, kneading the soft flesh, teasing the nipple with gentle pinches and strokes of his thumb, and he felt her quiver.

The mixture of sensations had Paige going wild for him and strained his control. He fought to prevent himself from coming just yet, and shifted the angle of his thrusts so his groin brushed against her with each stroke. When Paige threw her head back, spilling her hair across his pillow as she cried out and clenched around him in orgasm, he was utterly and completely lost.

He lifted his head so he could watch her face as she found her release. Those startling green eyes went blurry and soft but fixed on his, so she watched him as he plunged deep one last time and came harder than he had in memory, fighting not to roar with intense satisfaction. And an odd contentment.

Moments passed as they stared at each other, helpless in the aftermath of their release. Julian wrapped an arm around her before he rolled them, so she lay atop him, her head nestled against the curve of his shoulder.

They lay like that for several minutes until their breathing returned to normal. Paige wasn't sure what to say, choosing instead to lay a gentle kiss against the pulse in his throat. She didn't want to break the peace between them. Or worse, for him to say he'd regretted the most memorable experience of her life.

"I hope you're not too tired," he told her, just as she debated whether to get up or say something.

Surprised by the comment, she lifted her head and gave him a curious look. "Too tired for what?"

Lips curved in a lazy, wicked smile. "I said it was going to be quick that time. Now I have to make up for it."

Eyes widened when she felt him already hardening against her, and he gripped her hips to encourage her to slide onto him.

"And I plan to make up for it the rest of the night," he said, voice gone rough again with passion.

He kept his word, loving her twice more before letting her go to sleep, just an hour before dawn. And when she slept, it was with her curled up against his side, a smile on her face.

That smile was still in place when she woke, reaching for him even before she had opened her eyes. But he wasn't there. Her smile faded and she sighed. The sheets were still warm, so he hadn't been gone long. It would have been nice to wake up with him, but...he needed time. She knew that. And he'd taken a big step toward healing by not shoving her out of the room, not to mention sleeping beside her for the remainder of the night.

Facts that she was very grateful for.

Not wanting to push him too far, too fast, she put on her robe, gathered up what remained of her clothes, and slipped out. All while trying to convince herself that she wasn't disappointed.

Julian hadn't gone far. When he'd woken, still holding Paige, still hungry for her, he'd felt a sharp pang of guilt for the woman who'd once slept in his bed. The woman he'd once loved. Gently, he extricated himself from Paige's hold and made his way to the room he had forbidden Paige to enter when she decided to tend to the house, to his room. The room that had been Mary's sanctuary. The place that had been hers just as the workshop had been his.

He sat in her favorite chair, holding a portrait of them that had been done just after their marriage. In his other hand was the ring he had slipped on her finger so many years ago. The ring that Paige had found for him and that he'd retrieved only days ago.

His eyes were dry, but there was an ache in his chest he couldn't ignore. Not longing for Mary, not anymore. This ache was caused by the fact that he, finally, could admit he had begun to fall for another woman.

He was moving on.

A finger brushed over the image of Mary's face and he sighed. "I'm sorry, Mary. So sorry," he whispered. "I held onto you for as long as I could, but...they're right. You wouldn't want me to live the rest of my life like I have been. You'd want me to be happy, however that happiness was achieved."

He glanced to the doorway, thinking of the woman he thought still slept in his bed. "I don't know if it's...I care for her, and I was so tired of being alone. Forgive me," he said, voice barely audible even to himself.

Rising then, he set the portrait and ring in one of the dresser drawers, then slowly closed it.

Finally putting part of his past behind him, or starting to, he left the room and tried to ignore the memories.

And the guilt that he knew he needed to shed.

CHAPTER 20

Things changed in the house after that night. Julian would find Paige around the house or in the garden and pull her into an empty room or secluded place hidden by bushes. Then he'd take her with a need and intensity that delighted her and left her weak. Nights were spent in each other's embrace as well—though always in Paige's bed rather than his own—and she always woke up alone.

While their time together was better than she could have ever imagined, and made a mockery of all her prior encounters, it wasn't perfect. She kept her dismay to herself, understanding that Julian had made huge progress in finally moving on and that she shouldn't rush him. Nor should she try to take Mary's place. Not that she even remotely wanted to. She wanted Julian to care for her because he liked her, wanted her, not because she was a replacement for his dead wife. So she'd give him time.

There was still tension between them, just a different flavor than before. This tension she couldn't mind.

Wade recognized it, and the change that had occurred in his friends. In deference to them, he didn't mention it and tried to keep things light. Often, he had Paige laughing despite her concerns. Even Julian began to smile more often as his guilt began to fracture, grief replaced by growing affection for a cheerful redhead.

The day before they left, they finalized their plans. Planes to Antarctica weren't exactly simple to book, and getting as far south as they wanted would be problematic even with a plane, so teleporting was their best option. Again, Julian didn't want to strain his powers, so he called in a favor from Jeff Anderson, a witch he had helped to save several months ago. With his wife's full support, Jeff agreed to teleport to them the next day and take them south.

He arrived at noon, looking a little tired and begging for a cup of coffee, even before introductions were made. There was still half a pot left, so Paige quickly delivered.

After he had gulped down every drop, he grinned, a trace of sleep still in his eyes. "Sorry about that. I'm useless before my first pot of coffee. We're on the west coast—this week, anyway—so it wasn't even dawn yet when I left," he explained before he offered his hand to Paige, then Wade. "I'm Jeff."

Both shook his hand, with Paige smiling. "I'm Paige. Thank you for agreeing to help us. Not sure how we would have gotten there without you."

"Wade. And what she said," the shifter said with a wolfish grin.

"Jeff has some pretty impressive powers for someone who's only known witches exist for a little more than a year," Julian explained, giving one of his increasingly frequent smiles to the American witch.

Paige gave him a sympathetic look. "You were brought up ignorant as well? I'm sorry for that. It does make things difficult, doesn't it?"

"It does, but don't be sorry. If things hadn't gone how they did, I wouldn't have my Elise. And I'd fight a hundred Gurnovs for her."

Both Paige and Wade looked clueless at the name, so Julian explained. "He and Elise were guardians for a prison that held a dangerous demon named Gurnov. Wade, you might have seen something on the news about odd weather and darkness in Georgia about a year ago? Near Stone Mountain?"

Wade nodded slowly. "That was you?" he asked Jeff, brows lifting in surprise.

"Yes and no. It was Gurnov. I just helped kill him and get things back to how they should be," Jeff clarified. "But we can talk about that later. Right now I have a sleepy—and pregnant—wife who wants me home soon."

Paige noted the sheer satisfaction and pride in his voice, and couldn't prevent the wistfulness that rose, or a look at Julian. His face was completely unreadable and she sighed softly.

Forcing cheerfulness, she said, "Well, let's get ready so Jeff can get home." She put on her arctic gear, then immediately hoped that everyone else was getting ready just as quickly. In Antarctica, the warmth would be welcome, but in an already comfortable house, she was quickly getting overheated.

Fortunately, it was only minutes before everyone was geared up and had their packs on. They all laid a hand on Jeff's arm or shoulder so they wouldn't get left behind. "Everyone ready?" At their assent, Jeff nodded and focused on the picture they had given him for reference.

Dark colors, wood, and heat were replaced by miles of white and a temperature low enough that Paige was suddenly very happy that she was dressed as she was. Even with the gear, frigid wind stung her face and had her pulling her hood a little more tightly around her face.

Jeff seemed unconcerned by the chill, despite wearing short sleeves. He only turned in a slow circle, taking in the monochromatic landscape. "This the right place?"

"It is," Julian confirmed, though he didn't even glance around. "Give Elise my regards."

Jeff tipped an imaginary hat, then disappeared.

"How was he not freezing?" Paige wondered. "I'm dressed for this and I'm still cold."

"He's a fire elementalist. He tends to run hotter than anyone but an actual fire elemental," Julian answered.

She knew she'd heard the term, but couldn't place it at the moment. "What's the difference between the two?"

"Elementals aren't witches, they're a separate race altogether. Their powers are limited solely to manipulating or becoming their elemental, though their control over it is stronger than most everyone. An elementalist is a witch who is just strongly connected to an element, and can manipulate it almost effortlessly. In Jeff's case, he can actually turn into flame."

"I wish I could have seen that," Paige murmured.

Julian smiled. "I'm sure you'll have a chance. For now though, why don't you find out which direction we need to take. I, for one, would be happy for a cave, or even a cliff, to block some of this wind."

She shivered, knowing that she needed to touch the amulet with her bare skin to get anything, which would involve exposing skin to the elements. She drew out the amulet then moved closer to Julian, using him to block some of the wind. Before she could take her glove off, she had an idea and slid the amulet inside the glove instead. She didn't think she could put it away without taking her glove off, but with the seemingly endless snow and ice, having constant direction wouldn't be a bad thing. Getting lost here would be entirely too easy.

With her mind properly shielded, there was only a single tremor and sigh in reaction to the contact, though Wade noted that her glowing eyes stood out less here than they had in the Amazon or Julian's workshop. It was too blindingly white to really notice a green gleam.

Paige nodded after she took a minute to sort through the sensations from the relic half. "It's that way," she told them, before they started walking. By unspoken agreement, they flanked her, not just to help protect her from the cold, but just in case the amulet affected her negatively.

Hiking through the rainforest had helped Paige shed some of her softness, so she was in slightly better shape now than she had been, but it still wasn't an easy trek. Often the wind blew directly at them, making it difficult to walk with any speed. Worse, there were all sorts of natural dangers dotted around the landscape—snow-filled crevasses to fall into, jagged pieces of ice, as well as a cold more intense than any-thing they'd ever felt. And those hazards were expertly camouflaged by nature.

Wade was the first to slip on some ice and Paige reflexively grabbed for him. Instead of preventing his fall, they went down together, land-ing hard on their backsides. There was some padding, with the thermal layers and heavy coats, but Paige's butt still felt bruised by the time they'd gotten back to their feet.

It wasn't the last problem they came across either, or the worst.

There was little to distract from the walk, with the landscape changing so little. Ahead, Paige could see a mountain range, but they were still probably two days away from it. Even Wade had stopped cracking jokes, claiming that his brain was too frozen to be witty.

Julian had ended up a few steps in front of the others, and Paige focused on his back to keep herself moving forward. So it was a shock when he seemed to disappear. It only took a second for her to realize that he hadn't disappeared, he'd fallen.

"Julian!" she screamed as she moved to the now visible edge of a crevasse and dropped to her knees, Wade right beside her. Her heart stopped as she looked down hundreds of feet of ice, frozen rock, and snow, until she spotted the dark blue of Julian's coat. On his way down, he'd managed to grab hold of a piece of ice or rock that jutted out and stop his descent.

"I'm okay," he called, voice thin and winded.

"Wade, do something!" Paige demanded of the shifter.

Before he could speak, Julian yelled up to them again. "Just give me a moment and I'll pop back up there. I'd move away from the edge."

Wade tried to draw her back, but she gave him a deadly look that dared him to move her one inch. In surrender, he held up both hands and remained crouched beside her. "Better hurry. She's not going anywhere."

Julian's muttered curse carried up to them a heartbeat before he actually disappeared and reappeared behind them. "Now, will you move back before you fall in, too?" he snapped angrily, grabbing Paige's arm and pulling her several feet from the edge. The thought of her falling down that long drop made him colder than all the wind here had managed.

"I wasn't going to just leave you down there, Julian," she told him, chin lifted defiantly.

He sighed and wrapped his arms around her as best he could in their bulky clothing. "Just be more careful, okay?" he murmured while Wade looked elsewhere.

"I will," Paige promised, closing her eyes and clinging to him, relieved that he was all right. That had been close. Entirely too close. If he hadn't reacted so quickly, she would have lost him.

After they had both recovered, they found a way around the jagged gash in the ice, though it took them several hours to get back on course. By then, they'd been walking for most of the day and were getting tired, despite breaks to rest and eat a little.

"We should stop and make camp. If we don't sleep, eat, and warm up a little, we're not going to last for long," Wade said as he stopped.

"Already? What time is it?"

"Red, we've been out here for six hours with only short breaks."

Given that they'd gotten to Antarctica around one in the afternoon local time, this surprised Paige. "There's no way. It's still as bright as when we got here," she protested.

"Yeah, but we're near the south pole. There won't be any nighttime for another month or so, and for a few months it won't get any sunlight at all," Wade explained with a shrug. "But the point remains that we need to rest, warm up, and eat."

After that, Paige didn't argue at all, just helped erect their shelter. Once inside, she ended up happily pressed between Wade and Julian, soaking in their warmth, as well as the warmth of the tent heater. It relaxed her, enough that she almost missed the fact that her visitor was back.

"We're being watched again," she whispered, leaning more fully into Julian. A minute passed before she shook her head. "It's gone, but it's the same mind I felt when we were in Brazil." Unfortunately, that was the only thing she was able to discern. Whoever kept peeking into her mind was nearly an expert at shielding.

"I really don't like that I can't smell anything when that happens," Wade growled. "Means either that person isn't here, or they're really damn good at hiding from me."

"I haven't sensed anything either," Julian admitted. "But maybe that means that we're getting close to the next piece, since you only have this visitor when we're near one."

"We're closer, yes, but it feels like we've still got a ways to go," Paige said reluctantly.

"You doing okay having it touching you constantly? It's not draining you, is it?"

She smiled and shook her head. "No, it's not. It's pulling me, like an impatient kid who sees a toy he wants, but it's not doing anything bad to me."

"You tell me if that changes, though. And I mean it, Paige. No playing around with this."

"He's right. If I'm worth more than a piece of that relic, then you definitely are," Wade added.

"I know, and I will. Any changes, however small, and I'll tell you. Cross my heart," Paige promised with a smile for them both.

"You'd better, Red," Wade said with a bump of his shoulder against hers.

She smiled at their concern as they pulled out food, though she was a bit skeptical of the MREs that Wade had found them. Quickly, she decided she was hungry enough that mud would taste good right now.

Despite her hunger, with the warmth in the tent she had nearly dozed off by the time food was ready, and ate in a daze before she finally did pass out, head on Julian's shoulder.

"She held up longer than I thought she would," Wade murmured once he was sure Paige was out.

"She may prefer to spend her time with books or in the garden, but there's no quit in her," Julian said with a faint smile as he gently eased Paige down onto her sleeping bag. "Didn't Brazil teach you that?"

"Yeah, but that's part of what I meant. After Brazil and the way she reacted to joining the two pieces...she was pretty well wiped." Wade grinned wickedly. "Then add in how you keep exhausting her..."

"Don't go there," Julian warned, but Wade just kept grinning.

"Just let her sleep tonight, all right?"

"That was the plan, but we should both get some rest, too," Julian said, stretching out beside Paige.

"That was the plan," Wade echoed.

Paige floated, her body pushed lazily by some breeze she couldn't feel. She was somewhere unfamiliar, but there wasn't any concern, any discomfort. This was a dream, and she knew it, but it was still a bit of a shock to find herself in a green and gold *peplos*. Wearing a piece of clothing that she knew was worn in ancient Greece made her wonder just where she was. Or when she was.

Her body was pulled across the landscape, and she marveled at how beautiful, how untouched it was. There were homes, yes, and farms, but none of the stories-high buildings or roads she was used to. The structures she did see were smaller and more primitive in design, and she didn't see a single glimpse of technology. Wherever she was, it was before industry had arrived to spoil the land.

She was drawn down into a simple stone building, flying through corridors until she reached a large room. The walls were absolutely covered with shelves, some holding books, some tools, others jars of various materials. A few even held what looked like crude bricks of metal in various shades of silver, copper, and gold. In the middle of the room was a heavy, scarred worktable with what looked like chemistry equipment on it, but something told Paige it would most likely be alchemy equipment. From all she'd read, she would have thought that would have come later, centuries later, but it was the only thing that made sense.

There were two men and a woman there, all dressed in fashion similar to her own outfit. One of the men was fairly average in height, build, and appearance except for his eyes, which were an astonishingly beautiful pale blue. The woman was similar enough in appearance, right down to the eye color, that Paige wondered if they were siblings. They were huddled together at the table, holding something and speaking quietly. Despite it being Ancient Greek, Paige could understand them easily, and knew they were speaking of the final touches needed to complete their work.

But it was the second man who really drew Paige's attention. He stood in the corner of the room, shrouded in shadows. Larger than the other man by almost a foot, and much more muscular, he watched the pair with his arms folded over his chest. Paige couldn't make out any of his features, yet somehow she knew when he turned his gaze to her.

"What are you doing here?" he asked, his voice gruff and gravely, but it wasn't unpleasant.

"I...don't know. I'm asleep, dreaming, and this is just where I ended up," she admitted. "I'm not even sure where here is. Greece, I think, judging by the language, but I'm not sure why I'm dreaming about ancient Greece, though."

He grunted. "If you think about that hard enough, I'm sure it'll come to you."

She frowned. "But I don't..." Then she realized what he meant. "I fell asleep with..." No, she shouldn't mention the relic, not even in her dreams, not with someone spying on her. But the fact that she fell asleep with it touching her skin might have something to do with it. The first time she'd held it, Julian had said she'd spoken the very language she was hearing now. "With Greece and magic on my mind."

"Liar," he said without heat. "But I don't blame you for your caution. It will serve you well. And yes, that's the reason why. What do you think it is they're holding?" he asked with a nod toward the pair.

Her gaze shifted and she caught a glimpse of a familiar silver disc. "Are you serious?" Paige asked, suddenly excited. She wished she could get closer, but she couldn't move. "That's fantastic!"

"For them, yes, at least for a time, but it's also what gets them killed," the man said without any emotion.

She frowned. "And who are you? How are you in my dream? How do you know all this?"

He chuckled. "If you think on those questions hard enough, the answers will come to you, too. But it's time to wake up now. And don't worry, you'll see me again."

"Wait, but I have—"

Before she could finish the sentence, Julian shook her shoulder, dragging her from her dream and back to reality.

CHAPTER 21

The moment Paige was conscious, she sat up abruptly, almost head-butting Julian in the face. She looked around, expecting to see the gruff-voiced man here, even though she knew it had just been a dream.

Julian sat back quickly and his brows lowered in concern. "What's wrong?"

"I..." She closed her eyes for a moment and shook her head. "Nothing. Nothing's wrong."

"C'mon, Red. I can smell the adrenaline from here. Something's got you worked up, and it isn't Julian for once," Wade chimed in as he offered her a cup of coffee.

Her cheeks flushed, but embarrassment wasn't high on her list of priorities at the moment. "No, really. Nothing's wrong. I just had a weird dream," she insisted as she took the cup and sipped.

"What sort of dream?" Julian asked.

Paige hesitated for a moment. Her instinct was to brush it off and get moving. Yes, it was a dream, and it had probably been brought about by contact with the amulet, but what if it was more than that? On the off chance, maybe she should tell them. "I was flying over ancient Greece. At least I'm almost certain it was Greece, judging by my clothes and the language spoken. It was definitely sometime extremely far back, because there weren't any signs of technology." She drew a slow breath. "I was pulled into a workshop of sorts in this large stone building. There were two people there—brother and sister, I think—working on an amulet." She touched her fingers to the amulet beneath her glove. "*This* amulet. It's like I was seeing into the past, to when it was made. And there was a man watching them. He seemed familiar, but I don't remember ever seeing a man that tall or muscular. He spoke to me."

Wade and Julian exchanged a look before Wade asked, "What'd he look like?"

"I don't know. He kept to the shadows."

"Well, what'd he say?"

"He asked why I was there, and when I refused to mention the amulet, he seemed to just know what I was thinking about, though I didn't feel anyone in my head. He said I was seeing the amulet as it was made. I think that the relic is why I had that dream. That touching it while I slept took me there."

"Damn. I hadn't considered that. You shouldn't sleep with it touching your skin anymore," Julian told her.

"Maybe, but I wouldn't mind if I did get another one," Paige said with a shake of her head. "It wasn't a bad dream, just odd. Especially when he answered my questions by telling me I just needed to think harder on the answers and I'd know."

Julian frowned. "What questions did you ask?"

Paige shrugged. "Who he was, how he was there, and how he knew what he knew."

"I don't know who he is, but as to how he was there? Red, you've had someone poking around in your head. Don't your defenses drop when you're asleep? Other defenses do, so why not magical ones? Could be it's the same guy," Wade pointed out.

"Maybe? But I knew it was a dream. I was just as coherent as I am now, and I really do think I would have felt if someone had been poking at me. But even if that's the case, it still doesn't answer the question of who he is."

"No, but I have a feeling it'll come to you. You have a knack for gleaning information from touching things, after all. And what is a mental connection by a sort of touching?" Julian pointed out. He still frowned, and Paige picked up on the waves of concern radiating off of him. He was acting nonchalant, but none of them liked knowing there was someone spying on them. On her.

"Julian, I'm all right. I promise. I may not like that someone was able to invade my dreams, but I didn't get any sense from him that he was trying to hurt me." The strange man had been a little irritated at first, but at the end, Paige thought he'd been more amused than anything. She just wished she knew who he was. Maybe he was someone who could help them. Three people doing a task that the gods had forbidden wasn't a lot, and there was strength in numbers. But she knew better than to suggest it to Julian, especially when he was already worried.

Julian studied her for a moment before he nodded. "Okay. We'll worry about it later. Right now, we should pack up and get going."

"Hell yeah," Wade agreed and started to shove things into his pack. "I don't want to spend one minute longer in this frozen hellhole than we have to. I'm freezing my fur off!"

Paige grinned and downed the rest of her coffee so she could start helping. "Can't argue with you there. First thing I'm doing when we get home is taking an hour long hot shower."

Under his breath, Julian gave her a heated look and muttered, "That makes two of us."

For the next several minutes, she didn't need anything else to keep her warm.

An hour later, they were packed up and well on their way. The relic was more insistent than it had been the previous night, and seemed to vibrate constantly inside Paige's glove, a sign they were getting closer.

"I swear this thing is more excited than we are to get the next piece," Paige told them with a little smile.

"Still dancing, huh?" Wade asked.

"It gets stronger almost every step I take."

"At least we know we're on the right track."

"Very true, but I think I'd have to be half dead not to be able to follow its directions at this point," she said with a laugh.

"Well, let's try to avoid that particular state of being," Julian said dryly.

"I can't argue with that," she said with a bright smile.

Only half an hour later, the amulet was beyond insistent when they finally reached the mountain range and stopped at a cliff. It seemed to go up forever, with only one ledge visible from the ground.

"Let me guess," Julian said with a sigh. "We've got to climb that?"

Paige stared upward as she let the relic tug on her mind then gave him an apologetic look. "I'm afraid so. It's up, though I can't tell how far."

He sighed. "Right. Well, I'm going to pop up to that ledge and check it out. Hopefully, there are more of them, so we can jump from one to the other until we're as high as we need to go. It's more than I wanted to do, but it's safer than the alternative. I'll be right back."

"Sounds good." Paige waited a moment, two, then a full minute before she asked hesitantly, "Why aren't you going?"

Julian's brow was furrowed, his eyes narrowed in concentration. "I'm trying. It's not working. Nothing is. My magic is blocked. Damn!"

Wincing, Paige tested her own powers, and felt the loss of the comforting feel of Julian and Wade. They were still there, but sensing them was difficult, as though they were on the other side of a thick wall. "It's not just you." She shivered, but it had nothing to do with the cold. She wondered how she had missed that. Yes, Julian tended to shield his mind and emotions, but Wade tended to be an open book, and she hadn't noticed the lack of wolfish emotions. Had it happened gradually, perhaps? That was the only thing she could think of that might explain how she hadn't realized she couldn't feel either of them.

"Could it be the amulet?" Wade asked. "You did say it left Paige drained the first time she touched it."

Julian shook his head. "No, because I haven't touched it in days. And my magic isn't gone, it's blocked. I can feel that it's still there, but I can't access it. It's like the temple, except it's not just teleportation that isn't working."

"He's right," Paige agreed before she looked up at the cliff. "I supp ose...we'll have to climb." It wasn't something she was looking forward to. She'd never done it before, and though Wade had mentioned that he was an experienced climber, the thought of actually doing it still made her nervous.

"Yes, we'll have to climb, but I promise I'm not going to let you fall, Red. I won't let either of you fall," Wade assured her.

She gave him a weak smile as he unpacked the gear. He studied the ledge for a moment, before saying, "We might want to take a quick breather here and eat before we go up. This might end up taking us a few hours, and we don't know what we'll find up there. Besides, the cliff is blocking most of the wind. And it'll give me a chance to explain what to do."

The others agreed and Julian got out the tent heater while Paige unpacked energy bars and a thermos full of coffee. Luckily, it was still hot, so the combination of that, the heater, and the break from the winds did warm them up some. It didn't hurt that Paige plastered herself against Julian's side, making the most of their body heat.

Wade patiently explained the mechanics of climbing and how they'd be harnessed in, but with all of Paige's questions, it took longer than the few minutes they'd wanted to spend. Eventually, Paige ran out of things to ask, though, and it was time to head up. She watched nervously as Wade got her harnessed, double-checking that she was secure before he got Julian situated. Wade went first, with Paige and Julian tied to him with ropes. If someone fell, he promised that he was strong enough to support them.

But Wade and Julian gave the nervous Paige a look, then silently agreed. If something did happen, they'd save Paige over each other.

Paige was too busy staring at the cliff in trepidation to notice the exchange. When they began the climb she was terrified, but desperate to hide it. The first half hour was the worst, but it wasn't an easy climb, so it took the hours Wade had predicted for them to reach the ledge, especially with two inexperienced climbers. More than once Paige had lost a foothold or handhold, but with Wade's help, had regained her footing and continued on.

Once they reached the ledge, instead of finding someplace to just sit and rest for a few minutes, they were pleased to find that it was partially shielded and large enough for their tent.

Though Julian wanted to press on for a little longer and try to reach the next ledge, or even the cave, he saw the weariness on Paige's face, the heaviness of her limbs. This was a lot more than she was used to. Than he was used to, for that matter. "We'll camp here for the night."

"What? On a ledge?" Paige asked, eyes wide.

He smiled. "It's big enough for the tent, and you're not going to knock the tent over. Besides, we'll put you between us so you'll be warm and stay in place," he assured her. Though he still didn't like Paige sleeping beside Wade, he knew it was safer for her, and warmer. And he knew she wouldn't turn to Wade in the middle of the night. She would turn to him.

Her nervousness about sleeping a hundred feet above the ground warred with the absolute exhaustion she felt. It didn't take much to convince her to give in. It took even less to convince her to let them set up the tent while she rested.

By the time camp was set up she was half-asleep, so Julian carried her inside, took the amulet from her glove, and settled her in her sleeping bag.

She stirred when he zipped her in, her eyes half opening. "Julian?" she murmured.

"Yes? Do you want something to eat before you go to sleep?"

She gave her head a tiny shake. "No. Don't go far?"

"Wouldn't dream of it," he said quietly as he bent and kissed her temple.

Her lips curved sleepily, and she was out cold before he'd straightened.

Wade was watching them, and when Julian caught his eye, he smiled. "You're a goner."

Though he wanted to protest, Julian said nothing, just slipped into his own bag and pressed close to Paige.

He was very much afraid that Wade was right.

CHAPTER 22

They slept deeply after the exertion the day before, and only the alarm Wade had set on his watch kept them from sleeping too long.

Though no one was eager to leave the warmth of their sleeping bags or the tent, they quickly ate, had their coffee, and packed up. The sooner they found the piece, the sooner they could leave this frigid piece of hell.

Unfortunately, the climbing went no quicker than it had the day before, so it was nearly four hours later when they found a cave. The opening was little more than a horizontal slit in the side of the cliff, about twelve feet across and five feet high. It had been invisible from the ground and had appeared on none of the satellite images Julian and Wade had poured over. But no one could argue with the insistent thrumming Paige felt from the amulet as they stared at the icy mouth. A thrumming that had her starting forward. Clearer heads held her back, though, and made her put the piece away.

"Remember the temple. We don't know what's in here, or how it'll react to the amulet," Julian cautioned.

Sheepishly, she nodded as she slid the piece into an inside pocket of her pack. It was more difficult to stop touching it now than it had been, but she knew they were right.

They pulled out their flashlights—and Wade's headlamp—once they were free of the climbing gear so they could examine their surroundings.

The cave walls were smooth and looked to be made of ice as much as stone. Snow and ice had been pushed into the mouth of the cave and formed snowdrifts, but after a dozen or so feet, they all but disappeared. Paige almost regretted that fact, since otherwise the cave seemed somehow sterile, lifeless. Not, she thought wryly, that the rest of what she'd seen in Antarctica had been teeming with life. But the cave was essentially an oblong tube without the snow to soften the lines of it. There were no niches or tunnels she could see from their vantage point, not even any carvings. Just bare stone and ice. It even smelled barren. The only thing that the cave had in abundance was echoes. Like the temple, the smallest of movements against the stone was magnified, so all three stepped carefully to avoid deafening themselves.

Or alerting any guards this piece may have.

They started down the passage in silence, surprised when they'd walked several minutes without coming across another tunnel. The passage they were in sloped gently downward and curved back and forth like a snake slithering through the stone. But so far they'd found none of what they'd expected. No guards, no traps, no danger. The one oddity was something that Wade noticed.

He stopped and tilted his head back so his light shined on the ceiling of the cave. "This is weird...This tunnel is just nothing but the same, right? It twists and turns, but otherwise it's the same damn thing over and over. Which is kind of creepy, by the way. But look at this," he said, pointing to a section of the ceiling.

Both Julian and Page shifted their gaze upward, and she frowned as she studied the grooves in the stone. "What are those?" she asked.

"Not sure, but they started a few feet back," Wade answered with a shrug. "I get there not being any stalagmites or anything because hey, no liquid water, but these?" He shook his head.

"I honestly don't know, either. It doesn't look like anything natural, but I also can't say I'm an expert on caves," Julian murmured, curious as well. He backtracked some and followed the progression of the marks. The grooves were only on the ceiling, and they varied in length and depth. Some were straight, while others curved or zigzagged. "It could be that the cave was created by the gods when they hid the piece here. Not that I know what the purpose or meaning behind these may be, but it's the only thing I can think of offhand."

That answer was good enough for Wade, at least for now, and they continued on.

Paige was the first one to spot the skeleton ten minutes later. Before she could think better of it, she screamed. Wade pulled out a wicked-looking knife, while Julian shoved her behind him.

Embarrassed, she leaned against Julian's back. "Sorry. The skeleton...I've never seen one before, outside of a museum, and it...startled me," she told them, voice partially muffled by Julian.

Both men relaxed, and though she worried she'd lost face in their eyes, Wade just gave her an amused look. "Don't worry about it, Red. No one reacts well when they see their first," he told her, giving her shoulder a squeeze. "I may have given an unmanly shriek the first time I saw a skeleton."

She sincerely doubted that, but appreciated the effort.

Julian went a step further, drawing her into his arms while Wade checked out the bones. "It's okay, no harm done. Though if you see another, please spare my ears and just point?" he asked her, but there was humor in his tone. The scream wouldn't have been quiet under normal circumstances, but with the cave bouncing the sound back at them, it had been almost deafening.

Blushing, she nodded.

Crouched by the skeleton, Wade called, "Hey guys?"

"What is it?" Paige asked.

"There are teeth marks on these bones." He glanced up. "And I don't mean animal teeth," he said grimly. "Not that there are any animals living in this part of the continent anyway, but..."

"Cannibalism?" Julian asked with surprise.

"Looks like it, yeah."

"You mean like...someone got stranded here and had no other way to survive?" Paige asked. It wasn't a fantastic scenario, but it was far better than some of the ones running through her head.

No one answered, and she swallowed down her sudden nausea.

They got moving again, and when they found a second set of bones fifteen minutes later, Wade looked at them just long enough to determine that they, too, had human-looking teeth marks on them.

Before they could move on, they heard a scraping sound from behind them. It sounded big, but it was hard to tell if that was the cave amplifying the sound or a real indication of size. Paige's mind immediately flashed to the spiders from the Amazon temple and she shuddered. Wade lifted his head to catch the scent, but whatever he got made him frown and motion for them to continue further into the cave.

The sound followed them, so they kept going, with Wade searching for some place more defensible than an open tunnel. Before he could find one, they almost ran right into three figures.

They were humanoid, but Paige couldn't bring herself to call them human. They were shrunken and starved, with almost no meat on their bodies, so their bones protruded obscenely. Instead of nails, they had long claws that glittered like diamonds. The clothing they wore was ragged, hanging in pieces that covered almost nothing. Their skin had a faint blue tinge to it, while their hair was the same blue she had seen in photos of glaciers. But what frightened her the most was that their irises were an unnatural glowing red.

And every one of them radiated the same emotion, more intense than anything Paige had ever felt before. An emotion so strong it broke through whatever was hindering her powers.

Hunger.

One of the figures, the only woman, let out a low moan. "So hun gry..."

Behind them was the sound of something falling, and she glanced back to see a fourth figure. He must have been on the ceiling—which explained the gouges in the stone—herding them toward the others until he joined them, trapping the trio between four apparently starving ice elementals. For Paige could think of nothing else these four could be with their coloring and lack of discomfort from the cold. They could be elementalists, she supposed, but she was fairly certain that, being witches, they'd look more...human.

Julian tried to reason with them, even as Wade helpfully pressed a machete into his hand. "We have food. We'll be happy to share with you."

"Starving…" said another of the figures, this one a tall man. "Trapped so long without food…Can't even transform. Need to eat…"

No one doubted that they were intended to be the meal for these pitiful creatures, even before the first lunged toward them and latched onto Julian's arm.

Wade stepped forward, putting himself between Paige and one of the men as he warded off another with one of his knives. Paige didn't know where the second weapon come from, but she was happy to see it.

Not wanting to get in the way, and knowing she was unable to really help, Paige did her best to stay back while the other two fought.

Julian swung his machete toward the elemental that had released him and decided to try to get to Paige. He caught the figure on the arm, but Paige had to jump aside to avoid getting hit by claws. It was then that the smallest—and sneakiest—of the group grabbed her by the ankle and pulled. The combination of that and the slick ice of the floor had her landing hard on her back. It knocked the breath out of her so she couldn't even scream as she was dragged deeper into the cave.

Still, Julian noticed and yelled her name, but couldn't break away from the one he was fighting. He went berserk, striking faster, harder, but the elementals, for all that they were starved, were desperate, quick, and managed to avoid his blows. At least until the heavy blade caught his opponent across the throat. The elemental staggered back, hands flying to his throat, where deep blue blood poured out, staining the front of his body.

"Wade!" Julian yelled as he took off down the tunnel after Paige, trusting that the wolf was skilled enough to take the remaining man and the woman without dying. Though if he was honest, he could admit that he would have gone after Paige even without trusting in Wade's abilities. He couldn't let anything happen to her.

There was no caution in his steps, so he slipped as he ran, once going down entirely and landing hard on his side. His head cracked against the unforgiving stone floor, causing light to burst behind his eyes. Ahead, he heard Paige finally scream and, dazed, struggled back to his feet to follow the sounds, ignoring the sharp pain in his head.

The cries ended abruptly and made his heart stutter.

He rushed around the next curve and into a chamber, only to slide to a stop, his eyes widening.

Paige was scrambling back from the elemental, who lay on the floor, blood gushing from a wound on his head. A rock, coated in thick blue fluid, lay beside him. His movements were sluggish, almost imperceptible, but he was still trying to reach Paige. Still trying to feed.

"No, no, no, no..." Paige repeated, her voice low but tinged with hysteria as she pressed her back against the wall, as far away from the dying figure as she could get. Even then, it looked like she was trying to crawl backward up the wall to get away. One of her coat sleeves had been ripped off at the elbow and there was a deep bite mark on her forearm that was bleeding heavily.

"Paige?" he said gently as he went to her, and she threw her arms over her face as though expecting a blow.

"No! I had to!" she cried.

He reached for her and she struggled against him, but Julian wouldn't let her go until she was cradled in his lap, his arms tight around her. He turned with her head held against his chest, so she couldn't see the body.

"I know, baby. I know," he soothed, kissing her hair, her forehead, her cheek. "It's okay. You didn't have any choice. You were protecting yourself."

She was crying now, sobs that wracked her body and broke his heart a little. But she no longer fought him, instead clinging to him as she struggled with the fact that she'd killed someone. That it had been an elemental crazed by hunger didn't matter. She'd taken a life.

He murmured to her and began stroking her hair. Slowly, she began to calm, until sobs were replaced by hiccups.

Wade ran into the chamber, knives out, blood—blue, not red—on his arms and face, though one of his sleeves had been clawed and his blood stained the cloth. A similar wound was on his calf, but overall he wasn't hurt too badly. His appearance made Paige cringe and tense again, but Julian just held her.

"It's okay, sweetheart. It's just Wade. You're safe now. I promise, you're safe."

The shifter quickly took in the scene and sheathed his knives. When Julian nodded to the body, then out into the tunnel, Wade understood and picked it up, removing it from the chamber. Letting Julian tend to Paige, he moved all the bodies into another chamber so Paige wouldn't have to see them again.

Her frenzy of guilt had subsided by the time he returned, and she was laying calmly against Julian, sniffling occasionally.

"You okay, Red?" he asked gently.

Paige nodded once.

"Julian?"

"I'm not hurt," he answered, choosing not to mention the bump on his head, before shifting so Paige's gaze went to the far side of the room. "And look."

Built into the wall itself was an altar made of ice. Sitting atop it was another wedge-shaped piece of silver.

"We found it?" she asked softly.

"We did." He set her on her feet and gave her a light push toward it.

Hesitating only briefly, she went to the altar and picked it up with a gloved hand. With her other she drew out the half she had, unsurprised when the pieces yanked themselves together, forming almost three quarters of a circle.

There was no glow since she didn't touch the object with her skin, but there was still a moment where her gaze went unfocused before the amulet was put away.

"What happened? Did you get something from it?" Julian asked. If she had, it would be the first time without skin-to-skin contact.

"Not like you mean," Paige whispered with a shake of her head as she walked back to him. "Just got a jolt of happiness from it. I guess it was strong enough that I didn't need to be in direct contact with it."

"You have partially reassembled it, so it makes sense that it would be more powerful than when it was just one small piece."

Paige smiled, though it was thin. "Good point."

"It's too late for us to climb back down. I found an empty cave big enough for the tent. Why don't we rest here tonight, then tomorrow we'll get the hell out of this place?" Wade suggested. "It's the first tunnel once you go back toward the entrance."

"All right," Paige said quietly before leaving the chamber, her steps slow, her shoulders hunched.

After she'd left, Wade turned to Julian, both of them frowning. "Did she kill him?" he asked softly, so the sound wouldn't carry. When Julian nodded, he cursed under his breath. "Her first?"

Again, there was a nod. "And she's such a sensitive person, so careful not to hurt anyone that...she isn't taking it well." He sighed. "Help me keep an eye on her? Especially until we get home?"

"Of course." Wade smiled faintly. "I care about Red too, you know." Julian's eyes flashed darkly and made Wade chuckle. "Not in the same way, so relax. Not that she's ever looked at me that way with you around," he couldn't resist adding. Whistling tunelessly, he followed after Paige.

After tending to their injuries using the first aid kit Wade had packed, they collapsed in the tent, exhausted. Wade was out in under a minute, but Julian was awake longer, holding Paige as she was assaulted by nightmares of the life she had ended to save her own.

CHAPTER 23

The next morning Paige was still acting distant and depressed, and even Wade's antics couldn't draw more than a weak smile out of her, though he tried his hardest.

When Wade stepped out to relieve himself, Julian took her into his arms and kissed her, but her response was half-hearted at best.

He sighed and leaned his head against hers as he rubbed a hand over her back. "It'll be all right, Paige. You can't keep beating yourself up like this. You saved yourself, nothing more," he murmured.

"But he's still dead because of me," she whispered.

"No, he's dead because someone, probably some egotistical ass of a god, put him here where he would starve," he corrected. He thought it prudent not to mention that the elementals were likely guarding the very thing they'd come to collect. The thing that resided in her pocket. Guarding the relic and kept hungry so they would eagerly devour any who wandered too close to it.

Unconvinced, she said only, "Maybe..."

"There's no maybe about it, Paige. If you hadn't done what you did, you would have died." His arms tightened at the thought, until it was hard for her to breathe. When she squirmed a little, he relaxed his hold.

"Don't die on me. Promise me, okay?" he whispered hoarsely against her hair.

Stunned by the depth of the emotion in those words, Paige's arms crept around him. "I promise." It made sense to her that he wouldn't want to see anyone die, not after he'd watched Mary die. It also made her feel a little better. Besides, if the elemental had killed her, it might have gotten one of them, too.

"You two about ready to go?" Wade asked when he returned, his voice more cheerful than he felt. He was relieved to see that Paige wasn't just allowing herself to be held, but holding Julian in return. It was progress.

"I just want to check Paige's arm once more, then we can go." Reluctantly, he let go of her so he could, and though the color of the wounds worried him, he reassured himself that, once they were away from the influence that was blocking his magic, he could heal her. He had never studied proper medicine, not when magic was quicker and more efficient, but he decided to correct the lack as soon as possible.

After cleaning the bite as well as he could with limited supplies and putting on a new bandage, they gathered their things and went to the edge of the cliff. Going down was quicker than climbing up had been, but it still took time and its toll on the already worn trio. They took a short break for food on the ledge where they'd stayed the first night, before deciding to continue on. All three of them wanted off this continent and back to where they had their powers. Julian pushed harder than the others. He'd grown too dependent on using magic to heal, and he didn't like the fact that Paige's wound could potentially get infected. Not to mention Wade's several injuries didn't look that great either, and his own head was throbbing despite the painkillers he'd taken with breakfast.

Once on the ground, they only gave themselves fifteen minutes to rest before they started walking away from the cliff. They knew the moment that they were beyond the dampening field, because Paige could suddenly feel the strong concern for her from both men, and made a soft sound.

"It's back," she whispered, her tone wondering as she looked from Julian to Wade. To their surprised relief, she suddenly smiled at them. The guilt was still there, but it was no longer quite the burden it had been before she knew how much they cared. She didn't sense any sort of condemnation from them, just concern, and it lifted her heavy heart.

Just knowing that they had access to their powers again had some of the tension leaving both male bodies. Neither had liked having part of them inhibited.

Paige shivered and glanced around, frowning.

Wade caught the frown and his hand went to the hilt of his knife. "Someone watching us again?"

"Yes. The same person as before," she verified with a nod. She didn't believe he meant her harm, but that didn't mean he was necessarily on her side. "Julian, get us out of here, please."

He nodded once and reached out to lay a hand on their shoulders. "Happily."

When they appeared in the entrance hall of Mooreton, they all breathed a sigh of relief. Moving quicker than any of them thought they could, they dropped their packs and stripped out of the heavy clothing. Clothing Paige considered burning, since it was torn, dirty, and meant for a place she never wanted to return to.

"I hope your water heater can handle three showers, Julian, because that's my first stop, and it's going to be as hot as I can get it," Wade said, yanking his shirt off in anticipation.

"Healing first," Julian told him, though his eyes were on Paige.

When Wade started to protest, Paige simply said, "Please," and he subsided. His injuries were minor compared to theirs, especially Paige's bite, but he stood quietly while Julian healed him. He grinned and kissed Paige's cheek. "There, all better now, Mom." Before they could think of something else to keep him from the bliss a hot shower would bring, he ran up the stairs, taking them two at a time.

Turning to Julian, Paige lightly touched the injury on his head. She could feel the pain radiating from it, even though he'd never mentioned the wound. Within moments, the dull throbbing had ceased. The weariness remained, as did the swollen bump itself, but he could handle that easier without pain as a distraction. A hot meal and good night's sleep would take care of the weariness. What was worse was the lingering fear he had for her. Even holding her tightly while she slept hadn't eased it.

He cupped her arm beneath the bite wound, then laid his lips over hers while he healed the wound. It wasn't a hot, passionate kiss like the ones she had become used to, but tender and full of some emotion she was hesitant to name. It made her head swim until she felt dizzy and grabbed hold of him to steady herself.

By the time he drew back, her heart was pounding, and she felt a yearning more potent than anything she'd ever felt. She stared up at him and wanted to tell him how she felt, what she wanted, but held back. His heart was still healing, and it had taken a beating the day before. Taking that next step right now wouldn't be good for either of them. Resolving to give him time, she loosened her grip and said softly, "I'm going to go take a shower, too."

He nodded and let her go, but was only a few steps behind her as she walked up the stairs. Before she could veer into the bathroom off her bedroom, he took her hand, leading her into his room and through to his bathroom. Afraid to say anything and break this curious spell, she simply followed.

The water was turned on before he turned back to her. His hands were gentle as he pulled the remainder of her clothes off a piece at a time, taking care to kiss each inch of pale flesh the moment it was revealed. So by the time he drew her into the shower with him, every cell in her body was vibrating with a need that went beyond just the physical.

He was just as gentle as he bathed her, not letting her do anything to help. It wasn't a hardship to be tended to, either, she realized. The feel of his hands in her hair, working the shampoo into it, was immensely relaxing, and she couldn't help but moan softly and lean into him. And when he decided to forgo using a washcloth to spread soap over her skin and instead used his hands, she had to bite her lip to silence a whimper. His every touch was as careful as though she were some fragile, priceless object that he cherished, and it made her heart clench. She wasn't fragile, but feeling cherished was a new sensation for her. One she thought she could easily get addicted to.

There was no rush in his movements, though she clearly sensed a strong need within him. It was only then that she realized that he wasn't shielding his mind from her for the first time since they had met. He wanted this as much as she did, not just to touch and sate his body with hers, but to satisfy that yearning which went so much deeper. Though she'd wanted so badly for him to open up to her like this, she hesitated to look too deep. Hesitated to put a name to the emotion she felt from him. If she misread it, believed he felt more for her than he did, she wasn't sure how she'd handle it.

When he went to his knees to soap her legs and feet, she was forced to lean against the shower wall to brace herself. And that was before he gently lifted one of her legs and draped it over his shoulder.

Knowing what he intended to do, Paige's breathing quickened. He caught her gaze and held it as he started to caress her with his mouth. Each stroke of his tongue was like a brush of sweet fire against her and her breath caught. And, like in his care of her, he wasn't in any rush, taking his time to lick and tease her sensitive flesh. Her eyes fluttered closed on a groan and stayed that way until he nipped at her thigh, just hard enough to get her attention. Her eyes flew open and he kissed the spot he'd just bitten. "I want to watch your eyes," he told her, voice rough with hunger. "I want to see you watching me."

When she made no attempt to look away, his mouth found her again, and he was merciless in his loving of her. He used only his mouth to touch her, and she felt branded by it. Her legs weakened under the onslaught, but he easily supported her while his tongue delved inward. When she began to writhe against him, he moved slightly upward to torment her sensitive clit, wanting nothing more than to see her shatter for him.

Too breathless from the pleasure to scream when she came, Paige could only whisper his name as she trembled helplessly and gripped his shoulder, hard enough to leave crescent moon indentations from her nails.

With one last kiss, he set her leg down then rose to his feet. Using his powers to shut the water off, he gently picked her up and carried her into the bedroom. Disregarding the water that dripped off them both, he carefully laid her on the bed and settled himself between her legs. He slid a hand up to her thigh and drew her leg up, letting him move closer to her. In one smooth motion, he was buried inside her and his mouth was over hers, her sigh of pleasure mingling with his groan.

This was no frantic coupling, no rush for the physical release that would come at the end. As he kissed her deeply, as he slid into her again and again, the part of her mind that still functioned realized that she'd never felt so wanted or needed.

So loved.

Her mind tried to tell her that he still loved his wife, not her, but she couldn't hold on to those thoughts for more than a heartbeat. She was going to enjoy what she was given and not question it. Not now.

Minutes later, when she came apart for him again, he was there with her, tumbling after. Not yet done, he savored her body with his hands and mouth until he was recovered so he could love again, and again, until they fell asleep, limbs tangled together in a deep, dreamless sleep.

When Paige woke the next morning, it was with the expectation that Julian would already be gone, as had been his routine the week before they left for Antarctica. What she got instead was the feel of him sinking slowly into her, her body easily accepting him. She let out a soft, happy cry and lifted her hips to meet him, her arms finding their way around him once more.

He kissed her lingeringly, then whispered against her mouth, "Good morning," before he set out to exhaust her one more time.

CHAPTER 24

It was hours later when they finally dragged themselves from bed and each other, and even then it was only hunger that drove them. They found Wade in the kitchen, a very knowing—and happy—look on his face.

Paige found it hard to blush—she was entirely too happy and sated for that—and just smiled at him as she fixed herself a sandwich.

"Morning. You two sleep well?" Wade teased.

"When I slept," Julian answered as he watched Paige's every movement, looking and sounding utterly satisfied. The hesitation he'd previously had with showing affection toward Paige was gone. She was his lover as well as his friend, and he was finally acting like it.

"Red? Tell me you've got a sister. Maybe a cousin would work. Or an aunt?" Wade asked her playfully. "C'mon, throw a wolf a bone."

She grinned and patted his cheek. "Sorry, Wade, I'm one of a kind."

He feigned a resigned sigh. "Isn't that always the way?"

Julian grinned. "I'd say sorry, but...I'm really not," he said smugly.

"Who can blame you?" Wade asked with a laugh. "So, we going to venture down to the secret sanctum to find the next piece once you guys are done eating?"

"That's the plan," Julian confirmed with a nod.

Her sandwich made, Paige took a bite, then said, "It's still in my coat pocket. I'll grab it and meet you two down there?" After getting their assent, she went to the entrance hall, finding all of their gear right where it had been dropped. She started to dig for the amulet before remembering that she wasn't wearing gloves now. Instead, she dug in her pack for a bandage. It wasn't ideal, but it would keep the metal from touching her skin.

Just as she found the partially completed amulet and pulled it out, she stilled. The mental presence was back. It didn't *feel* dangerous, but it made her decidedly uneasy.

"Who are you?" she whispered, projecting her thoughts toward the unknown watcher. "Why are you watching me?"

Unfortunately, rather than any real answer, she felt the presence grow stronger for two heartbeats then recede to nothing once again.

"That's getting annoying," she muttered as she straightened and took another bite.

She'd finished her sandwich and shaken off the mild annoyance by the time she joined the men in Julian's workshop. She set the amulet on the table and unwrapped it before she sat down. Wade was, once again, standing, so she said, "We're going to need to get a chair down here for you. It feels rude to sit while you always have to stand."

Wade grinned. "No need for that. If I get tired, I know how to sit on a table."

Not entirely sure he was joking, Paige just smiled and moved on. "I got a glimpse of the next piece when I put them together. It was sort of lost in the surge of happiness, so I didn't realize it at the time, but thinking on it now, it's a little more clear."

"How? You were wearing gloves," Julian said with a frown.

"I honestly don't know," she admitted. "Unless we were right and having three pieces instead of one just makes it that much stronger, which does make sense. Why wouldn't it be more intense as it becomes more complete? What I don't understand is how it happened when we were in a place that magic doesn't work."

"Good point." Julian frowned at the amulet, more than halfway complete, and shook his head. "I have theories, but it would be hard to test them. It could be that it's because it holds more magic than we do, or maybe this particular relic was created by a god. I don't imagine we'll get an answer anytime soon on that one, though. For now, what did you get from it?"

"A lake. Which isn't much help, I know. There are thousands of lakes in the world."

"More like millions. You just be damn careful when you touch that thing, Red," Wade said seriously. "If that thing's stronger, given what it's already nearly done to you…it could be dangerous. You nearly got hypothermia from it last time." Which meant he was afraid she was going to drown holding the piece now. Not an unreasonable fear, she could admit, but not one she felt.

Paige smiled reassuringly. "I know, and I'm not going to be reckless about it. I've already shielded my mind very carefully. I promise," she said, directing that to both of them. "I've experienced intense pain and cold from this. I have plenty of reasons to be cautious, believe me."

Neither looked that reassured, but Paige reached out and picked up the amulet once more. No one was surprised or really reacted when she tensed or her eyes turned into green spotlights this time. She didn't cry out in pain or arch unnaturally, so they let her be. Even the quickened breathing was allowed, so long as it was the worst she suffered. But they hovered nearby, just in case the amulet chose not to be so benign.

"Deep. Gods, so very, very deep. It seems to go on for forever. It doesn't feel like I'm ever going to see the bottom," she panted softly. "But it's...I can see further than I should be able to, it's so clear. Not like a pool, the color's wrong for that, but not like any body of water I've ever seen. I...it freezes now and again, sometimes with ice thicker than a man is tall,"

Wade shifted slightly with recognition, but didn't interrupt, so she never noticed.

"I can't see the actual piece, but it's at the bottom of the lake somewhere, further than anyone should be able to go." She frowned and cocked her head. "I can feel...there's something—no, several somethings protecting it, but I can't tell what they are. I don't know if it's an animal like the jaguars or a person like the elementals." She shook her head, her body going taut. "Something's blocking me. Something—" She broke off and let out an anguished scream, dropping the amulet, so it clattered on the table. The scream didn't end when the contact did, so it was obviously not the amulet doing this to her. Not this time.

Not knowing what to do, Wade looked helplessly at Julian, who dove over the table. He cradled her head in his hands, then hissed with pain. "Something's attacking her," he said between his teeth. He closed his eyes and touched her mind, working past the invading entity—gods, it had simply shredded all her shields—so he could help her fight back and pull away from it.

Sweat beaded on his forehead from the effort as he shoved past the intruder and gave Paige all the strength he could. Minutes ticked by, but Paige's screams gradually turned into low whimpers as the attack began to abate. Having freed her, Julian remained in her mind, soothing her and easing the pain. By the time he was done he was breathing hard, but that didn't stop him from picking her up. He returned to his seat, settling her across his lap and holding her protectively in his arms.

"What the hell was that?" Wade asked, casting a wary look at the amulet.

"Something felt me looking, and didn't like it," Paige answered weakly. "It tried to..." She swallowed. "Tried to kill me."

"Was it the person who's been watching you?"

She shook her head before she rested it on Julian's shoulder. "No, it felt different. This one was entirely aggressive, but the other feels...curious. Like he only wants to see what I'm going to do. I keep getting the impression that he doesn't mean me any harm."

She was surprised to realize just how unafraid she was of the secretive watcher. She was curious, yes, even mildly annoyed, but not afraid. Whoever it was hadn't allowed anything of themselves to leak to her, but she would have wagered money that they didn't want to hurt her or stop them from reassembling the relic. More, she was certain the visitor was male, but she couldn't have explained why.

But the person who had attacked her today? That person she was terrified of.

Julian's lips brushed her brow, and the obvious display of affection in front of Wade had Paige relaxing a little more and even smiling a bit. "Are you sure?" he asked.

"I am. I felt him when I went to grab the relic, and I'm almost sure the man from my dreams is the watcher. This one? It just wanted to stop me from finding out where the next piece was."

"Too late for that," Wade said, dropping down into Paige's abandoned chair. He suddenly had two sets of eyes fixed on him, and he chuckled despite his worry.

"How so?" Julian asked as he stroked a hand gently up and down Paige's arm.

"A couple years back, I was tracking a rogue shifter," Wade began, putting his feet up on the table and leaning back nonchalantly. "Ended up going through Russia to do it. Along the way, I came across this lake. The water was insanely clear. It'd look like a boat was in just a few feet of water, but it'd be twenty or thirty feet deep. Now, as it happens, this lake also happens to be the deepest lake in the world. So it seems like it'd fit all the descriptions you gave me. It even freezes in places in the winter."

Excitement began to shine in Paige's weary eyes as he pulled out his phone. A few taps later, he was turning it around to show her a picture. "Was this the lake you saw?"

She took the phone from him and studied it, her brows furrowing as she considered. After a minute, she slowly nodded. "I think it is. It's a different angle, a different part of the lake, but this?" she said, circling her finger around one portion of the picture. "The area around it? It looks right."

"Well then, my friends. We're going to Russia. To Lake Baikal." Before Paige could get too worked up, he lifted a hand. "But there are problems."

Paige frowned and offered his phone back. "Like what?"

"When I said it was the deepest lake in the world, I meant it. I was curious enough about the lake that I did a bit of research after." He shot a grin at Julian. "I know that's your specialty, but don't worry, it was just a one time thing. But I found out that it's damn near a mile deep in some places. Keep in mind that the deepest dive, with scuba, is only around a thousand feet, and they recommend that most people don't go much past a hundred. You need special equipment to go down to a few hundred, even."

"Um...can you translate that to meters?" Paige asked.

Wade laughed. "You Brits. Deepest dive is about three hundred meters, but recommended is around forty. And we may have to go a kilometer and a half to get what we're after," he told her helpfully. "So, not even counting any guards or magical traps, we have to figure out how in the hell we just get down there. There are submersibles, of course, but I don't figure they'd be easy to get a hold of, or cheap." His eyes fixed on Julian. "Even for you."

The excitement was gone, replaced by dismay, but only for Paige. Julian was starting to smile.

"I think our fearless leader has an idea," Wade said, a brow arching.

"I might." Paige shifted around to look at him as he went on, and he just drew her closer to his chest. "There's a spell I came across once, and have a copy of, that's supposed to allow a person to not only breathe water, but also help with the pressure at great depths. It was meant for the ocean, which is a great deal deeper than this lake."

"That's fantastic! How long will it take you to do it?" Paige asked, beaming at him.

"Slow down," he warned. "I've never actually done the spell. I had no reason to, since there don't tend to be books underwater, and even water demons tend to stay in the more shallow areas. Besides, you know how tricky spells can be to use."

Her smile dimmed. "Oh. That's true..."

He smiled. "But I'm sure I can figure it out. I'll test it at the little lake not too far from here. Shouldn't take more than a day to get it worked out, which will give us all time to recover from Antarctica. You'll see. We'll be heading for Russia in no time."

Despite his confidence and assurances, it took several days.

The first day was spent locating the spell and doing research on it, to make sure that he'd be able to maintain it on three people for the length of time they were likely to need. On day two, he was ready to put it to the test.

At Paige's insistence, his first attempt wasn't made in the lake, but in a full bathtub, with both herself and Wade present. He'd warned them not to overreact if it didn't seem like it was working at first, which is why he inhaled more water than any of them would have liked before they yanked him out and did mouth-to-mouth. Neither of them would allow him to attempt it again that day, even after Paige had thoroughly examined him and he'd promised that he was perfectly fine.

The second try went better, after he'd corrected a few mistranslated words. After several tense moments it became obvious that he was actually breathing underwater. He'd told Paige via telepathy to let him stay there, so he could test the duration of the spell. Unfortunately, it wore off after only just a few minutes. Fortunately, they knew what to look for, so this time he didn't swallow quite so much water.

It took another day for him to work out the kinks—he hoped—for another try. He insisted that this attempt actually be at the lake, arguing that laying in a bathtub for an hour was boring and they knew that the spell would work at least for a few minutes. When Wade backed him up, Paige gave in, but only with the caveat that she link with him mentally in case something went wrong. He agreed, but the link turned out not to be necessary. For more than an hour he swam around the lake before surfacing. After the first few minutes, Paige and Wade joined him in the water, and they spent most of that hour with Julian splashing and dunking them both. Paige had to admit that what could have been a disaster turned out to be a lot of fun.

Giddy with success, he proposed that they all try it the next day for two reasons: to ensure that he could bespell all three of them at once, and to let them get acclimated to the experience. It was a good proposal, so all three of them ended up in the lake, playing and exploring for several hours.

After returning to the house, they decided they would leave for Russia in the morning, especially since Wade had already obtained the wetsuits that they'd need for their dive. Once he'd arranged for their plane, Julian went right to bed, too exhausted by his magical endeavors even to jump Paige, but he still drew her into bed with him and slept with her curled against his side.

To make up for the lack—or to repay his efforts, he wasn't sure which, nor did he care—Paige woke him the next morning in one of the best ways possible; first with her mouth, then by sliding herself onto him to ride him until he roared with pleasure.

All in all, it was a very good start to his day.

CHAPTER 25

Their moods were high as they flew across Europe and into Russia, with all three laughing and enjoying the company of each other. Only part of it was forced, as Paige thought about the presence that had *not* wanted her anywhere near this piece. Still, she wasn't one to spoil things if she had any other choice, so she joined in with the joking. Besides, it was her second trip on a private jet. This time she could spend less time gawking and pining over Julian, and more time actually having fun.

When the plane landed, they sobered only marginally as they transferred from aircraft to rented SUV. Once again Wade did the driving, since he'd been in this area before. He found an unpopulated spot near the part of the lake that Paige had seen and parked.

Paige changed into her wetsuit in the SUV, while the others—who had *no* modesty, she noted—just changed outside, mostly blocked by the vehicle. Wade had a diving knife already, but he pressed one onto both Paige and Julian as well.

"There was no magic last time, so let's not risk it, huh?" he told them.

"If there's no magic, we're in more trouble than being unarmed. We're going to be underwater with no way to breathe," Paige pointed out. Besides, she had no idea how to effectively use a knife.

"True, but take it anyway, okay? It would make me feel better."

She sighed, but took it. "Fair enough." Though she truly hoped she had no reason to use it. She didn't need more fodder for her nightmares.

"Okay, I'll need five minutes to do the spell. After I'm done, Paige, will you be ready to link us?" Julian asked. They'd decided that since communication would otherwise be limited to hand signals, Paige would connect their minds so they could 'talk' to one another.

"I am. And I'll get the direction we should start in while you're doing the spell."

Paige actually waited until he'd begun before she pulled the amulet out, hesitant to touch it again. Wade gave her a reassuring smile and nodded, so she took a breath and touched it with her bare fingers.

She braced herself for someone to attack her mind again, but felt nothing negative, just the tugging and emotions that she'd become so familiar with, though much, much stronger than it had been originally. "That way," she breathed, giving Wade the direction before she slid the relic into a bag, then tucked it into her wetsuit so it wouldn't be lost and could be easily retrieved.

They felt when the spell took hold of them, and Paige closed her eyes to focus on linking them together. *Do you hear me?* she thought at them.

"Yes, but it's freaking weird to have you in my head," Wade responded, amused as he slid his goggles on. In addition, he hooked a light to

his waist, and slid a wrist light on, which the other two had been given as well. The deeper they got, the darker it would get, after all.

"You get used to it," Julian assured him as he copied the action. *"Shall we?"*

With a grin, Wade was the first to dart toward the water then dive in cleanly. Paige couldn't help but smile as she followed at a more sedate pace, adjusting her goggles. She expected the water to feel cool, if not cold, but Julian's spell had apparently taken care of that as well. She hadn't noticed back home, with the water a more comfortable temperature naturally, but she knew the water should be colder than it felt. It was more lukewarm than truly warm, but it would suffice.

They all submerged and gave themselves a few minutes to adjust. It really was very odd to breathe water instead of air, even if they had practiced with it back in England. While bearable, Paige didn't think she liked it. That didn't stop her from swimming downward, however. She was meant to lead the way, given that only she had the direction, but after they had inadvertently allowed her to be taken by an ice elemental, neither man was taking a chance with her safety.

"It felt like it was in the deepest part of the lake. It shouldn't be far, judging by how hard the relic was pulling on me, but that could also just be because it's closer to being whole," she told them as she swam with them on either side of her.

"Did you get any indication of what might be guarding it?" Julian asked.

They felt her failure and regret before she could put her thoughts to words.

"No sweat, Red. We've got this," Wade assured her, giving her a thumbs up. *"And we'd have never gotten this far without you."*

After half an hour, afraid she'd lost her bearings, she paused, pulling the relic out. After considering the action for only a second, she tucked it into her sleeve, without the bag, high enough up that it couldn't slip out. The glow of her eyes gave the surrounding water an eerie feel, but it was a fair trade, she thought, for knowing where to go.

She swam off toward the right, getting more eager, more impatient with each stroke, until she was swimming as hard as she could.

"Slow down, Paige," Julian thought at her. *"It will still be there if we get there a few minutes later. Don't wear yourself out."*

Paige fought against annoyance, because she knew he was right. Worse, she knew that her sudden enthusiasm came from the relic, not from her. Still, she did slow her pace. She'd need her energy and strength if they were attacked.

It was right about ten minutes later when Paige stopped, arms and legs moving just to keep her place as she looked around. *"It should be right here, but I don't see it or any sort of guards,"* she told them, confused. *"Do either of you see an altar?"* The previous two pieces had been on altars, or at least something that resembled one, so it made sense that this one would be, too.

Julian looked before he shook his head. *"I don't see it either. We'll just have to search the bottom as carefully as we can."*

"Very carefully," Wade thought as he turned on the larger light. *"Stir up too much silt and we'll be blind."*

Working beside each other, they slowly sifted through the fine sand at the bottom. Minutes passed, but all their discoveries so far had been junk. Literally, Paige thought with disgust. Bottles, cans, even an old rotary phone.

Wade suddenly stopped and twisted around, staring into the water for a moment before yelling into their link, *"Guards!"*

He drew his knife and the Julian followed suit while they moved a little closer to one another, careful to block Paige from whatever was coming.

At first Paige thought the guards were mermaids, but it only took one good look to realize that she was a bit off with that guess. While they were half human, half aquatic, their tails were more shark-like than any benign sort of fish. There were no brilliantly colored scales, but instead a dull gray skin, complete with a rigid fin at the small of their backs. More, their fingers were tipped with deadly looking claws, and their teeth? Definitely shark teeth.

"Don't focus on that, Paige! They're armed!" Julian told her, which made her realize that each one of the shark people had a knife or spear.

There were six of them, and they formed a loose circle around their prey. Not one of them looked friendly. One swam forward, moving faster than Paige would have thought possible. It arrowed at Wade, who somehow managed to shift aside just enough to avoid being skewered. There was a murkiness in the water after it had passed, and Paige thought that Wade had nicked it with his knife. She hoped he had, at least, because the alternative was that Wade had been injured.

Another one rushed forward, knocking Paige back, but she didn't feel as though she'd been cut, just hit with a hard, fast object. She didn't have time to wonder why he hadn't used his weapon, but she was grateful nonetheless.

After that, the guards stopped toying with them and attacked in earnest. Wade fought with his knife and strength, letting the shark-people come to him so he didn't waste energy swimming after them.

Julian had his knife in his hand, but he wasn't using it. Paige saw ripples in the water and knew that he was using some sort of concussive blast to attack.

Unable to help, and cursing her lack of skills in this area, she mostly tried—unsuccessfully—not to get hurt. The next time one of the sharks rushed at her, it slashed at her with a knife, and she felt it slice along her belly. She cried out, clasping her hands over the wound. If she was lucky, it wasn't deep, but there wasn't any time to check it out.

But something happened, something triggered by the combination of injury, fear, and hating how useless she was. Some part of her that had lain dormant was awakened, letting her do something she couldn't have done before the mental attack she'd suffered at Mooreton. Unknowingly, her attacker had imparted knowledge as well as pain with the assault.

Without consciously realizing what she was doing, Paige lashed out toward the shark that had cut her, striking out with her mind. She mirrored the telepathic barrage she'd suffered only days before. It wasn't something she'd ever done before, or knew she *could* do. But her strike was clean and her foe less protected mentally than she had been. She blasted its mind, felt it wither and die. The body would live, for a few minutes at least, but the shark man was effectively brain dead the instant her power touched him.

Her horror was stronger than when she'd killed the elemental, and with her mind connected to Julian and Wade, they felt it, too. It distracted Wade just long enough to have his arm sliced open twice before he managed to grab the shark and plunge his knife deep into its chest, leaving four still attacking.

Julian was affected more than Wade, and his next blast was aimed poorly, just grazing one of the sharks. Undeterred, it speared through the water toward him, brandishing its knife. *"Paige! You have to calm down! Now! We're still in danger!"* he yelled into the link as he desperately shot magic at the approaching threat. This time he hit, even if it wasn't quite as centered as he hoped. It must have hit something vital, though, because the shark, while not dead, floated in the water rather than continuing its charge.

One of the three sharks still alive nudged at the still figure of the brain-dead shark, before it gave Paige a look of extreme hatred. She flinched at the force of the emotion, and only then did she break out of her panic long enough to realize the threat they still faced.

Wade and Julian were busy with the others, and there was no way that they could reach her in time to save her. She knew that if she didn't do something, she was going to die here, in the cold and dark of Lake Baikal. Worse, she was going to cause the deaths of Julian and Wade.

More hesitant now that she was cognizant of what she was doing, Paige struck out with her magic again. It took a tremendous amount of power, but she did it. This time she felt the mind snap cleanly under the intensity of her magic, felt it break and become useless. She let out a sob and covered her face, curling into a fetal position as she floated in the water.

She felt a touch to her shoulder and pulled herself into a tighter ball.

"It's me, Paige," came Julian's thought, even as she felt his magic healing the cut along her stomach.

"It's us," was Wade's just an instant later.

Neither man had any sort of condemning thoughts about what she'd done or how she'd done it. They were relieved the three of them were alive, happy she had a defense, but mostly, they were concerned for her.

At Julian's urging, she slowly straightened and he pulled her into his arms. *"It's okay. You helped to save us. You only did what you had to do. What we all had to do. There is no shame in that. No shame in surviving."*

"But what I did…it's worse than simply killing! I didn't even know I could do that…" she thought, appalled at herself.

"No, it was merciful. Quick, painless. And you're stronger now than you have ever been. It makes sense that you would gain new powers." He lightly kissed her lips. *"Come…let's find that piece and go home. I think you need a glass of wine, a back rub, and a full night's rest."*

He felt her hesitation, but smiled rather than pressing her. Wade did the same as he rubbed a comforting hand over her back.

"All right. Let's find it," she finally thought. She was careful not to let them hear that she wanted away from the corpses more than anything. Nor did she allow them to sense just how strong her guilt over her actions was. She hated violence, even if she knew there was a time and place for it. And while she was happy that she'd helped saved them, she knew the deaths—of both the shark-people and the elemental—would weigh on her for quite some time. But for now, she shoved it to the back of her mind and locked it away. They'd get the piece and leave the grisly proof of her power behind.

They split up, but Paige noticed that one of them was always close by, worrying about her.

Though they tried not to stir up the silt, they were only partially successful, especially since they were in a hurry to find it before any other sharks came to find out what happened to the first group. Despite that, it was another fifteen minutes before they found anything.

"Hey, over here. I think I found something," Wade called. The others swam over to him while he gently fanned dirt away from a crude, worn chunk of rock that loosely resembled an altar.

"Is it there?" Paige asked, trying to see if there was silver beneath the muck, but it was impossible to tell.

"I'm not sure. There's something here, but whether it's the piece?" Wade shrugged. *"I have no idea."*

"What do you feel from the relic?" Julian asked, looking at her rather than the altar.

Paige laid a hand over it and focused. It pulsed like it was trying to tell her something, and she focused on that sensation. She shifted forward and reached out instinctively, not for the top of the altar, but a hidden niche near the base. Her lips curved faintly as her fingers closed around something small. *"It's here. I have it,"* she told him, and felt a burst of excitement from Julian and relief from Wade.

When she drew her hand back, she had a piece of silver in her hand, so tarnished it was black. She was overwhelmed with sensation, and not just from the piece of the relic that lay against her skin. Despite the glove of her wetsuit, she keenly felt the newly discovered piece, and an elation that made a mockery of what Julian was feeling.

"Let's get out of here," Wade told her and pointed upward.

Paige absently nodded, but it still took a nudge from Julian to get her moving upward.

The search had kept them going after the adrenaline rush of the attack had faded, and now they all just wanted home. In lieu of that, a bed and several hours sleep as they flew home would do.

They hadn't yet reached the surface—were, in fact, still minutes from reaching the top—when the spell started to fade. A ripple of panic washed through their minds, and none knew who it had come from. Their pace increased, but Paige wasn't sure she could make it. She wasn't as strong a swimmer as the others, nor did she have their stamina. Yes, the spell had aided them in swimming, but it didn't make it effortless.

Only fifty feet from the surface, the spell gave out. Paige's exhaustion kept her from fighting against inhaling water. Her strokes went sluggish, her eyes wide, but after just a minute, she stilled and her eyes drifted closed. She floated in the water, moved only by the currents.

It was the sudden lack of mental contact with either Paige or Julian that alerted Wade that something was wrong. He glanced back and his heart stuttered in his chest when he saw Paige's still form. He wouldn't let her die. He wouldn't let Julian lose another woman he loved. He refused. Struggling to hold his breath, he dove deeper and he reached for her. Her hand was closest, so he grabbed it, yanking her upward with him. When she was level with him, he wound a strong arm around her and kicked toward the surface. Never before had he felt such urgency, but he had to get her out of the water.

Julian had stopped to see what was the matter, and his blood ran cold at the sight of Paige so unresponsive. Knowing that neither he nor Wade had any breath to spare, he reached out and used magic to help propel Wade upward. It was perhaps a touch too fast, but they weren't that far from the surface and she needed air, fast. He saw the two shoot out of the water and used the same magic to push him to the surface.

They got to the shore and Wade carefully laid Paige on her back. He turned her head, letting some of the water drain from her mouth.

Julian dropped to his knees just after that, his expression one of anguish. "We should have had enough time!"

There was nothing Wade could say to make it better, so he stayed silent. He watched as Julian started to give her mouth-to-mouth, forcing air into her lungs, just as Paige had done for him a few days earlier. Wade wasn't sure he drew a single breath as he prayed that the witch would start breathing again. Each moment that passed weighed more heavily on him, and on Julian.

It seemed to take forever, but the first sharp inhalation had him closing his eyes in relief.

Julian gathered her into his arms once she was done coughing up the lake water, burying his face against her hair. He didn't notice he was trembling with relief, but Paige did.

She lifted a hand to his cheek and he shifted to look at her. "I thought you were gone," he told her, voice hoarse.

"'m right...here." She frowned and looked around as well as she could without moving.

"What are you looking for? Wade's right here," Julian asked after glancing around to make sure they were alone.

"Saw...a man. In the water. Just before..."

Wade shook his head. "I was right there with you, Red. There was just the three of us."

"Saw him. Tall...tanned."

Wade gave Julian a look, but said nothing.

"How about we get back to the plane and get home?" Julian gave a weak, apologetic smile. "I'm afraid that I'm pretty much wiped out."

"Sounds...good."

No one questioned why they boarded the plane still in wetsuits. Paige's hair was still drenched and they all looked wretched, but then, Julian paid good money for the lack of curiosity.

Julian took care of the cuts Wade had sustained before he helped Paige get back into street clothes and took the relic from her, putting it away, separate from the new piece. When they got home was soon enough to worry about it. For now, he wanted to simply hold her and revel in the fact that she was still alive.

He hadn't lost her. And he vowed to himself that he never would.

CHAPTER 26

O nce they were back at Mooreton, Julian wanted to wait before dealing with the relic, but Paige ignored that suggestion and went straight to the workshop. She wanted it done, now. The sooner it was dealt with, the sooner she could try to put what had happened in Russia behind her.

"Paige, I think it would be a good idea to wait, just for a day or two, before we mess with that again," Julian said as he followed her. "It's been a long day, and you hardly slept on the plane."

"Considering what happened, considering that you nearly *died*, I think he's right," Wade added. "Let's grab some food, a shower, get a good eight hours sleep, minimum, then do this tomorrow."

They expected protests. They didn't expect for Paige to sit down and silently hold her hands out. Her brows lifted and she all but dared them to continue arguing with her.

To her surprise, Wade laughed and stole Julian's seat, stretching out with his fingers linked together over his belly. "She is a redhead," he told Julian unhelpfully. "Stubborn. Unless we hogtie her, I don't know that you're going to get what you want this time."

Julian scowled at him but walked over, hesitated a moment, then carefully placed the two pieces of the amulet in her hands, one in each.

Paige flinched lightly, but said nothing as the two pieces pulled together, leaving only a hole in the center where the last piece, the jewel, would go. Almost whole, the amulet was only two inches across. The symbols were complete now, though their meaning was still a mystery to her.

She sought the location of the last piece, but after only a few seconds she closed her eyes. She had to. With so many pieces of the amulet being joined, there was too much sensory input, and she needed to limit it however she could, even if it was just blocking out the sight of what was here and real. She was hyperventilating from the ferocity of the impressions, the images she was getting. There were too many to sort through easily, coming too quickly to process, especially with the amulet so pleased at being nearly completed, yet so eager to have that last piece.

She swallowed as she struggled to understand and relay what she was getting. "Desert. Not in any temple or tomb, nowhere near any structures of any sort. All I see is sand." She frowned. "No, there's an oasis, but it's miles away, past a dune."

Suddenly she cried out, and Julian plucked the amulet from her hand. Eyes blinked open and she shook her head. "I wasn't in pain. I'm all right." She shuddered and wrapped her arms around herself. "I saw snakes around the last piece. Hundreds—maybe thousands—of snakes. I'm...I'm terrified of snakes," she admitted.

"Hey, me too," Wade said solemnly, but even without her empathy Paige knew he was lying through his teeth to try and make her feel better.

"Thanks, Wade," she told him, grateful.

"I hate to ask, Paige, but..." Julian began.

"But can I look at some snake pictures to see if I can identify which one I saw so we can figure out which desert?" she finished with a tired smile.

He looked sheepish but nodded. "I'd rather you wait until you've rested, but if you're intent on doing this now, we may as well finish it out."

"I agree, and I can. I'd really rather not see another snake again for the rest of my life, but yes, I can do that."

He kissed her hair and took a moment to put the amulet in the safe before pulling up pictures. He and Wade took turns showing her different species, each one drawing a look of distaste from the empath, and occasionally a shudder of fear. Several minutes later, she wrinkled her nose and looked away, motioning toward Julian's phone. "That one. Times entirely too many."

Julian looked grim. "Egyptian asp. On the plus side, it does narrow it down—to all of the Sahara."

Wade snorted. "On the negative, they're extremely poisonous. And the Sahara is massive."

"There is that." He looked back to Paige and noted that she was nearly stark white, and her eyes were blurry.

"You should put her to bed," Wade said quietly.

"You're right." Julian drew Paige out of her chair, though she gave a feeble resistance. He saved her the effort of walking by just picking her up. "Good night, Wade."

"Night. Feel better, Red."

A small sound was the only response she could give. She felt so exhausted that she didn't even notice that Julian took her to his bedroom, not hers. "I know you're tired, but you'll sleep better if you wash off the lake water," he told her as he carried her into the bathroom. He braced her against the counter while he undressed her, then quickly dealt with his clothing. Once in the shower, he sat her on the narrow seat and began to quickly, but gently, wash her from head to toe. But even with his speed, she was half asleep by the time he shut the water off and started to dry her.

Finally, he carried her to his bed and laid her down before drawing the covers up to her chin. "Paige? You think you could eat some soup if I brought it up?" he asked, not liking how she was still too pale.

"Tired. Just want to sleep," she murmured.

He brushed her hair back from her face and nodded. "All right. Sleep as long as you want, sweetheart."

"Julian?"

"Hmm?"

"Will you stay with me? Just until I fall asleep?"

He brushed her hair back from her face and smiled. "Of course." Moving carefully so as not to disturb her, he slipped under the covers and drew her against him. He kissed the nape of her neck and she sighed once before sleep took her under.

Though he'd promised only to stay until she fell asleep, he remained long past that. Not for her, but for himself. He'd come close, so very close to losing her, first mentally then physically, so he was content to reassure himself of her safety by just laying beside her.

He lay awake for another few minutes before he, too, succumbed to sleep.

He'd been asleep for a few hours when the dreams began.

At first, he dreamed of Paige. They moved together in the morning twilight, each in sync with the other as he moved within her, stroked fingers over her smooth skin. She clung to him, her eyes warm and full of love. Soft kisses and quiet whispers did nothing to break the spell that they'd cast upon one another in the last few minutes before day broke. For this moment, nothing existed but the two of them.

As the sun crept over the horizon, Paige trembled in his arms with her release. Her head fell back on a gasp before he heard her whisper, "I love you."

Moaning, helpless to resist her pull, he followed, pouring himself into her, body, heart, and soul.

His eyes closed for a moment as he recovered, muscles shivering from exertion. Lips curved into a smile before he opened his eyes, but it wasn't the red-haired, green-eyed witch he'd just loved so thoroughly who lay beneath him now. Instead, it was a familiar blonde with blue eyes. A blonde whose image had once been so clear in his mind until time began to erode it until it was hazy. She was young, the same age she'd been when Julian had married her, not quite twenty yet.

"Mary," he whispered, shocked that he didn't feel instant pleasure and happiness at having his wife in his arms. No, he felt cheated to have Paige taken from him.

"Julian. Why didn't you save me? Why did you let me die and move onto another woman? Why did you save her and not me?" she asked sadly, unshed tears making her deep blue eyes bright and shimmery.

He jerked back, sitting on his heels as guilt lanced through him. Before he realized what he was doing, he yanked the sheet up, covering his groin. Though he was in a dream, it felt wrong to be nude around anyone but Paige. Even his dead wife. "I couldn't save you, Mary. I tried, you know I tried to find a way to prevent you from dying, but I didn't have the information then that I have now. I would have saved you if I could have. You have to know that."

She sat up and shook her head. "I don't. I don't know that at all. But because you didn't save me, I died." She began to age rapidly before his eyes, her beautiful hair overtaken by brittle gray, lines appearing on her once smooth face, her flesh withering away until she was as frail as she'd been the day she died. "I died, Julian, because of you," she whispered and lifted a hand that trembled out for him.

"No!" he yelled and scrambled off the bed.

The moment his feet touched the floor everything changed around him. Mary was gone. His bed was gone. His entire bedroom was gone. Now he stood in a workshop that wasn't his own, with shelves full of books and materials. He noticed that he wasn't naked any longer, but he wore some sort of cloth that was draped and folded about his body. A toga, maybe?

"What the hell is this? Where am I?" he asked aloud before he spotted a figure in the corner.

The person was tall, imposing, but whoever it was, he didn't want Julian to get a good look at him and kept to the darker parts of the room.

"Where you are isn't as important as your first question," came the reply. "You're nowhere, really, since you're dreaming. But as to what this is? This is me saving you from someone who wanted to mess with your mind."

"Who?" Julian demanded.

The figure shook his head. "I can't tell you that, other than to say it was the same person who attacked your companion. The name wouldn't really matter in any case. But to answer the question you're going to ask next, you already know why someone would want to mess with your mind. You're getting too close. Soon enough you'll have the last piece, and there are people who would kill to prevent that. For that matter, they have killed."

"And why are you telling me this? Why help me?" Julian asked suspiciously. "If you know what I'm doing, why aren't you trying to stop me, too?"

The man waved a hand and a large oval mirror appeared, floating in midair a few feet in front of Julian. In it, Julian could see Paige, still asleep, curled up against his side. "Because helping you helps her."

The idea that this man could want Paige made something hot and dark flare in Julian's chest. "What is she to you? Why do you care about helping her?"

The stranger sighed. "Temper, Julian. I have no designs on your woman. I'm just looking out for her. The reasons for it are mine and mine alone." He chuckled. "It's not like you're going to remember any of this when you wake, anyway."

Julian scoffed. "I doubt that. I always remember lucid or magical dreams."

The chuckle became a true laugh, full of genuine amusement. "Perhaps, but then, you've never shared a dream with a god. We're a whole different sort of magic. Now, wake up."

The god—if he was really a god—snapped his fingers and Julian woke instantly. He felt Paige against him and tightened his arm around her. He felt apprehensive and protective of her, but he couldn't figure out why. Reaching out with his senses, he didn't find anyone or anything in his home but for Wade, Paige, and himself. A frown marred his brow before he shook his head a little. It must have just been a bad dream.

He kissed Paige lightly, then closed his eyes and let sleep reclaim him once more.

CHAPTER 27

When Paige woke, alone, it was just starting to get dark. All the traveling to different time zones had her internal clock way off. Still groggy, she wondered how long she'd slept, because it didn't feel like she'd been out that long. Never one for lazing about in bed, she got up and shuffled into the shower. After the way yesterday had gone, one shower hadn't been quiet enough to make her feel fully human.

The water helped clear her mind a little, which was both blessing and curse. The thought of what had happened, as well as what was to come—specifically the snakes—had her shuddering as she toweled off. She really was terrified of the things. She'd never even been able to handle being around non-venomous pet snakes.

Even as she thought of snakes, which was the one really big reason not to go to the Sahara, she knew she would. Julian wanted so much to reassemble this relic, and she couldn't tell him no, especially not because of some phobia. She wouldn't let herself be the reason they failed. Her lips twitched as she dressed. Then again, if nearly dying hadn't put her off of their quest, she didn't know what would.

Hair still damp, she padded barefoot down the stairs. Hearing voices, she started toward them, only to stop when she heard her name.

Eavesdropping was wrong, she knew, and rude, but in this case, she'd make an exception.

"I just don't know if Paige should go with us to Egypt," Julian said.

"Believe me, Julian, I get your concern," Wade assured him. "She's been through more than her fair share of shitty situations the past few weeks, and if she's that scared of snakes, it's not going to get any easier."

Hands clenched as Paige felt herself growing angry. They had no right to decide what she did or did not do!

Wade continued, "But it's not really up to me. Or you, for that matter. Sure, we can present reasons for her to stay here while we go, but in the end, it'll be her choice." He smirked and stretched out his legs, resting his booted feet on the coffee table. "Besides, I have a feeling that if we did leave her here, then she'd find her own way to Egypt. And probably get to the piece before we did."

Julian sighed. "No, you're right. I just...don't want to put her through any more pain."

Just as quickly as it had started to build, the anger faded. How could she be upset that they cared about her? And it didn't sound like they were actually trying to make decisions for her, just talking out their concerns. She got it. In their situation, she'd probably want to say the same, but she couldn't stay behind. The Sahara was huge. No way could they find the piece without the directions only she could provide.

"Believe me, I know. I felt how badly she suffered in Russia. And Julian? I'm freaking mad for that sweet little red-head." Paige felt a stirring of annoyance and something darker from Julian. "Red's like the baby sister I never knew I wanted. I'd cheerfully kill if it meant keeping a smile on her face."

While Julian relaxed, Paige simply felt deeply touched. Then she started to feel guilty for eavesdropping and slipped out to the garden, unnoticed. Or so she thought. Wolf noses missed little, and Wade smiled as she left.

The sun was fully set when she came back inside, feeling a little better after her time in the fresh air. Gardening always helped relax her, too, knowing she was helping something live while bringing more beauty into the world. She stepped in the house to the smell of something delicious. Following the scent, she found the guys in the kitchen, with Wade snatching a piece of pizza from one of four boxes.

She laughed and drew their attention to her.

"What's so funny?" Wade asked before taking a bite of pizza, not minding how the cheese scorched the roof of his mouth.

"I smelled food and thought it was the most delicious smell ever. I like pizza, but I must be hungrier than I thought," she explained as she took her own slice and immediately bit into it. The yummy noise she made had both men smiling.

"Well, eat as much as you like," Julian told her as he studied her face, relieved that she no longer looked quite so worn out.

"With four pizzas, I should hope I'd be able to," she quipped.

"Have you not noticed how much furball over there eats?" he asked dryly, though one corner of his mouth twitched upward.

"I object to that," Wade said with dignity. "I never have furballs," he told them before taking a huge bite. "You're thinking of cats."

Paige giggled. "Fair point. So, three pizzas for him, one for us to share?" she asked Julian playfully.

Julian grinned. "Exactly."

She sat down and the next few minutes were quiet as they sated the worst of their hunger. After finishing her second piece, Paige voiced her concerns.

"I'm a little worried about the snakes. I'm not an expert on them, but aren't Egyptian asps supposed to be extremely deadly if they bite you?"

"Yes. *If* they bite you," Wade pointed out.

"You didn't see how many snakes there were," Paige said, shaking her head. "Odds are at least one of us is going to get bit," she told him and shuddered.

"It does seem likely," Julian allowed. "But here's what I can do. I don't know how well our brand of healing works on venoms like the more potent ones like we're talking about, but I know one person who would know how to deal with it. I can visit Suni and, if she says that our healing won't be effective, I'll get her to make up some magical antivenom for us."

Paige nibbled on her lower lip as she thought, not realizing that such a small action was making Julian's pants fit rather tightly. "Can you get the antivenom even if our healing will work?" she asked. "What if you get bit, and can't heal anything? Wade and I can't heal, but we can give you antivenom. And snakes aren't the only dangers in the Sahara. Aren't there scorpions, too?"

"Red's got a point. Hopefully we won't need it, but I'd rather have it and not need it than the other way around," Wade agreed.

"That's easy enough. And don't worry," Julian told her with a smile. "Suni is the best healer alive. Probably the best who's ever lived, if you discount a god or two. She'll be able to help us."

She returned the smile. "That sounds wonderful. Thank you."

"My pleasure. In fact, since I'm done eating, I'll go ahead and pop over to her place," he said, rising from the table. "After you eat, why don't you go rest in the garden? You're still looking a little pale."

Her reaction to his well-meaning criticism lost out to pleasure that he was concerned, so Paige nodded. "Okay." No reason to let him know she'd just come from there. She'd enjoy just taking a walk this time rather than working. Besides, the moon was up now, and she did enjoy the garden in the moonlight.

Julian looked to Wade and arched a brow, silently telling the wolf to watch her. He knew better than to voice the desire aloud, and he'd known Wade long enough for the shifter to understand instantly.

The wolf grinned. "As it happens, I like gardens. Don't know a damn thing about flowers though, so maybe you can teach me something."

Paige beamed at him. "I'd love to." She'd take any excuse to talk about one of her passions.

"Then that's settled." Julian bent and brushed a light kiss over her lips, which curved under his. "Be safe," he whispered to her before disappearing.

Paige sighed, happy despite everything else. It was only when she caught Wade's knowing grin that she blushed lightly. "What?"

"Nothing. It's just good to see you happy. And to see him starting to get the stick out of his ass."

"I...thank you. Though I'm not going to touch the stick comment."

He grinned. "What do you say we go take that stroll through that garden? Julian tells me it's almost entirely your doing?"

She put the rest of the pizza away and grabbed a bottle of water before leading the way outside. "Basically. Julian hadn't touched them in years before I showed up, so they were all but ruined when I got here. Overgrown, weeds everywhere, more grass than flowers. Since I love gardens and, especially at first, wanted to feel useful, I've spent a lot of time restoring them. Weeding, pruning, planting new flowers and bushes. I'm glad I did, too. The garden and library are my favorite places here."

"It shows," Wade said as he got his first real look at her handy work. He hadn't been lying about not knowing a damn thing about plants, but he knew when a garden was pretty, and this one was. It wasn't as regimented as he might have expected from her, either. It looked a little wild, like the house and garden had always been here, together. She'd done well. But he wasn't here just to compliment her. He wanted to get to know her a little better—and tease her a little, of course.

He smiled impishly. "So when are you going to thoroughly enjoy the garden with Julian, hmm?" She only blushed and he laughed, slinging a companionable arm around her shoulders. "I'm sorry, Red. I shouldn't pick on you, but it's so much fun to see you blush."

"It's okay. I'm just..." She sighed. "He is acting differently now, since Antarctica, but he doesn't generally spend the whole night with me. It...makes me worried that he's still in love with his wife. I don't want to compete with her, and I can't replace her even if I wanted to, but if he loves her..."

He gave her a squeeze. "And you're in love with him, aren't you?" he asked gently.

She absolutely was, and she couldn't figure out if she was worrying for nothing or not. Dealing with the relic was stressful, and it might be clouding things, but she just couldn't tell. Maybe Wade could help? It couldn't hurt to try. "I am. Does it show, too?"

"It does, but probably only to me, since I'm not in the middle of it. Impartial observer, if you will."

"Good. I don't want him to know."

"You don't?" he asked, surprised. Then it clicked. "Ahh...you don't want to make him feel pressured or scare him off?" he guessed.

"Pretty much," she agreed. "I have my pride, but more than that, I don't want someone to be with me out of some sense of obligation. I want to be in a relationship with someone who simply wants to be with me. I want..." She trailed off, not quite knowing how to put words to her feelings.

"I get it," he told her with a nod. "And he won't hear it from me. But I think you're worrying about nothing."

She frowned. "I don't think this is nothing, Wade."

He shook his head and found a nice little patch of grass that was circled on three sides by flowers and drew her down beside him. "Your feelings aren't nothing, no. And I get your concerns. But I think he cares more than you realize. If it weren't for Mary, he'd probably be treating you...like a normal girlfriend, I guess is the best way of putting it."

"He's not treating me badly, especially the last week or so, but Mary *is* a factor," Paige pointed out. Part of her knowing she was being stubborn, but facts were facts.

"In a way, yes, which means he's just feeling guilty that he's not thinking of Mary all the time. That he's opened himself up enough to actually care for a woman other than her. And you're right, he is treating you differently the last week. More affectionate, less grumpy?" He bumped her shoulder with his. "And you said he leaves after sex, right? That's an easy one, too."

"Doesn't seem easy to me," she muttered, which made him grin.

"Not emotionally, but to explain. Since Mary died, he hasn't been a monk. I'd be shocked if any man could avoid sex for that long, to be honest. But from the impression I've gotten from him, it was always very...impersonal. Not quite a wham, bam, thank you ma'am, but close. So sleeping, actually sleeping, with you is sort of a new thing for him. I'd wager good money that you're the first woman he's actually slept with since Mary."

Paige considered that, then sighed and leaned her head against his shoulder. She'd gotten very comfortable with the wolf since they met in Brazil, and had familial feelings for him as well. If she'd grown up with an older brother, she liked to think he would've been like Wade. "That...really does make sense."

"Of course it does! You think I'm just a pretty face?"

She grinned before taking a few minutes to just enjoy the beauty and scents of the garden.

"You want to tell me what else is bothering you?" Wade asked gently, wanting to rip all the bandages off at once.

She stiffened and lifted her head, but he wouldn't let her get up.

"It's the elemental and those sharks, isn't it?"

Paige had hoped he wouldn't figure that part out. Honestly, that weighed on her more than Julian at the moment. She knew Julian had changed, that he was showing her that he cared. That was all good. Was it stressful? Yes, to an extent, but she loved her budding relationship with Julian. She didn't love knowing that she'd killed, several times.

Her eyes closed and she nodded. "I don't even kill spiders, Wade, but I just ended those lives without hesitation. I hate knowing that it's in me to kill," she whispered.

He shook his head and hugged her. "Honey, it's in everyone to kill under the right circumstances, from the smallest child to the oldest man. Now, if you asked me if I thought that you had it in you to kill indiscriminately, I'd laugh in your face, because it isn't. You're not a bad person by any stretch of the imagination. But you were protecting yourself, Red. Yourself and me. And Julian. And speaking as someone who enjoys being alive, I really hope that if it comes down to it again, that you'll make the same choice." He tightened his squeeze for a moment. "Though I'm going to do everything I can to prevent you from having to make that choice."

She clung to him, letting the tears flow, though she knew she was getting his shirt wet. "It was just such an awful feeling. And I feel so terrible. So guilty!" She sniffled and looked up. "Does that feeling ever go away?"

He gave her a sad smile. "For you? Likely not. It's like losing a loved one. The pain never goes away, it just lessens, and you learn how to live with it and not think about it every second of every day."

There was another sniffle but she smiled at him. "How'd you get to be so smart?"

He gave a bark of laughter. "Baby, I was born this way. Now, no more of that. You've got a boyfriend who cares for you and we only have one more piece of the amulet to retrieve. You should be happy." He gently separated himself from her and stepped behind some bushes. His shirt came off and she blinked when he tossed it at her, color spreading up her cheeks. "I think it's time for you to smile."

His form shrank and she realized that he was shifting. When he leapt out from behind the bush in wolf form, she grinned. And for the next hour, he amused her by acting like no more than a silly—albeit smart—wolf who wanted nothing more than to play. He nipped and barked, wrestled and pounced, and by the time Julian returned, Paige's guilt was forgotten. For the moment.

CHAPTER 28

Julian appeared in the front yard of a ranch house in Montana. It was a nice place, kept neat and well-maintained. There wasn't so much as a single instance of peeling or faded paint, droopy gutters, or dirty windows. In addition to the house, there was a large greenhouse that was attached to the rear of the house and a red barn in the back yard. In the distance, behind a fence, he saw several horses grazing and galloping around.

It struck him as a very efficient, yet homey, place. The one other time he'd been here, he'd felt more comfortable than he did anywhere but Mooreton—or a library. But he expected nothing less from Suni. Healers were meant to make people comfortable, and she was the ultimate healer.

He strode up the steps and across the wide porch to knock on the front door. A moment later, it opened.

Suni barely topped five feet, and though she looked delicate, he knew that she was one of the strongest people he knew—and more stubborn than a herd of bulls. Her hair was black, short, and spiky, and though he always expected to see brown eyes to go with her dark hair and dusky skin tone, hers were a vivid, striking blue.

She smiled and leaned against the doorframe, her arms folded over her chest. "Well, this is a surprise."

Julian couldn't help but return the smile. "I know. Can I come in anyway?"

Her brows lifted. "Have I ever denied you before?" she asked as she motioned him inside.

The interior of the house had changed little since his last visit more than a century ago. The furniture was still rustic, handmade, and cozy, and it suited her to the ground. The decor was heavy on Native American art, all genuine and also handmade. But what really dominated her home was the greenery. She had potted plants on most flat surfaces and hanging from any empty space she could find. It made the otherwise civilized home seem a bit wild, but the way a wolf viewed from afar was—beautiful and a little awe-inspiring.

"You want something to drink?" she asked, waving him toward a chair in front of the empty fireplace.

"I wouldn't protest some scotch," he said, grinning when he saw she already had a bottle in hand. "You know me too well."

"I should after this long," she told him, pouring. She passed the glass to him before she sat in the rocking chair next to him. "How have you been, Julian? We didn't really get a chance to speak in Georgia."

"No, we didn't, and I'm sorry that I didn't take the time for it," he said apologetically. "I've been...busy. Not quite well, but I'm doing better, I suppose, than I was a few years ago."

"I'm glad you're doing better, but there's no need for apologies. We were there for a specific purpose, and you did seem....preoccupied by something else. I'm sure no one else noticed, but I've known you too long."

She wasn't half the empath that Paige was, but she'd always been extremely perceptive. Other than his new lover, and possibly Wade, no one could read him better than Suni.

"I was. And that's actually why I'm here, indirectly," he admitted.

"Ahh...I'm to learn what has gripped the stoic Julian so tightly that he left his home country for the second time in a century?" she teased as she leaned back and started to slowly rock.

"Not entirely," he told her. "I wish I could, but knowing exactly what I'm up to could be dangerous for you."

She snorted. "Boy, don't forget who's the older of us. I've survived more than you've ever dreamed of," she told him dryly.

He grinned unapologetically and shrugged. "That doesn't mean you should have to deal with this."

She rolled her eyes and waved a hand dismissively. "Fine, fine. Tell me what you're comfortable telling me."

It took him a second before he began. "I'm going to Egypt soon, with a couple of companions—"

"What companions?" she interrupted.

"My...apprentice, Paige," he started, with only the briefest hesitation, "and Wade."

She nodded approvingly. "Wade is a good one to take. If there's danger, he'll be very useful. I can't say one way or another about Paige, but your judgment is usually good." She smiled sweetly. "Go on."

"Like I said, we're going to Egypt, and thanks to a seer—" it was the only way he could describe Paige without mentioning the relic, "—we know that we're going to be confronted with Egyptian asps. A *lot* of them."

She arched a brow. "Define a lot."

"We don't have an exact count, but it sounds like it'll be at least a hundred. Maybe closer to a thousand," he reluctantly admitted.

Slowly, she shook her head. "Not wise, not wise at all. Those are vicious creatures, and definitely dangerous. You can't be talked out of this?"

"Sorry, Suni, but no. Which is why I'm here. After discussing the matter, we thought it would be prudent to see you."

A brow arched and she cocked her head. "And what do you want from me? I can't control snakes, and you're better in a magical fight than I'll ever be."

"No, I'm not asking you to come with us. I would just like an answer and a favor."

"That depends on the question and the favor, doesn't it?"

Remembering the glass in his hand, he sipped. "Can healing—not the sort you do, but the magic available to other witches—cure venom as easily as injuries?" He was certain he knew the answer after the incident with the bullet ants, but it never hurt to be sure.

"It depends on the venom, unfortunately, and the strength of the witch's power. I could cure an asp's venom, absolutely, but I don't know if you could," she admitted.

He sighed. "I was afraid you'd say that," he murmured.

Suni just shrugged and asked, "What's the favor?"

"Can you make a magical antivenom that *will* cure a bite from an asp? Or anything else we might get bitten by?"

She frowned. "I can't guarantee that, since I don't know what you'll encounter. I can guarantee that it would cure any bite or sting from any *natural* creature, but if it's magical, or magic is involved in any way, then I cannot promise that it'll do you any good."

He nodded. "That's absolutely fair, Suni. No one could ask more than that." Honestly, he was relieved that she could do that much, despite having told Paige he had no doubts.

She eyed him for a moment. "I guess you'd like me to make it now?"

He gave her a hopeful smile. "If you don't mind. We plan on leaving in the next few days."

Sighing, she pushed to her feet. "Well, come on then. And while I'm doing that, you can tell me what's really bothering you."

Groaning, he rose to follow, finishing his glass first. He knew he was going to need it. "And this is why I don't visit anymore," he joked. "You see right through me. Even Paige isn't as good, and she's an empath."

"Would she be what's bothering you?" she asked, leading the way into the greenhouse. The moment she opened the door he was assaulted with the scents of life. He had no idea how many types of plants she had in here, but he was fairly certain that some no longer grew anywhere else on the planet. If they ever had. He couldn't put it past Suni to have created entirely new species, just to see if she could, or to fulfill a need.

"You could say that..."

"But would you?" she asked. Picking up a basket, she walked along the uneven rows and began to pluck leaves or blossoms from plants, placing them in the basket.

He said nothing until she not-so-gently nudged him with her elbow. "Oof. Yes, I guess I would."

When it become clear he wasn't going to continue, she sighed. "Do I need to pry every detail out of you? I do have a potion that will have you spilling every secret you've had since you were three if I need to, but it would go much quicker if you'd just tell me what's going on.

Plus, I'm sure there are secrets you have that I really don't want to hear."

Knowing she would never do such a thing—or not without a *very* good reason—he shook his head. "No. It is Paige. And it's Mary," he began.

Suni nodded. "I see."

He had no doubt that she could, so he hurried on. "I rescued Paige from a mugger three years ago, and afterward she showed up on my doorstep. I'd never given her my name or address, and she didn't follow me there. She was a witch who'd grown up ignorant of her true self. And from that moment, I've always felt...protective of her. And intrigued by her powers."

Suni smiled. "You would. You've always been interested in the strange, unusual, or exceptionally powerful."

Ignoring that, he said, "The last month, things have changed."

Unsurprised, she nodded. "You became lovers."

"It wasn't quite that simple, but in the interest of keeping this short, yes."

"And you feel like you're betraying Mary. That caring for another woman, sleeping with her, has somehow lessened what you had with your wife."

Relieved that she understood, he nodded. "Basically, yes."

"That's stupid."

Those blunt words made him stop. "What?"

"I said that's stupid. The heart has room to love anyone you meet. And there are so many widows and widowers who would tell you that finding someone after your spouse has passed does nothing to your former relationship. It's not like it turns back time and makes you love Mary any less. So...you're being stupid."

Somehow, those words, spoken so matter-of-factly, reassured him more than anything Wade had said. But she wasn't done.

"If you care for the girl, then enjoy what you have with her. Don't make her suffer because you have a past. Personally, I'm happy to see you moving on. It's been entirely too long. I have no doubt Mary would say the same thing. She probably would have been smacking you upside the head after the first year or two."

The image of his sweet, eager-to-please wife smacking anyone brought a smile to his lips. "You have a point," he said as she started to mash and mix the ingredients she had gathered.

"Of course I do. Have you ever known me not to?"

"Also a point."

"Are you going to listen to anything I've said, though?"

"I am. Because you're right. Just as Wade was right. "

She nodded curtly. "I knew that wolf had a good head on his shoulders." She paused to give him a sharp look. "But do *not* tell him I said so. His ego is already bigger than the whole of Montana."

He laughed and nodded. "I won't."

"Good." She continued working for another moment before she stopped. The expression on her face was one he'd seen before. One that meant she was suddenly *knowing* something she hadn't before. It wasn't a power she had any control of, he knew, and not one many members of the Arcane had, regardless of what type of supernatural they were.

It could also be both blessing and curse.

He frowned and took a step closer. "What is it?"

She brushed her hands off and went to a wooden cabinet, placing her palm against it. It clicked open with a tiny pulse of magic and she pulled out a small green vial that reminded him of Paige's eyes, especially when she was holding the relic.

"Your Paige...what color are her eyes?" she demanded.

"Green." He motioned to the bottle. "That shade, actually. Or close enough."

She nodded and held it out. "Take it."

Baffled, he did. "What is it?"

She shrugged nonchalantly. "I have no idea," she admitted as she went back to mixing her antivenom. "I apparently made it one night in a sort of trance. But you're going to need it, and you'll know when and how to use it."

"Sometimes I really hate this cryptic shit," he muttered, but he dutifully slid it into his pocket.

"And how do you think I feel, occasionally having my brain invaded?" she shot back. "Now sit down and be quiet so I can finish what you came here for."

"Yes ma'am." He sat on a stool and fell silent, toying with the bottle.

And wondering what it had to do with Paige.

CHAPTER 29

T hough Paige looked fully recovered, and didn't seem to be suffering from the lives she'd taken, they still didn't leave the next day. Julian wanted to give her a bit more time, so insisted that they spend the day planning and making sure they had everything they needed. With some grumbling, and a discreet elbow to Wade's ribs, he got the others to agree.

Since the Sahara was in no way small, and they had nothing to go on as far as a starting to location, they were simply going to fly into Egypt and rent some camels—though Wade had protested that part until they pointed out that cars could—and did—break down or run out of gas. Then they would leave the city and use the amulet to get them to the right spot. And, to Paige's relief, each of them would be holding one of the antivenom vials Suni had given Julian.

He hadn't told them yet about the green bottle. He wasn't sure why he was holding it back, but it didn't seem right to explain about it just yet.

So it was the day after that had them on a plane as it landed in Cairo. From the moment she stepped foot on Egyptian soil, Paige forgot about all the reasons to be sad. It wasn't the first foreign locale that she'd been to, but it excited her more than the others. This was *Egypt*.

The home of the pyramids, the Sphinx, and who knows what magic. It was ancient and steeped in history. History she'd seen glimpses of her entire life, but she wanted more.

As they walked to where they planned to rent the camels, she dug out her camera and started taking pictures. She took pictures of *everything*. Wade and Julian, homes, locals, the shops. Nothing was safe from her aim, especially once she caught the outline of the pyramids in the distance.

Unable not to notice her preoccupation with the country, Wade and Julian had a quick, quiet conversation and found they were both in agreement. Their trip would be delayed for one more day.

"Paige?" Julian called and had her turning. "Wade and I were thinking that we'd spend today here in the city, and not leave until tomorrow. Would that work for you?"

"Are you serious?" she asked, gaping at them. At his nod, she let out a happy sound and raced back to them. Wade got a quick, tight hug, as did Julian, though his was followed up by a kiss. It was meant to be no more than a brief thank you, but it continued until an amused Wade cleared his throat.

Paige blushed and stepped back, but couldn't stop smiling. "Sorry. So, where do we go first?"

"That's up to you, Red. We've both been here before," Wade told her, grinning. "Consider this payment for playing guide for us. Today, we're at your beck and call."

She looked torn for a long moment. What to see first? Museums? Tombs? Monuments? There were entirely too many options, but then she realized one was at the top of her list and she laughed. "We have to start with the pyramids! Then the Sphinx, the museum, the bazaar, and whatever else you two can think of," she told them with a bright smile, linking her arms with theirs, so they walked down the street in a line. "You can be my guides today."

"I had a feeling that was going to be your first choice. But I think we'll make a little detour after the Sphinx," Julian told her, shifting his arm until her hand rested in his, fingers linked together.

Curious, but not opposed to detours, she asked, "Why is that?"

His voice dropped a little. "The pyramids and temples that archaeologists know about aren't the only ones that exist, sweetheart. I thought you might like to see the workshop of an ancient Egyptian witch." When her eyes widened until they were the size of saucers, he chuckled. "I'm guessing that's a yes?"

"Yes! Yes, yes, yes! Let's go," she told him happily and quickened her pace.

They spent several hours just on the pyramids and the Sphinx, with Paige taking so many pictures they had to buy another memory card for the camera. She listened intently to every word written or spoken about the ancient monuments, and she seemed to be in awe at the age of them. When they went inside the first pyramid, Julian thought she might faint from excitement. True, something was lost since they were there with a bunch of tourists milling about, but it was still grand and historical.

She loved every second spent there and every inch of carved or worn stone.

Though Wade and Julian had done this for Paige, to see her forget her grief long enough to be genuinely happy again, her enthusiasm was infectious and they found themselves getting caught up in her excitement. And that only doubled in intensity when Julian led her a short distance away from the crowds to what looked like nothing but a stone wall. After a quick glance to make sure no one was watching, a bit of magic was all that was needed to open a doorway she never would have found unless she knew what she was looking for. Inside nearly put her into a history coma.

The whole place resembled the inside of a tomb or pyramid, but unlike the ones tourists and scientists were able to see, this one was pristine. The paint hadn't faded, so it was infinitely more colorful than anything she'd seen before. It made a huge difference in the general appearance, and she couldn't resist tracing her fingers over the perfectly painted hieroglyphics and images of ancient kings and gods.

Someone had also found a way to deal with sand and spiderwebs, because she didn't see either one after they'd gotten inside. There were, however, several chambers that were filled with treasures. Books and scrolls, tools for mummification and magic, jars and pots, and many more things she couldn't identify a purpose for. Luckily, Julian was familiar with this workshop and was able to help her out.

The witch who had used this particular location had lived several thousands of years ago, he told her, and though there were quite a few modern witches who knew about the place, they'd all agreed not to take it over, instead leaving it as a piece of history for future witches. Anyone could see pieces of Egyptian history in a museum, and some of the artifacts stored in museums dealt with the true supernatural, but none of them were on this level. Fortunately, the magic that had preserved the workshop made it possible for Paige to open scrolls and look at the hieroglyphics inked onto papyrus without damaging anything. Julian was also able to explain what the various tools and pots were for. Egyptian witches, he told her, tended to like more ritualized magic than those of most other cultures. A great many magical rituals that existed today were either created by, or influenced by, the Egyptians, he explained.

To her delight, they spent several hours in the workshop, giving her plenty of time to explore. It wasn't enough, but there was too much for her to see and only one day to see it all in.

When they left the workshop, Wade excused himself. He wanted to give them some time alone and was feeling a bit like a third wheel. He didn't mind that when they were actually on the hunt for a piece of the amulet, but in a more casual setting, it occasionally wore on him. Besides, slipping away gave him a chance to book them a hotel for the night and get checked in. Even without having a clear direction to begin, he wanted to recheck the maps and satellite images, to avoid as many surprises as he could. It would be impossible to avoid them all, since some magic made it impossible for satellites to take images of certain structures or locations. Handy for hiding from the humans, not so handy when the Arcane were trying to find something that had been lost.

While the workshop was the highlight of Paige's day, Julian was happy to see that she thoroughly enjoyed the trip to the museum and the bazaar as well. Especially if the number of souvenirs she'd bought was any indication. She'd purchased papyrus, small statues, incense, a necklace, and even some clothes, draining what remained of her savings. It was worth it, though, and she was happy to give over every penny. But she'd actually bought so many they had to return to the plane to store them, since they wouldn't fit in the packs they were taking into the Sahara.

Once they'd dealt with the extra cargo, they went to dinner. Though it was hot, Paige asked they eat outside, so she could more easily see the pyramids as they ate. But even with that as a distraction, most of the meal was spent focused on Julian.

He'd changed so much since the day he'd first shown her the amulet piece. Not just in how he acted around her—which was amazing—but the way he interacted with the world. Some of the heaviness he'd carried since before her birth had begun to lift. He smiled, he laughed, he joked. No, he wasn't the jokester Wade was, but it was enough to turn him from someone she'd reluctantly fallen in love with, to someone she was more than happy to love. It felt, she realized, like he was becoming whole, just like the amulet was. That might have been coincidence, but she doubted it. To her, it felt like fate, which made her wonder how much more complete he would be when they found the jewel that would fit into the hole of the amulet.

And if he was whole, would he be able to love her in return?

They finished their dinner early and strolled down the streets of Cairo, hand in hand, until Wade sent them a text with the name of the hotel. It was dusk before they joined him. Though Paige was surprised that Wade had booked not a room, but a suite, she was too tired from the excitement and all the walking she'd done to do more than shower and collapse into bed.

Julian emerged from the room they were sharing only a minute later with Paige already asleep and a little smile on her lips.

"Out already?" Wade asked from the couch, offering a glass of scotch out to Julian.

"The moment her head hit the pillow," Julian confirmed as he dropped into a chair. "This was a good idea, Wade." One he wished he'd thought of. It was odd to understand he was feeling guilty now, not for caring for a woman other than his wife, but for not treating the woman he was with like she deserved to be treated. His first instinct was not to think too closely on that, but he forced himself to. It only took a minute for him to realize he'd truly begun to move on. He wasn't just considering it, he wasn't just being told to, he was actually putting Mary in the past. And for once, it didn't fill him with pain. He took a deep breath at that realization and noticed Wade had been speaking.

Wade grinned and toasted Julian, not for the first time since the witch had sat. "My pleasure. Was worth the delay to see her smiling. She looked like a kid at Christmas."

"For her, this might as well have been Christmas. She loves ancient history. I don't think she realizes just how long it's going to take her to go through the pictures she took, though."

Wade laughed. "Probably not, but it doesn't matter." He sipped at his whiskey. "Plan still the same for tomorrow? Rent camels, head out into the desert with Paige playing compass again?"

Julian shrugged. "It's really the only idea we have, and it has worked well so far."

"True. And with that in mind, I'm going to crash. The desert's gonna be a bitch," Wade said before he drained his drink and headed to his room to sleep.

"Yes, yes it is," Julian murmured to himself. Here was hoping it would be worth it.

CHAPTER 30

The sun had only been up for an hour when the trio loaded up their rented camels and started off into the desert.

They waited until they'd lost sight of any buildings or people before they stopped so Paige could take out the amulet. The demanding pull from it was stronger than before, so intense now that she gasped and nearly dropped it. "Gods, it's strong. I think it knows we're close, that we're almost done." She'd begun to think of the amulet as a sentient being, no matter how it looked or had been created. It may not think or feel quite like a person, but it had emotions and awareness, which was enough for her.

"It's so far away though...It may take us days," she told them after she put it away, feeling the regret from the relic, and her own eagerness to see it whole again.

"We're not on a deadline, so if it takes us days, then it takes us days." Julian smiled. "Don't worry Paige, we'll find it."

At first she wanted to be disappointed that it would take so long, but he was right. She should just try to enjoy the adventure while she could. She did wish it wasn't so hot, but at least they weren't surrounded by ice or a jungle full of dangers.

But a dry heat was still heat, no matter what anyone said.

Unfortunately, she discovered that riding a camel wasn't as much fun as she had thought it would be. It took less than an hour for her backside to start hurting, and an hour after that for it to go numb. And while Antarctica should have prepared her for dealing with unchanging landscapes, she'd expected more from Egypt. Not that she was allowed to be bored, no. Both Julian and Wade did their best to entertain not only her, but themselves as well. A good thing, since they would have otherwise lost their minds after the first few hours of sand and sun.

By the end of the first day, despite slathering herself with sunscreen, her face was almost as red as her hair. Worse, she'd needed Julian to help her off her camel, because her legs simply refused to work. After some healing, she felt well enough to help Wade fix their dinner.

That night they sat around the campfire, happily chatting until they decided to turn in.

The second day passed much like the first, with one notable exception. Just before they made camp that evening, Paige saw a figure standing in the distance.

"There's someone here," she whispered, unsure of how well sound carried out here.

Wade's hand went to his knife and both he and Julian turned. The wolf relaxed after just a moment. "I don't see anyone, Red. I don't smell anyone either."

She glanced back and frowned. "Oh, they're gone now. But I swear, there was someone there just a second ago," she insisted.

"We believe you, but whoever it was, they're not there now," Julian told her, rubbing a hand over her back.

"I suppose…" But she still watched the now empty space for a minute before she resumed helping set up camp.

The third day wasn't any better. Not only was she beyond sore after two days on a camel and in the desert, they still hadn't found anything. And though Paige never saw anyone except for Julian and Wade, she felt like she was constantly being watched. More than once she felt a brush of a semi-familiar mind against hers, but the contact was always brief.

Come mid-afternoon, her ever-present watcher was the least of her concerns, and not just because she was tired of the heat and relentless sun.

Wade brought his camel to a halt and pulled out his binoculars.

"What is it?" Julian asked, easing his camel closer to Paige's.

"I'm not sure," Wade murmured. "There's something ahead, but I can't really make out what it is. At first I thought it was a mirage, because it's sort of shimmering, but I don't think that's it. It's too big and I can see *something* solid there, I'm just not sure what."

"Can I see?" Wade passed the binoculars over and Julian peered into the distance.

"Well?" Paige asked.

"I'm afraid I can't tell you anything more than what Wade already said. I can't make it out any more than he can," Julian said as he lowered the binoculars. "I'm not sure if it's something we should head toward or away from. What do you get from the amulet?"

She drew it out of her pocket and rubbed a thumb across its surface as she concentrated on the feelings she got from it. "If we're going to avoid it, we're going to end up just circling around it. That's the direction we have to go."

"Let's just get a little closer until we can figure out what it is, then we can decide," Wade suggested with a shrug.

"Works for me," Julian said before he urged his camel forward again.

There was a short burst of power from the amulet before Paige could put it away. It left her hand tingling, but not in an unpleasant way. "I think the relic agrees," she decided with a faint smile. It was as impatient as she was. More, even. It had been waiting millennia to be whole again.

The shimmering landscape was farther than they had initially thought, so the sun was low on the horizon by the time they could make out what it was they were heading toward.

"Are those...trees?" Paige asked, voice full of wonder.

"Not just trees. That's a whole damn city, Red," Wade said as he studied it.

A city that had to have been built around a lush oasis, one with enough water to boast hundreds of trees. Stone walls surrounded the city, at least twenty feet high. Both they and what buildings he could see over it were all stark white, which accounted for their inability to distinguish it from the desert any sooner. The style of those buildings wasn't anything from a recent century, but more closely resembled structures from thousands of years ago. What worried him the most was the fact that he only saw a single entrance—a heavy metal gate flanked on either side by a black and gold figure who stood half as tall as the walls themselves.

"Well...here's the good news," he told them when he exchanged his binoculars for his GPS. "That many trees? There's got to be more than enough water to refill our canteens and probably bathe off some of the sand. And for you history buffs? That city or oasis or whatever you want to call it isn't a new place. For that matter, it's not on any map or satellite image I've looked at."

"That's wonderful! Undiscovered ruins? I've always dreamed of finding something like that," Paige said excitedly, nearly bouncing atop her camel.

"Isn't that what you already did in Brazil?" he teased, but she just grinned.

"If there's good news, I'm guessing there's bad news, too. What is it?" Julian asked.

"There are at least two inhabitants...I think. Guards. You see those black shapes on the outside of the walls?" When they nodded, he continued, "They could be statues, but they could also be alive. From this distance, it's hard to tell. They look human other than the fact that they're black and gold and probably around ten feet tall. I have no fucking idea what they could be if they are alive, though. No Arcane I've ever met looked quite like that." At his words, Julian got a look of realization on his face. "You know what they are?"

"No. Well, maybe. But I think I know what the city is," Julian answered. "It came to me when you were talking about the guards. I remember hearing about an oasis or city that was somewhere in the Sahara. I don't remember much, except it was guarded by black giants and contained a sleeping king, queen, and their treasure. It was called...Damn, what was it?" He thought for a moment, sorting through his mental files. "That's it. Zerzura."

Both Paige and Wade shook their heads. "I've never heard of it," Wade admitted. "You remember if it's dangerous or not? We can still skirt around it if we need to."

"I honestly don't remember anything except what I just told you."

"Damn. Okay, so how about this? We start for it, but if those two giants act like they're going to fe fi fo fum us, we run like hell?"

"If by running you mean making the camels run, then I'm absolutely all right with that," Paige said. At this point, there was no way she could walk, much less run, not without help.

"That's fine by me," Julian agreed with a nod. After a moment, he smiled. "I think this is a good sign."

"A creepy ass city hidden in the middle of the desert is good?" Wade asked incredulously.

"Mmhmm. Don't you remember what Paige said when she held the amulet to get this location?"

Paige's recollection of what she said while holding the amulet was often fuzzy, at least the first time she touched a new piece, so she said nothing. Wade considered for a minute before he, too, smiled. "The piece was beyond an oasis, right?"

"Exactly. Yes, we've found a few small ones, but nothing on this scale. It might not be this oasis, but I would say it would be an extraordinary coincidence if it wasn't."

Paige joined them in smiling. "Then let's go."

Despite that revelation, all three were cautious and kept their camels at a slow pace as they approached the city. After a few minutes, Paige glanced apprehensively at Julian.

"Steady," he murmured.

When they got closer, they expected the guards to react in some way, but they remained as still as stone. Paige wasn't convinced they *weren't* statues, despite what Wade had said.

They were able to ride right up to the gate without being intercepted. Though the gate was made of metal bars, they were twisted until they formed the shape of a bird of some sort, with its wings outstretched. They could see through those thick bars to the city beyond, and Paige was stunned. The buildings were white, yes, just as they'd seen, but they hadn't been able to see the gold decoration that was present on every building. The intricacy of the designs was astonishing and absolutely beautiful. Plants grew everywhere, and not just the palm trees they'd seen from a distance, but brightly colored flowers in every shade of the rainbow. But that was the only color that could Paige could see from her vantage point. If the buildings were anything but white and gold, it was hidden from the gate.

Another thing she couldn't see were people. Though the city looked lived in rather than crumbling ruins, there weren't any signs of human—or inhuman—inhabitants.

"It's beautiful, but so empty," she murmured as she nudged her camel a little closer.

"Think you can get the gate open, Julian?" Wade asked, frowning as he looked around.

"Should be able to. When I get it up high enough, hurry through. I'm not sure how heavy it is, so let's not take any chances, okay?" Only after he'd gotten the assent of the others did he stretch out his hand and magically begin to lift the gate. It was heavier than he'd expected, but the gate was in better repair than he could have hoped, so there wasn't any resistance from rust or corrosion. "Go, now," he told them, and Wade urged his camel forward, grabbing the reins of Paige's mount to ensure she hurried as well. Only once they were both clear did Julian start forward. His mount was slower, since most of his focus was on keeping the gate from crashing down, but he made it with seconds to spare. And through it all, the guards didn't move.

"You smell anyone?" he asked Wade.

"No. This place just smells like the desert, aside from all the gold."

"You mean that's real gold, not just gold colored paint or something?" Paige asked in surprise.

"No, it's the real deal," Wade assured her.

"Let's check it out and see if we can find anyone. It's almost sundown, so if this place is abandoned, it might work for a camp for tonight," Julian told them.

They dismounted and began to search the buildings closest to the gate. The first one they entered was someone's home, or had been at one point. The furniture remained, as did knick-knacks and other decorations. Julian even found a chest full of clothes, but there was no food and nothing that could be considered truly personal.

The next building had been a shop and it still held its wares. Stone shelves were built right into the walls and held fabric and clothes, pottery, ropes, jewelry, and a number of other things. But like the home, it was impersonal and empty of life. Paige itched to take a small handled jug she saw, painted in vivid blue, gold, and red, but it felt wrong. Even though no one was around, it seemed too much like stealing to her.

Every building they searched after the first was in a similar condition; fully furnished, but no sign of any actual occupants, past or present.

"I don't get it. If they abandoned this place, why leave all this stuff? And why does it look like it could have been built yesterday?" Wade wondered as they moved toward the bright blue water that occupied the center of the city. "There's no erosion, the sun hasn't faded any of the colors...there aren't even any signs of insect or animal habitation."

"The witch's workshop we saw back in Cairo was just as new look-ing as this place," Paige pointed out. "Could be the same magic."

"Yeah, but doesn't explain where they went. Or why."

"I haven't seen any sort of journal or anything that could give an answer there," Julian said. "We could keep looking, or we could refill our canteens, get some sleep, and move on in the morning." They'd found the oasis easily, situated in the middle of the buildings. It was larger than Julian had expected to find, probably two acres in size, and hopefully the water would be suitable for their needs.

"Why don't we check there before we stop for the night?" Paige asked, pointing to a large, temple-like structure on the opposite side of the oasis. "I haven't seen any other buildings that were so big. Could be important."

"Red!" Wade said in a fake tone that radiated shock. "Didn't anyone ever tell you that size doesn't matter?" When she blushed bright red and sputtered, he laughed and gave her a wink. "Just teasing. We can check it out after we fill the canteens. The water smells clean."

They filled the canteens and did their best to bathe off some of the sweat and sand with clothes dipped in the water. Only then did they circle the water until they reached the steps of the building. Halfway up, Wade stopped and growled low, taking a single step back. At the same time, Paige jerked to a standstill and flinched as she was hit with a jolt of emotion and power.

"What is it?" Julian asked, retreating with them.

"I smell people, but it's not any sort of people we want to meet," Wade answered, voice still rough and dangerous.

"Demons?"

"I don't think so, but they smell...Powerful."

"He's right. I can feel them now," Paige whispered as she slowly moved backward down the stairs. "They're...not dead, but not awake, not quite. I think that if we went in there, they could wake up. That would be very...very...bad."

"Okay. Back out now. We'll camp once we're away from here," Julian said, turning to hurry down the stairs, an arm moving to Paige's back to urge her to move quicker.

"You don't have to tell me twice."

They ran through the streets, and the whole place felt ominous to Paige now, rather than simply empty and sad.

When they reached the camels, Wade plucked Paige off her feet and onto the animal before leaping onto his. "Time to get the gate up, Julian," he said urgently.

Julian slid into place on his mount and focused on the gate. He grunted softly. "It's heavier than it was."

Paige could see that he was straining much harder than before and guided her camel beside his. She took his hand and lent him strength and power, just like he'd done for her not so long ago. Though it wasn't the first time she'd done so, it clicked to her now that a kiss wasn't necessary to give someone power. She almost smiled. She'd revel in that once they were well away from the beings within the temple. With a grinding sound, the gate slowly raised, and they raced through it the moment it was high enough.

"What the hell was that?" Wade asked as they rode away. They needed to be on the other side of the city, but by unspoken agreement, they gave it a wide berth as they circled around.

"I don't know. The people you two sensed trying to keep us there?" Julian answered. "I'll ask around and see if anyone knows what happened to that place, but right now I'm happy just being away from it."

"So am I. The stuff I got from that place..." Paige shuddered. "It was dark. Worse than some of the things I've felt from people in the last few weeks."

"I've got the GPS, so I'll send that to you." Wade glanced back to the receding city. "I want to know what's there, but I'm not sure I want to know enough to check it out myself."

Coming from an adrenaline junkie, that said quite a bit.

They rode in silence for half an hour before they made camp, and said nothing when Paige huddled closer to the fire than usual.

CHAPTER 31

N one of the three slept well or long that night, though Julian was the least affected. He hadn't felt or smelled the things Paige or Wade had, and it was those experiences that had the two tossing and turning, when they were able to sleep at all. So they were slow to get going the next morning, though the anticipation from the amulet revived Paige somewhat.

She smiled tiredly. "We're getting close. If all goes well, I'd say we'll find it before the end of the day."

"Red, I could kiss you. That's the best news I've heard in days," Wade told her before impulsively giving her a loud smacking kiss right on the lips.

It had her laughing, so Julian just smiled. He'd been feeling less jealous lately of the affection between Paige and Wade. It really was more along the lines of love between siblings or best friends, and he had no doubt that Paige cared for him. He *knew* it was platonic between her and the wolf, and that neither would ever betray him. Truthfully, he could admit it was more the latter that had allowed him to relax. "Let's pack up and head out, then. The sooner we find it, the sooner we can put a lot of distance between us and that oasis."

The first verification that they were, in fact, going the right way was the snakes. Not a nest of them like Paige had seen, but one or two at a time, slithering across the sand. Her phobia kicked in, and even the best efforts from Wade to make her laugh only marginally worked. His jokes did keep her from panicking, which he settled for.

It was almost noon when her camel suddenly reared back before trying to rapidly sidestep, nearly unseating her. She cried out in surprise and leaned forward, clinging to the animal's neck. From the new vantage point, she could see why the camel had acted that way. There was a snake in the sand at the camel's feet, but it didn't look as though it had actually bitten her mount.

She urged the camel to move again, to go faster even as Julian called out, "What's wrong?"

"Snake! It tried to bite my camel!"

After a few minutes, both woman and beast relaxed, and though they saw more snakes, none were close enough to cause them harm.

Half an hour later, another snake appeared, again targeting Paige's mount. Then again, fifteen minutes after that. Somehow they all missed the camel, but each time it caused her mount to rear or shy and scared the hell out of Paige.

Fed up and worried for Paige, Julian rode close and pulled her off her camel and into his lap. She leaned against his chest, her back to an alert Wade, and tried to calm herself. But the change of camel didn't do much to ease her fears, no matter what her companions told her, not until Julian decided to try another method.

His hand slipped just under her shirt and he silenced her protests with a kiss. At first she was a little embarrassed at the display of affection, but the stroking of his fingers over her belly and persistent press of his lips had her softening for him and forgetting all about snakes. Wade's presence nearby was only heeded enough to keep Paige from moaning aloud, though it took her digging her nails into her palm to manage it.

She was considering asking Julian to find a boulder they could ride behind for some privacy just as everything went to hell.

The camel collapsed beneath them. Julian twisted so he landed on his back with Paige on top of him. He grunted at the impact, but it was lost in Paige's cry of surprise. Next to them, Wade was having the same problem, though he managed to jump free of his camel before it hit the sand. Even the one that Paige had started out riding had fallen.

Wade helped them get free of the camel before he bent to check one of the downed animals. Eyes grim, he looked up. "Dead," he said flatly.

"But...how?" She shook her head in denial. "We stopped for water only two hours ago, and they don't have a mark on them! There aren't even any snakes nearby." She did admit to herself that she might not have noticed passing any snakes with Julian distracting her, but surely she would have noticed one if it was here now. Not only that, but there's no way Wade would have allowed himself to get distracted, not now.

Wade shrugged as he got to his feet. "I honestly couldn't say. It's the damnedest thing I've ever seen," he admitted.

With nothing more to do, they got their packs off the camels. The last one had only just been picked up when small scorpions began to swarm out from under the lifeless bodies, completely covering them. Though the three quickly started to run, several scorpions followed and managed to latch onto their legs. Slapping at the arachnids got most of them off, but not before Julian got stung by one.

He hissed and stomped on the offender, which made it impossible for Paige not to notice. "Julian! Did it get you?"

"Yes, but we have bigger problems." He nodded, and, dread pooling in her belly, she looked back to the camels. The mass of scorpions was starting to move in their direction.

Anger and pain fueling his magic, Julian threw out his hands and fire spilled over the arachnids. Still, some tried to make their way across the sand toward their prey, but he didn't let up until every last one was little more than a charred husk.

The smell made Paige nauseous, but when Julian's hands dropped she grabbed the one that had been stung and started to fuss over him.

"I'm okay. I'll just take Suni's anti-venom now. It should work as well on scorpions as it would on snakes," he assured her. When she didn't look convinced, he smiled. "Suni's the best, as she'll happily tell you if you two meet."

"She will, too. Not a modest bone in that woman's body," Wade agreed with a nod. "Unfortunately, it's all well deserved, too. So if she said it's a universal antivenom, then you can put money on it."

Still, Paige wouldn't let up until she'd seen him drink the vial down and heal the tiny puncture mark. Once he'd gone several minutes without showing any ill effects, she agreed to continue on.

Their progress was slower than before now that they were on foot. Paige was more jumpy than she had been, since there was no distance now between her, the sand, and the snakes it hid. Each time she saw something move, she flinched, certain it was a serpent about to slither at her or a scorpion to sting her.

Oddly, they didn't see either creature. Not until they crested the top of a sand dune. Below was a sight familiar to Paige, the one the relic had shown her. Hundreds upon hundreds of dark, sleek bodies writhed together in the valley between dunes, so many that the sand beneath them was completely hidden.

Paige made a small sound and stepped closer to Julian's side. His arm slid around her, but he was staring in astonishment at the display before him. Even Wade was shocked into silence. Though they had expected quite a few snakes, this was beyond anything they had imagined. Paige's reaction to the vision back in England made a great deal more sense now.

Wade pulled out his binoculars and peered down into the squirming mess. "She was right," he said without taking his eyes off the snakes. "Definitely Egyptian asps. I was really hoping you were wrong about that, though, Red. That and the jewel being *in* the sand instead of on a nice, neat altar." He lowered the binoculars with disgust. "I can't see a fucking thing except snakes. No wonder you were so worried about how we'd get through them. Is the jewel in the middle of all those things?"

"I hope not, because if they're anything like the things guarding the other pieces, then they're not going to be easy to deal with. Paige, can you pinpoint where the relic is?" Julian asked, but Paige didn't hear him.

She twisted around to look behind her. That presence was back again. Every other time she'd noticed the intrusion, it had always disappeared, but it wasn't going away now. She took a step away from the men as they continued to talk, and reached out with her magic. Pinpointing it was impossible. It seemed to come from everywhere. Nor could she get any sort of emotion or a thought.

But she was able to sense how powerful it was.

"Paige? Did you hear me?" Julian asked again.

"Hmm?" Right, he'd asked her a question. "Oh, sorry. No, I can't." Knowing that neither Julian nor Wade would be able to scent or sense anything, Paige said nothing about the watchful presence when they retreated a few feet. They set the tent up so they'd have shade while they figured out what to do, but Wade insisted that all the windows be opened so he could see if anyone or anything approached. No one argued with that.

"There's too many for any sort of weapon to do any good," Wade said, even as his fingers drummed lightly on his sheath. "I could get some of them, but we'd end up overrun if I tried." He nodded to Julian. "Could you burn them? Like you did with the scorpions?"

"I don't know how well it would work with there being so many," Julian admitted. "Though if we don't think of anything else I can certainly give it a try."

Since strategy—especially fighting strategy—wasn't her forte, Paige only half-listened while she watched for snakes venturing near them.

After a few minutes, she frowned when she noticed other minds nearby. Their thoughts were unformed, fuzzy, but they were there. More, there were a lot of them.

"I'll be right back," she murmured as she climbed out of the tent, and though Julian glanced up, he assumed she was just going to relieve herself.

She didn't go far, just a few feet out of the tent, enough to allow her to see the snakes. It took more effort than she would ever had admitted to get so close to them without Julian or Wade by her side, but she did it.

Concentrating on the snakes, those amorphous minds became clearer. There was an instant of joy as she realized that she wasn't limited to human minds, and it was quickly followed by an idea. She glanced back to the tent, then bit her lip and focused on the snake closest to her. She reached out to it, thinking at it to turn back. Nothing happened. She concentrated harder on trying to force it back to the other snakes, so intent on her task that she didn't realize that both Julian and Wade were standing beside her, and the former was speaking.

When the snake turned around and slithered away, she let out the breath she'd been holding and the tension that had built in her body relaxed. It happened so abruptly that she lost her balance and fell directly into Wade. Luckily, he caught her and held her up until she was steady again.

"Want to explain what just happened?" Julian asked, confused and a little concerned.

She realized that neither had seen the snake's actions, and even if they had, they wouldn't understand the significance. Elated, she pointed toward the reptiles. "I turned it back!"

"What?" Wade asked, just as perplexed as Julian.

"The snake! While you two were talking, I realized I felt all these other minds. But they don't think like we do. It's all sort of...unfo cused. But with so few people around, and since I was kind of...not paying attention," she admitted with a guilty smile, "I realized that I was feeling the snakes, that they were all the minds I sensed. Then...I don't know. For some reason, I decided to try to control one of them. I've never had that sort of ability before, but I focused on one of them and made it turn around!"

For a long moment there was no reaction other than Wade giving her a worried look. Desperate for one of them to believe her, she turned to Julian, astonished to see that he was starting to smile.

"I've got an idea." He grabbed her hand and pulled her over to where they'd set their packs just outside the tent. He began to search through his as he talked. "There are a couple of things you've never been able to do before that you've done lately, right?"

"Yes, actually. But—"

"And it all started when you began wearing your mother's ring, didn't it?"

She blinked, then lifted her hand to look at the ring. "I hadn't thought about it before, but...yes, I think so." She considered a moment before she nodded more definitively. "Yes."

He pulled the green bottle out of his pack and sat back on his heels, grinning up at her. "I told you the ring was magic, probably a relic, and the timing is right. I think somehow it's given your magic a boost. Your empathy and telepathy, anyway. I haven't seen you try anything more physical since then. This," he lifted the bottle for both to see, "was given to me by Suni."

Paige took it when it was offered, but there wasn't much to see. Just a liquid, probably clear, shifting inside as she moved the bottle. "What is it?"

Wade took it and carefully removed the cap, sniffing at it. "Smells herbal. And magical," he told them before closing the bottle again. "It probably won't hurt you if it came from Suni, though."

"That's the thing. Suni didn't know what it was for. She just asked what color your eyes were, then gave it to me, saying that I'd need it."

"Need it for what?" Wade asked.

"She said I'd know when and how to use it, but that was all she could tell me."

"Ugh. She did the prophetess thing again, didn't she?"

"Exactly."

Paige took the bottle back from Wade, leery of its contents, no matter who gave it to Julian. "And you think that I need to drink it now?"

"I do. I think it'll help you with the snakes," Julian said with a sure nod.

"You're right," said a familiar gravely voice from behind Paige.

Wade was closest and shoved Paige behind him so quickly she almost fell. Before she was fully behind him, he had a knife in his hand.

Julian leapt to his feet and stood shoulder to shoulder with Wade, effectively forming a living wall in front of Paige.

The man was tall, more than six and a half feet, and well muscled. His arms were the most impressive, shown off as they were in a white tee-shirt that had tiny little holes dotted through it. His hair was short and dark brown, his skin was tanned and only a few shades lighter, while his eyes were a shade darker. He wasn't a handsome man in any conventional sense. His features were a little too off-center, too asymmetrical for that, his nose a touch too big, his lips a touch too thin. It was also obvious that he had a limp, and his bad leg, mostly exposed by the cargo shorts he wore, looked like half the muscle had simply been removed. Worse yet were all the old burns and scars that littered his flesh.

The most notable thing about him wasn't his size or appearance, but the sheer power that radiated from him. It was potent enough that all three could sense it without trying.

Seeing the defensive posture of both men, the stranger said, "I don't mean any of you harm." His lips twisted into what might pass for a smile. "But I'm one of the few who can say that at the moment."

Julian frowned as something about the man tugged at his brain. He seemed familiar somehow, but at the same time, Julian would swear he'd never seen the man before in his life.

Paige could barely see past her guards, but a glimpse of the stranger was enough to trigger recognition. This was the man from her dream, the man who'd been watching her since Brazil. He'd even been there, in person, when they emerged from the water in Russia.

She knew she'd seen someone there!

In a rush, all the pieces came together in her mind. A man with intense power, who was around when a millennia-old relic was created, who took notice of craftsmen, and could see and do more than anyone in the Arcane could. Add that to her knowledge of mythology, and she knew exactly who he was. It was a leap, she knew it, but she did know it, just like she'd known Julian's address three years before.

She pushed at Julian's back, but he didn't move, so she simply stepped around him, shrugging off the hand that shot out to stop her. For once, she was unafraid. "You're Hephaestus," she said with utter certainty.

Julian went very still behind her. "Hephaestus?"

"The god?" Wade asked, body thrumming as he expected a fight. The gods were the ones who destroyed the relics, so was Hephaestus here to kill them for trying to put one back together? It wasn't out of the realm of possibility, but he didn't know how they could stand against a god.

Hephaestus inclined his head to Paige. "You are very perceptive."

"You're the one who's been watching me. Following me." It wasn't a question.

"I am." He looked toward Wade and Julian. "So you see, if I wanted to harm any of you, I could have done it weeks ago."

"But sir...why are you here? I thought the gods would be against us doing what we're doing," Paige said respectfully.

"Not all of the gods," he said firmly. "But yes, some are. If you take the last piece of that amulet, they've already ordered assassins to kill you."

"It wouldn't be the first time," Wade muttered.

"Then why are you here?" Julian asked suspiciously.

Hephaestus gave him a bored look. "You *do* know what I'm the god of, don't you?"

Wade shrugged and answered, "Fire."

The god snorted. "Yes, with all these burns, I'm the god of *fire*," he said sarcastically.

He was associated with fire, yes, said to have his forge inside a volcano, but that wasn't where his powers were centered, she knew. "Blacksmiths," Paige said quietly. "You're the god of blacksmiths."

He touched his nose. "Bingo. In other words, I make things. Hell, I made most of the magical objects that the gods used. So why in the name of Olympus would I want to see them destroyed? But...I was overruled," he added bitterly.

"Are you here to help us, then?" she asked hopefully.

He drew in a deep breath. "Can't. Not how you want me to, any-way." But Paige thought he sounded apologetic. "I *can*, however, give you a bit of advice. That ring of yours? It does exactly what your man said it did. If you're wearing it, your telepathy, your empathy, will be much stronger. Better yet?" He grinned slyly. "I've hidden it from the other gods. They don't know it exists. Not that they'd care about a relic such as that. It's not powerful enough. Still, better to be safe than sorry, right?"

Wary of gods, Wade asked, "Why would you do that?"

The grin faded and he gave Wade a sharp look. "You ask a lot of questions, pup. But it's because the women in her family have always been good and kind, and one of them is the person who made it. Seemed fitting that she be able to wear the blasted thing."

Paige gasped and cradled the hand wearing the ring against her chest. "One of my ancestors *made* this?"

Hephaestus's manner softened. "She did. So keep it safe, and use it well." There was a pause. "I can't help you any more than I already have. Good luck." He gave Paige a paternal sort of smile, then vanished.

Paige stood there, absolutely stunned by the whole thing. Suddenly she felt giddy, even hopeful, despite the countless snakes nearby.

"What the hell did he mean couldn't help more than he has? Other than telling us what the ring does, he hasn't done anything, has he?" Wade muttered, snatching up a water bottle and drinking deeply.

"But he has..." Paige said slowly.

"What do you mean?" Julian asked.

"Think about it. I told you that he was the one who's been watching me. I think he gave us little nudges here and there," Paige said as she turned to face them.

"Like what?" Wade asked, curious.

"Well, like now. How did I get the idea to control the snakes? It wasn't something that would ever occur to me. I don't control people.

I don't *want* to control people, for that matter. And Wade, all those times when you would just suddenly veer off and tell us there was water that way, how did you know? Or Julian, in Russia...I know you were drained. You'd bespelled all three of us, then used a lot of magic in the fight. So how did you have the power to get us out of the water?"

Wade was the first to speak, his tone uncertain. "I...am not sure, to be honest. I just knew."

"Like Suni just knew we'd need what's in this bottle?" Paige asked with a smile, holding it up and wiggling it.

"I think she's right," Julian said after thinking it over. "Subtle things, nothing that could really be construed as out of the ordinary."

"I hope he comes back," Paige murmured wistfully.

Startled, Julian asked, "Why?"

"After everything he's done, I want to tell him thank you."

Unsurprised at Paige's generosity, he pulled her into his arms. "Of course you do."

"Okay, save that for later, you two. Are we doing this?" Wade asked.

Julian leaned back so he could see Paige's face. "You up for it?"

She smiled, bolstered by the presence of her two favorite people, and the support of a god. "Let's do it."

CHAPTER 32

They got everything packed up before they did anything, knowing that if this worked, they wouldn't have time to grab their
things before Julian teleported them home. Once done, they stood
atop the dune overlooking the snakes.

"You ready for this?" Julian asked, the potion held toward Paige,
but he didn't release it immediately.

"As ready as I'll ever be. I can do this, Julian," she told him with
a confidence she only half felt. But she knew if she couldn't, then
there was no way they were going home with the gemstone. Not
today, in any case. But that didn't necessarily have to be the end. They
knew where the stone was now. They knew what was protecting it.
If they did have to leave today, they could plan better and come with
something guaranteed to work against snakes.

He hesitated a moment before relinquishing the bottle to her. "All
right, but if you need to stop, just let us know and we'll get you out of
here."

"I will. Promise." Before drinking the potion, Paige sniffed it. Herbs
and magic were the perfect way to describe it, though she couldn't
identify any of the ingredients in it. She gave the others a smile and
cheerfully said, "Bottoms up!" before she drank it. It tasted exactly as it

smelled, and pleasantly so. A hard shiver worked through her body and she gasped when she felt power pouring through every cell in her body until she was full to bursting. "Oh gods," she whispered. "That's…" She closed her eyes as she tried to adjust. "Amazing," she breathed. It felt as though she'd just stuck her finger not in an electrical outlet, but straight into a power station.

"You okay?" Julian asked. When her eyes opened, he was shocked to see that they were glowing, even without the amulet touching any part of her skin. It made him wonder if the relic itself had somehow boosted her power in the past, perhaps lending it to the person it sensed could help reassemble it. If that were the case, then the glowing eyes weren't really a side-effect of the amulet, but of her power.

"I'm wonderful." Better than wonderful. She'd never felt this amazing before. She felt invincible, like she could do anything, but also a little drunk. Just pleasantly so, not fall down drunk. Part of her knew the feeling was dangerous, but she also trusted Julian and Wade to prevent her from doing anything foolish.

Not quite so pleased, Julian gently turned her toward the snakes. "Time to move the snakes then, sweetheart. We don't know how long the potion will last."

She gave him a brilliant smile before her attention shifted to the snakes and the jewel they were guarding. Even without touching the amulet she could feel the stone, the power it radiated, somewhere in the midst of all those serpents. So close to its other pieces, it pulsed with power. "I can feel it there," she murmured, lifting a hand and pointing to a spot almost dead center of the mass of snakes.

Wade stood ready at her side, hand already on his knife. He trusted Paige, but he didn't trust the gods or their tricks, and he wasn't going to let her suffer because of them. "Move the snakes and get us there, Red, and I'll grab it for you."

Her arms lifted, palms facing toward the snakes, and she closed her eyes to help her focus on the task before her. She drew in a deep breath and touched the serpentine minds. After only a few seconds, the first of the snakes started to turn, slithering away from the trio. Her mind left those and moved to the next closest group and turned them back as well.

As the leading edge of the mass receded, Paige stepped forward, slowly working her way toward the center of the knot where she felt the stone. Giddy with the power, her phobia was temporarily shoved to the back of her mind, letting her move easily toward the reptiles. Julian and Wade walked with her, sticking close to her sides to protect her in case any of the snakes slipped from her control.

Their progress wasn't quick, and the longer it continued, the slower it went. After the first few minutes, the snakes seemed to realize what was going on, and unless they were under direct control, they tried to reach the trio. This meant that Paige had to focus on more minds at once than she'd counted on. Before long, it was a struggle to remember to move forward. Worse, even with her temporary power hike, it became harder to keep all the snakes contained, much less move them where she wanted them to.

Sweat dripped into her eyes, but she only blinked it away, not daring to lift a hand even for a second. Her body trembled with the force of the magics moving through her, and the effort it took to command so many at once.

When they reached the spot she'd initially felt the jewel, they were surrounded on all sides by dark, hissing figures. Even the normally carefree Wade looked uneasy at their current position.

Paige's eyes opened and she gave a soft cry. "It's not here! It's moved!" Her dismay temporarily disrupted the hold she had on the asps and they gathered themselves, preparing to strike. The first snakes were surging toward them when she clumsily reached out and took control of them once more. It was harder for her to hold them now, her power drained. She only had minutes, at the most, before they broke free and attacked at will.

Julian and Wade knelt and searched through the sand, hoping that she'd been overwhelmed by her task and overlooked the jewel, but she hadn't. The stone, if it had ever been in this spot, had been moved, perhaps by the motion of the snakes as they retreated from Paige.

Wade stood and looked over the snakes, looking for some sign of the jewel. A shimmer, a gleam, anything that might tell him that it was still here somewhere. All he saw was sand and snakes. But something, perhaps Hephaestus's influence, made him look in just the right direction. There was one snake that was different from the rest. It was bigger than the others, and though he had to squint to see it, he could make out a spot on the back of the snake's head that was just a shade or two lighter than the rest of its scales. A spot that formed a symbol. He didn't recognize it, but he didn't need to. It was enough for him to understand that it meant this snake was special.

He drew his knife from its sheath, and though it wasn't made specifically for throwing, he still flung it at the snake. It struck the reptile just behind the head, neatly killing it and pinning it in place. Before the others could ask what he was doing, he darted forward and snatched up the limp reptile. He was quick, but not quick enough to prevent one of the other asps from striking and latching onto his wrist.

"Get us out of here, Julian! Now!" he demanded as he rushed back to them, laying a hand on Paige's shoulder.

"No!" Paige cried. "We haven't found it yet!"

"Just do it!" Wade roared.

Julian trusted Wade's judgment, and he was concerned about what this was doing to Paige, but he wavered.

The decision was ultimately made for him.

At the break in Paige's concentration, she completely lost control of the snakes, who darted for the three, moving over boots and trying to climb legs.

Julian grabbed Paige's arm, then flashed them back to Mooreton.

They didn't travel alone.

The snakes that had been touching them when they teleported were pulled along with them.

Paige screamed, her fear back in full force, even with her eyes still shining, just a little, with power. Instantly, she ran backwards until she hit a wall.

Wade stomped on and stabbed the snakes he could reach, while Julian used magic to blast them. Fortunately, there were only eight snakes, so between the two of them they managed it quickly. Just not quickly enough to prevent both Paige and Wade from receiving bites.

"Quickly, take your antivenom," Julian snapped to Wade, while he fished out Paige's vial and held it to her lips until she swallowed. He'd already taken his, but he hoped there was still enough in his system to be effective.

After Wade had taken his, Paige gave him a betrayed look. "Why did you tell him to go? We don't have the jewel yet!"

"Tsk. Doubting your favorite wolf," Wade said in a mock hurt tone as he retrieved the snake he'd killed in Egypt. "This one was different from the others." He turned it so Julian could see the symbol on the snake's head. "And look, it's bigger than the others, and there's this little bulge right here." He picked up his knife, then hesitated. "Close your eyes." Paige may not be innocent in the ways of violence or death any longer, but he didn't want to traumatize her further.

Paige didn't argue and closed her eyes immediately.

He slit the snake's belly open, then smiled. He reached in and drew something out of the snake, wiping it off on his pant leg. "Open your eyes," he murmured.

She did, though reluctantly, only to gasp at the round, iridescent jewel held between his thumb and forefinger. "I will never doubt you again!" she told him as she rushed forward, eager to complete the amulet.

Before she could reach him, they were surrounded once again.

CHAPTER 33

F our men and one woman, all wearing black robes, appeared and formed a circle around them. None of them looked happy, and all of them were armed.

Paige moved closer to Julian, while Wade moved in front of her. They couldn't fully protect her, not from all five, but they were going to try.

One of the men spoke. "You should not have gone against the gods and retrieved the pieces."

When another of the men spoke, there was no pause. Their words flowed seamlessly from one to the other like they had a hive mind. "If you give us the pieces, all of them, without first completing the amulet, the gods will allow you to live."

A third man added, "But you must not ever seek to reassemble any other relics the gods have decreed taboo."

The woman picked up their speech. "If you do not agree to this, then we will kill all three of you, here and now."

The last man said only, "Choose."

Acting quickly, Paige linked her mind to Julian and Wade. "Please, can we have just a moment to discuss this?" she asked.

They neither spoke nor moved for several heartbeats. "You may, but do not attempt to escape, or leave the room," said the first man.

The woman added, "You cannot teleport, and you must not complete the amulet."

The trio huddled together, but spoke mentally.

"I'm so sorry Paige, but if these are assassins of the gods, we're going to need your help," Julian thought. *"They'll be extremely well-trained and very powerful. Can you take care of one of them?"*

"Can't we just give them the amulet? It's not worth our lives," she thought back.

"I'm pretty sure they're going to kill us either way, Red," Wade thought with a shake of his head. *"The gods lie, and they don't like it when people ignore their rules. They'll make an example of us."* He hesitated, then added, *"I'm not sure why they didn't just attack and take the amulet already."*

The thought of her impending death, much less that of Wade and Julian, made something inside her snap. She was furious. The gods would kill them even if they gave up the amulet? How dare they? They were not going to take her best friend and the man she loved away from her. She hadn't even had the chance to tell Julian she loved him. A week with him wasn't nearly long enough. No, she wouldn't allow the gods to do this. She could not allow them to be made into examples!

Still high on the power Suni's potion had given her, though it was largely depleted from controlling the snakes, Paige looked at the assassins. She looked each one in the face as her anger built until she couldn't contain it any longer. Before the thought had fully formed in her mind, she struck out with a ferocity and skill she'd never possessed before. The ordeals with the shark people and the snakes had taught her much about herself and her powers. Things she wished she'd never learned, but she would still use them to protect those she cared about.

She didn't just attack one of the assassins. With their minds linked together, lashing out at one meant she struck out at all five simultaneously. Her magic hit their minds and in the first instant, she felt that connection, almost identical to the one she shared with Julian and Wade. In the second instant, she shoved magic at their minds, overloading them. Joined as she was with them for that moment, she felt an echo of the agony they felt. Invisible spikes rammed into their minds, tearing through them. Killing them.

As one, the five assassins screamed in pain before the sound ended abruptly, like a switch flipped off.

Astonished, Julian watched as all five simply crumpled to the ground, their eyes open but unseeing. Unbelieving that Paige had not only attempted to do such a thing, but managed it, he looked back at her and stared. The unearthly light was almost gone from her eyes, but she still looked absolutely livid. And absolutely amazing.

But he knew that the enormity of what she'd done hadn't hit her yet. When it did, she would suffer, far more than she'd suffered for the killings in Russia or Antarctica.

"Paige..."

The arrival of seven more figures interrupted him, and he noted that while the last five had looked determined, these assassins looked supremely pissed.

Paige's borrowed power was almost spent, but she wasn't going to go down without a fight. Instinct guided her to the weakest of the seven assassins, and she latched onto his mind. She didn't have the strength now to take out this group like she had the last, but she had enough to control, at least for a minute. Her target hadn't been expecting that sort of attack, so the struggle for his mind was surprisingly brief. Obeying her commands, he threw his knife at one of his companions, hard enough that it sank into the man's chest up to the hilt.

Seeing the light fade from the assassin's eyes, Paige cried out with horror at what she had done and inadvertently signaled the start of the fight.

Trembling with effort, she held onto the assassin's mind. She was unable to force him to attack his allies again, but neither could he break free of her hold. Since it kept one person out of the fight, kept one person from attacking her friends, she refused to release him.

Wade shifted into his wolf form. His clothes tried to stretch to accommodate him, but ended up on the floor in tatters. Even before the change was complete, he was moving. He leapt at one of the assassins, who brought a knife up to protect himself. Wolf and man lunged and circled one another, both suffering in the attack as claws and blade sliced over skin. Wade feigned a lunge to the right, only to dart in and tackle the man to the ground and go for the throat.

The moment he felt the life leave the man, he leapt at another assassin. This one blocked his teeth with her arm while she shoved a dagger into his side. He snarled at the pain, but kept attacking.

Magic was Julian's weapon of choice, and he started to throw blasts of raw power at the assassins. That was the type of attack the gods' executioners had expected when they came, and they were more prepared for it. They blocked his attacks and started to throw their own. Magic hit all around the foyer, destroying paintings and smashing vases and furniture, but little got through to the people locked in battle.

The balance changed when Wade managed to deal with his oppo-nent and leapt right into the fray, taking the three against one battle down to two against one.

The witches were at a stalemate until Julian switched tactics. "Wade! Move!" he yelled, and the wolf's trust was true enough that he didn't hesitate. Julian aimed his next blast at the chain holding the heavy iron chandelier and sent it crashing downward. One of the assassins managed to avoid it, but the other was crushed beneath it. Not dead yet, but he would be soon.

With the odds down to one against one for both Julian and Wade, and Julian felt a spurt of triumph.

No one saw the second woman sneaking around the edge of the fight until she was behind Paige. An arm wrapped around Paige's throat at the same time that a knife pressed against her ribs, hard enough to break flesh. Paige gave a soft cry of pain and lost her control over the other witch.

Free to do his job, the man threw a fireball at Julian, then another, and another.

Having heard Paige's cry, Julian looked to her and got hit square in the shoulder. He wasn't braced for the attack and it knocked him onto his back, but that caused the next two fireballs to fly over his head and hit the wall. Lying prone, he retaliated, hitting hard enough that the man flew back and smashed his head against the staircase railing, knocking him out. Not trusting that the man would stay down, he started for him, but the woman's voice—cold, lethal—had him stop-ping mid-motion.

"Stop. Hand over the relic, all of it, or I'm going to kill the little murderer here." She pressed the blade a little deeper, making Paige whimper.

After shifting back to human, Wade was nude and still mentally linked. *"Control her, like you did the other one. Save yourself, Red!"*

Guilt rode Paige hard, the assassin's words, 'little murderer,' sending ice deep into her belly. *"I can't!"* she cried to them.

"You can, Red. Do it!"

"No, I've used too much. I don't have the power!"

"Take mine," Julian thought.

"What?" The thought terrified her.

Julian looked calm despite his offer. *"Take my power. As much as you need. Use it, save yourself. Save us!"* he insisted. He was desperate not to lose her, but alongside that thought was his complete faith in her ability to protect herself. That faith helped give her courage.

It was dangerous, she knew. It was one thing for a witch to give power, but to forcibly take it, even if the witch was willing? That wasn't a thing to be taken lightly. Magic didn't give life to witches, they could survive as mortals with their powers stripped, but it was much a part of them as hearing or the color of their hair. And Paige knew she'd have to take a lot to do what they were asking her to do.

Reluctantly, she closed her eyes and tugged on Julian's connection to her, drawing power from him. It felt different from the time he'd lent her power. Instead of a comfortable warmth, the stolen power was icy and itched beneath her skin, but still she drew more of it.

Wanting to give Paige time to draw enough power to save herself, Wade spoke. "What assurances do we have that you won't just kill us all the moment you have the amulet?" Out of the corner of his eye he saw Julian jerk, the drain affecting him physically as well as magically, and continued quickly, hoping that he could keep the assassin from noticing. "For all we know you don't even work for the gods, you just want the amulet for yourself."

The power from Julian filled her, almost as heady as Suni's potion. Paige had known he was strong, but she hadn't realized how strong. Pride for him pricked at the back of her mind, but she forced herself to focus. She prepared to try to control the woman, but she heard another voice, one that was just a whisper in her mind. Neither male nor female, she couldn't identify it. All she knew was it wasn't either Julian or Wade, and neither gave any indication they heard it. It didn't even sound like Hephaestus.

"It won't work, child. She's prepared for you to try to control her. If you want to save yourself, don't think. React. *"*

The woman ran out of patience before Paige could ask what the voice meant.

"Give it to me now!" she screamed, digging the knife in deeper, pressing it between two of her ribs. Much further and it would strike something vital.

The pain of it made Paige scream and she forgot about her control. She forgot about her moral code that made her feel guilty for acting in self-defense. She stopped thinking and reacted, just as the voice had commanded.

The magic within her almost had a life of its own as it attacked the woman threatening her life. There was no attempt made to control her, no trying to destroy her mind. It was pain she inflicted on the assassin, as sharp as the blade invading her body.

Legs no longer able to hold her, the woman shrieked and fell, dragging her knife down Paige's side and hip before she hit the floor. The pain didn't end there, and neither did her screams.

The sting of the blade hit Paige's senses and she started to fall forward. Only Julian's timely catch prevented her from landing face first on the hard floor.

He knew what Wade would do next and turned Paige, shielding her from seeing the wolf snap the woman's neck.

The screams stopped.

Julian kept holding Paige until Wade had ensured that the unconscious man wasn't going to try to harm them ever again. "You okay?" he asked roughly.

"It hurts," she said in a small voice.

He lowered himself to the floor with her in his lap, so he could look at the cut. While it was nearly a foot long, it was only deep near the top. "I'll bet." He went to lay a hand over the injury when Wade shouted, "Don't!"

Julian scowled at him. "She's hurting, Wade," he snapped.

Wade was kneeling by the woman and had her blade in his hands. "I smell poison on this," he said bleakly. "You remember the poison from Brazil? This is a variation of that."

The poison made from gorgon blood. The painful, quick-acting poison. Julian nodded and closed his eyes. Now that he was looking, he could sense the poison that was even now working its way through Paige's veins. Veins that hardened with each passing breath, slowing the blood that pumped through them.

Though weakened, he still had enough power for this, he thought, and tried to neutralize it.

It took three attempts before he realized that it was no use. His magic couldn't save her. He was going to lose the woman he loved. Again.

Wade saw the panic on Julian's face and knelt beside him. "Get Suni," he said quietly. "I'll stay with her."

"What's wrong?" Paige asked weakly, unable to lift her hand or even turn her head.

"I...I just need to get Suni," Julian said in a choked voice. He carefully shifted Paige off of him and grabbed Wade's discarded shirt to wad up under her head to cushion it against the unforgiving stone floor. There was so much fear for Paige that he couldn't even care that Wade was naked around his lover. "Watch her," he told the wolf before sending himself to Suni's house.

There was no polite landing in the yard this time. Julian appeared right in her living room, finding her sitting in her rocking chair, knitting, of all things. Later he might be amused to find the formidable Suni knitting, but he barely noticed at the moment.

She set aside the yarn and needles and surged to her feet. "You do *not* just teleport into my house!" she snapped. It was a rule she'd set centuries ago and had firmly enforced.

Julian shook his head. "Suni...It's Paige..."

The worry and the look of terror on his face penetrated Suni's outrage instantly. "Tell me."

He swallowed thickly. "We were attacked by assassins sent by the gods. And I don't know which gods. One of them stabbed Paige with a poisoned knife. I couldn't do anything. Suni, please, *help her.*"

She paled. "I don't know if I can. Not if the poison came from the gods," she told him, half-running toward her greenhouse. "Do you know what kind of poison it is?"

"You have to try, Suni. Please. I don't know what kind of poison it is. Wade said it smelled like it had powdered gorgon blood in it, though."

The curse muttered in a language even Julian didn't know ramped his worry up. If Suni was that concerned, then it wasn't good.

She quickly gathered what she might need and laid a hand on his shoulder. "I swear I will do everything I can."

"Thank you."

He took them back to his house, but the moment he saw Paige, he yelled, "No!" and fell to his knees beside her.

In the few minutes he had been gone, she'd deteriorated rapidly. Her breathing was weaker, and a quick check of her pulse showed that it was too slow, too faint. Her skin had developed a blue tinge to it, and worse, he saw that her veins had begun turning black. He watched one and could almost see the blackness spreading further.

"What kind of poison is this?" he whispered in a voice full of pain. "Gorgon's blood couldn't do this, could it?"

"I don't know," Suni admitted, apology in her eyes. As much as she hated to admit it, she was very much afraid that Julian was going to have to bury another woman he loved. Still, she tried, using every piece of knowledge she'd picked up in all her long years, and that knowledge was extensive. Various herbs were tried, along with every antidote that Suni had in her possession. Even the magic she used for herself, magic long forgotten by the rest of the world, couldn't help.

Minutes passed and Paige only got worse. It tore at Suni to see Julian clinging to Paige's hand, murmuring reassuringly, though the woman was barely conscious. Every vein in Paige's body had turned black, and the blue over her skin had deepened, giving her an otherworldly appearance. She was about to tell Julian the bad news, that she had failed, when she felt something odd in the air.

Both Julian and Wade lifted their heads, an out-of-place look of hope on their faces. The power felt familiar to them, and it took no time for them to recognize it as Hephaestus. For a moment, they were certain he was going to show up and help Paige, but no one appeared.

"What? Why do you two look like something good happened?" Suni demanded.

Instead of an answer, a small bottle appeared, hovering in place a foot above Paige. There was a label on it which faced Suni, the writing faded nearly to invisibility from age.

"What the hell is that?" Wade asked, angry that instead of coming himself, Hephaestus had sent some sort of tonic.

Suni leaned in to better read it, though it was difficult to make out the letters. When she managed it, her breath caught, the same moment that Julian snatched it out of the air. "Give it to me!" she told him, reaching for the bottle.

He scowled, but knew better than to argue with her and held it out to her. "Why? What is it?"

"Mithridate! Other than divine intervention, it's the only thing that has a chance of saving her," she explained as she opened the bottle and carefully poured a few drops on Paige's tongue. She wasn't certain of the dosage as she'd never had the privilege of using it herself, and watched Paige carefully in case she needed to administer another few drops. She wasn't entirely certain it would be enough, as its creator,

Mithridates, had been a talented human rather than Arcane, but it was all they had.

And there wasn't much in the bottle.

"I think in this case that the bottle was divine intervention," Wade murmured to Julian, but he got no response. Julian was too busy watching for signs that it was, in fact, the cure.

Paige gave him a weak smile before her eyes closed and she went completely still.

"No! Paige! You can't die!" he cried, dragging her half into his lap. "What did you do?" he yelled at Suni.

"Calm down, Julian," she told him, sounding infinitely more calm than she felt. "Mithridate is an antidote. A very powerful one created millennia ago that works on any and all poisons. Even those created by the gods." Or she hoped. She'd never read anything stating it could cure divine poisons, but Julian needed to believe for as long as possible.

"But she—"

He stopped when Suni gave him a sharp look. Satisfied for the moment, she examined Paige and breathed a silent sigh of relief. "She's just passed out. The poison worked very rapidly. While a cure, mithridate can only neutralize the poison, not instantly reverse its effects. It may take some time for her to heal, even with my assistance, but there's no danger of her dying now. I swear it."

He wanted to believe her. "If mithridate is so good, why didn't you have any?"

"Oh, I wish I did, believe me. Unfortunately, the recipe was lost before I was even born. I didn't even think that any more of it still remained in this world. Or any other, for that matter. Someone must have saved some." She looked at Paige. "And given that just a few drops of this stuff are worth any amount of riches, this someone must like either you or Paige very, very much."

"Paige. It's her, all her," he whispered, kissing Paige's brow before he loosened his grip somewhat. He didn't want her to regain consciousness with her body full of bruises.

Suni smiled. "She must be very special. Now, I can see you two are hurt, so why don't you let me heal you, then you can move Paige to a bed until she wakes up? And before you ask, yes, I'll stay until she's fully recovered." At their assent, she touched a hand to their arms, healing the cuts and burns they'd suffered in the fight. Unlike Julian, who had to struggle to heal serious wounds, her healing was effortless. Part of that was her power, while some was simply centuries of practice. "Better?"

"Much." Julian got to his feet and picked Paige up.

"Definitely. You take care of her, Julian, and I'll take care of the trash. Suni, would you mind helping with the disposal?" Wade asked.

"Of course. But only if you find some pants. Hasn't Julian suffered enough today?"

Wade only grinned and shrugged, unconcerned about his state of undress.

"Thank you. Both of you. If you ever need anything, just let me know and I'll be there," Julian said, unable to appreciate the light banter between Suni and Wade. Not yet. Not until Paige woke up. And she had to wake up.

"Oh, I'll collect one day, but right now you just get her to bed," Wade told Julian with a grin before he started removing the bodies.

Julian nodded once, then took Paige upstairs and laid her in his bed. Where she belonged.

CHAPTER 34

The first night, Julian bathed the blood off of Paige's skin. Though it was all hers, he was worried that if she woke with such a visible reminder of the fight, of the lives she'd taken, she'd panic. Afterward, he'd dressed her in her favorite pajamas before he crawled into the bed with her and held her while they slept. He'd hoped that she'd wake the next day, but she lay as still the second day as she did the first, so he remained with her. The blackness of her veins had receded, and was completely gone by that evening. The blue tint of her skin was slower to fade, but Julian could see her normal fair complexion was returning.

During this time Wade and Suni took turns checking in, not just on Paige, but Julian as well. He barely slept, and when he did it was in spurts that were spent holding Paige like he was afraid she would fade away if he let her go. He wouldn't let either of them tend to her, though he did let Suni examine Paige to ensure that she truly was getting better. Despite her reassurances that yes, Paige was improving and the poison was leaving her system, Julian refused to leave just in case something else did happen.

They would bring him food, but if he touched it, it was only to pick at it, even when they brought his favorite foods. Suni considered drugging his food so he would actually sleep, but rejected the idea only a moment later. He wasn't eating enough for most of the concoctions she could make to have much effect, and it hadn't yet reached a point where sleep was critical for him. So not only would it be useless, but if he found out, he'd never forgive her.

Wade was nearly as worried about Paige's condition as Julian, and spent a good amount of time near Julian's room in case he was needed. This resulted in Suni being concerned about him as well, but since he slept more than an hour at a time and ate more regularly, she let him be.

Just before noon on the third day, Paige stirred. She felt oddly warm and turned her head to find Julian plastered against her side. She smiled weakly and stroked her fingers over his cheek. The motion tired her, but it did serve to wake him from his light doze.

His eyes opened and it took only seconds for him to register that she was conscious. "You're awake!" he said in a hushed voice, but he couldn't disguise his happiness, or his relief. Yes, she was paler than normal, but she was no longer blue or unconscious, which was enough for now.

"For the most part. What happened?" she murmured, letting her hand drop so it rested on his chest.

He frowned, not yet releasing her. "What do you remember last?" For her sake, he hoped she'd forgotten most, if not all, of the fight. They weren't memories that would do her any good.

She thought for a moment, brow furrowed. "I...remember the people showing up. The woman cut me, and I hurt her. I almost fell and you caught me." She struggled to remember more, but had to stop when it caused her head to pound. "The rest is too fuzzy."

He closed his eyes, teeth clenched, but he made himself relax. "There was poison on the blade that she used on you. It was similar to the poison powder we found in the temple in Brazil. It must have been from the gods, because nothing Suni could do worked."

"Suni? I'm sorry I missed her," she murmured absently while her mind raced. She'd been poisoned? And by something potent enough that even the fantastic healer couldn't provide an antidote? Fear abruptly countered the heat she'd been feeling only a moment ago. "Am I..." She trailed off, unable to finish the question.

"No, you're not dying, sweetheart." He kissed her lightly. "And you'll get your chance to meet Suni," he told her.

"Okay. Good. But how am I alive if she couldn't help me?"

Now he smiled. "I think you made a friend, sweetheart."

Confused, she asked, "I like making friends, but what do you mean?"

"You...you were nearly gone, and Suni had tried everything she could when I felt something familiar. A certain watcher's presence."

Paige brightened a little. "Hephaestus was here?"

He shook his head. "Not in person, no. We never saw him, but this bottle appeared over you that stunned Suni. And not much surprises her."

"What was it?"

"Some mythical antidote she thought was lost forever. It can, apparently, cure any and all poisons. She gave it to you and you passed out." He hesitated. "That was three days ago."

"Three days?" she gasped before sitting up quickly. Too quickly. Pain flared in her side, sharp enough to have her falling back against the bed. Slowly, she pulled her shirt up to see the wound the assassin had given her remained. It had healed only a little while she slept, and she lost what little color she had at the sight of the nasty looking gash across her flesh.

"Careful," he warned, stroking a hand over her hair. "I'm sorry, I should have warned you. We didn't want to heal it and risk sealing poison in your body. One moment." He lightly touched her, and she watched as the cut knit back together, disappearing but for a faint scar. "Better?"

"Much. But...three days? That explains why I'm so hungry," she said, hand resting on her belly.

He chuckled. "Then let's get you food, shall we?"

To her chagrin, he insisted on carrying her, claiming she was still weak, and even with her protests, he got his way. It was probably wise, as she really didn't have the energy to make it downstairs.

Suni and Wade were already in the kitchen, sitting at the table talking while something simmered on the stove.

"Whatever that is, it smells heavenly," Paige said after inhaling deeply.

"Red!" A grin split Wade's face. "About time you got your lazy ass out of bed," he joked, but his pleasure in seeing her alive and awake was obvious.

"I thought about trying for another day, but I just couldn't do it," she told him, smiling warmly at the wolf. "And you must be Suni. Thank you so much for helping me," she said sincerely as she was carefully settled into a chair.

Julian sat in the one next to her, then pulled it closer, making Wade and Suni laugh.

"You're very welcome, Paige. I'm just happy that I was able to help, though I can only take a small amount of the credit." Suni smiled. "And it's good to see you up and about."

"Believe me, it's good to be up and about. Now, what's that I'm smelling?" she asked, her stomach growling loudly.

"Chicken and dumplings. I had a feeling you might wake today," Suni admitted, rising to ladle some into two bowls, setting one in front of Paige, and one in front of Julian. "*Both* of you need to eat your fill. There's enough for an army, even when the soldiers eat like wolf man over there," she said, inclining her head toward Wade. "And yes, Julian, I will be watching to make sure you eat, too."

He got such a sheepish look on his face that Paige couldn't help but giggle, pressing her face against his shoulder in an attempt to muffle it. "And here I thought you were be on my side," he protested, trying to sound serious. But she only had to smile at him before he gave it up.

Conversation was light and mostly kept up by Suni and Wade, since the other two were busy delivering spoonful after spoonful to their mouths. Finally Paige sat back, waving her hands in a 'no more' gesture. "I can't. I'm done. If I eat another bite, I'll pop."

"I hate to admit it, but I am, too. But it was delicious, Suni. Thank you." Julian cocked his head. "Speaking of thanks…That antidote. Whatever is left in the bottle is yours. It's the least I can do."

"That's assuming that Paige's benefactor lets me keep it," Suni said, well aware of the fickleness of the gods. "But thank you. Might I also ask for one small favor?"

"Name it."

She smiled. "A quick ride home?"

"Oh! Yes, I guess that would be good." He kissed Paige's cheek. "I'll be back in a flash."

Suni had apparently expected this outcome, because her things were neatly set nearby, so she only had to grab them and be ready to go. "Bye Paige. Be well. And Wade?"

"Hmm?"

"Stay out of trouble."

"Hey!" was as far as he got before Julian, mid-chuckle, teleported them both to Suni's home.

In under a minute, he was back and retaking his seat.

Paige laughed. "That was quick."

"Red, you're talking about the guy who wouldn't leave his bedroom for a minute while you were out," Wade offered with a smirk.

She gave Julian a surprised look. "Really? You stayed with me the whole time?"

Julian looked a little uncomfortable, but nodded. "I didn't want you to wake up alone."

Extremely touched, she leaned over and kissed him gently. "Thank you."

"If you guys start that shit, I'm out," Wade said, though there was no true annoyance in his voice. His grin would have given him away in any case. He was too pleased to see them both up, healthy, and happy.

"Sorry," Paige told him, smiling and only mildly apologetic. But she did change the subject. "Did you get the amulet assembled?"

Julian shook his head. "No. I found your piece, but it didn't seem right to do it without you."

"Not to mention it seems like it should be you who does it," Wade added. "You did the most to find it, and you sure as hell earned it.

Besides, you put the other pieces together. We can't break our routine now."

"That's so sweet. Except...is it safe to reassemble? The gods did send assassins to kill us before we could put it together."

The men exchanged glances, both frowning. "At this point," Julian began, "I don't think anything is certain. Nothing has happened for three days, but that's no guarantee they'll leave us be."

"On the other hand, having the pieces can't be any less dangerous than having the amulet, can it?" Wade asked.

"No, I suppose not." Julian considered for a moment. "Maybe they feel like it isn't worth it to send more assassins, since the first twelve never returned."

Paige nodded slowly. Those were all logical points, and she agreed with them. She also wasn't sure Hephaestus would have helped them if he thought completing the amulet would simply end up with them dead. She also couldn't quite bring herself to think of the assassins too much. If she did, she would remember what she'd done to them. Better to focus on the present.

Her mind made up, she sat up a little straighter. "Can we do it now?" They were so close to finally doing it, to completing the amulet. While yes, she was excited to see it whole again, and give that gift to Julian, she would also be happy to see their task completed. She was so very tired. Despite her jokes about Indiana Jones, she didn't know if such an exciting, adventurous life was really for her. She'd rather stay home, researching, gardening, and spending her nights with Julian.

Julian nodded. "If you feel up for it, yes, we can."

"I do. I'd really like to see it done."

"Then I'll go get your piece. Wade, you have the jewel?" he asked as he got to his feet.

"Yep." He leaned back to dig in his pocket, then set the gem on the table.

He'd cleaned it sometime in the last few days, because it showed no traces of the snake it had been within. It was slightly oval-shaped and as big as her thumbnail. More, it was every bit as beautiful as Paige had seen in her visions of the amulet. As she moved, the colors shifted, going from a rainbow to individual shades depending on the angle. When she leaned right, it seemed predominantly blue, but when she shifted left, it was almost golden.

Her palms itched to touch it, but she resisted, waiting for Julian to get back. It only took him a few minutes, she knew, but it felt like so much longer.

She got so antsy that Wade laughed. "Relax, Red. He'll be here in a minute. The jewel isn't going anywhere," he teased.

She sighed deeply. "I know. But I want to see it whole again."

As if on cue, Julian stepped back into the room and offered the nearly complete amulet to Paige, not wanting to set it on the table. It would be a shame if it assembled itself and robbed her of the privilege.

She held her breath when it dropped into her hand, but it was strangely quiet. There was a low vibration, and a definite desire to be complete again, but there wasn't any jolt of power or emotions from it. No pain or images so rapid it made her head spin. She knew that her eyes were lit from within again, but that was the only reaction she had to it this time. She realized the men were watching her—Julian curious, Wade amused—and she flushed a little. "Sorry, it just feels different."

Wade chuckled. "Well, go on then."

"I'm kind of nervous now that I actually have all the pieces here," she admitted.

"Understandable," Julian said gently. "Do you want me to do it?"

"No, just...give me a minute." It took more than one, with her breathing slow and deep to steady herself. She finally reached out and her fingers brushed the jewel.

She didn't know what she expected, but it wasn't for a shaft of pure joy and energy to rush into her. Her body jolted once in reaction and her eyes widened. "God!"

"Is that a good 'god' or a bad one?" Wade asked.

"Good. Very. Very. Good," she panted softly. "I feel like I could run a hundred marathons and climb a thousand cliffs. Forget coffee. This is so much better."

Julian gave her back a quick rub and she offered a smile to him before she stopped fighting what the amulet wanted.

Just as the metal pieces had, once the amulet and jewel were close to one another, they simply pulled themselves together and the seams were repaired. The second the amulet was whole, a shock wave of magic exploded from it. They all felt it hit them, felt the magic that pounded against their bodies, but though they swayed against it, it didn't knock them back as they'd expected, nor did it damage anything in the kitchen.

They watched in fascination as the tarnish melted away, leaving the silver bright and clean.

Paige ran her thumb over the markings, which were perfectly clear now, grinning like a fool. "It's so beautiful," she murmured.

"It really is," Wade had to agree.

While holding it, everything inside Paige insisted that she keep the amulet, but she found herself holding it out to Julian.

He met her gaze, held it, then without looking away, asked, "Can you give us a minute, Wade?"

"Err, yeah, sure," Wade said, giving them each a quick glance before he hot-footed it out of the kitchen.

Out of view, he paused a moment to smile.

It was about damn time.

CHAPTER 35

Paige glanced to the retreating Wade, then to Julian. She could sense nothing from him, his thoughts, his emotions locked up tight. And after everything that had happened, she didn't know if she could handle another confrontation, even with him. "What's wrong?" she asked as dread curled in her gut.

"Nothing's wrong," he denied, shaking his head. "But I don't want the amulet."

Nonplussed, she could only say, "What?"

He smiled a little. "I don't want the amulet," he repeated.

"But...all we've been through...everything that's happened," she sputtered. "After everything I've done to get this...You *have* to take the damn amulet!" she snapped. If she nearly died just so he could give the amulet away, she was going to seriously consider taking drastic measures. Perhaps she could enlist Wade's help to knock some sense into Julian.

He chuckled—chuckled!—but bit off the sound when Paige let out a low growl of anger. He couldn't help that his often serene lover getting so worked up was amusing him. It was actually a bit of a turn on, he admitted to himself, but he pushed that to the back of his mind for now. Mostly.

"Don't get me wrong, I'm not giving it back to the gods," he assured her, and saw the worst of her irritation vanish. "The majority of them can kiss my ass. But I want you to have it, not me."

She frowned, then quickly shook her head. "No, you need to keep it, and give it to someone you love, Julian," she insisted. "That was the whole reason we started all this, isn't it?"

"It is." He covered her hands with his own, trapping the amulet between them. "And I am," he whispered.

Her eyes grew damp, and he could see the hope—and the uncertainty—in them, now that the glow from the amulet had faded. In a voice that was barely audible, she asked, "Are you saying...you love me?"

He cocked his head and gave her a smile, brushing his thumb lightly over her cheek. "Do you really doubt it? I don't spend three days doing nothing but watching over someone because of duty. Should I need to prove it, though? I've gotten so used to shielding from you it just became habit, but..."

The barrier that had kept his feelings private vanished, and Paige could suddenly feel everything he was feeling. The amusement, the arousal, but most of all, the intensity of his feelings for her. The love. It washed over her, erasing the anger she'd felt only moments ago. It was intense and warm and more than she'd ever dared to hope for. Tears fell as she let out a happy cry and threw her arms around him. She kissed him eagerly, holding nothing of herself back. There wasn't any need, not now. He loved her and she tried to show him with that single kiss that she felt the same way about him.

More than willing to accommodate her, he pulled her out of her chair and into his lap, deepening the kiss until they were both panting and restless with need. But just when he considered taking her up-stairs—or out into the garden—she drew back and cupped his face, unable to stop touching him.

"Why didn't you tell me?"

Apologetic, he brushed her hair back from her face. "I couldn't. At first I was so caught up in guilt that I wouldn't even consider it, then later..." He shook his head then shrugged. "I was just stubborn, I suppose. But when I thought you were going to die..." His words broke and he had to take a few breaths to calm himself. "I couldn't stand it. I wished I had told you, and decided that if you woke up, I wouldn't waste my chance." He rested his forehead against hers. "So yes, Paige. I love you, and I want you to have the amulet, so you never have to grow old and die," he murmured. "I don't think I could bear that."

"I understand. All of it, I do," she said before kissing him again. "But you should keep the amulet, Julian."

He frowned. "What? But you know why I want you to have it."

"Yes, and I appreciate that, on a number of levels. And I absolutely understand why you want me to have it, but...I love you, too. I don't want to lose you anymore than you want to lose me. But...well..." To his delight, she squirmed and he had to bite back a groan as he hardened against her backside. "You *are* older than me, by quite a bit," she finished in a rush. "You're going to grow old before I do, so you need it more."

He chuckled. "True," he allowed. "But still—"

They both felt the quick rush of magic, and the aura of power that followed, but it only took a quick glance to the side to see Hephaestus standing there. Paige jumped a little in surprise, but before she could speak, Julian scowled. "Is this to become a common occurrence?"

The god chuckled and shook his head. "Oh no. But given what I'm here for, you might want to be a *little* nicer to me," he said, leaning a shoulder against the wall, his arms folded over his impressive chest.

Recovered enough to speak, Paige gently elbowed Julian in the belly. "Be nice anyway. He's a nice man, and he did help save my life," she pointed out in a low voice.

Mildly chagrined, Julian nodded. "Fair point. And I do thank you for that with every fiber of my being."

"No thanks are necessary. There are too few women like her around. I couldn't just let one die," Hephaestus said with a shrug. "And like I said, I never agreed with the decision to destroy the relics. It was a waste, to my mind."

Paige smiled. "I'm still going to give you my thanks. But you said you were here for a reason? What might that be?" she asked, her tone much more friendly than Julian's had been. "Oh! I didn't even think. Would you like some tea? Or there are really good chicken and dumplings if you'd rather have food."

Hephaestus's rough face softened at the offer and he shook his head. "No, but thank you. I can't stay that long. But my reason for coming involves two things. First? Given how hard you fought, and the reasons you fought for it, I've managed to convince the other gods to let you keep the amulet." The shocked and pleased looks that crossed both faces had him continuing quickly. "You cannot, ever, seek out another relic of that magnitude, though, and you cannot ever give it to anyone. It must remain with you or the assassins will return."

Paige smiled brightly at him and answered without needing to consult Julian. "We can absolutely agree to that."

Julian nodded. "We can. What's the other reason for your visit, though?"

Hephaestus inclined his head toward the relic. "That trinket you two are holding had a ritual that was created to go with it. One you might be interested in."

Julian's scholarly mind was now intrigued. "A ritual? Of what sort? And might I ask how you know about this ritual?"

"Other than being a god?" he asked dryly.

Julian cleared his throat and nodded. "Yes, other than."

"That stone there in the center?" he began, inclining his head toward the amulet. "I provided it to the one who made the amulet. And Paige knows I helped with its creation. So I know damn near everything there is to know about that particular bit of jewelry," he said smugly.

Julian gently drew the amulet from Paige's fingers, examining it more closely. Paige, however, just grinned at Hephaestus. "That makes sense. A craftsman—*the* craftsman—helping others."

"But what about this ritual?" Julian asked without looking up.

Hephaestus rolled his eyes at Julian's single-mindedness, and earned a low laugh from Paige. "Is he always like this?" he asked her.

"For the most part, yes," she admitted.

"Good luck," he muttered. "So, the ritual was meant to bind two people together, and to that relic. But only—" and he paused to stress that word— "if they truly loved one another. And I don't just mean romantic love. The love of a parent for a child, or for a friend, would work just as well."

"Or siblings?" Paige asked, remembering the dream she'd had and the pair she had thought were brother and sister.

Hephaestus nodded. "That was the original intention, yes. But none of that really matters since, for the two of you, it's romantic love."

"What do you mean that it binds people together and with the relic?" Julian asked.

"Well, after the ritual is done, all three are connected. So as long as the amulet is touching one of the people it's bound to, its effects will work for both." He smiled at Paige. "So you could wear the amulet, but he wouldn't age either."

Julian was so stunned he only stared at the god. Paige, on the other hand, made a happy sound, nearly radiating that emotion, and slid off Julian's lap. Not caring about what Hephaestus was, she strode over to him and gave him a warm hug.

Only Julian saw the look of complete shock on the god's face at such a simple—but powerful—gesture.

It took him a moment before he smiled and awkwardly returned it. Awkwardly enough that Julian idly wondered if it was the first hug Hephaestus had ever received. If the stories about him were true, it might just be, and his heart swelled with pride for his caring lover.

Paige looked up at him and smiled. "Thank you, sir. We will never, *ever* forget this, I promise you."

"You're welcome," the god said gruffly. "And you can call me Hephaestus. Sir is too stuffy. Sir is my dad, and I am way more laid back than he is."

She beamed and stepped back, delighted to be given the honor of using a god's name. "Thank you, Hephaestus."

"If I may," Julian began. "Why would you go against the other gods again? You'd already helped us, and convinced them to leave us be, but now you reveal a secret of something they forbid to exist? Why would you do such a thing?"

Hephaestus inclined his head toward Paige. "Because of her."

"Me?" she asked with some surprise.

"Yes, you," he grumbled. "You think just everyone is as kind to me as you are?"

Paige thought about the same stories Julian was just thinking of, remembering how it was said that his own parents had thrown him off Olympus for being deformed. How he was known as the ugliest of the gods. How even his wife cheated on him constantly.

Sympathy for this strong, abused man welled up, and she gave him another tight hug. "I will always be kind to you. I swear it."

Hephaestus cleared his throat and patted her back. "Thank you."

"Thank you again. I promise to cherish what you've given me. Given us," Julian told him.

Hephaestus gave him a dark, menacing look. "You damn well better. If you don't, you'll be getting another visit from me. And *I* promise that you won't like it if I do." He looked down at Paige as she drew back with a grin. "You let me know if this boy doesn't treat you right, okay?"

She laughed and nodded, looking back to Julian. "I will, but I don't think I'll have any problems on that score. But I do have two more questions."

"What's that?"

"First, do you truly think they'll keep their word and leave us alone?"

Hephaestus nodded. "I do. I wouldn't put it past my father to reconsider later, but you took out several of his assassins. In the grand scheme, the relic you hold isn't enough to truly worry him, so as long as you stay under the radar otherwise, you should be safe."

Relief swamped her and she closed her eyes until she'd absorbed the information. "That's fantastic news. Thank you." She cocked her head slightly as she looked up at him. "The other thing…When the…assassins…showed up, I heard a voice in my head that wasn't Julian or Wade. It gave me advice, told me basically to use my instincts instead of thinking. Was that you?"

He shook his head. "It wasn't, but I think I know what happened. I told you that one of your ancestors made the ring you wear. All of the women in your family have been very skilled with any magic that involved the mind. There's a little bit of her mind in that ring. I've always known it was there, but I'll admit that, until now, I thought it was just a sacrifice of her power to boost the power of whoever wore it. So my guess? It was her trying to help her descendant."

That made Paige tear up again and he shook his head. "No, no crying. I don't do crying," he said, eyes wide as he almost panicked. "Remember, treat her right, Julian. Or I'll hear about it." With one last glare at Julian, he disappeared. A second later, a scroll appeared on the table.

Paige wiped at her tears and returned to Julian then, sliding back onto his lap, her arms around him. "What's that?"

Julian unrolled it with one hand, unwilling fully release her, and skimmed over it. "It's the ritual. A very detailed one, but it's doable. It just might take some time to make sure we get everything right."

"He's such a sweet man," she said, knowing that she was still smiling. She couldn't seem to stop.

"You're probably the only one who thinks so," Julian said dryly.

"Hey! Be nice," she admonished.

"I am. He doesn't come across as sweet to anyone but you. I really do think you've made a friend there, love."

"I hope so."

Wade poked his head in. "Is it safe?"

"Yes, it's safe," Paige told him.

He sniffed at the air as he started toward them. "Was that god here again?"

"He was. And he left us a present." Julian explained about the ritual, and had Wade whistling, impressed.

"Nice one. I've just got one question."

"What's that?" Paige asked.

He grinned impishly. "When are you going to make me a best man? Or man of honor. I'm not picky as to which, just so long as I don't have to wear a dress."

Paige laughed, but Julian just smiled and said, "Soon."

EPILOGUE

Six months later

The bedroom Paige had lived in for three years hadn't been used in months, but today she was in it once more, and she wasn't alone. Suni, as well as Jeff's wife, Elise, and mother-in-law, Michelle, were there, too.

They were helping her get ready for her wedding.

She stood in front of a mirror, trying her hardest not to cry. That would ruin the makeup that Michelle had so carefully applied, but she was so happy! She wore a sleeveless satin gown that was paler even than her own skin. The bodice and hem of the gown had lace blossoms that held just a touch of pink to them, as did the short train.

It was the most gorgeous dress she'd ever seen, though she was well aware that she could be wearing a burlap sack and feel the same way. Any dress she married Julian in was an amazing dress.

"I never, ever thought that being mugged would turn out to be such a good thing," she told them, sniffling. "Not to mention all the attacks and everything."

Having heard the full story before, the three ladies just grinned.

"Good, immense good, can definitely come out of bad," Elise told her. "That's how I met Jeff, too. Though it didn't start out quite as bad as your meeting with Julian did."

"However you met, you got here, which was the hard part," Michelle said, fussing with Paige's hair. Julian was so enamored by her thick red tresses that he had put his foot down and demanded she not wear a veil or anything else that would cover it up. Paige hadn't had strong feelings either way, so had happily complied and chosen a gold headpiece that looked like a leafy vine that held her hair back from her face. That, along with her gown, made Paige feel more beautiful than she ever had before.

Sadness struck Paige suddenly, and she pressed a hand to her chest. "I just wish my dad had accepted the invitation."

"Oh, honey," Michelle said, rubbing Paige's arm. "He still loves you. And it's not like there aren't people here who love you, too. But maybe he'll surprise you. He didn't say no, he just didn't respond."

During the planning for the wedding, Paige had gotten to be good friends with all three women, so she knew Michelle spoke the truth. Still, her smile was tinged with sadness.

"Hey now. None of that," Suni said briskly. "You're getting married. You're in love. Focus on the good and ignore the bad, at least for today." She paused. "Though I'd suggest ignoring the bad until after the honeymoon is over, too," she added with a wicked gleam in her eyes. "He *is* taking you on a honeymoon, right?"

It had its intended effect, and Paige laughed. "Of course. He hasn't told me where we're going, but he gave me a list of all the things I need to pack as a clue."

"And what'd he tell you to pack?" Elise asked.

Now it was Paige's turn to grin, even as her cheeks turned pink. "Sunscreen and sunglasses."

The other three roared with laughter. "So a private beach some-where, where clothes are optional?" Suni asked.

"Sounds like it!"

There was a mental nudge to all four witches to signal that it was time, and Paige turned and grinned. "Do I look like a proper bride?"

"You look gorgeous," Elise assured her. "Now let's go get you married!"

Downstairs, she found a man waiting for her just outside the closed doors that led into the garden where all the guests—and Julian—waited. She smiled brightly at him. His features weren't familiar, but she recognized him all the same. Hephaestus's power was something she'd recognize for the rest of her life.

After her father had ignored her invitation, Paige had figured out how to get in touch with Hephaestus through dreams and asked him to do her the honor of walking her down the aisle. He had been stunned but agreed—but only if he disguised himself so none of the guests would recognize him. Paige had stubbornly argued, but when he said it was safer that the gods not know, she had relented. The last thing she wanted was for any of them to get into any more divine trouble.

She took his arm and leaned up to kiss his cheek. "Thank you for doing this."

In the gruff voice she now knew meant he was pleased, he said, "You're welcome. You look beautiful. Julian's a lucky man."

One by one, Paige's three attendants walked through the door and down the aisle, with Suni going last as the maid of honor. Then it was her turn.

With no trace of nerves, Paige was led between the rows of chairs, proudly escorted by the god of blacksmiths. She saw a hundred faces, recognized about half, but her focus was all on the man standing at the end of the aisle.

Julian looked amazing in his black tux, a look of absolute love and pride on his face. Beside him as best man, Wade grinned, but the wolf also nodded into the guests. Wondering what that was about, Paige followed his gaze, and almost tripped. Only Hephaestus's strong arm kept her from falling.

Her father was here! He stood awkwardly, dressed in a suit that didn't fit quite right, but he was here! He met her gaze, his face stony, but she could see the apology in his eyes.

By the time that Hephaestus gave her away, tears were sliding down her cheeks.

Julian kissed her cheek and whispered, "Are these good tears?"

Unable to speak, she simply nodded and gave him a big smile.

She was so filled with happiness that she barely heard the words that joined her to Julian, though she somehow managed to give the proper responses at the proper times. All too soon she heard, "You may kiss the bride," and found herself receiving the most intense kiss of her life.

Wade had to nudge Julian and clear his throat loudly before the newlyweds heard the chuckles from the guests and broke apart, Paige's cheeks flushed with pleasure and embarrassment.

The reception took place there at Mooreton, and after Paige had greeted all the other guests, her father approached her uncertainly.

"Dad..."

"I'm sorry, Paige. I'm so sorry," he said, looking ashamed as well as remorseful. "I was a bloody idiot." When she started to speak, he shook his head. "No, let me finish, please. Then if you want me to go, I will."

She wanted to tell him he could stay, but she held her tongue and nodded. If he needed to say something, she'd listen.

"I never should have treated you that way. Hell, if your mother was alive, she would've torn a bloody strip off me, and she would've been right to." He took a deep breath. "And while I know I don't deserve it, don't deserve a damn thing, I just wanted to say I was sorry and ask for your forgiveness."

Paige smiled and put her arms around him, giving him a warm hug. "Of course, Dad. I'm just happy you came!"

He held her tightly, not caring that he was tearing up. If a man couldn't tear up at his daughter's wedding, then when could he? "You were beautiful, you know. Even more beautiful than your mother was, and I thought no one could be so fine as she was the day I married her." She let out a soft cry and tightened her hold. "She'd be proud of you, you know. Proud of who you've become."

"Daddy," she whispered, crying again.

He sniffed once, then carefully drew back, nodding to Julian, who now stood only a few feet behind her. "I think it's time for you to have your first dance with your new husband, Paige. But I'll be around more, I promise."

"I'm going to hold you to that," she told him with a laugh.

Julian took her hand and led her onto the dance floor. As they moved to the slow, romantic tone of the music, he asked, "What did your father say?"

"He apologized," she breathed, still finding it hard to believe. "Said he never should have thrown me out." She rested her head against his shoulder. "Said I was a beautiful bride."

"He was right about that. It was all I could do not to grab you and run away to have you all to myself." She laughed and he tilted his head against hers. "Would you change things if you could?"

"What do you mean?"

"If you could go back and make it so he never threw you out, would you?"

She lifted her head so quickly it nearly smacked into Julian's chin. "Of course I wouldn't! I would go through that, through everything, over and over again, so long as it always led to this moment. To me dancing with my husband."

"I'll hold you to that," he teased, before taking her lips in a tender kiss. He'd been seeking eternity, and instead found something so much more valuable. Now he just had to get her away from the wedding guests, so they could begin their new, extremely long life together. A life that would be filled with knowledge, adventure, and love.

COMING SOON

A Fury's Heart

Releasing April 25, 2023

Wade never expected to come home and find a demon in his bed.

Along with most of the world, the wolf shifter hated demons, so when he saw her, his first instinct was to attack. But this demoness came with a grave warning. Something much worse was coming.

Instead of killing the intruder, he's forced to work with her, as well as a small group of demon hunters. They only have until the next full moon to find a way of preventing the demon lord of another dimension from coming to Earth and claiming it as his own. And it won't be easy.

Not only do they need to discover exactly when and where the demon lord will arrive, they're also being tracked. Every time they turn around, they have to deal with yet another attack. They're good, but it will only take one wrong move to end them and doom the world.

About Author

Meg M. Robinson is a fantasy author who lives in north Georgia with her husband, a teenager, and a small menagerie of animals. She's goofy and a little dorky, which greatly amuses her family.

She's obsessed with crows, sea turtles, and houseplants. And, of course, books. When she's not focused on either reading or writing a book, she enjoys playing video games, archery, and baking.

www.megmrobinson.com